FROM THE
WORLD
OF
GALLIZE
SHIFTERS

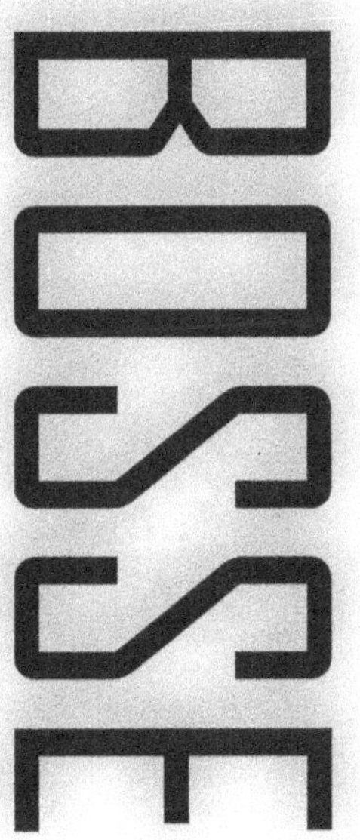

Wild Wolf Pack

DIANNA LOVE

DEDICATION

DEAR READERS:
This is the new *Wild Wolf Pack* series, which is a spinoff from the League of Gallize Shifters. If you've read the League of Gallize Shifters, you'll know how this new wolf pack happened and who is alpha. If you haven't read the Gallize series yet, that's fine.

This series stands alone.

But for those who *have* read the Gallize series, these shifters are not Gallize but unique in their own ways. Also, you'll see many of the characters from the Gallize, as well as the Guardian, in these stories.

There will be more Gallize books, some of which will be about the Guardian.

It's just now a bigger world.

Thank you for reading my books.

Dianna

PRONUNCIATION GUIDE

Alifair – *Al uh FARE*
Bosse – *BOSS* (rhymes with loss)
Cierna – *see UR nah*
Ivo – *EE voh*
Jothan – *JOE than*
Krol - *KROWL*
Lammogo – *lah MOW goh*
Linota – *Lin OH tah*
Magdelina – *mag duh LEENA*
Zuzani – *zoo ZAHN ee*
wilkotauk – VEE kuh TAAHK

BOSSE
Wild Wolf Pack

"Spellbinding action and steamy romance."
~ Goodreads on Wild Wolf Mate

Can a gifted female on an impossible mission and a tortured wolf shifter doomed to die in a cage risk trust to save each other?

Bosse will never escape the cage he's been locked in for the past two years. Used as entertainment for an insane lion shifter pretending to be a king, he's forced to battle other shifters to the death every day. His life is over, thanks to the pack alpha who sold him for refusing to breed females not suited to be mates. A chance for escape comes from a strange female servant who secretly gives him meat he needs to heal and… cookies. Who bakes cookies for a monster? The more he watches her, the more his numb heart begins to feel again, which is dangerous. What if she's trying to trick him like others who betrayed him?

Alifair inherited the duty of finding the missing leader over her clan of gifted beings in America, but her magic is flawed. Even her best asset of clairvoyant dreams has occasional hiccups. That's how she ended up captured in Slovakia to secretly toil as a servant where the female leader is being held. Her latest dream identifies the person who is key to succeeding at her duty, but her dream godmother must have been on a drinking binge. Alifair's first step is to free the most dangerous wolf shifter locked in the basement cages.

Alifair enters the cage of a predator, prepared for the worst, and discovers a man who touches her heart with one surprising action. Bosse's cookie fairy offers him the freedom he never expected but with an unacceptable condition.

———— ∽∽∽ ————

Note: All the Wild Wolf Pack are stand-alone paranormal romances.

Please join my **https://authordiannalove.com/connect** to stay up on all my releases.

For signed books, bookplates, and swag, visit **www.DiannaLoveSignedBooks.com**

Chapter 1

BOSSE HEAVED ONE ragged breath after another, battering the tiger shifter's chest while dodging brutal strikes. Fighting a boulder would be less painful. Blood streamed into his eyes, blurring his vision.

Tangled, dung-colored hair hung in wet strands over the tiger shifter's face. Bosse looked no better, and their naked bodies smelled of sweat and grime.

He whipped his head aside from a blur coming at him.

The tiger shifter's massive fist still caught him with a sharp right hook. New blood spewed from Bosse's cheek.

He stumbled to the side and kept moving. Fists up and ready, he shook off the stars sparkling across his vision and blinked. Soaked hair clung to the hot skin of his neck.

Titan snarled a low grinding sound inside him. His wolf wanted out now.

Too soon to shift. Bosse had to wear down their opponent first while they were both in human form to give Titan a chance at defeating a tiger that he guessed could be a couple hundred pounds larger than his wolf.

"Now, Makari! *Kill that wolf!*" Krol shouted at them from a platform thirty feet above the battle arena where he perched on an obscene gold throne. With the sides shaved, he wore his pale-blond hair long on top, tied in a ponytail at the crown of his head. Jeweled rings sparkled on his fisted fingers, and dark eyes outlined in black gave him an older appearance than being a mid-twentyish tyrant.

Whatever ancient Egyptian ruler Krol pretended to

emulate with the blue silk tunic and matching pants had to be cringing in his cold linen-wrapped body.

The tiger shifter lifted his death gaze upward and roared at the crazy lion shifter who had captured him for lethal entertainment.

Noisy guards protecting their leader up top and those down here beyond the steel bar gate rumbled with excitement. They'd lost a lot betting against Bosse.

Good.

He took a step toward the distracted shifter.

Makari yanked his gaze around, not too distracted at all. His lips pulled back, exposing long, sharp teeth in a black maw. Bloody claws tipped thick fingers. He had an arm span a foot wider than Bosse's.

Makari moved with purpose, closing in on his prey.

Bosse growled. He was no one's prey. Arms loose, he waited for the tiger shifter to expose a weakness. None so far.

Makari rushed forward, claws reaching for Bosse's throat.

Bosse locked his hands into a club of a fist and swung around in a blinding move to smash the tiger shifter's head.

That strike would have killed a human or knocked out a smaller shifter.

Makari stumbled away, turning as he did to keep his opponent in view. He hadn't gone down, but that knock rattled his brain. He hunched over, shaking his head and blinking. Muscles wrapped his arms like a giant python.

Bosse ran at him, jumping up to kick Makari in the jaw. That snapped the shifter's head. Blood and saliva flicked from his mouth.

Makari flailed his arms to stay upright, then shook off the hit and snarled.

Damn. Bosse had yet to find the best place to hit this guy. Until then, he had to avoid those claws. One misstep, and he'd end up gutted.

Titan grumbled in Bosse's head, *Biggest shifter yet. Will be an elephant next. Time to shift.*

Not yet. Bosse clenched his jaws. He avoided thinking about how their chance of survival diminished with every new capture Krol dropped in here.

"Attack! Kill the wolf!" Krol's maniacal screams for bloodletting drowned out everything else. That lunatic lived in a fantasy world. He believed himself a monarch over this crumbling castle in a remote part of modern-day Slovakia.

Makari shot forward, fists swinging.

Bosse ignored the noise above him, took hits in his sides, and struck back viciously. He stayed up on his toes, feet dancing. There had been a time when he could do this for hours, but not now. He began to breathe harder and blocked hits with sluggish movements.

Time narrowed to seconds—to each gulp of air.

He ducked a blow that barely missed his head and shuffled back thirty feet quickly.

The tiger shifter paused and cocked his head, confused. Then his cold blue eyes filled with arrogance. Sweat covered his pale skin, and stringy hair slapped his shoulders. Makari's upper body muscles bunched for an attack.

Time for a new strategy.

Bosse dropped his shoulders and moved with a limp.

"Yes! Yes! Yes!" Krol crowed and clapped. His voice scraped across Bosse's raw nerves.

Makari roared. He started forward slowly, prowling like the cat he hid inside.

Bosse stood still, eyes focused, not blinking.

Makari chewed up ground, closing in at fifteen feet … ten feet …five feet, then lunged with arms up to deliver a downward death blow.

Bosse drew in a deep breath. Claws shot from his blunt fingertips.

Inches from Makari's fists coming down like a sledgehammer, Bosse leaned his body over and spun hard on one leg. His hands slashed across Makari's middle. Blood spewed from the gut wound.

Unable to stop his forward motion, Makari slammed into Bosse.

Losing his footing, Bosse clasped the wound, trying to grip entrails and drag them out in the chaotic collision.

An enormous fist bashed his head, knocking Bosse aside before he could do more damage. He rolled away. The world spun. Dirt blew up and covered his body. Titan howled inside him. He had double vision. He shook his head and now saw only one tiger. Forcing himself to stand, he wobbled sideways.

Makari wrapped an arm around his middle and leaned against the arena wall.

Attack now! Titan urged.

As if Makari had heard Bosse's wolf, which was absurd, he shoved off the wall with a grimace and charged back into the battle, wielding his free arm.

Bosse couldn't believe that shifter could move again so quickly.

He went on defense and made a clumsy attempt to swing away from Makari.

Four dagger-sharp claws ripped the bare skin on his back. Bosse locked his jaws to keep from yelling in pain and drove his elbow into Makari's lower back, sending the tiger shifter to the ground.

A good time to attack if Bosse could move faster than a slug.

He stumbled all the way across the dirt floor in the hundred-foot-wide arena, then flipped around to prop his side against the wall. From the gritty dirt beneath his bare feet to the rusty sheen of death rotting on the stone walls, putrid air clogged his lungs.

Hot pain seared the ragged wounds on his back. His ability to heal became less dependable each day. At one time, Krol fed him well for longer fights.

Not anymore.

He needed a minute. Or fifty.

Stupid tiger shifter rose and turned to stand against a wall with blood still oozing from his gut, but more slowly. His freaking wound had begun to heal. Of course, Makari had only just shown up last night.

Stay here a week and live on slop, then fight.

Krol banged on the arm of his throne and warned, "Disappoint me and face worse than death. Shift to your animals!"

Neither of them paid the despot any attention.

Cupping his middle, Makari eyed Bosse slowly, then huffed a confident sound.

One of victory.

Delaying would not help. Bosse straightened away from the wall, took five steps, and lifted his chin—a silent challenge to *Bring it.*

He got a nod in return. *Challenge accepted.*

Makari lifted both arms, leaving his wound unprotected, and ran forward with shoulders hunched to keep his middle too far back to be touched. With Bosse away from the wall, Makari had more reaction time to avoid hitting it.

Bosse dropped down and leaped high, kicking the hard heel of his bare foot at Makari's filthy face.

Crack! A howl of misery followed.

Bosse twisted away as the hit sent him backward. His body glanced off the wall. He landed hard, felt a snap in his ankle, and stumbled to the side. Ah, shit. He'd damaged his ankle. He hurt in so many places that they all blended into a single knot of agony.

This couldn't last much longer.

Heaving to draw in shuddering breaths, he waited for Makari's next move.

Grabbing his head, Makari bellowed in pain and fury, but he kept an eye on Bosse.

More than a broken nose. Bosse's heel had slid to the side and crushed the left eye socket. Solid hit and one Bosse would pay for with every step he took on the same foot.

Makari's hand clawed at the bloody hole in his face.

Shifter healing would not regrow that much damage to his eye. He smeared blood when he wiped his face.

Gasps came from the gallery. The female servers, not the crazy king.

Bosse took a step to test his ankle and gritted his teeth. There would be no more jumping up to strike Makari.

Krol yelled like a petulant brat. "Twenty minutes of battle is not enough entertainment for what I paid. Do not dare end this too soon."

Titan growled, *Stupid lion shifter.*

Bosse muttered back, *A real alpha would jump down here and fight us.*

We would kill the pussy, Titan deadpanned.

After the first year of Bosse winning battles, Krol had begun putting more effort into finding a shifter that could kill him and Titan. The castle king had no idea that his obsession only fueled their drive to be the last one standing for as long as they could.

He and Titan would never escape this place.

After two years of living in a twelve-by-twelve cage, winning was more a game than anything. One day, he and his wolf would lose.

Not today. He hoped.

Makari growled threatening sounds, but he made no move to strike back yet. Finally, a sign of his weakening.

Another prime time for Bosse to attack.

An opportunity was only as good as his ability to use it.

Krol chose that moment to shout at servers delivering him food and drink. "Stupid bitches! I do not want *that* wine."

At the sound of a glass breaking and a female crying out in pain, Bosse's head yanked up.

Of the three women serving Krol, the one with two different colored eyes stood closest to that moron.

Bosse's cookie fairy.

Krol stood and slapped the wooden tray holding the insulting wine bottle from her hands. Terror racked her pretty face surrounded by coffee-brown wavy hair. Red liquid splattered over her olive-brown skin and faded cotton tunic.

Growling as loud as a pack of fierce wolves, Bosse took a step from the wall.

Titan ordered, *Look out!*

Bosse got knocked off his feet.

He went flying and hit the ground hard, rolling to get away. His ripped-up back caught loose rock and gritty sand. Hell, that hurt. He pushed past the pain and reached his feet fast again.

When he did, he found out why Makari had not continued to battle him.

Loud pops and groans squeezed from the far side. Makari had begun changing into his tiger first. He just took the upper hand.

Without a word from Bosse, Titan forced a blast of energy into the shift.

Body twisting and burning in agony, Bosse yelled telepathically, *Damn it, Titan!*

Your fault. Stupid to look at woman. Again!

Standing on all fours at the same moment as their opponent, Titan shook off the change and readied himself.

Krol cheered and pumped his fist. "Yes! Now we see who is best."

Now my turn, spineless lion, Titan spit out internally. Head down and eyes locked on the gigantic Bengal tiger, Titan backed up until his rear legs touched the wall. He declared, *We do flip-flop.*

Bosse warned, *The cat may be too fast for it to work.*

Titan argued, *Cat not that quick.*

Ignoring his wolf's arrogance, Bosse focused on how they could take down over eight hundred pounds of pissed-off tiger with fully extended claws capable of shredding anything that feline could pin down. Blood dripped from the tiger's underside, but more slowly.

Titan preferred to remain still until attacked. He'd wait an hour if he believed that strategy would win. Energy fed into the damaged ankle, patching bone.

Bosse trusted him. His wolf understood their poor ability to heal meant they were running out of time for any strategy.

The tiger roared over and over, showing off his short, brutal canines with pressure-sensing nerves. Those allowed a natural jungle cat to quickly identify the optimum spot to sever a prey's neck. His damaged eye remained a bloody hole.

Do not allow the tiger to get behind you, Bosse reminded Titan.

Understood, was all his wolf said. The deeper Titan got into a battle, the less they communicated.

Without a flicker of warning, the tiger took three fast strides and lunged forward, leaping twenty feet through the air.

Bosse tensed, but Titan held firm.

At the last second, his wolf flopped on his side, rolling away with his legs tucked and coming up on all fours. Pain shooting from gouges in his back blinded Bosse momentarily.

Titan endured the same pain, but he showed no weakness.

The tiger hit the ground, legs backpedaling and paws sliding over the loose ground as he barreled toward the stone wall. A dirt cloud blasted out from his large paws. His powerful legs cut away from the stone mere inches before slamming into it.

Damn. Had the flip-flop worked, it would have ended with the tiger suffering a few broken bones. Maybe even his neck.

Titan wouldn't wait for the cat to crash into the wall. His wolf raced in a half circle and leaped onto the tiger's back from behind. He clawed deep into thick fur, digging hard against muscle as the massive cat wrenched his body and tried to throw him off.

Natural tundra wolves were large, growing seven feet long. Much bigger than those, Titan had earned his name honestly by reaching ten feet, not counting his bushy tail.

But their opponent still outweighed Titan by over three hundred pounds of muscle.

Titan's claws kept tearing at the thick skin.

The tiger pushed up hard on his hind legs, then teetered and fell backward.

Bosse yelled, *Jump!*

Sliding off, Titan clawed for purchase, then gave up and pushed off as he hit the ground.

A thick golden hindquarter striped in black landed on the same leg where Titan had just patched the broken ankle. Bones crunched. Air squeezed from Titan's lungs in a sick sound.

The tiger's body ended up corkscrewed with his back leg jammed against the wall. His tail swatted back and forth, hitting Titan in the face.

Bosse's wolf struggled to wrench his body around until he could lock his jaws high on the tiger's back leg. Grinding and yanking viciously on the lower part of Makari's leg, Titan did not let up until he'd dragged tendons and muscle from the wounded limb.

Makari howled, jerking back and forth in a frenzy to escape. He lunged hard, trying to snap his jaws over Titan's muzzle.

Missed.

The tiger used his powerful front paws to claw his body away from Titan's jaws.

Weight on Titan's damaged leg eased, allowing him to drag his body to freedom as well. When he could get up, he scuffled away like a broken crab to put distance between them.

Bosse saw stars, and bile churned inside him.

Unable to do more than suffer with his wolf, he wished once again to rip Krol to shreds for what his wolf suffered every single day.

Appearing to stand on four legs that worked, Titan snarled a sound that threatened more mauling. Bosse's head spun. That crushed rear paw felt useless. Titan would not be able to jump or hide this limp when he moved.

Blood soaked through the Bengal's striped fur on his back and dripped into a puddle beneath him. His back leg hung unnaturally. He kept that paw off the floor.

Titan had done his best to even the odds.

The cat still had three powerful limbs, but his bright blue eyes changed from a savage animal to a deeper human color filled with misery and sadness.

Two majestic predators reduced to little more than cock fighters.

Such a shame. The tiger had wanted to live. He'd been captured and forced to fight but so had Bosse and Titan.

Only one would be allowed to survive.

Keeping the injured hindquarter still, Titan scratched the dirt with his opposite front paw and continued rumbling a terrifying sound nonstop. Blood ran warm down his back as well. They'd bleed out if this battle went on much longer.

Titan lifted his head and howled… an arrogant sound of victory meant to humiliate.

Hate replaced sadness in the cat's blue eyes. The tiger took a step toward Titan. Unable to lift his damaged leg, he hobbled sideways in slow, deliberate moves.

Bosse had no idea how they could stop that animal. *Can you move, Titan?*

Only once. Must wait for best chance.

That didn't sound promising.

Titan's head turned slowly as he tracked the tiger. When the large cat paused as if he were about to leap, muscles along Titan's body tensed.

Unable to jump without two functioning back legs, the tiger rushed forward with an uneven gait, jaws wide open to rip a large bite out of Titan.

In a move Bosse didn't expect to survive, Titan twisted his body at the very last second and rolled over on his back as if submitting. Legs folded and head pointed toward the tiger.

Krol leaped up, shaking his fist in the air. *"You lose, you miserable dog! You lose!"*

The guards erupted in matching shouts of joy.

If Makari's tiger stopped in time, he would only have to drop his body and crush Titan. With that much body already in motion, the tiger would hit the wall head-on if he didn't slow himself down first.

As the tiger reached him, Titan lunged up to attack his throat. His claws dug into the soft skin and held on for his jaws to rip a large gash. He got yanked around as the tiger fought to stop and shake off Titan. Adrenaline overrode pain from Titan's abused body. He jerked his head back and forth like a rabid animal. His claws dug deeper, mutilating skin protecting the underside of the tiger's throat.

Blood spewed over Titan's face. Mangled body parts fell loose.

All that happened in the blink of an eye as the tiger dragged Titan with him while trying to get away.

Makari's tiger arched up, snarling and slapping his paws at Titan, anything to escape the bludgeoning.

Being smaller had advantages in close contact, but the advantage ended there.

Running out of energy, Titan made one more desperate attempt to reach the vertebrae deep in the tiger's neck. Blood rushed over his muzzle.

Making a mighty lunge upward, the tiger stood on one leg.

Bosse couldn't believe it.

As if the thread holding him together snapped, eight hundred pounds of tiger fell.

Chapter 2

AT THE SOUND of Krol's roar and his guards' jubilant shouting, Alifair paused on her way back to the kitchen in her wine-soaked clothes.

She could handle Krol slapping wine all over her, but she wished he had not distracted the wolf shifter known as Bosse.

The tiger appeared to be winning as it was.

Her stomach churned at that possibility.

She needed Bosse to survive. She'd have nightmares about his wolf's bloody fangs ripping into the tiger, but that would not stop her from her responsibility. She had to convince Bosse to help her.

If he lived.

Guards rushed her out of the room, shoving her. "Stay in the kitchen and wait for new orders."

She curved her shoulders forward to look fearful and humbled when she wanted to lash out at the idiots. Once they returned to Krol's side, she lifted her head, straightened her back, and trudged to the kitchen.

Her heart clutched with constant worry. If the wolf shifter died, her sacrifice to end up in this Slovakian hellhole would have been wasted.

Hard to blame Bosse when he had no idea she depended on him. They had yet to speak a word to each other.

Slipping quietly into the medieval kitchen, she internally grumbled over this place. Four women were prepping and cooking food. Hessie, the evil bitch in charge, had her hands busy cleaning a wild boar a guard had killed earlier.

Bosse would not see any of that meat if Hessie kept it under her control.

He fought nonstop while being fed slop a starving animal would pass on. Alifair had learned he'd been here for a couple of years. How had he lasted so long?

Hessie yelled, "Serve da food now!"

Krol forced everyone, even native Slovakians, to speak English. Hessie only knew a handful of words.

Alifair rushed over to a bucket of water where servants had been instructed to wash up. She cleaned her hands and scrubbed the wine from her skin and face with no idea if she got it all. Her tunic would have to wait for laundry day.

Servers who'd responded to Hessie's bullhorn voice filled their hands and headed for the great hall. Alifair snagged a tray loaded with Pogača. It reminded her of focaccia a friend at home in the States made, except this baked offering was stuffed with potatoes. If she were home now, she wouldn't be eating this food or living like a slave in a dreary castle.

Her mother had once said, "With exceptional gifts comes responsibility."

Sounded reasonable if Alifair had been given an exceptional gift.

Guards in the arena area yelled again as she entered the great hall.

Her stomach rolled at the thought of Bosse being killed. She gripped her tray so tightly it shook as she lowered it to the coarse wooden table. She silently scolded herself. *No reacting to anything, ever*.

It was difficult enough to maintain this submissive servant role daily while fearing how much could go wrong with her plan.

Relaxing her fingers, she raced back to lift another tray holding bowls of Kapustnica and returned to the table. If she spilled even one drop of the succulent soup, Hessie would probably have her strung up by her thumbs.

Linota, a thin young woman with brassy red hair who sounded British, glanced at Alifair from across the wide tabletop. "Ya look gutted, mate."

Starting to understand the woman's odd phrases, Alifair made a show of shaking her left hand to prove she was not upset. "No, I've just got a cramp."

Linota nodded and moved on.

Alifair picked the tray up again and continued placing a bowl next to each hammered metal plate along the fourteen-foot expanse. She'd come from a world of electronics to this ridiculous place. She wanted air conditioning in July regardless of the current outside temperature in the seventies. Her tiny sleeping room was suffocating with no air movement.

She'd enjoyed Ren Faires, which were created for fun. Nothing like this nightmare.

Krol made everyone live this backward life for real.

Her rescue mission would go down as the worst task she'd ever faced, beginning with having to get close to a dangerous wolf shifter.

She'd never known a shifter of any kind before allowing herself to be captured and brought to this castle three weeks ago. Her one dependable gift, clairvoyant dreams, recently showed her that Bosse would be critical to the success of her mission.

Raised in a clan of gifted beings, she'd been taught to fear and avoid all shifters.

That had clearly not been explained to her dream godmother.

Sounds from Krol's arena died down, giving her a moment of relief at the thought Krol might be disappointed with another win by Bosse. Such inhumane entertainment, but a psychopath had no conscience.

Had all the shifters been captured? She couldn't imagine where someone would find that Frankenstein rhino shifter in the basement cage everyone called Beast.

Even she doubted he'd been born that way. Had dark magic been involved?

Krol's people fed most of the caged shifters well until it was time to fight.

All except Bosse.

In the short time she'd been here, the castle king seemed to resent how the wolf continued to win bloody matches and showed it by sending only nasty gruel occasionally to his cage.

A shifter wasn't human, but her heart had still whimpered at her first sight of Bosse's scarred and naked backside as he'd slept in human form on a dirt and steel bar floor in a dark cage.

Shifters had terrified her forever, but … something about him had made her want to comfort the wolf shifter in any small way she could long before she'd dreamed about him helping with her rescue mission.

Lifting the empty tray, she smiled to herself about maneuvering around Krol's guards to secretly feed Bosse meat when she carried food to the other shifters. She'd begun helping more in the kitchen and baking so she could sneak Bosse spiced honey cookies known as Medovníky in this country.

Wonder what the big bad wolf thought about her treats?

An angry shout from Hessie had her and Linota hustling back to the kitchen.

Just as she reached the kitchen door, a loud animal's scream of horrendous pain soared through the castle. Every server stopped and turned to stare at the arena observation entrance.

Alifair stumbled, her heart beating a crazy thump in her chest.

That sounded excruciating and final.

Chapter 3

BOSSE WATCHED IN horror through Titan's eyes as time splintered into seconds.

The tiger had Titan pinned against the stone.

Panic tore through Bosse. How could he help his wolf?

Titan twisted and stretched to claw his way free of being trapped.

The mighty cat screamed a hoarse sound and tried to lift its head, then fell back, dragging in gurgling breaths. Weight shifted, but he still had Titan's body pinned, trapping him from the chest down.

Jerking his head to the side, Titan began fighting harder to drag his body from beneath the tiger before he suffocated. He pushed with his two front legs and strained with every move, but exhaustion turned the struggle into a futile effort.

When the air quieted, Titan huffed one hard breath after another. Warm and sticky liquid oozed all over his coat.

A specter of death hovered over the dirt floor once again, ready to claim the loser.

The tiger struggled for one last breath, having bled so much too quickly to heal his throat.

Bosse and his wolf had survived once more, but not for long unless Bosse could come up with a way to get the dead weight off Titan's body. If he failed, his wolf would eventually be unable to expand his lungs enough to keep breathing.

Titan, turn your head to look at Krol.

Groaning, Titan complied. Bosse assessed the castle

king's actions to see if he was sending guards to finish him off.

No, the drama queen had his head dropped back, staring up at the ceiling. Probably infuriated that Bosse and Titan had once again squashed his attempt to lord over their defeat and death.

He may get his wish yet.

During the silence, the metal gate where Bosse exited the arena each time whooshed open. Guards came in, moving carefully. One carrying a crossbow loaded and ready entered, then stood back. The other guards poked their rifle barrels at the tiger, checking to see if it had expired.

The stink of expelled body fluids at that moment should be confirmation enough.

Bosse had only one option, and it was not going to be fun. *I'm sorry to hurt you more, but give me the body, Titan.*

After a strained wheeze, Titan dropped his head down and initiated a change that stopped halfway.

Hell.

But enough of Bosse's human head had made the transition. When he could speak, he rasped out in a rough whisper for the closest two guards, "The tiger skin can be sold for what all of you earn in a month. But if you wait too long, the skin will be nothing more than a dirt rug."

Those two had leaned forward to hear his words.

They straightened up and murmured to each other, then quietly addressed the other four. Evidently, a deal had been made while Krol stared at the ceiling.

All six began dragging the tiger's body away.

Inside Bosse, Titan whimpered once when the dead tiger's paw dragged across Bosse's back, and the huge cat's head banged Titan's badly injured foot.

Bosse forced himself not to shout at the guards. He did not want Krol to discover his men were inadvertently helping him. Once the pressure had been removed and Bosse had room to squirm around, he finished shifting all the way. Lying there a moment to catch his breath, he prepared for the pain, then got to his knees. The room spun. He sucked in more air and made it to his feet. To remain upright, he had to put a hand against the wall.

His stomach rolled. He suffered a dry heave for his effort.

We are healing slowly, Titan said, sounding weary and beaten down from suffering.

Taking in shallow breaths to keep from throwing up, Bosse sent back, *That's good. We'll stand here a minute. If you can heal at least the foot and leg, that would be most helpful.*

Energy seeped slowly into the damaged appendage. Not as powerfully as it would have been flowing if they were a hundred percent, but a start.

"*What are you doing?*" Krol shouted. He jumped up from his throne.

Bosse kept quiet and watched without moving a muscle.

Every guard froze. The one in charge said, "Uhhh … we wish to save this hide, uh, for you, Alpha."

"Do not *ever* help that wolf again, or you will face worse than the tiger next time."

They all dropped the hold they had on the tiger's body. As one, they shouted, "Yes, Alpha."

Nobody moved.

Grabbing his head, Krol ordered, "Get the body out of there, skin it, and bring me the hide."

Panicked now, every guard used both hands and dragged the carcass free of the arena.

Bosse tried putting weight on the foot. *Oh, mother.* Not yet.

Krol swung his black gaze to Bosse. "You were lucky again today. You will not always be so fortunate."

If this was luck, Bosse and Titan could do without it. He found saying nothing to Krol worked best, especially since that lunatic liked hearing his own voice more than anyone else's.

"You will stand there for ten more minutes before returning to your cage."

Inside him, Titan snickered. *Ask him to punish us with twenty minutes.*

Bosse did his best to maintain a flat, give-a-shit expression and avoid chuckling at Titan's twisted humor. He might be able to walk in twenty minutes.

Krol turned his back, and two female servants rushed to his side, asking what they could do.

He sent them running with a sweep of his hand. "Get out!"

Neither had been the female with mixed-colored eyes. Just as well. Titan had been right to be pissed at Bosse for getting distracted.

Krol stalked out behind the two women running away.

Bosse's shoulders and chest muscles eased, but nothing stopped the pain racking his body. He had to keep his bad foot flat on the ground to heal correctly. Nerves in his back burned to life all at the same moment. Reaching a hand around to check the lump on his head aggravated the headache pounding his skull.

Titan growled, but the ache they suffered meant they stood tall to battle another day.

Bosse listened to the movement of guards outside the arena. They spoke quietly, grumbling about getting screwed on the tiger skin. They thought no one could hear them whisper. Stupid humans had gotten too comfortable with shifters.

He would not kill them for doing their jobs unless he got a chance to escape, and they stood in his way. Ridiculous thought. He was never going to escape. Krol had armed the guards with titanium-coated bullets, arrow tips, and swords.

Harming Krol had never been off the table.

Bosse would shred that miserable lion shifter if he ever had the chance to battle the castle king. Two years of abuse he would never forgive.

Sadly, Krol treated Bosse no worse than his own family and pack alpha.

They'd sold him into slavery.

In fact, the entire pack where he'd grown up in Ávži at

the north end of Norway had turned their collective backs on him.

The only woman he'd thought cared for him had come to his bed nightly for a month. He'd welcomed her soft and willing body until she went into heat. At that point, he refused to bed her until it passed. He wouldn't even risk having sex and pulling out. She'd shown no interest in him beyond the sex, which had been fine since she was far from mate material.

One minute, she loved on him, and the next, she turned into a harpy, screaming at him, "What are you doing refusing me?"

He'd been adamant. "I will not bring a child into this world to be raised by the pack that has mistreated me my entire short life."

"You self-centered piece of shit! The alpha expects me to deliver a monster cub. If I don't, he'll make me mate with that pig Skott."

That's when he realized she and the alpha had played him. How many other women were waiting to convince him to breed them?

He sent her away, stating that he would no longer bed females from the pack. That was the day he decided to make other plans. Going lone wolf had become dangerous with the human population now aware that shifters existed, but he could not stay.

All he'd ever wanted was to live free and settle down with a mate. Unlike other lone wolves who needed a pack for support, he didn't need one. His alpha had just confirmed that for him.

The alpha of his wolf pack brought him up in front of everyone the next night and gave him a choice—breed the females in heat or leave.

Bosse had crossed his arms and calmly declared, "My mother and I will leave." It would have to be better somewhere else. He and his mother did not get along, but he would not abandon her. As the original alpha, Bosse's father had died a month earlier beneath the claws of this unscrupulous shifter who had blindsided him in an ambush. From that moment, Bosse had accepted his duty to his only family and kept his mother safe.

During the pack meeting, he sure as hell hadn't expected her to slide over next to the new alpha and curl her fingers around his arm or admit, "I'm staying."

The woman had never been much of a mother, but Bosse couldn't believe she'd stand with that miserable excuse for an alpha who had killed her mate.

Done with her and the entire pack, Bosse said, "Very well. I will leave immediately."

"Not exactly." The alpha gave that cagey reply, then waved his hand as if calling someone forward.

Two shifters in human form and smelling of jackal emerged from the dark shadows.

Bosse had never seen them before. He angled his body to keep everyone, including the strangers, in view. "What's this about?"

The alpha casually explained, "You will go with them."

With a dismissive glance at the two shifters, Bosse scoffed at the stupid comment. "No. I'll leave, and you'll never hear from me again. Stand in my way, and you'll regret it."

"You are partially correct," the alpha mused. "I tire of you refusing to do your part to build up this pack. I will not allow you to join another pack where you might breed their females and build an army against me. A powerful man has paid well to take you off my hands."

What the hell? Bosse stabbed an incredulous look at his father's killer. "You *sold* me?" His gaze swept sideways to his mother, who showed zero reaction. "And you *knew* about this, didn't you?"

She sighed heavily as if he inconvenienced her with such a question. "Everyone has a duty to be a good pack member. You never even tried."

Was she serious? "I am *not* going to breed a female I have no desire to mate with and then hand off my cubs as if they have no more value than livestock. For that, you stand with a man who thinks to sell your only child?"

Placing a hand on her middle, she looked longingly at her new alpha. "Not my only child for long."

Unbelievable. Bosse released a harsh laugh. "You and this entire pack can't force me to go anywhere."

Shrugging with indifference, the alpha said, "I have been assured these two shifters sent to transport you to your new home will be sufficient." His lips curved into a sly smile.

What the hell had been put in motion here?

Bosse backed away, warning the strangers, "Get your money returned. I have no desire to kill you, but neither will I come willingly."

He continued to back up another five steps.

Not a person spoke or made a move. They were smarter than he'd given this bunch credit for. Once he had reached the dense woods and was too far for someone to rush over to grab him, he turned and lunged into a run.

Within several steps, something sharp stabbed his back and burned.

He ran harder, but his legs became rubbery. His jaw went slack. He stumbled.

Drugs! Titan yelled in his head.

Bosse's vision blurred, and his stomach revolted. His last thought was that his own mother had betrayed him.

Women had proven to be his downfall.

Bosse shook off the bad memory. He glanced at the empty arena covered in the dried blood of past slaughters, none of which he felt proud about, but neither would he regret surviving. He tested his injured foot. He'd limp, but he could walk.

Ten minutes had come and gone. With Krol no longer present, the guards weren't as worried about returning Bosse to his cage. No reason to move yet while the guards ignored him.

He stayed put for what felt like another fifteen minutes.

Titan said, *Walk now.*

Bosse took a couple of careful steps. Not bad. Blood might finally be drying on his back, but complete healing would require food. For now, he'd take being able to walk to the cage.

He went to the steel bar door and shouted, "Krol said ten minutes. I don't care, but your boss must."

Someone cursed and came pounding over to the gate. "Get out." The guard carrying a crossbow loaded with a barbed titanium tip arrow, who most often walked him back to his cage, waited.

While he would survive a stab that didn't slice up an organ too badly, the titanium would kill any shifter if left inside the body long enough.

For that reason, he strolled quietly down the dirt corridor and passed through a wooden door hanging on handmade metal hinges and into the basement area. Captured shifters were kept in cages. He paused next to a doorless room on his left the guards called *záchod*—a toilet.

Dark and noxious smelling, it held only a rusty bucket.

The crossbow guard nodded. Disgusting, but Bosse's cage stayed cleaner than most of the others.

On his way to his cage again, Bosse passed the stairs on his left that led up to the main floor of the castle. Just beyond the bottom of the stairs, two guards sat in wooden chairs and used an empty barrel for a table. They played a card game called Zasran until a new pair came at midnight to relieve them.

Bosse rarely thought about what day it was or the time.

What purpose would that serve?

His cage waited twenty feet ahead, the second one on the left and one of the two largest in a space that contained an additional eight when at full capacity. Revolting scents of shifters in animal and human form permeated the stale air.

A shifter should not live in captivity.

When Bosse managed to sleep and not suffer nightmares, he dreamed of Titan feeling the air rush over his coat as he ran wild.

As he neared the first cage on the left, Beast lunged,

slamming into the inch-thick titanium bar wall. Metal creaked at the seams.

Could he break free? The guards had better hope not.

Unfazed, Bosse paused to glance over, grin, and wink at what was thought to be a black rhino shifter.

Beast went berserk, uttering crazy snorting sounds.

Everyone called this shifter Beast because even in his semi-human form, he was a creature from night terrors. Coarse dark hair with white tips sprang from his head like curly serpents. Patches of gray-brown dense fur covered most of the shifter's ruddy skin. Thick bands of slick black carapace had formed over parts of his back.

Bosse was nothing special to look at either, but he'd never spent so much time in animal form that he'd lost his humanity. He'd heard the guards whisper about the only time they'd seen Beast shift fully into his rhino form. Evidently, it looked nothing like the natural animal except for sharp hooves. The twisted part-human-and-part-rhino head had wide jaws filled with fangs. Shaggy black fur streamed down from indestructible black plates covering its upper body.

Human eyes the color of a ripe pumpkin stared back with no hint of emotion.

Bosse had doubts about Beast shifting into anything other than his present appearance.

When would Krol toss that monster into the arena with Bosse?

Not until the castle king believed his favorite beast could win.

That time had to be coming soon. The only reason Krol hadn't outright killed Bosse by now was because the castle king wanted to enjoy watching him die from the safety of his throne.

Plus, he would not lower himself to risk losing.

Beast raged and made hoarse honking noises Bosse interpreted as bloody threats.

"Stop bothering Beast," the guard escorting him ordered.

As he turned slowly, inspiration struck Bosse. He stared

at the guard and shrugged. "I can't help that the smell of fresh blood sets him off."

Beast quieted at that, an ominous change in him.

Whoever used magic, power, or both to alter that shifter's animal shape would have laughed at the suggestion this abomination got upset at the smell of blood. He lived for it. Who had remade a shifter into this creature?

Bosse's bet? This thing had been the result of a Black River Pack experiment.

He shuddered at the thought of being experimented on by that sick group.

Beast slammed the cage, and the steel-plated floor welded to the bars rocked.

The guard following Bosse lifted his crossbow higher. "You know the drill. Stop two steps past the door to your cage."

Once Bosse had complied, the guard opened the door to his cage and stood behind the open door as if that would protect him.

Bosse entered, hesitant to lie on his still-wrecked back and glad he had no mirror to assess the damage. He had to sit or stretch out soon to offer his body a better chance of healing. He decided to do a psych-out and stiffened his body before falling forward with his arms bent. His hands landed first. Like shock absorbers, his elbows took the brunt of his fall.

Titan's displeasure rumbled.

Bosse sent back, *Sorry. Best way to get down on the floor without more damage to our back or exposing a weakness.* He did ten pushups for show, then rolled over on his side with his back facing the cage exit. He forced his pained sigh to come out quietly under his breath.

No one could sneak in to catch Bosse with his back facing the entrance without him hearing them. More than that, none of this group wanted any part of him and kept their distance.

After a few minutes, he heard two guards straining to walk and cursing with each step. His taunt about Beast not liking the smell of fresh blood may have paid off, but he tensed. The result of his goading would hurt like a mother.

He told Titan, *Brace for the cold bath*. He got no answer, but muscles in his back and chest tightened.

When the splash of ice water mixed with salt hit open wounds, Bosse fisted his hands white-knuckle hard but kept quiet.

Heaving shallow breaths to hide his reaction, he slowly opened his fists. With the initial shock and acidic scald passing, Bosse smiled at feeling cleaner. Krol believed the salt broke down dried blood faster to keep the area cleaner. He must not realize salt aided in healing. Even if it was a brutal method, Bosse would rather be clean.

Exhaustion swept over him. Sleep dragged him under. Titan had gone quiet, doing his part to first repair major damage and then work on smaller injuries.

The deep voice of an angry guard woke him. "Who sent healers at this hour? You know what? I don't care. Just get it done."

Healers? Bosse stirred awake. Why would anyone be here now when he was the only injured shifter?

The women who came down to the cages weren't really healers but servants who brought water and food. When forced, some would do their best to treat shifters in human form who were too injured to heal fast. The women would do it only if a guard armed with a crossbow stood watch, but not for Bosse. The most he'd gotten from all but one servant in recent months had been dirty rags tossed through the bars and water sloshed in the direction of his bowl.

Then the female with two different colored eyes who smelled of cinnamon and cardamom began visiting the basement late at night.

She had a distinctive soft step. She'd started occasionally leaving part of a goat or deer leg hidden in a rag that she'd discreetly push through the bars and drop beside the empty pottery bowl used for water or porridge. In the last two weeks, he often found his chipped and cracked bowl filled with water. She did it without entering his cage.

Then there were cookies. Spicy honey cookies.

He hadn't known what to think the first time she'd left the treat, but he never hesitated to scarf them down. Those extras appeared at odd times, usually while the guards on duty were deep into a game.

He sniffed the air. *She* was here.

Had she brought him a surprise? Was he a fool to hope? Maybe. He'd survived disappointment at the hands of other women. He could suffer anything so long as he and Titan received meat.

Why was she down here in the dark hours of early morning? He only knew an approximate time because the two guards present were new ones.

One of the guards smacked the table with his fist. "Get movin', or I'll make ya both pay for bein' a nuisance."

Two servants? Bosse relaxed his muscles to appear asleep and waited to find out what was going on.

"She doesn't want to go into the wolf's cage," a deep-throated female sounding like his cookie fairy said.

Stupid guards. No woman should have to enter a cage with a monster, especially not a human female.

Bosse considered helping the women, then hesitated. If he spoke up to say he needed nothing, his comment might draw negative attention to the women once the guards reported the incident to Krol.

He could hear the heartbeats of four people, two of which pounded wildly. Lifting up slowly, he caught sight of the second woman, a younger girl with brassy red hair.

That one was terrified of the guards, shifters, and her shadow.

The big-nosed guard in charge yelled, "Get in there and patch him up!"

"Please, no. I—I can't do that." Red's breathing got faster and shorter until she fainted.

"For the love of … Get this bitch out of here."

Bosse glanced through the only opening between the bars on Beast's cage and the rhino's grotesque shape for a slim view of what was happening.

The second guard flopped the redhead's body over his shoulder and stomped his way upstairs.

That left only the cookie fairy.

What woman baked cookies for a monster?

He didn't want her forced to enter any shifter's cage, especially his.

The guard glowered at her and warned, "I won't be so nice to another female who refuses to do her job."

His cookie fairy muttered angrily, "I'm not a healer. Just a servant."

"I don't care if you can heal or not. If Krol said to get his pet wolf patched up, *you* tell him you refused."

She argued, "No. I don't—"

The sound of a loud slap cut her off.

Bosse jerked his head up, rage igniting inside him. He'd never allowed a female to be harmed, no matter if he liked her or not. For the first time since being captured, he suffered an emotional reaction he hadn't in years.

He'd felt nothing in so long that the sensation surprised him.

Titan interjected, *We will not win against armed guards.*

I know it. Damn guard. Bosse could barely see past the blaze of anger threatening to blind him. He curled his fingers into fists that could break rocks. He hated being caged. Wanted to pummel the spineless slug who struck a female, especially that one.

Why he felt this strongly about it now confused him. That didn't mean he possessed the ability to care about someone other than himself and Titan, right? But somewhere deep inside, he still possessed the need to protect a woman.

His sense of honor had mattered nothing to the pack females who sat silently as he was treated like a slab of beef.

The sudden quiet pushed bad memories away for the moment.

That female servant should be weeping, making some kind of sound.

What had happened?
Had the guard killed her?

Chapter 4

ALIFAIR BIT BACK anger at this ingrate. Losing her temper with a guard would ruin her act of being meek. *Never forget the goal.* She'd been told that since childhood by a mother whose footsteps she now tried to step into.

Her face didn't sting from the guard's slap.

It throbbed.

She blinked away tears. The hood of her black robe and the lack of light beyond the torches made it easier to hide her face. Guards only lit torches around their table at night. This entire place felt like she'd fallen down a rabbit hole and ended up in the Middle Ages. No electric lights or kitchen appliances. No phones, mobile or otherwise. No medical services or law enforcement anywhere around here.

A movie set couldn't be this sterile of technology.

This scum would not see her cry. What a waste to have used her limited power on this spineless guard only for him to hit her, but her idea had worked.

So far.

Sadly, she had not used her magic to protect herself but to gain her way inside a dangerous wolf shifter's cage. Friends from her clan back home would be shocked at her for taking such a risk, but they were the same ones who decided *she* was the only one who could succeed at this hellish task. She'd inherited the duty of protecting them.

It would have been nice if she'd inherited her mother's

level of power and experience gained from so many years protecting the clan. Alifair was a poor substitute.

She followed Cyrano, the name she'd given the guard in charge of the basement security until midnight.

With a supersized nose, that guard would be perfect in the role of Cyrano de Bergerac.

He opened the door to Bosse's cage and shut it after she entered, clamping the lock in place.

She kept an eye on him as he turned to walk away, then whispered the words of a simple spell to interrupt his hearing and memory. His gait hitched momentarily, but he kept walking back to his wooden chair.

Her gaze skipped from him to the freaky rhino in the next cage. Its orange eyes flickered open and then closed.

She should be thankful she didn't have to meet that monster. Easy to understand why they called him Beast. If this was his human form, he was neither fully animal nor human.

Not that she was any safer in the cage of the castle's undefeated wolf shifter.

She scrunched her nose against the nauseating smell of animal and human body odor coming from Beast's cage but not the wolf shifter's. She'd have to breathe through her mouth.

Her heart pounded like a frightened horse in a dead run. It didn't want to do this either.

Calm down, she ordered quietly. Hopefully, this wolf shifter recalled she'd left him meat … and cookies.

Convinced they were not paying attention to her now that the second guard had returned and Cyrano had restarted their card game, she spoke a spell softly on both sides of this cage to protect conversation in here.

Then she crossed her fingers and hoped her plan worked.

Not a professional action for someone from her gifted clan, but she depended upon being lucky more than expecting to wield dependable magic many days.

She lowered her gaze to take in Bosse's human form,

lying very still with his back to her, and stopped short of crying out at the damage.

That tiger had slashed him open. Red, inflamed skin swelled all around his injuries. Blood still oozed from one.

His body barely moved with soft breaths.

Should she disturb him if he slept?

Taking a deep breath to calm her racing heart, she blew out her frustration and wiped the tears from her eyes. Her clan believed such unnatural beings shouldn't exist.

But she didn't accept all their ideas. Why should she tell someone born to be a shifter that they didn't deserve to live?

She'd never expected to be close to a shifter, especially one so powerful, but her dreams drove her decisions and actions. Realizing what she had to do, her hands shook. Regardless of her clan's influence, she did possess a healthy fear of someone who could change into a dangerous animal and kill her.

She'd taken a leap of faith by entering this cage.

Stalling wouldn't help.

This would be easier if she'd been tasked to save someone she liked.

Her parents would expect her to accept her new role and carry on the family legacy regardless of who she protected.

Squatting down, she dropped to her knees and ran her gaze from Bosse's head to his feet, not missing one inch of that beautiful naked body so severely hurt. The scraggly hair and mountain-man beard dented his looks, but those cut muscles … Goodness! He had to be at least six-four. Every day, that beautiful body got ripped to pieces, and yet he still managed to survive.

And be in constant pain since Krol never sent help. Thankfully, these two guards stayed down here more than up in the main hall.

She didn't want to think about what that sicko Krol would do to her if he found out she'd been down here on her own. He had a particularly cruel streak when it came to this shifter.

Inching forward, she had to maintain her balance to avoid falling on Bosse.

That would have started them out on the wrong foot. He'd probably rip her apart before she had a chance to gain his trust.

If her dream proved to be correct, he wouldn't kill her.

At least, not yet.

A comforting thought.

As comforting as staring down a rattlesnake that only shook its tail in displeasure. One mistake and it would strike.

Wrong mental image.

She needed to do a better job of psyching herself up to deal with a shifter. Delaying what she had little time to execute would bite her in the butt if the spell wore off too soon.

Tell that to her nerves.

A shortcoming for someone with her job description for sure, but she'd lived with the flaw her whole life.

Exuberant shouts went up from the guards over some move in the game they played.

A positive sign. She needed them distracted and not paying attention even while the spell worked.

Her right-hand fingers ached from gripping the cloth. She'd pulled the ends together to make a sack she could hide inside her cloak.

Pulling the sack forward to sit between her legs and allowing her cloak to fall around her like a tent, she considered her next move.

His wounds turned her stomach.

How could even a shifter's body take so much abuse?

She reached a trembling hand out to tap him on his shoulder.

Just short of touching him, he flinched. Of course, he was awake and knew someone was in his cell. She'd been foolish to think he'd slept through all this.

Snatching her hand back, she started to whisper what she had to tell him.

Before she could, he ordered, "Get out."

He hadn't even rolled over to speak to her first. Of course, she'd seen him move in a battle as if he and his wolf had eyes in the back of their heads. Surly man, wolf, whatever, if he thought she'd just scamper away at his command.

She had a worse flaw than intermittent magic.

When someone dared to order her around, a stubborn streak showed up. It had been hard enough to keep stifled during the past four weeks she'd been here, but she'd expected to be given orders as a servant.

Not from a person with even less freedom than her.

Sweetening her sarcasm, she assured him, "I won't hurt you."

Had he snorted or chuckled? Was he laughing at her?

She narrowed her eyes, a wasted effort when he could not see her.

He lifted a hand and ran his fingers through tangled hair the color of peanut butter, then dropped his hand back to the dirt-covered metal floor. "*I* am not the one in danger." His words came out low and gruff.

She almost detected the hint of an accent buried under his flat tone.

He spoke again. "Call the guard to release you. I need no healing."

Leaning close, she whispered, though her words still came out sharp, "I didn't go through all *that* to get in here just for you to tell me to leave. Find some manners."

He stilled, and then his head lifted.

When he twisted around to face her, his mop of pale brown hair covered his face except for one confused orb. A fascinating brown one that reminded her of dark whiskey.

"What did you say?"

"Keep your voice down," she hissed. Could he not just wait to find out why she was here? Why had her dream chosen this man to help her?

He'd understand one thing for sure.

She dug into the woven sack and pulled out a hind quarter

from the boar brought in today. It had taken all she could do to sneak it out of the kitchen in the garbage she offered to carry to a spot where guards would burn it later in the week.

Unwilling to touch him, she flipped the meat over his waist and gave him an order. "Quick, take it before the guards see."

He snatched the leg from the air before it hit the dirt. The meat disappeared into the dark shadow between him and the back of the cage.

She knew without question that was the most protein he'd received for days, even with the additional meat she brought when possible. A wild dog deserved better than the grunge they fed this man.

She'd brought him cookies twice.

He'd been asleep, so he may not have realized the gift had been from her. Maybe she should have included a note, but that might have gotten them both killed.

She wanted her rapid heartbeat to slow down, but she couldn't wish away her fear.

After several minutes, his body moved and settled with a deep breath. He sounded angry or put out when he said, "Tell me who hit you. I will kill him, and we will be even."

He'd do what?

Her heart pounded even harder at his fervent words. She doubted not one of them.

To be honest, his offer to retaliate over her injury touched her. No one had protected her since she reached the age of eighteen, seven years ago.

Her fear settled into worry. "No, please don't do that. It was necessary to antagonize that guard, or I could not have come in here. They wouldn't trust me if I had asked."

Bosse turned his head again. That single eye now stared at her as if he should fear her. "You got thrown in here on *purpose*?"

She sighed at his confusion and glanced to her left to confirm the guards were still enthralled with their game, and the rhino monster continued to sleep. Turning back, she quickly explained, "Yes. I must leave soon, or they'll become suspicious. I have something to tell you."

"Tell me." Simple and loaded with suspicion. With one quick exchange of words, he'd become wary of her.

She understood. She'd heard whispers about the invincible wolf shifter from Norway. Had he been here so long he'd lost his original language? Or did he speak English because Krol forced all his people to speak English? Linota had warned her to keep her distance from this wolf shifter. That hadn't been possible.

Based on what Alifair had learned about him, she could understand how he would not be receptive to a stranger—not yet.

She hurried to share what she could. "I don't have time to say much. I'll be back again and explain when I return."

"Why did you come now?"

His attitude was beginning to wear on her. Yes, he had reason to be cautious around anyone, but she'd brought him extra food more than once, including tonight. The best way to tamp down her terror was if someone riled her up.

He was doing a great job of it.

Every time he spoke, he made it sound like she was an idiot lacking any basic sense. Thanks to her damn dream, she had to deal with this unappreciative brute.

She kept her reply simple. "I'm here because you need meat to heal, even though you claim to be fine, and I need you to win your next battle tonight."

He sat up halfway, leaving from his waist down in the shadows. She hadn't been this close to him until now. Every time he moved, she admired more of his seriously carved muscles. He looked fit enough to toss an elephant over the moon.

If she stayed here much longer, she'd perspire from a sudden hot flash.

Had he kept his manhood turned away from her as a courtesy?

He grumbled, "Tonight? I never fight twice in one day."

That rocked her back on track. "Krol left after your last

battle. I heard him tell the guards he would return in four to six hours and to have the arena ready."

Bosse scoffed softly. "He could be sending Beast in to fight."

She shook her head. "Krol said to bring *you* the minute he returned." Her neck tingled at the sensation that time was running out. She had to go. "When I come back, we'll talk. I wanted to meet you first and to let you know you can … trust me."

"I trust no one." His words came out dead and unyielding.

Her heart plunged at his brutal declaration. "I understand why you would not, but we both want to escape this place. You can't do it alone. Eat the rest of the meat as soon as I distract them by getting me out of here." To end any further conversation, she stood and called, "Guards!"

The card game stopped amidst curses.

She whispered, "Lay back down like you're unconscious."

"Why?"

"Seriously? Just. Lay. Down." She put a growl into her words.

He smirked and relaxed his body, turning his back to her again.

The bigger guard who had carried the woman upstairs came over. "What are you doing in there?"

She now stood near the cage exit and let her voice tremble. A tear escaped to run down her cheek. She sounded pitiful and tiny when she said, "That other guard made me come in here. The wolf never woke up. I don't know how to fix his cuts and bruises."

She caught her breath but couldn't risk turning around to be sure Bosse looked asleep. She begged, "Please let me out. Please. I have more tasks to do."

He cursed and unlocked the cage, then shut it quickly once she was out, relocking it behind her.

Sniffling, she hurried past the next cage, where Beast growled and slammed the bars.

Wasn't he asleep? Had he heard her words?

The spell should have muffled her conversation with

Bosse. Plus, she'd never heard of Beast speaking. She ran to the steps and rushed up to the main floor where she paused.

Behind her, Cyrano asked where the hell she had come from.

The guard who had let her out of Bosse's cage replied, "She said ya made her go into the wolf's cage."

"The hell I did."

"Then how could she have been in there? Only you and I have the key right now. I was gone carrying that other sack of sniveling crap upstairs."

She waited to see if either guard figured out what had happened.

Cyrano ordered in a low voice, "Do not mention this to Krol. I don't know how she got in there, but you were here, too. Keep it between us."

"Agreed."

She exhaled a breath of relief. Now, if she could only make sure that the wolf shifter survives tonight's second battle, but she did not have that kind of power. She'd dreamed of him helping her save Rez, the leader of her people and her mother's best friend since childhood.

Once Alifair's mother died, Rez became a ruling tyrant around her. None of the clan realized what they had asked repeatedly of her mother and now expected her to do, but Rez should have. She had to have known what Alifair had lost and the mourning she'd gone through.

Duty came above all else, even personal feelings.

That's why Alifair had been tasked with joining Rez on a trip to Romania to meet with clan families wanting to relocate to the States.

Alifair would find Rez and send her home, but she would not accept criticism from that woman again. Not after being captured, on purpose, and forced into slave labor at this miserable castle just to find her.

Such a simple plan at first glance.

Not so much now that Alifair stood neck-deep in an impossible situation.

She'd staked a lot on dreams that had directed her to this castle. Where exactly had Krol hidden Rez, and what plan did he have for her?

No dream had answered those questions yet.

Thankfully, Alifair had been able to hide her abilities from Krol and his people.

If Bosse died tonight or even ended up injured too severely to heal quickly, she'd fail at her sole reason for existing. Watching Bosse die would hurt her as well, which surprised her. She'd been taught to fear shifters as mindless creatures that attacked any breathing being, but Bosse didn't seem to fit that stereotype.

He hadn't said thank you for the food and cookies, but he *had* wanted to punish the guard who had hit her.

She'd been a child the last time she felt safe and protected.

Men who had shown an interest in her as a young woman would never have put themselves in harm's way for her.

She shook off her wandering thoughts and returned to pondering on how to gain Bosse's trust.

After she'd had the same dream three times with him playing a role in this escapade, she'd devised a way to convince him to help her. The dream godmother had been otherwise stingy regarding Rez's location in this castle.

Alifair's path could not change now. Once one of her clairvoyant dreams gifted her with information, it was up to her to act.

Based on what she knew right now, Bosse was the only one who could save Rez, though the details were still murky.

The dream did not include Alifair being rescued, but she hoped to find a way out on her own once Rez was safe.

Chapter 5

K ROL LEFT HIS guards behind for this trip. He could travel quicker alone, and the less anyone knew what he was up to, the better. He patted the neck of Cierna, a raven-black Dacian horse descendant and fit for a king.

The lean, muscular animal had been a gift from a local farmer who bred a few horses a year to sell and pull his wagons to market. He offered the best horse he owned and asked only for his family to be ignored.

An amusing request. Humans were funny creatures.

Krol accepted the equine gift, of course, which had been well-trained, and told the man he'd think about the request.

Bright spots of sun shooting through the leaves had dwindled in the past hour. He hoped to reach what ruins were left of another castle before dark. After traveling for two hours, he came upon a cemetery overrun by weeds due to neglect. Just past that point, he guided his mount off the beaten trail and wove his way through thick woods to approach the meet point from an unexpected direction. Another ten minutes later, he located the weed-encroached trail he and his pride once used to hunt prey near the ruins of another castle.

Those lions were gone.

They could not keep up with his ambition. Worse, the males complained like old women.

In fact, he killed them as easily as a group of old women.

They should never have angered him. Sadly, the females were killed in the bloodbath. Just as well. With all the shifters he continually acquired, he'd eventually find the perfect mate and queen for his castle.

His horse sidestepped, interrupting Krol's mental wandering. He pulled up, pausing for a moment to study the area. The mage he'd been communicating with had sent word he was ready to discuss a deal and included directions to locate the abandoned castle at *Uhrovske Podhradie.*

Krol chuckled at how he'd sincerely thanked the mage for directions. He knew this land well and chose his own path to arrive at the castle from a different direction. He avoided the dirt road normally taken.

Good place to be ambushed.

As if he'd trust anyone, especially a powerful magic maker.

All seemed at peace here. Fresh air filled with pine scent lifted above the rot of leaves in the mud. Small animals scurried from one spot to another. Birds flew overhead, confirming no unusual threat nearby. He goaded Cierna into walking again and forced himself to move steadily without rushing.

In this forest, dark would arrive before the sun fully dropped out of sight in another hour.

Besides, he would not risk injury to his mount by hurrying through a treacherous route overgrown like a tangled rat's nest of weeds and debris from storms. If Cierna stepped in a hole and became lame, Krol would be forced to shift into his lion to kill his magnificent ride and then return to the castle in animal form.

It was undignified for a king to do such a thing. He shifted only when he wished to hunt and kill for sport, not to exercise his lion or travel like a peasant.

Everyone in his kingdom, including his lion, lived only to serve Krol.

Finally, the trees thinned out, allowing a gentle breeze to snake around his face. He slowed his horse before entering the unkempt open space surrounding a once impressive stronghold.

As a young cub, he'd escape his father's pride and spend

days here rambling through the stone fortress. He laughed, recalling when he'd chased a small bear across the wooden walkway stretched between two points of the structure like a bridge.

On the other hand, he cringed just thinking back at the damp and moldy smell of rot from decaying furniture scattered around. Peeling wallpaper spoke of a majestic time in the past.

This place had inspired him to have his own castle.

While the main building and wall structures appeared sturdy at first glance, he'd had a floor covered with a threadbare rug fall away from beneath him. His lion's quick reaction and ability to leap a great distance saved him from injury more than once.

He walked Cierna over to a tree at the edge of the forest, then dismounted and tied the reins to a low branch. While doing so, he listened for any unexpected sounds.

None yet.

Strolling across the open area that had once been kept scalped to prevent enemies from sneaking up on the castle, Krol stopped in the middle of the field.

The mage should be here already. He likely observed Krol at this moment.

Krol would not take insult unless the mage delayed appearing for longer than social etiquette allowed.

That thought had no sooner crossed his mind when a ball of golden energy appeared above the thirty-foot-tall stone wall. The ball of light glowed against the deepening twilight as if the sun had fallen from the sky.

When the swirling energy dissipated, Zuzani appeared, staring down his nose at Krol.

Zuzani stepped off the wall, floating down with the ease of a feather carried on the light breeze.

Krol managed to keep a straight face and not roll his eyes at the show of power.

The mage moved smoothly across the thirty-five yards separating them. His loose clothing hid the shape of his body, but Krol sized up human forms all the time. Though not entirely human, this one had an average body with adequate muscle but nothing that matched a lion shifter. Thick russet hair appeared blown back from Zuzani's youthful face as if he'd been racing forward against a strong wind. Diamond studded earrings sparkled at his ears.

For them to sparkle, there had to be magic at work, with no light available to shine on jewels.

Krol had met this man once before.

Zuzani had worn the same Persian gray silk tunic with long bell sleeves ornately embroidered in gold. Black pants of similar material flowed with the slightest encouragement from the air befriending him. Most notable was the silver pendant hanging against his chest on a thick chain braided of gold, silver, and bronze threads. A walnut-sized ruby set in the center of the pendant glowed.

More magic.

Was the show for Krol's benefit? A wasted effort. He only cared that this mage could do what he claimed.

Zuzani's arms were folded in front of him with his hands hidden inside the sleeves.

Anyone with a lick of survival sense knew those hands were his weapons.

As the mage neared, he said, "I am prepared to make an equitable agreement if you are."

"Of course, I am. My presence should confirm I am more than ready." Krol had no patience for people who talked in circles, but he would only have to suffer through talking to this one until he got what he wanted.

Was the mage truly ready to make the delivery now?

Krol hid his excitement beneath a layer of relaxed indifference. This was a negotiation. He had yet to find out what the mage wanted in exchange for Krol's request.

Zuzani stopped fifteen feet away. "Your presence can mean many things, but I will take you at your word until you give me a reason to not."

Wasn't that understood? Krol kept his arms relaxed at his sides, leaving it up to the mage to make the next move.

"You asked for a creature capable of capturing and

carrying a grown man while not leaving a scent trail. Correct?"

Did Zuzani think he had forgotten? Krol could make capturing shifters and other unusual beings so much easier with no way to be tracked afterward. He nodded. "That is correct."

"I will present my creation. Do not move until I tell you."

Krol couldn't stop the twitch of his fingers, ready for the unveiling.

Zuzani swept his right arm away from his body and pointed at a spot on the ground. He whispered words Krol could not discern even with his sensitive shifter hearing.

A circle of light appeared, and then a huge bird stood in the center. It had the head of an eagle but the wrong coloration. Low on its chest, the body blended into a four-legged animal with a long tail.

Krol's lion snarled inside of him and battered his sides. Krol silently ordered, *Cease now or pay the price later*.

Smells bad, his lion replied, but his agitation slowed.

Yes, the creature carried an odor of magic, but Krol could accept that. He kept his voice even with a touch of interest. "What is it?"

Smiling slyly, Zuzani said, "I call it a Lammogo. I took the upper body of a lammergeier, a great vulture from the mountains of central Asia, and merged it with a Mapogo lion."

Shock hit Krol before he could hide his reaction. "Mapogos were said to be extinct in 2013." He knew this because he'd scoured South Africa searching for one.

Zuzani shrugged. "I have my resources. One was rewarded handsomely when he informed me of a Mapogo lioness heavy with cubs. She gave birth to a pair, which I took before the homicidal males destroyed their own pride. I raised the twin cubs to maturity."

Krol dipped his head in respect for that move. He could barely take his eyes off the Lammogo. It had black markings along the vicious hooked beak, iron-red colored head feathers along the neck, and then black across its body. Bright yellow eyes ringed in red could not be any more natural than the rest of it.

"How much can it carry when flying?" Krol asked, concerned about the weight of the creature alone.

"The natural lammergeier has a ten-foot-wide wingspan, but this one's wings spread to fourteen feet and are far more powerful. It can carry a full-grown man as requested. It is also capable of capture only when killing is not required."

Krol shook his head in awe. "I will be honest. I am without words. This is impressive, to say the least." The mage had been brilliant to use a Mapogo lion. Its body was covered in a dark brown coat with powerful golden legs. Razor-sharp claws curved from paws the size of a man's head. Mapogo lions had been a pack of related males who stayed together instead of creating individual prides. They were responsible for the deaths of over forty lions and cubs in one single year.

Vicious killers.

Krol salivated to have this creation. He could admire the creature back at his castle. Right now, he had to find out what the mage wanted in payment, which would not be money. "I am ready to hear what my part of this deal will be."

Zuzani took a moment and said, "I want something from Austria. I can't go as I have enemies watching for me there."

Krol saw no issue traveling to Austria. "Go on."

"I will send the Lammogo with you to train, which will only take one day once I give it a command. For now, it will not kill, only transport a person or follow any other non-attack orders. You will travel with it to Austria by whatever means you deem workable. Once there, you'll go to a location I'll provide and extract the mate of a bear shifter. She is pregnant. I want her unharmed."

So far, nothing Krol could not manage. "I see no problem with that task."

"Excellent. As of this minute, you have seven days from

the moment you leave here to capture the female and deliver her to this spot."

Krol did not reply yet. He would like to have some leeway on the deadline in case he ran into some unexpected trouble.

Zuzani was quick to pick up on his hesitation. "Have you changed your mind on our exchange?"

"No, of course not. I am only concerned that I might need more time to ensure the female is not harmed while traveling. I wouldn't want to rush and her deliver the cub too soon."

"That would be a mistake if you allowed such to happen. She has another month to go."

See? That's what Krol hated about Zuzani talking in circles. "Are you saying I can't have another day or two if I need it?"

"I want the female in one week. I have been quite clear. You must decide if you wish to make this deal. It is the only time I will make this offer."

Krol had harbored a bad feeling this mage would be like that. "I'm in. I want the Lammogo."

"As we proceed, there must be terms of agreement and consequences for failure," Zuzani stated.

Krol's skin chilled, but he had confidence in his ability to execute a plan. "I'm listening."

"If you succeed, I will give you unfettered authority over the Lammogo forever. You will have all the control you require during the next week but no orders to attack. Until you have fulfilled your part, I will still hold the full reins to my creation. Fair enough?"

"Agreed. If the Lammogo follows my orders without harming the bear shifter mate, that's fine by me." Krol could barely wait until completing his part of this bargain to make plans for using that flying creature as a weapon to build his empire. "I get that you have a consequence in mind for me if I drop the ball, but what if your Lammogo does not perform as expected?"

Zuzani gave him a flat look.

Had he insulted the egotistical mage? Krol put this in simpler terms. "Hey, I'm negotiating, just like you are. I'm putting any question out so we're both clear on what might and might not happen."

Sounding put out, Zuzani said, "If my Lammogo does not perform successfully, in addition to keeping the Lammogo, I will gift you the only living Mapogo lion, which I have no intention of parting with for any price. If you fail to deliver Magdelina, mated to Ivo of his bear clan in Austria, to this location at the time agreed upon, I will send a message to the Lammogo to capture and deliver you at my feet to do with as I wish."

If Krol were in his lion form, fur would be bristled at his neck, the only warning of an impending attack.

"You still may choose to walk away," Zuzani offered in a mocking tone.

"How do I know you won't call to the Lammogo to bring the mate to you without me delivering her?"

The mage sighed so loudly that Krol expected birds to scatter from the trees.

Staring past Krol, Zuzani gave his answer in an exasperated tone. "I am one of the Power Barons."

Nodding that he knew this, Krol kept silent. "Explain."

"A Power Baron known as Robert lied and manipulated others in a bid to unseat the leader of our council recently. Once he was executed, the ruling council dictated a rule that all Power Barons had to take an oath to pay a substantial price if they broke their word or lied. If they did, the penalty would be to suffer ten times the fate of the person he intended to undermine or injure."

"What if someone died?" Krol needed convincing.

"If a Power Baron caused a person's death by breaking his word, he would die a horrible, dragged-out death, then be brought back to life to go through nine more similar terminations. I will make a simple demonstration to prove the truth of my words." Zuzani looked around until he found a tiny bug crawling on the ground. He crushed it under his heel.

Krol had to keep from laughing. What would killing a tiny bug prove?

Ignoring Krol's smirk, the mage explained, "Now, if I say, 'I did not kill that bug,' I would be—" Zuzani could not finish. His fingers seized, and he choked. His face lost blood, and he panted through clenched teeth.

Krol had no idea what to do to help him. He didn't think anyone was that good of an actor. He didn't dare move. He glanced at the Lammogo that stood still, blinking languidly as it watched.

After a long minute of watching Zuzani suffer, the mage caught his breath and shook his body as if freeing it from a binding. "I will *never* do that for anyone again," he muttered angrily.

That demonstration showed Krol how important this pregnant mate was to Zuzani. What would the mage do with her?

Did he care? Silly question.

Now would be a good time to get them back on better footing. "Thank you. What's next?"

Zuzani had paced a few steps away, shaking his hands, then returned to where he had stood before. He pulled his emotions under control, closed the distance between them to six feet, and took a commanding tone again. "Prepare to make the formal commitment."

Then Zuzani removed his hands from his sleeves and held a knife clutched in one. He reached up and cut a lock of his reddish-brown hair.

For a mage to clip a lock of his hair in the presence of someone who might take a strand and use it was shocking.

Following his lead, Krol produced his own knife, bigger than the mage's weapon, and lopped off a length of blond hair from his ponytail.

Zuzani said, "Our words spoken here today are understood and agreed upon by both sides, constituting an unbreakable contract and deadline. You must tell no one about this agreement or speak my name." The mage made that statement and pointed his knife at the ground between them, where grass immediately cleared away, leaving the shape of a perfect two-foot diameter circle. He stepped closer and dropped his hair, which floated to the exact center.

Krol couldn't do that, so he tossed it into the circle.

Damn, if his lock didn't land exactly on top of Zuzani's.

The mage lifted his hands above the small pile of hair and murmured something only he understood. Thick roots shaped like a three-clawed witch's hand burst through the dirt, curled around both clumps of hair, and pulled them underground.

The earth rumbled, and the circle glowed red as if on fire, then quieted.

Suddenly, Krol felt the burden of time beginning to weigh on him. "How do I find this female?"

Holding the palm of his hand facing the sky, Zuzani closed his fingers and then opened them again. A piece of paper with neat printing lay on his palm. "The bold black line on this map will take you to their clan."

"What does she look like? I need as much information as you can provide. I might even find her and return ahead of schedule," Krol boasted, ready to get moving.

"Magdelina will be easy to locate. She stands above the other females in the clan at six feet tall and has snow-white hair to her waist. Her eyes are a pale blue you will not see on one of the other females."

She sounded unique to Krol. Was she some form of shifter royalty? "What's the name of this clan?"

"The clan is called Braunbär Bastarde. Ivo is the alpha and a Gallize bear shifter. You must be swift once you capture her."

Blood drained from Krol's face. He knew nothing of the Braunbär Bastarde Clan, a name that translated to the Bastard Brown Bear Clan, but Krol *had* heard of the Gallize shifters. He had no desire to meet up with one and sure as hell never thought to put a target on his back from a group of shifters rumored to have extraordinary power.

What the hell had he gotten himself into?

Could he even do this with a Lammogo?

He had no choice.

Chapter 6

——~——

BOSSE WAITED IN the arena with its usual odor of sweat, despair, and death.

He would add disgust and hate, but no one coming in here knew anything about him. His matches had all been against strangers he had no reason to hate.

That emotion was saved for Krol.

Bastard had him fighting twice in one day, which sucked, but his cookie fairy had told the truth. Technically, this was a new day. It had only been an hour or two since she visited him.

Was this a new curve from Krol? Why?

He'd done his one disgusting service for the day. Or what seemed a day to him since he never saw the sun rise or set.

If this were to be Krol's new plan, Bosse and Titan wouldn't last much longer.

He hadn't slept much in a long time, but he fell into a deep slumber after eating the deer hindquarter. Titan was stronger even if they'd had little rest.

He still could not understand why that servant had taunted a guard into striking her.

Those meaty hands might have killed her.

Bosse really had to do something about that big-nosed guard. Not tonight, but soon.

What was taking so long? The steel door on the opposite side of the arena had not opened yet, but Krol also had yet to appear above the battlefield.

Maybe the alpha wants to play, Titan said in his mind.

We fight every day to survive. His cat is lazy. We could leap up to his throne and kill the human or the lion.

We could, Bosse agreed. He wiped his face with his hand. No way to clean his hand since he was naked, as always. He reminded Titan, *But the two guards protecting Krol have thirty rounds of titanium bullets in those rifles. They'd cut us to pieces before the titanium had a chance to kill us.*

I am always thinking of ways to escape.

Bosse smothered a chuckle at the running joke he and his wolf had on how to escape a castle in the remote wilds of Slovakia. Impossible wish. He and Titan agreed when they were captured that they would fight to their last breath.

Some days, he forgot what it had been like to wake up, get dressed, and eat a civil meal like any other man, human or otherwise. Having food and cookies given to him brought back those memories and made him long for a life again.

He'd done nothing wrong to end up here. In fact, he'd shown respect to the female in his pack who'd thrown it back in his face and said nothing as he was condemned to this life.

He and his wolf had accepted there would be no escaping this castle.

They'd considered every possibility.

What about that female servant? She'd spoken as if they needed each other to escape. She was dreaming if she thought either of them would survive an attempt. Bosse had begun to watch for her and caught glimpses of her dark hair peeking out from behind a curtain at Krol's back.

But he'd sensed her when she came in late at night and left him food. At first, he'd wondered if she was trying to poison him. Titan dismissed that concern when he smelled nothing odd about the food and ate the raw meat. His wolf always left her cookies for Bosse.

How had Krol not realized she was present when she hid near his throne? Had his lion lost its ability to scent a human?

When he finally got a clear view of her, he'd been surprised by the two different eyes.

A few days ago, he'd dreamed of a mystical black-haired female with one brown and one blue eye. Then she appeared in his cage. She'd riled a guard to get thrown into his cage.

The red imprint on her face still boiled Bosse's blood.

A man who hit a woman possessed no backbone. Coward was too nice a name for the guard.

He kept trying to make sense of her actions. What servant, especially a woman, put herself in danger like that for an imprisoned shifter?

Meat was good for healing, Titan noted.

Bosse grunted his agreement. He'd figured she was the one who had slipped extra food into his cage late at night. He'd never heard her or even caught her scent at those moments before she was gone.

That wasn't entirely correct. Bosse *had* noticed the lingering trace of cardamom and cinnamon twice after food had been slipped into his cage over the past two weeks. He'd wondered if the sweet smell had clung to his cookie fairy from baking the sweets.

She'd left the treats for him twice—three times, counting the ones from an hour earlier.

He ate them immediately. He should have thanked her for the cookies and extra meat earlier, but she'd pissed him off by risking death to talk to him.

He would tell her thank you if she returned to his cage again and not to come back to see him anymore.

He carried too many deaths on his soul and would not live with her innocent bloodshed for some harebrained idea about escaping.

Sadly, he'd miss the moments of calm he enjoyed when she'd visited him. While that had helped him sleep one night, he couldn't risk becoming too relaxed, not with Krol throwing more vicious opponents at him twice a day.

Our king has arrived, Titan announced sarcastically, having caught Krol's annoying feline smell.

Bosse lifted his head and tried to figure out what that crazy shifter was up to now.

A strange bird with animal legs followed Krol into his high seating area.

In the past two years of imprisonment, Bosse had never seen a domestic pet around Krol.

As for Bosse and the other captives, none of them were domesticated.

They would all kill the castle alpha, given a chance.

The bird-animal creature stood taller than Krol's human form. It had a sharp beak and feathers. A head shaped like an eagle flowed down a wide neck to where the bird blended into what appeared to be a lion's body, legs, and even a tail.

Who had made this abomination? The Black River Pack? They were known more for experimenting on shifters, most often wolf shifters. He'd never heard of them combining two creatures.

Titan murmured, *Magic*.

Bosse took a deep inhale and regretted it. The stench of dark magic floated down to him, contaminating the already repulsive air in the arena.

Krol turned his evil gaze on Bosse and grinned. "I see you've noticed my Lammogo." He walked several steps with an air of superiority, pausing to continue bragging. "It is a lammergeier vulture mixed with a Mapogo lion. Very rare. The only one in existence, in fact."

Did that man ever tire of his pompous attitude or hearing himself talk? Bosse kept his arms crossed over his chest and tried to perfect a mask of indifference.

Krol waved his hand across the room as if it were filled with disciples. "Unlike you and the others, this one can be trained and will perform every order exactly."

When a silent Bosse refused to show a sliver of interest, Krol snarled and ordered, "Watch."

He shouted an order in Slovak at his guards, which was strange since he would not hire them unless they spoke English.

A guard released a full-grown sheep into the seating area. It began wandering around. The minute it neared the

Lammogo, the sheep panicked and raced back to the now-closed door through which it had entered. With no way out of the closed door, the poor animal ran around the far side of Krol's seating area while the castle king roared with laughter at the terrified prey.

The Lammogo did not so much as twitch a feather until Krol gave it a verbal order in a soft voice.

Flapping immediately, the Lammogo lifted its unholy body into the air and headed for the sheep.

Running to the front of the viewing area, the sheep tried to climb the wall, screeching. If the sheep had gotten over the protective railing, it would have fallen and probably broken its neck.

Maybe the sheep understood the consequences and wanted to die quickly.

The guards and servants had backed up to the curtains, eyes wide in fear. Silent as a bird swooping through the sky, the Lammogo flew toward the sheep and dove fast.

If Bosse had blinked, he'd have missed the attack.

But it wasn't an attack. Though the sheep screamed when the Lammogo snatched it into the air, no blood dripped down from being clawed. The giant bird creature dropped the sheep carefully next to Krol.

The sheep stood stunned and paralyzed.

Why? What had the Lammogo done to it?

Settling back to the floor, the Lammogo stood in place, once again quiet as a statue.

Clapping at his new toy's performance, Krol said, *"Bravo!"*

The Lammogo appeared content to stand that way for the rest of the day and not touch the sheep.

Titan said nothing as they watched the demonstration that had surely been for their benefit.

Bosse told Titan, *If we ever face that thing, we must avoid the claws at all costs. I think they have some type of poison to stun prey.*

Yes, that would be unlike any other battle we have ever faced.

No question that Lammogo would annihilate something it wanted to kill.

But why had Krol trained that creature to retrieve? Before Bosse could think on that, Krol shouted a new order at his men.

"Take this sheep to be killed and dressed for the cook." Two guards crept down slowly and moved around behind the Lammogo to lift the comatose sheep off the ground, then scurried away quickly.

Krol chuckled. "I have entertained you enough. Time for you to return the favor." That said, he promptly ordered a very tired-looking servant to bring him food.

The only favor Bosse would ever consider giving Krol would be a fast death just to avoid any chance he'd survive the torture he deserved.

As a lion shifter, Krol had ruled here since his father had settled their pack in Slovakia and killed every human in this castle that Krol had requested as his inheritance. That information was based on what Bosse had heard the guards talk about in hushed late-night rants. Then Krol challenged his father to a battle, winning it easily so that he became alpha.

He had no lion pride to rule as he'd slaughtered them all.

King must give us a bigger steak tonight for fighting a second battle this soon.

Bosse rolled his eyes at his wolf.

A vision of the crap the guards fed Bosse came to mind. Three days ago, two rabbits had been tossed into his cell while Titan lay on his side, trying to heal. His wolf had to capture and kill each one as fast as he could just for a meal. Titan could eat ten of those small animals and still be hungry.

The guards enjoyed watching Titan try to capture food before it ran through the bars. Everyone expected to be entertained.

Not his cookie fairy. She'd gifted him with the best meals he'd ever had in here over the last week and had asked nothing in return.

Titan must have picked up on his thoughts and said, *Woman wants something.*

I know, but I'm not turning down food we need to heal.

I agree. I say we help her.

That surprised Bosse. Titan generally thought zero of humans. Was his wolf getting used to the extra food? *We have to find out what she wants first,* Boss cautioned. *I don't see how we can escape, which makes me wonder why she's trying to befriend us.* He wished he could inhale her sweet scent and wipe away the stench from the arena.

Bad idea. That would result in relaxing him.

Deep growls came from something huge that banged the steel door on the other side of the arena from where Bosse had entered.

Pushing stringy hair off his face, Bosse told Titan, *Show time, my friend. I'll fight first in this form. Push your healing as usual and take the body when I run out of juice.*

I will be ready. Then Titan added his usual sarcastic warning after they'd suffered a bone-chilling salt bath. *Do not dirty our body again.*

Bosse replied, *I'm sure the king will have a tub filled with hot, soapy water delivered to our cage.*

Yes. I sometimes forget the rewards that always await us. Titan made a muffled chuckle.

Bosse could not have survived or tolerated the endless days of being caged without Titan.

Rusty hinges squealed as the steel door began to move.

All joking ended.

Titan did his part. Energy raced through Bosse to what was left of his lingering injuries, which would heal faster once Titan took over. His back still ached, but the energy rolling through him now gave Bosse a burst of power.

The steel door opened all the way, and a massive Cape buffalo pounded in.

Titan was done joking. *Give me the body.*

Not yet. Bosse barely got the words out in his mind when the buffalo charged him.

He dove to the side, telling his wolf, *If we try to shift now, it could kill us mid-shift.* He jumped up and ran to the other wall.

We do the flip-flop. That will give us time, Titan suggested.

Good idea, but Bosse wasn't sure he could trick the buffalo into biting or if the buffalo would stop in time like the tiger had. *I'll try it.*

He took a deep breath and ran at the buffalo, who lowered its head, snorting and scratching the ground. The buffalo flicked sharp horns in Bosse's direction, ready to rip him open. At the last minute, Bosse sidestepped, kicking a hard foot under the black throat.

Great kick, but his foot and ankle felt as if he'd attacked a stone wall.

A sick sound squeezed from the buffalo's throat as it quickly jerked around.

The sharp tip of a horn caught Bosse in the side and ripped open skin, damaging muscle. Pain seared his skin, and blood spilled. Attempting to flip-flop meant pretending to be injured.

Thanks to the buffalo, Bosse wouldn't have to pretend.

He cursed and made it to the far wall. Leaning against the cold stone, he gasped for air with a hand covering what he could reach of the cut on his side.

Blood ran through his fingers.

A captured tiger that had shared a cage near his before dying in the arena once told Bosse the natural Cape buffalos were vegetarians but had been known to hunt and kill a human who had angered it.

He warned Bosse to avoid pissing off a Cape buffalo shifter.

Too late.

It took only seconds for the buffalo to swing around and stomp its front hooves on the ground. That wide head lifted, and huge jaws opened. It bellowed in rage.

Bosse stumbled backward and put his hand on the wall to stop his fall. The flip-flop worked best if he could step out into the open. His gut twisted like a pretzel at the idea of leaving the wall.

From far across the arena, the buffalo started striding toward him.

Bosse shoved away from the circular wall and tried to walk confidently but ended up limping a few steps into the arena.

The buffalo snorted loudly and once again stomped front hooves big enough to smash large rocks. Then it charged, nose down and horns headed for Bosse's body.

That bulky animal was damned fast.

Bosse had one second to make his move. Sweat ran through his eyes and dripped off his chin.

One second with over two thousand pounds of fury coming hard.

He had to allow this one to come closer than the tiger had.

Keeping his eyes on that towering animal, Bosse watched through wet strands of hair.

The easiest move would be backward and rolling away, which would also be obvious. Too risky.

At truly the last second, Bosse called forth Titan, then dove forward and to the side, barely missing a collision by less than an inch.

The buffalo rammed the wall. A deep-throated moan followed.

Pain ripped up Bosse's insides with shifting, the gash still raw.

He might be hurt worse than he realized. No time to think.

Stumbling, the buffalo pushed up from its knees and shook off the brutal hit that would have killed many animals.

Bosse had dropped to the ground on all fours to help Titan however he could. Titan pushed power into the last part of the shift. It happened so fast the pain blinded Bosse. When his vision cleared to see through Titan's eyes, the buffalo wove from side to side, still shaking its head.

Blood streamed from the injury on Titan's side. His wolf would show no pain but could still pass out if they lost enough blood.

That buffalo hadn't truly been enraged before.

Not compared to the insane beast eyeing him now and snorting so hard fire should be shooting from its nostrils.

Titan tried to run to the left, then to the right, but the buffalo moved quickly, cutting all that weight back and forth like a rodeo horse blocking a calf. Nothing would appease that black demon except Titan's body ripped to pieces.

Titan said, *Not sure this works, but we lose too much blood to fight long.*

Bosse had no chance to ask what his wolf was going to do before Titan spun in a fast circle that started moving to the right. He'd confused the buffalo that paused, staring hard, grunting aggressively, clearly waiting for the optimum moment to attack.

When Titan came out of his spin, he wobbled with dizziness.

The buffalo lifted its head and made a loud chuff sound that might have been laughter. Then it came in a fast walk for Titan and picked up speed.

Bosse warned, *Get ready.*

Titan turned toward the buffalo, shaking off his blurred vision.

Not seeing a good outcome, Bosse urged, *Run. Try to wear it out.*

We will tire first, Titan argued.

The buffalo rushed its last steps. Titan rolled to the side, shoved up, and leaped on the buffalo's shoulder. He struggled to dig in a claw, but nothing was breaking through the tough skin.

The buffalo bounced and bucked, wrenching one way and then the other.

One of Titan's claws snagged a hold, but not enough for his body to hang against all that jerking and jumping around.

As Titan started sliding down, a horn caught his softer wolf body and tossed him against the wall with a sickening smack.

Bosse groaned, and fire burned their insides, but he urged, *Get up, Titan. Don't let him stomp you.*

His wolf had landed upside down in a pile of legs.

At the sound of the buffalo bellowing in victory, Titan rolled over and forced his legs under him. Then he turned to face another attack. He told Bosse, *I can try one more thing. If I fail, we die.*

Bosse would never stop fighting with his wolf ready to battle on, but part of him sometimes longed for an end to all of this.

He said, *If it doesn't work, then we finally escape forever.*

Either overconfident or fearful of hitting the wall again if tricked, the buffalo headed for Titan at a steady trot with its head up and ready to kill.

When the buffalo was six feet away, Titan dropped low and launched his body over its head, landing on its back but closer to the neck.

That shocked the buffalo for all of a second before it erupted in a jumping fit.

Titan slid to one side, claws digging hard to hang on. He bit the buffalo's neck and got his body tossed on top with the buffalo's next buck. Titan clawed the softer skin and took a bigger bite this time.

Bosse had faith in his wolf, but this was like riding an angry building trying to throw them off. How long would it take Titan's claws to reach something vital?

The buffalo jumped around and rammed its side into the wall.

Titan picked up his hind leg before the bones were smashed.

In that one tiny moment when the buffalo had hit the wall and was not bouncing around, Titan stood immediately and spun his razor-sharp claws fast, digging deep into the vulnerable neck skin and shredding muscle. The buffalo howled in pain, jerking its head up and around, so desperate to get free of the wolf attacking its neck that it lost battle focus.

That's all Titan needed to finish ravaging its neck until the head flopped forward and blood spewed.

You got it, Titan. Bosse was so proud, but their worst injury bled in a faster stream. They needed to get out of here and to the cage where Titan could lay down and slow his heart. Stop the bleeding.

As the buffalo fell over on its side, Titan stumbled off its back before getting caught beneath that mountain of animal. He headed slowly for the exit door that would lead to their cage. If he moved any faster, he'd stumble, fall, and not get back up.

The steel bar door wasn't open.

Titan turned his head to look over his shoulder, allowing Bosse to see the alpha sitting high above them. Krol looked sick. Not happy at losing his new pet, huh? Maybe that would stop the maniac from turning his flying creature loose on Titan.

Krol might not have realized that Bosse feared whatever that bird did to paralyze the sheep.

Standing, Krol's eyes flamed bright with retribution.

What? Did he think Bosse and Titan had been unfair with the buffalo? They gave it an honorable fight and a quick death.

Krol's hands were fisted and shaking. He struggled to talk for a moment, then spoke in a dangerously low voice. "You will not always win. The day will come when you have no choice but to lose, and I will be there to see it."

Bosse spoke to his wolf. *Face Krol and sit like a puppy.*

No questions asked, Titan stepped around carefully and sat with his head tilted up at Krol.

That made the alpha king crazy. He screamed, *"Get out of my arena!"*

The arena door opened. Titan stood and calmly walked through.

Bosse could feel the agony his wolf suffered as he acted as though he could fight another battle right now. Hopefully, Titan could make it to the cage without passing out.

Titan complimented Bosse. *Good move. Pussy does not know how much damage we suffered.*

Not as lighthearted at the moment, Bosse said, *It worked this time. We may not get a second chance to use it. Give me the body, and I will try to stop the blood.*

Bosse's eyes crossed at the pain of shifting, but in the next moment, he stood with a hand against the wall.

"Keep moving," a guard shouted.

Another one said, "No. Wait up."

What could those idiots be doing now?

Cold water crashed over Bosse's head and back. He sucked in a breath just as a second one was thrown at his front from the side.

"Krol doesn't like blood in this area, and I'm not cleaning up anymore today," the guard with the bucket shouted.

Drawing in a deep breath to tamp down on his urge to rip all of them to pieces, Bosse used both hands to wipe water off his face and shove his hair back. "Assholes."

"What'd you say?"

He started walking toward the cage area, refusing to answer. Stars ran through his gaze. He was getting lightheaded from the blood loss.

By the time he reached his cage, he was dry. His bowl was not in the cage. "I need water."

"So?"

"If I die from dehydration, Krol won't be happy."

The guard laughed. "You think he cares if you die?"

"I think he'd be furious if I died, and he was not here to witness it in person."

That shut up the fool. He called over for someone to bring a water bowl for the dog.

Bosse sat down on the ground, clenching his teeth against the pain and wave of dizziness. Once the bowl of water was shoved inside, the guard locked the door and left. Grimacing, Bosse leaned over to pull the bowl to him. He drank it all and dropped the bowl, then fell over on his side facing the cage door.

With nothing else to use, he slapped his hand over what he could cover of the gash. Blood oozed through his fingers, but Titan couldn't heal this much before tomorrow. He struggled to stay awake.

Krol may have beaten them this time.

Chapter 7

A LIFAIR WALKED QUIETLY in case the spell she had placed on the guards and Beast failed to work on one of them. That would be disastrous.

This spell had taken a greater effort than the one earlier because she needed more time tonight. This would be an awful time for a her magic to fail.

She'd hoped to get the regular early morning shift guards who were not as on the ball as Cyrano and his sidekick, but Eriko, Krol's right-hand man, had ordered those two to stay on duty until three in the morning.

Maybe their exhaustion would work in her favor.

Cyrano snored so loudly through that big honking nose that she worried he'd wake the entire castle.

She continued forward, paused next to the cage holding Beast, then counted to ten. That thing's distorted rhino form had bedded down with its legs folded and head on the ground. A natural rhino would be scary enough, but this one seemed to stay in a perpetual half-human and half-beast state.

Breathing a tiny sigh of relief because her magic had a life of its own and occasionally malfunctioned, she hurried to the cage where Bosse's wolf lay on its side facing the cage door.

Her pulse had ticked up with feeling reckless the first time she'd entered his cage. The wolf shifter hadn't jumped up and attacked her, which gave her a bit of confidence for this trip. She had no reason to believe for sure she'd be safe again this time but hoped after feeding him extra food and sewing his wound, he'd allow her to talk. He'd permitted her presence in his cage on her first visit, even if he'd sounded like a jerk.

Maybe he had just been tired and in pain.

She could be making a huge mistake tonight, but she had no time left to come back again.

Staring through the bars, she ran into a new problem. The man was not in there. She faced the wolf.

Would his animal attack a defenseless human woman who had fed him?

Did she have time to ponder that at this moment?

No.

She used the key from Cyrano's ring and opened the cage door as quietly as possible. Before walking in, she looked to her right at the other cages on each side of the walkway deeper into the basement.

Nothing stirred.

Should she trust her spell? It had been a simple one. It should last three hours or more, which she figured would give her time to gain a bit of trust with Bosse and get him on his way. Also, to do it quietly, which required not making a mistake by rushing.

She'd originally intended only to share how she was working on Bosse's escape plan when she came here tonight.

Krol had been livid when Bosse won the last fight. The castle lunatic's announcement slashed the time she had for planning to nothing. Now she had to convince Bosse to escape immediately before she could accumulate enough information for a successful exit strategy, or there would be no freeing him or saving Rez.

For the first time since being here, she had two goals. One was Rez, but even if Bosse could not help Rez, he still deserved to escape.

Stop mentally meandering and get moving, she ordered her hesitant self.

Right. No plan allowed for cold feet.

"Fine," she grumbled under her breath and opened the cage door, slipping inside. Keeping her voice down, she softly called out, "Bosse." She waited, then again said, "Bosse."

Still nothing. Didn't wolf shifters have excellent hearing?

The wolf lifted his big head and turned to eye her. Wide jaws opened, exposing fangs she'd never seen this up close.

Her heart tried to beat its way out of her chest to save itself.

She froze. This had been a mistake. One she might not survive.

But her dream had picked a wolf shifter. *This* wolf shifter.

Shaking, she said, "Please don't attack me. I hope you understand my words. I need, uh, the man part."

Had the wolf smiled?

As she watched, the wolf began changing into the shape of a man. She could feel energy rolling across the cage. When the change finished, she was facing the front side of a muscular male body, complete with…

Heat flooded her face. She looked away. "Uh, please turn around."

"You did say you wanted to see the man part," he deadpanned.

He had to know she hadn't meant *that* part, which was now burned into her mind. This place normally chilled her. Where had the rush of heat come from? Her cheeks had to be flaming.

Sounding as if he laughed, he said, "You're safe to look now."

She peeked a little. He was sitting up with his hands covering his private area. That reminded her of what she'd brought. But then she saw blood dried in spots and some still trickling down his side. "How badly are you hurt?"

"I'll live. I think." He kept his voice low.

"Show me."

"Why are you here?" Then he looked around. "How'd you get in without waking anyone?"

"I put them to sleep. The more questions you ask, the less time you'll have to escape."

That wiped the smile away. "What are you talking about?"

She didn't say a word, just gave him her I'm-in-no-mood-for-fools look.

His scary eyes got darker. "Start talking."

"I will as soon as you show me your injuries." She cocked her chin to make her point. It also helped to hide the terror racking her body.

Could he tell her heart was beating inside her chest like a brat having a fit?

Probably.

He grumbled worse than an eighty-year-old man when he couldn't be thirty yet. Rolling away from her to leave his backside exposed, he said, "Should be obvious."

She dropped the sack she'd brought, a larger one this time, and knelt. It had been an hour since his battle, and that gash was still open. From what she'd learned about shifters since being in this castle, his healing should have kicked in by now.

He might escape, but he wouldn't get far.

For him to turn his back to her while injured and vulnerable surprised her. Clearly, he saw her as no threat. She had her weapons, but he would be right. The wolf would shred her before she could draw her magic up to work.

Regardless, this felt like she was gaining a smidgen of trust after all she'd been doing.

Pushing the hood of her robe off her head, she rolled up the wide sleeves halfway up her arms. "I'm going to touch you."

He grunted.

Should she take that as yes or no?

She decided on yes.

First, she pulled a gourd of water and a towel from the sack. She used the wet towel to wipe blood from the injured skin and gently touched the wound. He remained still. She asked, "If I sew this, it will stop the bleeding until you heal, correct?"

He took his time answering and sounded suspicious again when he said, "Yes."

"Prepare yourself." She dug out the needle and thread she'd brought just in case.

"You can't hurt me."

Taking him at his word, she tried to sew quickly, grimacing for him every time she pushed the needle into his skin.

He didn't so much as twitch.

If she had a wound like his and someone sewed it with no pain medicine, she'd be crying and screaming. That thought led to wondering what Krol would do to her if he caught her in this cage now or found out she'd aided Bosse in any way. She forced her mind to stay on task and not think of the hideous punishment he would dish out.

"Why are you doing this?" Bosse asked.

Careful with her words, she replied, "I'm trying to help you and someone else at the same time." She'd never expected to be in this situation or to put her life at risk for anyone other than someone she loved. She didn't even like Rez, but her mother had loved the woman. Although Alifair did love the rest of their gifted clan, she would not do this again. It wasn't the fear of death.

No, it was the fear of facing something worse than death from a demon.

If Krol found out, would he feed her to his new flying creature?

Bosse knocked her mind away from dwelling on the worst-case scenario when he asked, "Who is this other person, and what do you want from me in return if I can escape?"

"Please don't ask me to tell you more than I can. You'll understand once you're free."

"That makes no sense."

She agreed, but if she told him everything now, she'd fail to get him out of here.

After all this, would Bosse escape? By not sharing what she needed from him to help save Rez, she could be dooming her true plan to fail, but she would not risk him being captured again. She'd fretted over what to do for hours, but saving Rez fell on *her* shoulders. This man had suffered enough without adding her problems to his.

If the dream were to be fulfilled, it would have to happen on its own.

Would she fail Rez by wanting this wolf shifter to be free of Krol?

Or would she get everyone killed if her dreams while in this castle turned out to be as undependable as her magic?

Chapter 8

WHERE HAD THIS crazy cookie fairy come from? Sure, Bosse had seen this female servant for the past few weeks since Krol's guards brought in a new batch of captured females to be servants, but she was no servant. She didn't have that beaten-down look like so many others, such as the redhead. He'd heard that some of the women had been expected to provide personal service to Krol beyond delivering food and drink to his bedroom.

He ground his teeth in rage at the idea of Krol touching this woman.

"What's wrong? I'm almost done, but your back muscles have tensed hard as stone," she grumbled.

What *was* wrong with him? He relaxed his back muscles and smiled.

He couldn't help it. She was clearly terrified to be in here but dared to sew him up with no idea if he'd attack her. "How did you put the guards to sleep?"

"I have a gift… sometimes."

What did that mean?

He started to ask, but her hand trembled when she placed it on his shoulder.

A buzz of energy shot through his skin, making him jump. "What was that?"

She'd snatched her hand back. "I, uh, don't know what you're talking about."

Lie.

Before he could think of what to say, she went back to

sewing. He could feel a tingle from her light touch but not the shock from before. He didn't know what to make of this woman, who sewed his injury while shaking with fear.

She shouldn't be so trusting. Not just of entering the cage of a monster.

He'd heard the guard with the big nose talking about the females.

For the miserable time Bosse had spent here, he'd paid no mind to the rumble of stupid chatter. He'd lived every day expecting to die and had no way to help the women here, or he would.

They might not turn on him the way his own mother had.

Over the endless days, Bosse had learned to tune out whatever trash talk went on among the guards. But after returning to his cage tonight, the guard with the big nose had boasted how he intended to get his hands on the female servant with two different colored eyes and ride her hard.

If there were any real hope of escaping, that would be the guard's last mortal mistake before Bosse ripped his head off if he touched the angel sewing his back.

She wasn't his to protect, but she had shown him the only kindness since he came here.

And cookies. How would he ever eat a cookie again and not think of her selfless action?

He should have been nicer to her earlier. After nonstop months of constantly fighting to survive and living naked in a cage, he'd lost the ability to be kind.

Then she showed up and confused him.

Titan told him, *Be careful.*

Of what? His wolf was usually more specific.

Titan said, *She has no scent.*

Bosse kept still to help her finish sewing more quickly. He argued back to Titan, *She does have a scent. It is like no other woman—cinnamon and cardamom.*

Titan countered, *She masks her natural scent with those spices, but not now.*

Bosse searched his mind for the few times he'd caught whiffs of her.

Titan was correct.

Now that he thought about it, he could not recall a human scent. Another odd thing to go with her mismatched eyes, none of which he saw as a negative.

Not yet.

Closing his eyes, he shut out the smells of the guards and other prisoners.

He'd like never to inhale the odor of that beast rhino again. An unholy smell he'd never forget.

Yet now that he was concentrating… she had no human scent or spicy smell tonight.

She pulled hard to tie off a thread.

He clamped his teeth at the sharp pain, unwilling to flinch and make her feel bad. A muscle in his jaw twitched.

She paused. She had been calm for the last few minutes, but now she smelled of fear again, and it sickened him.

Keeping his voice as nonthreatening as he could, which was an effort, he said, "You did nothing wrong. The tighter the stitch, the sooner I'll heal. They'll rip out when I shift."

"Okay." She placed one hand lightly on his side, pinching the edges of his wound together. There came that buzz of energy again. She took a couple of deep breaths and got back to work.

He forgot about the needles and the pain in his side, only the sweet touch of her fingers stroking a buzz across his skin. He struggled not to shudder under a touch so foreign he couldn't recall what having a woman's hands on him had felt like. She'd misunderstand his sharp reaction as pain from being sewn and not the hard-on he struggled to keep hidden.

For now, he closed his eyes to keep track of every second her fingers brushed over his skin. He wanted to soak up her gentleness.

Oh, he'd had women before being captured, but they had only wanted what he carried between his legs. None had been memorable.

Not gentle and sweet like this one.

His cookie fairy made him think of a life he'd once

dreamed of long ago. After all the time here, he accepted he'd never have that life or any other normal existence. He had been gutted emotionally and changed after two years as a monster.

He was not worthy of a mate.

If this strange woman did have an escape plan, he would get her to safety first, then run as hard as he and Titan could to find their own freedom.

What was she? No human female could have put the guards to sleep. He glanced over to where even Beast slept.

Magic.

Did he care? Not a damn bit.

His angel paused her ministration and made a ruffling sound, and then her hand appeared in front of his face. She held a raw steak. A big one. "Sorry, but you have to hurry."

He took the meat and started eating. Then she handed him a baked potato. His mouth had been watering at a smell he was sure he'd imagined. He'd been more intent on finding out what she had in mind than asking what she'd brought him.

He took the potato, wolfing it all down as fast as he could without choking. A gourd full of water appeared next. He paused to take a deep swallow, then put it back in her slender hand, waiting for the container to be returned.

A pile of clothing was dumped in front of him.

She answered his unspoken question in her soft voice. "Those were the best I could find for a tunic and pants that would fit you. You won't make it far without clothes. It's from the servant supply area and belonged to someone Krol killed."

Sitting up, he pulled the tunic over his head and drew back at the strong human scent, but that should help him if he really did escape. He was almost starting to believe this was not him hallucinating from lack of rest. Standing, he stepped into the pants that were a bit short but with baggy legs. He could move in them.

"Here. You can use this as a belt."

He turned at her voice. She handed him a thin rope from where she stood a step away.

As he finished tying the rope, she leaned forward to ask, "Will you be healed tonight?"

"Yes, because you closed my wounds and fed me." He dug around and found some manners. "Thank you for this and the food you brought other times."

Sadly, his words surprised her. "You're welcome."

Bosse noticed the large cloth bag gripped in her hands. The ends of the material had been tied to make a sack. "You truly think we can escape tonight?"

"You have no choice. You *must* leave tonight," she whispered. "Krol plans to make you fight two shifters at the same time after daylight. I did not hear what kind of shifters, but if you survive them, he will pit you against that one immediately after." She'd tilted her head toward the rhino shifter and added, "He was furious at losing the Cape buffalo."

Bosse kept his surprise hidden. The castle alpha intended to kill him after all.

He had known it in the back of his mind but thought Krol would not give up his best fighter. That was before the castle alpha exploded with rage after the Cape buffalo died.

Titan had said they should help her earlier, but his warning minutes ago about her lacking a scent made Bosse pause.

Was this woman leading him into a trap? Why? How would she benefit?

Had he gotten soft over some food and her attention to his wound?

He had questions. This was as good a time as any to ask. "Explain how you are here now without disturbing even the prisoners. I hear no shifters in their cages stirring."

She gripped the bag even tighter and sighed with frustration. "I told you I have some gifts. I put the guards and other captives to sleep with a spell. I believe it allows for around three hours, of which we've probably used close to thirty minutes. We don't have time to talk about all that right now."

He heard no lie, but there were times he no longer trusted his shifter abilities to know the difference after so much abuse for years. If she was sincere about showing him how to escape, her words made sense.

He asked Titan, *Should we trust this woman for a chance to leave here?*

Titan replied, *Like you, I trust no one, but I do not sense trickery from her. She tells the truth, but not all. We should try.*

What did Titan think she was hiding? If it were important, Titan would say so.

Bosse let it go and went with Titan's instinct. His conscience berated him for showing little appreciation in the face of what this woman offered and the danger she put herself in. "I have no idea if I can really escape this castle, but you are giving me a head start to try. Thank you for coming to warn me." That sounded decent, right?

A mix of emotions from concern to worry played over her face. "Unfortunately, I don't have all the information I'd hoped to have by now. I had intended to wait and help you escape once I found everything I could to ensure success, but Krol's plans for you changed my timing." She paused before adding, "Here's what I do know. I can show you how to reach a tunnel hidden below the castle. The tunnel entrance is hidden behind stacks of wine casks that haven't been touched in years because they leaked, ruining the wine. Once you get into the tunnel, go to the end. You'll exit far enough away not to be seen from the castle."

"A tunnel? How do you know of this when you have been here less than a month?"

"One of the guards is too old to do much except simple tasks, but he was here when Krol took over the castle. Krol decided to keep him after the man said he knew everything about the castle. Most of the guards think he's off his rocker, but I got the old guy to talk one night while he was sleeping." Her cheeks blushed as if she'd admitted to committing a crime.

Not in Bosse's mind. She probably used another spell on him. "Go on."

Speaking faster, she said, "Anyhow, I know which direction you'll be facing when you exit the tunnel, but I don't have a safe passage route for you from there. I've seen you battle often from where I hide above the arena. You and your wolf are resourceful. You'll find your way once you are free. I'll fill you in and point out which way to go, but you must get out of here before daylight."

He hadn't missed that she'd failed to answer his question about the two of them leaving. Did she intend to stay?

A chance at freedom gave his heart a burst of hope he had never felt in this place. He would not leave alone, though. "Come with me so you will be free, too."

Shaking her head, she said, "I can't leave yet. Krol has someone I must locate and take out of here."

What could she be talking about? "Is this person worth your life?"

After a tiny hesitation, she said, "Yes."

Could it be a mate or lover? An unexpected flash of jealousy rolled through him. Why? This woman was not his. He would never have a mate, much less a human one. Still, he demanded, "Who?"

She backed up, gutting him with the speed of her pulse. He'd scared her again, but the hardheaded female still spoke her mind. "You don't know her, and I haven't found her yet, but she is definitely here."

A female.

That quieted his ridiculous reaction. He blamed his reaction on the dreams of his cookie fairy that had come to him time and again since seeing her face. He struggled to keep from tearing out of here, but he would not leave this woman to face Krol. "I will help you find this woman and take both of you with me." Not the best plan since he wasn't sure he could get two women to safety as well as himself.

"No." She clenched her jaws and argued, "If you fail to leave now, you will only cause both of us to remain prisoners here."

Shoving fingers through his ratty hair, Bosse thought of any way he could to change her mind and take her with him. He had enough humanity left not to take advantage of her offer and leave her a prisoner.

She put her fingers on his arm. Those soft fingers dragged a sigh from him. Until she stepped in here tonight, he had not been touched in forever. He'd thought he was immune to women after they'd screwed him over.

Evidently not.

Now was not the time to be distracted.

Whisper shouting, she pleaded, "Don't fight me on this. You'll only waste valuable time and all my efforts."

He had to make her understand. "I can't leave without you. They'll know you helped me."

"No, they won't."

"That monster next to me…" Bosse cast a long look at Beast before returning to her. "Did you also make him sleep through this?"

"Yes." No explanation, just an absolute confirmation.

Shaking his head, he pushed harder. "That one will know your scent and that you were here this evening. He will tell the castle alpha just to get an extra meal." Bosse wasn't sure anyone could make sense of what the almost-human side of that rhino shifter said. The few words he'd heard at all were babbled, but Beast would hurt this delicate woman if he could.

"He will not smell any scent from me," she assured him in an exasperated voice. "Not tonight."

How could that be?

Inhaling sharply, Bosse tested the air again. He truly could not smell her human scent, not even the spicy smells. How had she managed that?

Was she a witch, or did she possess gypsy magic?

He admonished himself to let it go. He judged only Krol. As far as he was concerned, this angel was a wise woman.

Moving around frantically now, she hoisted the bag toward him. "I put food, water, matches, and a knife in here. It was all I could get my hands on. Traveling in human form will be easier for you."

"I agree, but I just can't..." He took the sack from her and released a frustrated growl, unable to accept this gift and gain his freedom without hers.

"Stop." Her ferocious gaze held his. "This is my decision alone. You don't have a say. I need you to leave now so that when I escape, I can do so immediately without anyone else to worry about." She looked around at Beast, then turned back and wrung her hands. Her gaze pleaded with him to understand. "If you stay, you'll wreck my rescue plans."

Titan shared his thoughts on her words. *Truth, but she holds something back.*

That brought Bosse's head up. Why would she hide anything from him at this point? He'd try one more time to take her with him even though he hated spending time searching the castle.

She didn't belong in this despicable place any more than he did. He pushed again. "What of this other woman? Let me help you find her."

Pulling her hands apart, she stared at him as if about to shriek at him but kept her voice down. "You *will* help me by escaping. I'm hoping the guards will realize you're gone no sooner than two hours from now *if* you get out of here soon. When that happens, I expect the castle to be in chaos and Krol to send everyone after you. With him distracted as well, I'll finally get a chance to search the castle more thoroughly. If you're as fast as I think you are, they'll be gone half a day or more and come back empty-handed. I hope to use their absence to find my friend and get her out when Krol sends them back out to hunt again."

Could she really pull that off and stay safe from Krol?

His heart battered his chest. He had to get out of here. Damn this situation.

She paused in her frantic rambling and stared at him as if she could hear his thoughts. "If you don't go tonight, there

is no way I can help you after this. I… don't want you to
die."

Truthful and humble, to say the least.

Once more, her concern went against all he'd believed
since being sold to Krol. Why would this woman care
when no one else ever had? He could not drag his feet
on deciding to accept her aid. This was not the time to be
questioning an unexpected gift.

He cupped her face with his rough hand. "I hate this."

A sad smile wobbled into place. She breathed out the
words, "Just go and be safe."

"Why do you care what happens to me?"

She glanced away as if answering that question was asking
too much. Then her mismatched colored eyes returned to
his, along with a feisty attitude he found endearing. "I
shouldn't care since you don't seem willing to take this gift
in the spirit it's being offered. You must want to stay here."

Everything about the honorable man he used to be
revolted against leaving this woman behind. His angry
sigh could bend a tree. "No, I hate this place."

Those warm fingers covered his arm again.

He managed not to react to the sizzle of energy the touch
spawned.

Sounding convinced she would have her way, she moved
ahead. "You will also be far faster on your own. Even if
we could all leave now, we would only hold you back, and
all three of us would die because she and I can't outrun
shifters. Krol sometimes has shifters stay overnight who
hunt and bring food to the cook. He will probably send
them as well as the guards. With a head start, I hope you
can escape those monsters."

She hadn't called *him* a monster.

Bosse confirmed, "I will leave them in my dust or die
fighting. They will not bring me back."

"Do not die!" she ordered in a fear-laced order.

Why had he never found a female like this when he was
free?

Because he had not been allowed near humans.

He placed his hand over hers. "I will do all in my power to live for the simple reason of not disappointing you. When you escape, where will I find you?"

Her eyes widened, and she went silent.

What had he said wrong?

"You would look for me?" She seemed astonished.

"Yes." He rubbed his thumb over her soft skin. He had to see her again. Was it just to be sure she'd escaped? Of course, but that was not all. Was it because she'd taken such a risk to give him freedom?

Again, yes, but not exactly.

Could it be both of those reasons and the fact that in the short time they'd interacted, he felt drawn to her in a way he couldn't explain?

He was losing his mind and had to stop being foolish.

They'd only spoken to each other for a short time since midnight. What had gotten into him? Maybe it was simply loneliness and years of not having anyone who cared if he lived or died. She'd stopped talking.

Had he made her uncomfortable?

She wanted him to go without her. He should do the one thing she'd asked of him.

His damned feet refused to get moving. He was burning time he and Titan needed, but his stomach churned with the possibility of Krol punishing her for this.

Her words came out in a rush. "We've used maybe forty minutes now. You need every second to elude capture! When I escape, I will also find my way to North America and see you there. Follow me."

His heart floated like a happy balloon. She *did* want to see him. Then he realized what she'd said.

She had the cage door open and stepped out.

Bosse whispered, "North America?" It wasn't as if he'd been tutored in geography when wolf shifters in his pack were not allowed to leave their compound without permission, but he knew of this country an ocean away. "You want me to go *there?*"

Nodding, she waved him forward. "Yes. The United

States, specifically. Humans know of shifters there. You have to find a pack, or you get sent to a sanctuary camp of some sort."

"If I survive this, I will not be locked up anywhere again." Bosse didn't have to consult Titan about fighting to the death if someone tried to restrain them again.

She made a sympathetic sound of understanding and then looked around at the silent basement area before explaining, "I gained some directions from listening to a shifter who delivers fresh fish to the kitchen. He likes to chat with the young females. When you climb out of the tunnel, you'll be facing the direction you must go, which is west. You'll have to take a southern turn once you're out of the mountains and look for Venice, Italy, which has a shipping port on the Adriatic Sea. And don't take the risk of staying nearby to watch for me after you escape. I will not use the same route as you. My plans could change as quickly as yours have. Once I'm able, I'll go to a small town in an area called Mississippi."

He would find her again now that he knew her home was in Mississippi. How hard could it be to find her?

Not finished giving him directions, she said, "Don't look for me any sooner than a month from now. I may return by then, but it could be later. I must be careful and ensure Krol's people do not follow me."

He ground his back teeth at the idea of her trying to outrun Krol.

While he was thrilled at the idea of living free, his heart twisted painfully at leaving her unprotected. She proved to be as stubborn as she was courageous.

He would heed her advice, hurry to North America, and find a safe place to wait.

Those unusual eyes met his with unspoken words.

He wished for more time to get to know her and understand the woman behind these actions. Hell, he hadn't spoken this much with anyone in two years and hadn't realized how much he missed having even a friend.

She shook herself from her stupor and noticed her hands

clutching his shirt. Pulling her hands away, she backed up to the steel bar door, cleared her throat, and ordered, "No more talking. Go." Then she turned and slipped out of the cage he thought would be his last home.

He muttered, "Stop worrying. I'm fast." Stupid words when his feet dragged as he followed her past Beast's cage and still sleeping guards.

Taking the lead, he ran up the stairs ahead of her and paused to scope out the area before taking the last step. He'd never seen any of this castle beyond the basement containing captured shifters.

She tugged on his shirt and hissed, "Are you listening?"

What a temper. Would she be a fireball in bed?

He started to slap himself. There would be no bedding this woman, not by a monster. Turning to her, he said, "I'm listening."

"Let me pass."

He gave her room to pass and stepped up beside her into the great hall.

The only guards were far away at the end of the hall next to the front doors.

Pointing, she quickly explained how to locate access inside the kitchen to another basement area where he'd find the tunnel. "Try to bar the entrance behind you if possible once you enter the tunnel."

He'd figure that out when he got to it. Holding the bag in one hand, he placed his free hand on her shoulder. "I don't know how I could be so fortunate for someone like you to help me with food, water, and healing. Your cookies turned me back to a ten-year-old pup with excitement. No gift has ever meant as much."

Her lips curved, and her eyes smiled as if a new day of promise had just dawned in this ugly place. She lifted a hand to his face.

He sighed at how the sizzle had changed to content energy pouring through him.

What was it about this woman who confused and comforted him at the same time?

All he had to give her in return for taking a huge risk were words. "Thank you for being nice to a monster."

"Don't say that. You're not a monster." Her irritation on his behalf touched a place deep inside him no one had reached, even when he lived a decent existence.

She was wrong on one point. He was every bit a monster—one who would never have anything as precious as her.

Because of that, and after years of living on the edge of death, he wanted one more thing from this sweet woman. He didn't deserve it but had nothing to lose by asking. "I will cross the ocean to this other country, but I have one request before I go."

That broke the spell of her eyes fixed on his. "What now?" She sounded grumpy.

He chuckled out loud, so taken by her quick temper. "I wish for a way to remember a precious and courageous woman." Then he leaned his lips slowly toward hers. If she showed any sign of hesitation, he would stop, but she didn't resist a bit. She even closed her eyes, looking as if she'd anticipated the kiss when he hadn't known he would want one.

He kept the kiss gentle, careful not to scare her. He felt a lightheaded sensation down to his toes.

She clutched at the ragged shirt he wore, pulling him close.

His control slipped, but he dragged it back in time to prevent ruining one more generosity from her by going too far. Lifting his head, he murmured, "You are truly an angel. Thank you."

If she didn't stop staring at him with that look of wanting more, he might never leave. He could die on the run and never have this opportunity again.

He finally accepted he had to go.

Shoving a hand over his unkempt hair, he tried to say goodbye. He'd been through gut-wrenching situations in this place, but none as difficult as leaving without this woman who had put her life at risk for his freedom.

Then he realized he didn't even know a critical piece of information.

She glanced around. "I must return to my room under the stairs soon."

Bosse caught her arm gently, pleased when she didn't flinch this time. "What is your name? I have only heard them call you *sluha*." The guards used that Slovakian word for a servant when addressing all the women.

She looked around as if making sure no one could hear her and spoke so low he had to bend his head close, even with his shifter hearing. He drew in a deep breath, wishing to smell her unique mix of spices one last time, but she did not even have that tonight.

Fidgeting, she chewed on the corner of her lip, deliberating on something. "We are both taking risks. I trust you to protect my true name, which is Alifair."

I trust you. Three simple but powerful words.

He had trusted no one.

Until now.

"Alifair." He whispered her name to feel it flow over his tongue. He recalled a story he'd read as a child about Romanian gypsies with a character of that name and thought it meant elf warrior. Fitting.

He would hold what she had shared safely as a cherished prize. "Two gifts in one day. I have treasures which no king can match."

Her gaze flashed with surprise, but her parted lips said she'd liked the compliment.

It felt good to give her something to smile about.

Releasing a slow stream of air, she shook her head. "I had not figured you for a charmer."

"I'm not." Pulling her to him, he dropped his head to hers. "Know this as carved in stone. If you do not show up in Mississippi, I will come back here to find you."

Alifair blinked, leaving her eyes shiny with emotion. "I was raised to fear shifters, which colored my view of them. I never expected to meet one with honor. You have challenged my beliefs. I was sure you'd race out of here the minute you were free to escape, not use critical time trying to take me with you."

She was wrong. A man of honor would not leave her here.

Titan's words flowed through his mind. *She said to stay is to put her at risk.*

You're right, Bosse conceded.

Alifair straightened her back, all business again. "When you reach the shipping port on the Adriatic Sea, I think you can find a ship headed to America, and your wolf can stow away. Do not stop running until you find a safe place to live."

He stepped up until they were at eye level with each other. "Thank you for your trust. You have mine and a vow to help you in any way you ever need."

She licked her lips, and her heartbeat picked up.

Oh, hell. She could tempt a statue to life.

He leaned in, put an arm around her, and kissed her again. This might be the last time he'd ever hold heaven in his arms. He would have stopped after one kiss, but she gripped his shoulders and kissed him in return with enough heat to send his brain tumbling off the nearest cliff.

She trembled but not with fear this time.

Why had he met this woman now and not when he'd lived as a free man?

He knocked that thought away. When had he truly been free? Life with a pack had been confining, and then he ended up in this castle.

Still wrapped up with her, Alifair made a tiny sound that reached inside him, shaking his resolve to do the right thing. If this woman were sending him into a trap, he was going willingly.

We must go, Titan urged. *I hear someone rustling.*

That reminded Bosse that he owed freedom to Titan as well.

He broke the kiss, breathing deeply. "My wolf says we must hurry."

Her eyes widened. She looked at his chest as if she could see the wolf inside him.

He would never ask for another thing if he could take her with him, but that would clearly not happen.

Alifair whispered, "Guards up here in the main hall should still be asleep, but I could not put the servants to sleep with them in different rooms. You must be careful and go now."

He ran his thumb over her soft cheek. "Take care with your life. It pains me to leave you, but I will do as you ask."

She slowly pulled away from his arms, which now felt empty. Walking on soft steps, she wove her way toward a hall set along the side of the main staircase going up to the next level. She'd said she slept under the stairs.

Looking back, she pointed to the left and mouthed, *Tunnel. Go!* Then she turned in the opposite direction, took two more steps, and stopped.

When she looked back again, he hadn't moved.

His feet were as heavy as two boulders holding him in place, and he had a sick feeling that he was making a huge mistake leaving her behind.

Giving him a stern look, she waved him off and mouthed, *Please!*

What a warrior she would make.

He winked and nodded. As soon as she was out of sight, he turned and moved silently past guards sleeping along the wall. He crossed the wide room to the kitchen, made sure no one was in there, then hurried to the stone stairs she'd told him would lead to the tunnel.

Of course, it had to be below this level. His skin itched at the idea of being caught underground again.

Racing down the steps, he entered a chaotic storage room with boxes of supplies stacked in random areas. The smell of mildew and rat feces layered over scents of flour and stored vegetables. Ignoring everything except finding a stack of old wine casks, he squeezed through tight spots and moved what he could out of the way.

I smell vinegar, Titan told him.

Bosse paused and sniffed. *That would be the leaking*

casks she said no one bothered with because the wine had gone bad.

Following that scent, he had to move more old trunks and garbage out of the way until he could see the casks covered in spider webs. Without his shifter vision, he wouldn't have seen them at all this far from the stairs, where a dim light dusted the darkness.

He had to quietly drag that stack of kegs out of the way to find the tunnel access.

What if it wasn't there?

Stop thinking and start doing. That had been his mantra since being captured.

He grabbed the side of the cask support structure and hoped it did not fall apart as he pulled it away from the wall. Even with his strength, this thing weighed a ton. No rotted wood. This place was as black as Krol's heart.

Bosse remembered the matches she'd mentioned and dug them from the bag he'd placed on the ground. With the casks pulled three feet from the wall on this end, he struck a match and held it low to keep from blinding himself.

There was the outline of a three-by-four-foot board covered in thick dust. It had to be there for some reason.

He put out the light, kept one match he stuck behind his ear, and stuffed the box back in his bag. Pulling the casks farther away from the wall, he dropped to his knees and tugged around the board until the right side moved. Grunting, he dug his claws into the opening and pried the door open.

The metal hinges squeaked. Damn.

He dragged the bag to him and lunged inside the hole, scraping his back and arms. He managed to pull the door shut and fish the match from behind his ear to strike.

A torch half-covered with dirt lay next to where he sat. Would it even light?

He hurried to brush it off before his match light died.

The torch lit. He turned to make sure the door was closed but had no way to lock it. Even if he did, he had to leave the casks away from the wall.

You take too long to escape, Titan pointed out.

Bosse rolled his eyes.

He had to walk bent over for thirty steps. Then, thankfully, the tunnel opened wider and tall enough for him to stand if he kept his chin tucked into his chest. He moved quicker, gripping the cloth sack in one hand and the torch in his other.

Alifair had the mind of a tactician.

Without clothes, he would have no hope of passing through the countryside as a human.

It seemed he jogged forever, but it had probably been only fifteen minutes when the ground began dropping. Why would it descend?

Had he missed a turn?

With no time to question anything, he pushed ahead, his heart racing with excitement and no small amount of concern.

The path ended with no exit door.

Chapter 9

ALIFAIR STOOD IN a dark shadow created by the stairwell and watched Bosse until he crossed the room to the kitchen.

She wanted to go with him more than she'd ever wanted anything else, but her life had not been her own since the day she was born. Wouldn't it be nice to escape and meet up with him just like the picture she'd painted for him?

Of course, she would do all in her power to escape, but thankfully, he had not asked what her chances were of getting Rez out first, then herself.

If she'd told him the truth, he would not have left. She touched her lips. Had she really kissed a shifter? She hadn't even thought about that when Bosse leaned in to kiss her. The men she'd known had been more disappointing than enticing, and no one had put her first. If she'd said the word, Bosse would have abandoned his escape to help her find Rez, even willing to take them both with him.

What man suffered two years of hell and put her safety first ahead of racing for his freedom?

An honorable man.

Her clan had been wrong about shifters, at least some of them.

It didn't matter if he shifted into a wolf or not. Bosse had a good core. He could also detect a lie, so she'd stuck to stating her simple plan and directions. She'd told the truth about needing to stay to find someone. The rest had been bits and pieces of truth.

She had no idea if she could escape or not.

She wouldn't bet a plugged nickel on her chances.

Turning, she hurried through the main hall but stayed close to the walls, careful not to step on a sleeping guard. This place was so medieval. Yes, it was built during that period, but anyone in today's world would want heat, plumbed water, and power for electric lights.

Water had to be hauled inside from a well.

Her clan lived somewhat off the grid, but they had modern conveniences.

Krol lived in another time in his messed-up head. Had he been named Krol or just taken that moniker because it translated to something sounding like king?

To his credit, he'd chosen a perfect location. The lion shifter could not have this enterprise near any major city or town. He had to be in the middle of nowhere to limit contact with the outside world. She'd learned that shifters living secretly in the area made good money supplying the castle with fresh game and hiding his secret.

Why would they tell anyone and lose their income or their lives?

They even helped him by stealing humans. Krol and his men captured shifters to abuse and use as entertainment.

What about that flying creature? Had he stolen it?

She didn't think so. He'd left alone and had been gone for close to five hours before returning with what appeared to be a well-trained frankenbird. He must have gotten it from someone powerful enough to create a unique monster.

Why? What purpose did Krol have for his new creature?

She'd heard enough of his ranting before he left to know he was bringing back something that, in his words, not even Bosse could kill.

That reminded her she had to be in place when he was found missing. Her heart pounded wildly with worry all the way to the narrow corridor leading to her room. It was more like a large closet with a puny mattress on a single bed. More than Bosse had been given in his cage. She'd hated seeing him in there with no privacy, no comforts.

At least she had use of the one bathroom for all the female servants. If she ever got out of here, she would never take a cold bath again.

So far, Krol had not expected her to warm his bed. She had to find Rez and get her out of here before that happened to either of them. Was Rez sitting locked up somewhere, wishing Alifair's mother still lived so someone would save her? She had likely dismissed Alifair's ability to find and rescue her outright.

Rez had taken her along for the trip to Romania because the clan elders had been adamant about Rez having protection. The minute they left home, Rez had told her to stay out of the way and try to be helpful.

Bitch.

Hurrying to change into her sleeping shirt, an oversized one she'd found in the servant supply area, Alifair laid back on her bed, trying to think through all she'd told Bosse. With no wristwatch, she had to guess the time. Recounting from the point she'd entered his cage to now, she estimated he'd be in the tunnel by now and maybe even deep into it.

Bosse should get another hour or more before some of the guards woke up and figured out that he'd escaped.

She wished she'd had more information on that tunnel and the route to Italy, but he had proven capable of remaining alive for the last couple of years by his intelligence as much as his strength. Krol had something awful planned for Bosse in a few hours. He had reached the point where he wanted to watch him die in the most brutal way. He would be—

Guards started shouting in the main hall.

No! This was too soon. She sat up and hugged her knees to her chest.

Bosse might not reach the tunnel exit before the guards rushed out of the castle to search for him. She had no idea how far the passage ran. Her heartbeat raced like mad. What would happen to him?

Had she set Bosse up to die right now?

The deep voice of a guard shouted from outside her door, *"Get up and into the main hall!"*

She debated what to do but had only one option. If she stayed in her room, Krol would wonder why she had not been out with everyone else. She raked her hands through her hair to mess it up and grabbed her cloak to wrap the covering cockeyed around her body as if done so in a rush.

As ready as she could be, she ran out of her room.

What if Krol asked everyone if they knew anything about this?

He was a lion shifter capable of catching any lie.

When she reached the main hall, she ran to the other female servants huddled together. Many were dressed worse than her.

Guards raced around the castle, looking more chaotic than in control.

Krol stood at the bottom of the stairs with his flying monster at his heel. Frightening yellow eyes turned toward her group. She could swear it stared at her. Its beak opened, exposing crooked fangs that could tear a body to pieces.

Possibly sensing where his creature stared, Krol turned to the females.

She had no trouble looking shocked like the rest of them because she couldn't believe the guards had roused so quickly. What had gone wrong?

Krol asked, "Did any of you go to the cage area tonight?"

One trembling hand lifted. Alifair didn't know that woman. She only knew Linota's name. The hand-raiser was barely a woman, maybe twenty, and short with thin blond hair. "I t-t-took food to the g-g-guards."

His stare made them all begin to tremble. Alifair hugged the cloak around her like a bath towel, barely covering her arms.

"Did you see anything odd while down there?"

"No." The girl started bawling. "I just took the food and b-b-brought the plates back." She cried harder by the second.

Another woman closer to forty asked, "What's wrong, sir?"

"One of the animals has escaped."

Time to put on a show. Alifair slapped her hand to her mouth and thought about Bosse being captured, which allowed her to tear up. She spoke in a terrified and squeaky voice. "Is it loose in the castle? Will it kill us?" Tears ran down her cheeks. Good thing since most of the other women were crying.

Krol snapped back, "No. It appears the animal found a way out."

"Was it that beast?" another female asked in a shaky voice.

"The wolf shifter."

Guards ran over to Krol. One spoke quickly in a low voice.

Another door opened, and the old guard, half-awake, stepped out, looking around the room. He yelled, "What's going on?"

Krol turned sharply to him, glaring the man into silence. Then he swung back to the women and ordered, "Servants, back to your rooms. Do not leave until I send someone for you."

One of the girls wailed, "What if that wolf gets in?"

Now, the castle ruler looked impatient. He waved her off. "Stop crying. All will be secured in the next hour."

As soon as the first female turned to leave, Alifair fell into step right behind her. She hurried into her room and shut the door, then sat on the edge of the bed. Had she put Bosse at greater risk by helping him escape based on a plan with holes?

He would hate her for it.

She could live with that if he just survived.

If the guards and trackers caught Bosse, Krol would be merciless in dragging out his death.

What had gone wrong? Had something awakened a guard in the cage area, and he saw them leaving the dungeon?

No, that guard would have informed Krol immediately.

What about Beast?

She wasn't entirely sure her magic would affect him, but he appeared sound asleep. Had her spell not worked on him, and he fooled her by pretending?

Could he talk or not?

She'd told Bosse he was out of time, but now she might be the one out of time. Panicked at the idea of Krol setting Bosse up to die today, she hadn't thought this plan through enough at all. With the guards remaining in the castle on high alert, it would be even harder to slip away and hunt Rez, but she had to find Rez soon and free her.

If Alifair managed to do that, she would still have one more impossible task.

She had to get away from this castle before Krol discovered her role in both escapes.

Chapter 10

BOSSE FOUGHT THE first twitch of panic at finding no way out of the tunnel. He could figure this out. He hoped.

Titan warned, *Listen.*

In the far distance behind him, a howl sounded. He could barely hear it down here in the tunnel, but someone had discovered him missing and searched the kitchen.

There had been no chance for Bosse to cover his scent yet.

Had one of the shifters Krol often paid to deliver fresh game stayed last night at the castle as Alifair had warned? He'd heard talk of some being sent for a servant who escaped.

Trackers in animal form would move more quickly than him on two legs. He hadn't shifted to hold out until he needed Titan more than the human body.

What to do? He couldn't go back.

He stabbed the torch into the ground to the side of him, put the cloth bag below it, then let his claws out and started digging like mad. Three feet in, he scratched wood. He dug harder and began knocking the dirt away from the wood. The ground above had collapsed, covering what had been the way out. He located the rusty hinge first and clawed across to the other side. He flattened his hands and pushed.

It gave a little.

Dirt fell on his head. Would this tunnel collapse again?

He knocked dirt aside wildly until he found the top and

bottom of the structure. Leaning back, he kicked the wood. That hurt with no boots, but it gave a little more. Two more kicks and the wood fell apart. He grabbed the bag and doused the flame in a pile of dirt, leaving the torch behind.

Clawing his way out of the tunnel, he dragged himself free. When he stood, he took a deep breath of fresh air that almost sent him to his knees with thanks.

Freedom—a dream he'd given up on.

He owed Alifair and would pay her back when the time came. He didn't care what help she ever asked of him. It was hers.

Ahead of him lay a forest where a partial moon sent light diving through the branches and leaves overhead. His shifter eyes could see well enough to run now, which is exactly what he did.

He would reach North America and find the place with her people, but only after waiting a month as she'd asked. That would give him time to be sure no one followed him to her clan.

If she did not show up in the Mississippi place by five weeks, he would come back here for her.

A wolf howl shrieked through the air. That one was on the hunt.

He ran harder, plowing through thick undergrowth when he couldn't leap over it. His feet were tough enough to handle this terrain. He did not know this land well, but Alifair had said he'd have to make his way west from the tunnel, then turn southerly to find Italy. He tried his best to stay in a straight line, but without the sun, he would not know for sure if he stayed on track until daylight.

He could make all this work better if he didn't have to contend with a half-moon blazing overhead.

Level ground beneath the trees began to descend. He tied the bag differently so that it lay across his chest with the loop hooked over his shoulder with the bag under his arm. Hands-free now, he could grab at trees to keep him upright as he ran without his feet sliding out from under him.

When the branches thinned, he found the peak of a hill in

the distance where moonlight outlined it. He slowed before breaking free of his dense cover, watching everywhere as he reached the edge of a gradual drop-off.

Titan informed him, *I hear something above us.*

Bosse froze and dropped flat on the ground. A frisson of worry ran up his spine. The flapping sound grew louder until a huge shape passed between the moon and the ground. As it did, the silhouette of Krol's creature ran across the flat ground ahead.

His wolf could outrun a tracker, but having that abomination flying overhead just ruined their chance to make good time across the open plain beyond this slope.

He told Titan, *We have to skirt the flat land between here and the next hill to avoid drawing the Lammogo's attention.*

I run faster.

You do, but I doubt we'll be able to run fast through the thick woods we'll take to circle this area. Let's save you for now. Even when I tire, you'll still be strong enough to take over.

Bosse searched straight across the wide opening and made a mental note of where to pick up in the same direction he'd been running. He worked his way to the right around the slope, taking every chance to head downhill by running from bush to rocks.

He kept an eye on the Lammogo that continued to hunt across the flat area as if expecting Bosse to run straight across it.

Did that creature have any tracking flaws? He'd take one right now.

Krol's wolf, still far behind him, howled again.

Bosse crept cautiously around the edge of the field. His mind jumped from escaping the castle to if he could find Italy. That would only happen if he outran another shifter and a flying abomination on his tail.

He'd promised Alifair he'd stay alive for her.

Was she safe? He never heard a lie in her voice when she said he'd put her in danger by staying. He hoped that was true, and she found her way back to her sleeping area undetected.

When he stumbled, Titan growled, *Pay attention.*

Bosse grunted and kept moving.

When he'd completely circled the open area, he hunted for boulders on the hill he'd used to mark a spot for continuing west.

The spot had been a broken tree laid over a boulder.

He hurried to his left, knocking branches aside. There was the marker he needed. As he closed in on the tree and boulder, loud flapping sounded overhead. He jumped behind a tall spruce tree and leaned around to peek.

The Lammogo landed on flat ground, tucked its wings, and trotted around on four legs with its head high in the air.

Could that thing scent him?

Bosse stayed very still while trying to decide his next move.

The Lammogo opened its beak and screeched a loud noise over and over. Bosse had to cover his ears until it stopped.

Howling answered.

Was that creature calling in the shifter hunting Bosse?

The Lammogo couldn't have found any tracks out there. It had to be sounding an alarm based on losing his trail.

A low rumble of thunder rolled around to the west beyond this hill.

He'd welcome the fresh water.

Backing away as quietly as he could, Bosse waited until he could no longer see the Lammogo, then turned and made his way uphill and over the top. He hurried in the direction he hoped was west. Once he had covered about a kilometer, he ran every chance he was not in thick undergrowth. The land went downhill again, sometimes gently, but other times in sharp drops. But it smelled magnificent. He thought he'd never take a breath of fresh air again.

Once he ran out of significant cover, he had no option but to take the fastest path straight down.

He leaped over a bush instead of circling it in the interest of time but landed badly and fell into a roll, bouncing hard. Rocks jabbed his back and arms. He clawed to slow his fall, finally catching the base of a bush and sliding to a stop. The first thing he thought about was to thank Alifair for clothes, or that would have been even more painful.

Heaving gulps of air, he watched to see if the Lammogo had taken to the air and had seen the dust blown up from his tumble.

Not yet.

Getting up, he groaned at more abuse to his body and kept moving.

From here, he had a valley with scattered trees to cross and then a shorter rise to cover, but there was good news. Behind him, the sky began to lighten and define a horizon. He kept that eastern sunrise point at his back to keep moving west.

Thunder rumbled. That might be why the sky was still so black ahead of him. A crackle of lightning streaked across the sky.

Yep. He was running toward a storm.

That would slow him down, making it easier for the Lammogo to catch him, especially if he had to cross a river. He had no idea if he'd have to cross one, but he was better prepared than his wolf to take on a river.

A loud screech lifted the hairs on his neck. He twisted around to see the Lammogo high above the last peak and heading his way.

Could that thing really see him from so far up?

Well, it did have an eagle-like head. Might have the eyes of one as well. Plus, the partial moon still shined in this area. Where were the rain clouds when he could use them?

He struck out, running hard.

The thunderstorm built fast, moving quickly toward him. He had no dense forest down here for camouflage.

Chilly water began to sprinkle. It was a welcome relief to keep him alert, considering he'd had little sleep in the last few days. If not for Alifair, he wouldn't have eaten at all.

Wind whipped through the trees and blew hard in his face.

The Lammogo sounded closer now.

Bosse looked back, and the damn thing had set its wings to drop on him.

He made a fast move, running to his right.

An angry squawk sounded first, and then rapid flapping was his only indication the Lammogo had to fly up and away again.

He ran a hundred yards and switched directions to the left, looking up into the rain coming faster.

That strange thing flapped and turned in a big sweeping circle but dropped lower with each rotation.

Bosse had no idea how to escape something that could fly as fast, maybe faster than he or his wolf could run. But if it landed, could it match his speed on four legs? Possibly, if Krol told the truth about the bottom half being a lion.

With another glance at the predator, his stomach dropped.

Krol's flying creature had descended enough to fall quickly and grab him no matter which way he ran. He couldn't reach any type of cover for another twenty or thirty minutes. He'd have to face that creature at some point.

Here it came, dropping quickly.

Bosse spun to his right again.

The Lammogo must be getting better at flying that kind of body. It made a quick twist in the air and stayed on Bosse.

He could feel the creature closing the gap and finally decided to face the attack rather than be hit from behind. He turned to walk backward, watching it come for him.

Titan said, *I will fight it.*

Dipping down to pick up a rock the size of his head, Bosse said, *I trust you to fight any time, but I would feel a coward to hand you the body in an impossible situation. You would be forced to make contact to fight it. Those poisoned claws might stab you. I will do my best to bash its head before it can touch me.*

Sounded like a plan, but Titan would know they had little

hope of surviving that thing. Bosse hadn't heard the wolves tracking him for a while now. Maybe wolves couldn't keep up with a relentless Lammogo.

Rain came down harder, hitting him with water bullets.

The Lammogo finally landed and started trotting toward him. It paid no attention to getting soaked.

Bosse tightened his fingers around the big rock. He had one chance to make this work.

When the Lammogo got within ten feet of him, he slowly moved his loaded hand back, preparing for a hard and fast throw.

Lightning struck nearby, close enough that he got a deep whiff of sulfur and felt energy buzz across his skin.

The Lammogo screeched and shuffled to the side, flapping. It stopped, eyes bulging, then ran back to him as if unable to stop hunting.

Thunder and rain pounded. Lightning popped the ground again. Too close for Bosse's comfort.

Eyes panicked, the Lammogo took off flying and squawking.

Huh. It's afraid of lightning.

Bosse dropped the rock and fell to his knees as water hit him like sharp needles. He stayed there for a moment, caught his breath, then got up and started walking to what he hoped was still west. Just because he didn't hear the wolf shifters howling didn't mean he was safe. They could have decided to run quietly.

With the storm upon him, lightning struck over and over as if it could not decide what to destroy.

He reached a small stand of trees and trudged through them at a slower pace, but he'd run so hard he was wearing down. He and his wolf could go for many hours at a steady pace with some rest.

After passing through the trees, lightning chased across the sky.

He'd heard rushing water and, with another twenty steps, could see it during the next lightning display. A fast-moving stream of water followed the crooked path carved out along the base of a mountain on the other side. Not too wide if the creek ran slower, but this one raged, probably created by a flash flood. He had to get across before the turbulent water got worse. Maybe this would slow down the wolf hunting him.

Or were there more than one by now?

He climbed a tall boulder to stand and scout the area for rocks the water had to flow around. Lightning continued to offer occasional glimpses of a mountain soaring high above. In one bright flash, he saw a black spot halfway up the side of the mountain.

Was that a deep shadow from a rock outcropping or a cave?

A cave would be welcome, but he had to consider if any natural predators lived there. It could be the lair of a bear. Didn't matter. If he and his wolf could reach that height and rest for a bit, Titan would be even stronger to run the rest of the way.

Who knew how far the Adriatic Sea was or if he was still headed toward it?

He slogged upstream to his right, thinking he'd find a narrower crossing.

Ten minutes later, he was rewarded with a pile of rocks that the water ran around, leaving a froth behind. He leaped from one rock to the next and landed on the other side, where his feet sunk into mud.

Perfect.

Turning back to his left, he began to climb uphill at an angle toward what he hoped was not a mirage.

With the last flickering of lightning, he pinpointed the black spot and scrambled over rocks, clinging to any handhold until he could make out a ledge.

Definitely a cave.

Hooking a hand, he hoisted himself until he could grab with both hands and pull himself up and over the ledge, breathing hard from the exertion. He rolled over and sat up to look at the land he'd crossed, surprised at the distance visible from here. Thanks to the flashing storm moving to what he hoped was east, the sky appeared clear for miles. He saw no sign of the Lammogo or any preternatural wolves. Water drenched the flatlands, which might help disturb his scent trail, especially where he'd run back and forth in a zigzag, trying to avoid Krol's pet.

That was all he could do for now.

He had no idea if the Lammogo could track him even after the rain.

He snuck close to the cave entrance and listened, hearing no obvious sounds. Taking a few steps in, he sniffed and caught an animal scent. Might even be a bear, but the scent was old. He went deeper inside and stopped short of going too far.

He'd rest near the mouth of the cave. Right now, it smelled like freedom.

Pulling the bag strap of the cloth bag over his head, he sat down on the dirt floor, shocked that he'd made it this far. How was Alifair? Would she be safe as she claimed? His conscience warred with common sense now that he had a break from running. He could save no one if he failed to escape Krol's hunters.

Adrenaline drained from him faster than water from a broken bowl. Exhaustion took over, dragging his eyes closed. He had done all he could for now and hoped Alifair slept safely in her room under the stairs.

He lay on his side, using the lumpy bag to prop his head, and told Titan, *Wake us if you hear anything.*

I will.

But could Titan hear a flying threat in time before the Lammogo was on them?

He was too exhausted to worry about what-ifs.

Chapter 11

————⁓⁓————

BACK IN HER room, frazzled nerves dissipated under a blanket of weariness. Alifair flopped on her bed, exhausted. She listened for any sound of Bosse's voice. Every disastrous situation ran through her mind.

The longer silence reigned outside her door, the more oncoming fatigue forced her to close her eyes, but she fought sleep until she had to shut her eyes.

Just for a moment.

Her eyelids fluttered a couple of times.

She'd barely slept in three days for worrying and preparing. She hadn't dreamed since the one fingering Bosse as the key to success. She had her doubts. If he did make it to the States, and she wanted that with all her being, how could he possibly come back to save Rez?

That left it up to Alifair, but she had yet to spot Rez in the castle.

She began mentally listing places she hadn't been able to search yet while trying to stay awake.

Her eyelids got heavier. She was done.

Dropping deep into sleep, the next thing she knew, she was running through the castle, trying to find Bosse before anyone else did. Rain began falling, then driving down hard. How could that be going on inside the kitchen?

Dreams usually made more sense. She had no idea what was going on.

She wasn't inside. The world had turned into a black void, brightened only by lightning. A wolf howled. She froze. Could that be Bosse's wolf? No, he would keep quiet. She started running and struggled to find her way through oversized trees. Then the trees thinned out and opened to a large flat field.

Lightning popped and struck everywhere. Terrified, she ran across the field. How was she doing that when a turtle could outrun her?

A high-pitched scream yanked her around to look back.

Krol's monster flew high up in the turbulent sky. If it caught her, it would kill her.

She ran across the field, and the fast-moving storm passed over her. As she looked back, the flying creature turned around and flew away. Thank goodness.

She couldn't keep running. She was no athlete.

The wind swirled and spun. She was turning round and round until she floated in a tornado. When it stopped, she stood on a ledge thousands of feet in the air and screamed, backing away.

An arm wrapped around her body and lifted her off the ground.

She screamed again.

"Hush, it's me."

He sounded like Bosse. She calmed down and fought to catch her breath.

He'd stepped inside a cave and lowered her feet to touch the ground. "What are you doing here?"

"You're safe!" Relieved, she hugged him. "I don't know how I got here. It just happened."

His arms wrapped around her, making everything better. He asked, "How did you find me?"

Shaking her head, she said, "I really don't know. I was in a storm, and wolves were chasing me. Then Krol's creature chased me but got frightened and flew away. The wolves never got to me, either. A tornado picked me up and dropped me on that ledge. None of it makes sense." The longer she held onto his warm body, the more her body was ready to quit. "Let's talk in the morning. I'm so tired."

She tried to keep holding on but ended up leaning against him as her hands lost their grip.

"You're soaked," he grumbled, lifting her into his arms. He carried her to where he sat against a wall with her in his lap. "I don't know how you did it, but I'm glad you're here."

"You are?" she asked in a sleep-deprived slur. He was so warm and held her close. She never wanted this moment to end. She hadn't felt this safe since being a child.

"Of course, I'm pleased. I told you I wanted you to come with me."

"I know… I just…" She couldn't sort out her thoughts, not while in his arms. She hadn't forgotten his kiss or how she'd never felt so bold or appreciated by a male.

Not like she did now. "Kiss me again."

Bosse tightened his hold on her. "I should not have stolen one from you."

She pushed herself to wake up and find out what had changed. "Why not? Are you saying you regret it?"

"Hell, no. I'd steal one again if I had it to do over." Bosse kissed her hair. "I should have waited until we were out of this mess to ask you, but I feared never having the chance again."

He worried too much.

She hadn't complained. In fact, those kisses had been the best thing to happen to her in a long time. "I like kissing," she admitted, turning her face up to his even though she could not see him.

She placed a hand on his shirt and then slipped her fingers inside to touch his warm chest. His heartbeat bumped hard.

He muttered something that sounded like, "… will be the death of me," then captured her lips again.

Never had she enjoyed kissing anyone as much or wanted more. Her fingers grazed his chest, feeling the hills and valleys of his muscular build. All that power, and he held her close yet carefully.

His free hand rubbed up and down her arms. He made

hungry sounds at her being wet one minute, then sounding as if he'd been starved for touch the next, which he had been.

Then his fingers ran down her arm to play along her stomach and lift the edge of her shirt.

With no input from her mind, she leaned closer to his hand, a blatant invitation she wanted him to accept.

This might go down as the best dream ever if he didn't stop.

She'd never had sexual dreams and now understood why. She'd never been with a real man, one who made her feel as if no other woman in the world existed.

His fingers stroked, moving higher over her hypersensitive skin until he touched her breast. She arched and drew a shuddering breath. "That feels so good."

Invitation accepted.

His fingers cupped one breast, rubbing softly but missing the point of her need. Literally. Her nipples ached, impatient for him to notice them.

When he brushed his big finger across the first one, she reached up and gripped his shoulder, anything to keep her anchored to this world. He kept teasing each breast, driving her body crazy with wanting more.

He kissed her lips, demanding her surrender.

She'd already tossed in the proverbial towel.

Fingers on one of his hands journeyed south, taking time to stroke every inch they met along the way until dipping inside her panties. Had she traveled here in a sleeping shirt and underwear?

She never answered that question because his fingers got busy and yanked her attention to the spot he found. The one that wiped out all ability to think.

He could have anything if he promised to keep going.

He started slowly, sliding his finger through her folds, then picked up speed, teasing her until the tension threatened to shred her brain. She panted and dug her nails into his firm arms. He pushed the pinnacle she reached for a tiny bit farther away every second. Close to tears from clinging to that sharp edge with no end in sight, she begged, *"Now! Pleeease!"*

With a quick change, his fingers focused entirely on one spot.

Her climax cut loose the tight cable twisted into a knot inside her. She flew into another dimension, or maybe her mind just snapped free. Pleasure raced across every nerve in her body. Stars scattered through her vision. When the fireworks settled down, she slumped in his arms.

He pulled his hand free and held her as if fearing she'd disappear. "I'm not sure how you got here, sweetness, but I don't want to let you go."

Struggling to regain her ability to talk, she mumbled, "I have something I need to do but can't recall what it is. Must not be important. I'm not leaving you." She hadn't ever been this relaxed and happy. Why would she walk away from Bosse?

Safe in his embrace, she fell asleep to the sound of him whispering soft words and his warm lips kissing her cheek. She wanted to stay awake and be with him, but she couldn't keep her eyes open any longer now that she knew he was safe.

A loud pounding woke her.

Alifair jumped up, looking around for Bosse. Where was he?

Someone knocked on her door again.

She was back in the castle. Not in some cave.

Disappointment, like she'd never known, swamped her.

More pounding.

Her brain believed it was only a dream, but her heart swore that time with Bosse had felt real. Accepting the reality of being stuck in this castle, she pulled her cloak over her and made it to the door. She opened it to find the short guard from the cage area standing there. Not happy.

She'd go toe to toe with him on being unhappy this morning. Still wrestling with disappointment, she struggled not to fidget or do anything that would make him suspicious of her. "What? Is Krol ready for us to go to work?"

He frowned at her surly tone, probably making him snap at her. "Yes. No one is allowed in the cage area without a guard escort. Understood?"

She finally woke up and realized she was blowing the whole subservient act. Nodding quickly as she expected someone submissive would do, she also wrung her hands. "Thank goodness. I prefer someone with me any time I'm sent down there. It's frightening."

"Get to work." He stopped scowling but was clearly untouched by her fear for her personal safety.

She closed the door and slumped back against it. Her legs felt like noodles. *Suck it up, buttercup*, as her mom used to say. Alifair hurried to use the bowl and pitcher of water she kept in her room. She felt the need to wash between her legs, which was bizarre. She never went to bed without washing her body. The moment she touched the rag to her most intimate area, she gasped at the frenzy of sensitive nerves.

That was the moment she recalled last night's erotic dream with Bosse.

Had she touched herself?

She shook off the strange feeling she'd been with Bosse in person, where he hid in a cave from Krol's flying creature. It had just been a dream. Dressing quickly, she stepped out to find the jerk at the next door snapping at another servant. And here she thought she was special. Laughing to herself, she scooted past him and continued to the kitchen, where the bustling activity of preparing food would have felt normal if not for the unnerving silence. Women in here generally chatted as friends.

Today, suspicious gazes cut around the room.

Everyone had to realize by now that Bosse had help getting out of his cage.

Would Krol think it was a guard or a servant?

He had no evidence of her being down there.

She hoped.

But neither did she want someone else to pay for her actions. Please tell her that Bosse had been gone long enough to put distance between him and those tracking him. In hindsight, she should have devised a different plan, but none of this was within her expertise. She created spells. Some worked. She had clairvoyant dreams that tended to be more spot-on. She used the power she had been born with, which wasn't all that impressive.

Her greatest skill appeared to be the ability to get herself into jams like this.

She felt responsible for continuing her mother's legacy, stepping in and becoming the clan's go-to person in times of direct threats to their existence. Her mother possessed a natural power for wielding magic. If only her mother could have saved herself as well as the three missing children that she'd tracked down. The men who stole the children had no idea they belonged to a clan protected by a third-generation gypsy queen gifted with powers.

As the rescued children told the story, her mother unleashed a whirlwind that sent cars and trucks flying. When the men burst from the cabin with rifles, she'd spun each one in a different direction. She never wanted to kill anyone so long as she could neutralize them.

One of the children had been so terrified her mother had to carry her outside while pulling the other two holding hands. She started telling them, "Mr. Thornton is waiting close by to help once we get into the woods ahead. When I tell you—"

"Nice trick, witch, but I'm a warlock," one of the men shouted.

She put the little girl down quickly to face the threat. When she swung around with the children behind her, he shot her with a titanium bullet, striking her stomach.

As she fell to her knees, she yelled at the children to run and wielded a last surge of her magic at the same time to shield them with a thick fog.

The clan called law enforcement, saying nothing about magic being used. As one of their council people, Thornton had been racked with guilt over leaving her mother, but he had done exactly as she'd ordered—save the children first, no matter what. He led the police to the area where he claimed to have found the missing children, who told him about Alifair's mother saving them. Playing the role of the community leader, he'd explained that her mother had not returned after hunting the children on her own.

With a short search, the police found the cabin where no male bodies remained.

Evidently, the kidnappers had taken their time torturing her mother before cutting off her head and leaving her dismantled body to be chewed on by animals and vultures.

Alifair had been seventeen at the time.

With her mother gone, the clan turned to her for protection the minute she turned eighteen. She was a flawed replacement for her mother. Her father had been a lumberjack, just a human who loved her mother dearly, was fine with her unusual gift, and died in a logging accident.

Now Alifair faced the strong possibility she would not survive coming to this castle. She tried not to be angry, but she was.

Not for the first time, she wondered why her female lineage had been chosen to sacrifice everything for the clan.

Duty. Such a simple word with a high cost.

Shaking off that dark memory, Alifair searched for where she could be of the most use in the kitchen. She walked over to Hessie, the woman in charge of servants.

Alifair inquired, "What can I do to help?"

Taller than Alifair, thick with rough features and frizzy gray hair, Hessie paused from cleaning greens. She wiped sweat off her wide brow. "We will have no fresh game tonight with the hunters out tracking the wolf shifter. Peel and cut up fifty potatoes and thirty onions. I'll have more when you finish."

Nodding her understanding, Alifair ran over to the pile of potatoes and got to work. As the morning wore on, the other women finished baking bread and pies. One woman came in with an apron full of carrots and began prepping them.

How would a vegetarian meal go over with Krol?

Not very well.

Linota had been washing and drying dishes for a while. Based on the stack growing taller than her head, she was getting behind.

Alifair finished her task and found Hessie. "Do you want me to help clean the dishes?"

Hessie had her hands full of rabbits that one of the guards had surprised her with and waved her off. "Do that. I must get this meat ready. Krol will be happy for more than vegetables."

Every servant would be glad to see something more than vegetables for the castle alpha. A hungry lion shifter scared even the guards.

Jumping in to help Linota, who smiled her thanks, Alifair went through the dishes quickly, directing the young woman to start drying. There was a side benefit to joining this woman in her duties because Linota had to set the large table with these same dishes. That meant Alifair could go out to the main room with her where Krol and nine of his best guards devoured meals every day.

She hoped to learn something about the hunt for Bosse.

It was past time for the noon meal when she and Linota set the table with heavy metal plates and mugs of beer. The men were tough on the flatware, but Alifair had spent time straightening the fork tines while drying them. Using metal plates served Krol's need to keep a medieval air about the place and provided dishware the guards could not break.

Knives were kept in the kitchen and out in plain sight. Servants were not allowed to put them out for place settings. They were only used to prepare the meals. The men carried their own knives. Alifair had been fortunate to find a knife down in the storage basement when she went to look for the tunnel. She failed to find the tunnel access due to everything piled as high as her head and too heavy to move, but the knife had been a win. It could have used a sharpening. Still, that knife was better than nothing if Bosse needed a weapon besides his wolf.

Alifair had just placed the first fork by a plate when Krol came striding into the hall. "Why is food not on the table?"

Linota began to sob. That wouldn't help.

He glared at her. "Get out of here until you stop bawling."

She ran into the kitchen. Alifair stood still, sure that she should only move when told.

He glared at her. "Well? Where is the food?"

"We are bringing it out next, sir. We're normally on time when we start early. We—"

"Shut up and bring us food," Krol ordered. His guards filled in around him.

Dipping her head as she assumed a servant would to a king, she hurried to the kitchen. Such a joke to pretend she would bow to any of those monsters in earnest. Thankfully, Hessie had loaded trays for them to carry out.

Not that any of the servants had been fed yet.

Alifair whispered to Linota, "Don't let his bark bother you. Wipe your face and come back with me. Never look like prey to them."

Nodding quickly, Linota lifted her skirt to wipe her eyes.

Once she, Linota, and another woman had distributed the trays of fried rabbit with carrots, a strange potato salad, wine for their cups, and bread to fill the table, they backed away to stand against a far wall.

Krol liked to have them near, so when he lifted a finger, someone came running. To him, that was true power.

His arrogant act was standard at the meals, which was why she'd tried to endear herself to Hessie. Not a simple task when dealing with a woman who liked no one and had a face no mother could love. Correction. Hessie lived to keep Krol happy. To do that, she needed everyone to pull their weight.

If Alifair had not come here specifically to rescue Rez and hopefully get out as well, surviving this place would be even harder. If she did manage to make it home to America, she was going to find a way to send help for the other captives here.

She pretended to listen to the two other women standing next to her and whispering to each other, but she cared nothing for their gossip. She needed to hear what had happened to Bosse.

One of the guards finally asked Krol, "How long will the hunters pursue the wolf shifter?"

How many hunters? she wondered.

"Until they find him if they wish to be paid and keep their heads."

Several burly guards paused long enough from eating to snort a laugh, which pulled a smirk from Krol.

Another guard asked, "Are they to bring Bosse back alive?"

Shrugging, Krol said, "I have offered more money for him to be returned alive, but if it comes down to killing him to survive, I have agreed as long as they bring me his head."

Alifair did her best not to react. She had to clamp her lips shut tight, or she'd have thrown up. She hadn't considered that Krol would allow anyone to kill Bosse without his being able to watch. She never wanted Bosse to return, but she had thought that if they captured him, he'd have another chance to escape.

Of course, he said he would outrun them or fight to the death.

"What of your new… creature? Will it kill him as well?"

Krol bragged, "My Lammogo has the exceptional ability to retrieve anything I wish brought here without harming what it carries."

"But it paralyzed the sheep," another guard mentioned.

"Only for a short while," Krol countered, waving his fork. "That sheep was active before you slaughtered it, right?"

The guard nodded, raising his eyebrows. "It was."

Krol swung a rabbit leg around when he said, "See? No damage, but I told my Lammogo to return to the castle by one o'clock today. Unfortunately, I have another task for my pet that takes precedence." He ate the rest of his rabbit and put his fork down, which drew the attention of every guard sitting with him. They usually ate fast with no idea when Krol would call an end to any meal.

Leaning back against the heavy wood chair, Krol announced, "I will be leaving as soon as it returns. I want the castle locked down. I will allow game to be delivered to the kitchen again. You are responsible for anyone who comes on these grounds. Understood?"

"Yes, sir." All the heads nodded.

His lead guard, Eriko, asked, "How long will you be gone, sir?"

"I'm not sure yet. Hopefully, less than three days, but possibly as long as five."

Alifair would explode if they didn't talk about Bosse soon. It was good to know Krol would be leaving, but having the guards beef up security might get in her way. She still had a plan once she found Rez, but moving around the castle on her own was going to get risky.

Shouting erupted outside.

Krol and his men turned toward the giant double doors made of thick wood beams joined together and hung on iron hinges.

The doors swung open. The two guards pulling them open hid behind the doors.

Krol's creature came striding in, head held high. How had it known what time it was since nobody around this place wore a watch?

Alifair would never get that abominable image out of her brain.

Standing, Krol walked over to meet his four-legged bird creature, the Lammogo.

When he reached his new pet, it sat like a dog and fixed its eagle-like eyes on him. He asked, "Is the wolf shifter still running?"

The bird's head dropped low and came back up.

"Are the hunters still on his trail?" He got the same response to this question and then asked, "Do you think the wolf will escape the hunters?"

Turning its head from side to side, the bird made it clear what it believed.

Alifair's heart thudded with disappointment.

Krol laughed. "Very good. Wait here, and I'll be ready to leave in a few minutes." He crossed to the staircase and went to the upper level Alifair itched to search.

She'd gotten a little news on Bosse but wished for a hunter to return to tell them Bosse had vanished.

The other two women started for the table because once Krol stood, everyone knew the meal was over, and they were dismissed. Alifair joined the women in clearing the table left in a mess by guards standing to leave.

Every one of Krol's mighty guards gave the Lammogo a wide berth and departed the hall through the open doors.

She had carried one tray into the kitchen and then returned to gather more plates and forks from the table. As she bent over to reach for another dish to add to her stack, she paused at the sound of Krol's boots pounding down the stairs. *"Guards!"*

The first guard who rushed inside called out, "Your wagon is ready, sir."

Wagon? Alifair couldn't believe the man did not have a modern vehicle. No mobile phones, sure, but no powered vehicle? She had lost her mobile phone the night they captured her, but she'd since learned there was no reception here. There was no reason for even Krol to have one, she supposed.

It felt like she'd fallen into a hole and traveled back hundreds of years in time. Or more like getting cast in a horror movie that wouldn't end.

She watched as Krol headed for the door. His bird creature stood and followed him outside.

Finally, Krol would be out of her way. She had searched almost all the downstairs and below, which had required patience she'd never thought she possessed. If she were caught in the wrong location, she and Rez would both lose. Now that Bosse was gone and hopefully outrunning his trackers, she could focus only on Rez.

For the first time since being here, she felt energized at finding Rez. If only she could dream about her clanswoman. Her vivid dream of finding Bosse in a cave had been more real than her other projective dreams. Very real.

She had to get her mind off that wolf shifter and think about her duty.

When the double doors were pulled closed, Alifair lifted her gaze to scout the area.

Eriko came striding in and addressed one of the lower guards. "Krol has put out word that we're hiring new guards. Some may arrive soon. He wants fresh blood in our security and some to hunt game for the kitchen. Also, I will begin interrogating our guards later today. The servants will be next. I intend to find the person who helped the wolf shifter escape."

Not all guards watched over the cage area. The one speaking with Eriko had a short, squat body with bushy red hair that matched his eyebrows and had been down there.

He told Eriko, "I assure you it was not me. I couldn't stand that animal."

She bit her tongue to keep from yelling at him that Bosse was not just an animal.

Eriko gave him a long look before saying, "Krol has determined that either someone who liked the wolf wanted to help him escape or someone who hated the wolf freed him just to be rid of another shifter."

The guard's face turned ashen. "I would never cross Krol. Besides, who likes any of those things in cages?"

"That is good to hear, but I will speak to everyone who was in this castle last night. Krol has told me to find the person behind this or face the consequences myself. I assure *you* I will not accept failure."

Stomach in a knot at that news, Alifair turned slowly to keep from dropping the dishes. Her whole body shook as she shuffled to the kitchen. What way did Eriko have to determine who told the truth or not?

He was not a shifter who could smell a lie.

He must have something up his sleeve to make such a bold statement.

Panic urged her to escape this minute, but she couldn't leave without Rez first.

Chapter 12

S UNLIGHT SPEARED THROUGH the opening, waking Bosse. Why was he sitting up against a wall? Still sleepy, he called to his wolf. *Titan?*

I am here and ready. We are rested.

Bosse rubbed his shirt-covered back against the wall to ease the itching. Good sign that his skin had healed. Alifair's stitches would rip free when he shifted, but he had healed better than he'd thought by now. He stood, and dizziness hit him.

Sitting on the ground again, he told Titan, *We need food and water first.*

The woman put food and a gourd in the bag.

Smart wolf. Bosse had to shake off his mental cobwebs. He dug inside the gray cloth bag to find rolls, meat jerky, a gourd of water, and… cookies. Of course.

He hadn't smiled in two years, not a real smile that warmed his heart, but she managed to lighten his mood anywhere, even in his dreams.

What a dream that one was last night.

He paused. Hadn't he been sleeping on the floor? How had he ended up sitting against the wall? He'd dreamed Alifair came to this cave, and he'd carried her over to the wall, where he sat down to dry her off. He did way more than that to her body. His cock stirred just thinking about the erotic dream he'd love to enjoy in real life.

That dream had been so real—more than he wanted to admit.

He muttered, "Stop being ridiculous." He'd slept sitting against the wall in his cage at times when he had chest injuries. Nothing new there. That dream was born of the stress from escaping the castle and that Lammogo. Nothing else.

He quickly ate the meat and rolls, saving the sweets for later. He chugged the water and stuck the cork back into the empty container to use again.

Titan needed an easy way to carry this bag. Alifair had given Bosse a rope for his pants, which he wouldn't need while Titan had their body. He shed his clothes, then retied the bag into two halves with a rope attached to each side. He set it up so that Titan could slip his head through the loop and work the bags into place over his shoulders.

Between the rain, the sleep, and the food, he felt refreshed in a way he hadn't in two years.

Woman was good to us, Titan said.

Yes, she was. I still feel bad about her not coming with us. Guilt put a wet blanket on his upbeat mood. Bosse's struggle over continuing alone was not going away any time soon. He admitted to Titan, *Like you, I don't think she told us everything.*

She spoke truth when she said to leave without her.

Sighing, Bosse said, *I agree. Except for us being free, I don't like the way this all worked out.*

Titan was correct. Bosse had to respect her wishes even if he did not understand them. He had a bad feeling the guilt eating at him would not go away until he found her again. She'd reached inside him and discovered a spot for her when he'd have laughed at anyone else who thought they could.

Just thinking about her brought a shining light to the darkness he'd fought through day after day.

I will take the body and run fast today, Titan said.

Bosse happily handed the body to Titan, who hooked the satchel strap over his neck. Once Titan had it to his liking, he stepped out of the cave, taking in the vast landscape.

Bosse reminded Titan, *We must stop at some point to drink water and fill the gourd.*

I will find water, Titan said, then turned to a sound coming from the northeast.

One of the tracking wolves appeared maybe two kilometers back.

A tiny speck flew in the air.

Clear skies held no promise of protective lightning today. Time to go.

Over the next few hours, Bosse wished for a way to help Titan, but his wolf was better at picking up scents and moving quietly across rugged terrain. If the Lammogo caught up to them, they'd have to shift for Bosse to have a chance of striking it without getting close enough to be paralyzed.

He hoped he was correct in believing Krol would not allow anyone to kill him and steal Krol's desire to watch Bosse suffer as he died.

The Lammogo had proven it could deliver prey without killing it. That worried Bosse more than the wolves.

Until they ran into an unexpected obstacle, Titan would continue in the same direction until they found the sea. Once the land leveled out to normal terrain of occasional trees and some open fields being farmed, Titan would set a reasonable pace he could maintain day and night.

Luck smiled on them when his wolf encountered a two-lane road and shadowed it from the tree line, watching as vehicles came by two or three at a time.

Titan said, *Our scent will be strong today with no rain.*

Bosse asked, *Are you thinking of hitching a ride on a vehicle?*

Yes. When I find the right one.

His wolf kept moving and watching until a truck approached, hauling logs on a trailer with vertical steel posts holding them in place.

It was also traveling in a southwestern direction.

The commercial trucks they'd seen before had been followed by a couple of cars close behind and itching to pass. This one had rust on its faded blue cab and rambled down the road all alone at a leisurely pace.

Titan ran ahead to where the road curved to the right and waited until the truck slowed as it neared the curve. Perfect. Titan raced after the truck, running right behind it in a blind spot, and leaped, clawing to hang on, then climbed up the pile. It wouldn't have been so difficult for him if he hadn't been carrying the makeshift saddlebags.

He found a spot on the side of the logs where his body shape and the bag would not stand out, then turned to face behind the truck. He settled in with claws hooked in logs on each side. His Tundra wolf had a deep gray coat with dashes of rust color, which would blend in from the air. Getting off the ground would end their scent trail for a while.

This one move should allow them to shake the trackers.

Bosse hoped.

After what seemed to be an hour, the air carried a new scent.

Titan lifted his head. *I smell salt in air. Might be near sea.*

Bosse replied, *I think you're right. Pick a good place to jump off, and let's find out.*

The landscape along the road had flipped between trees and shrubs to occasional wheat fields being farmed. Waiting until a car that had run up close behind passed, Titan edged to the back and leaped off the truck, curling into a ball. He landed hard on the shoulder of the road and rolled down the drop to bushes where he finally stopped.

Bosse said, *Sorry about the bags.*

Titan lay there for a minute, breathing hard, then righted himself and stood. He wiggled to get the saddlebags in place. *We are good. We must cross the road to follow the smell.*

Sounds like a plan, Bosse said. *We're gonna need drinking water soon.*

Yes. I will find it.

After loping a short distance, fortune smiled on them

when they found a small pond that appeared to be part of a farm. Titan drank his fill and started to shed the bags looped over his body, but the cows began to moo as a group.

Bosse told Titan, *Let's fill the gourd later. The cows sound agitated. They may realize we're here.*

Titan took off before the cows alerted someone to investigate. After that, he made fast time weaving through sparse woods until blue sky and water began to show through the trees. He slowed and paused at the edge of the tree line.

A salty breeze brushed his muzzle, lifted in the air. No cloud interrupted a soaring blue sky, and emerald water rolled over a gray stone beach.

Titan said, *I am happy. This is the life we deserve.*

His wolf's words choked up Bosse after years of them clinging to life together. He wanted Titan to enjoy the life that had been stolen from them. This wolf had been his greatest friend since birth.

Staring at the scenery through Titan's eyes, Bosse had expected white sand from what he'd heard of beaches, but this one had more of a smooth gravel look and boulders running between the shore and the trees.

He told Titan, *We must be at the right place. We should go north to find a road. There must be one that follows this coast in a way that would be shorter to reach a port in Italy.*

Yes, good idea. Titan turned and headed north. In a short while, they located the road, but it was a busy highway. Titan had no trouble paralleling the route by moving swiftly through nearby trees.

With a bit of luck, the hunters lost their trail once Titan jumped on that truck.

It felt like two hours had passed when they encountered a small airport between the road and the water.

For Titan to continue would be risky as he'd had less and less cover over the last kilometer. Moving between two thickets of brush, they shifted. Bosse dressed in the tunic and pants again, then retied the bag to loop across his chest.

He looked like a poor person with no shoes. They must have those people in Italy. He figured no one paid attention to the poor. He struck out, walking past the airport where small jets were moving around, ready to fly—nothing he ever wanted to do.

Alifair had been wise to suggest stowing away on a ship. He hoped he and Titan did not get seasick.

Once he passed the airport, he kept his distance from the highway while still using it as a directional path. The sun was high in the sky when he began encountering more people, many of whom looked hard at him.

Perhaps he appeared too physically fit to be a homeless person.

He needed information and spoke no Italian. If not for being taught English while a cub and Krol demanding his people speak English, Bosse would have been at a loss trying to communicate with the guards.

When he located a large hotel complex, he took advantage of the lush landscaping and a thick stand of trees on one side. He climbed a tree and settled in to observe and listen.

Many people communicated in different languages. Several spoke English but only discussed their vacation plans. That was no help.

He'd noticed people sticking a card into a slot to enter one end of the building. That prompted him to slip down the tree and watch for the sun to set. Once twilight wrapped the city, he waited for someone alone to use their card. When it happened, he rushed to catch the door before it closed, waiting silently for the person to disappear at the end of the hall. Then he climbed a set of nearby stairs, which he took all the way to the top of the fourth floor. From there, he leaped over a metal bar, preventing others from going higher on the next set of steps. He found a door to the roof and located a place where he could see far out over the water.

He spotted what he hunted. Giant ships were lined up in a port.

But the road to the docks was a long bridge.

How could he traverse that without drawing attention?

After leaving the hotel, it took him another hour of searching to locate where to enter the bridge. He leaned against a brick building to watch cars and trucks crossing the bridge, frustrated at no simple way to get there.

Had he made it this far to be defeated by a bridge?

No. He just had to find a way to cross it without being seen.

A whiff of succulent-smelling food made his mouth water and his stomach complain. Using that as a beacon, he followed the scent to a long building and busy parking area where trucks were loading pallets of produce.

But he'd smelled something cooked and kept hunting until he found the source.

The food was locked in sealed metal carts. Damn.

Nothing to eat yet, but then he spotted a truck with the same logo and words on the side as one he'd seen cross the bridge to the port. While the men inside the building spoke and signed papers, he climbed up between the cab and the box bed.

He'd had to claw holes in the smooth metal top for a way to hold on and hope the dark slot he hid in would shield him from view.

The door to the truck opened and closed. The engine rumbled to life. Bracing himself, Bosse was prepared when the vehicle began to move.

Then a bad thought hit him. What if this truck was not heading to the docks?

He couldn't look around without lifting his head, but with every couple of turns, he caught the lights of the port. Then the wind blew his hair to one side as the truck motored across the bridge.

He grinned like an idiot.

This was the moment to celebrate all he and Titan had done to get here, but none of it would have happened without Alifair. His grin fell. The closer he came to leaving this side of the ocean, the more his insides twisted into a tangle of guilt.

How could he sit back in another country for a month enjoying freedom when she was still a prisoner?

The truck slowed as it passed through an automated toll area and then worked through short streets until it turned on the last road to the docks.

Bosse surmised this because he stared at a massive ship at the end of the path. Up close, the idea of Titan jumping on that behemoth seemed impossible.

Lights got brighter in this area. He had to get off this truck, or someone from up on those ships would see him.

When the truck paused at a stop sign with no vehicle behind it, Bosse climbed up and over the back end of the truck, then down to the bumper, and leaped away. He ran to a side street along an office building with no lights on.

Now what?

This looked hopeless, but he worked his way to the closest point behind a long metal container ten feet wide and just as tall to observe where they loaded supplies onto one ship. It appeared to be a passenger vessel. He needed a ship made for hauling cargo. He started walking from one dark area to the next, searching around this island.

His heart was wrecking his head.

Could he really jump on a ship and leave? If he did, this was final. Alifair made promises based on escaping. It had been difficult enough for him and his wolf. How would she outrun Krol's Lammogo or cover the ground he and Titan had?

Was the truth she knew she would not escape?

She hadn't lied when she said she needed to rescue someone else, but Titan had pointed out that she hadn't told them everything.

Bosse should have asked if she knew for sure she could escape.

She would not have been able to pass off a lie on that question.

He'd been exhausted and confused the night she'd come to him with a plan that had to happen right then. With some distance and time, he now saw the holes in it for saving herself. He could not leave this country and live with himself.

Swallowing hard, Bosse said to Titan, *I must ask you to do something terrible.*

What do you want?

Was he really going to do this to his wolf, who had been with him step by step over two horrific years? He and Titan had always discussed everything. He could not do what he wished for without Titan's help.

No matter what he did, he would let someone down.

I can't leave this country with no way to return for Alifair and live with myself, Bosse admitted. *I know you will not like what I feel I need to do, maybe even hate me, but she risked everything to free us. I believe we can free her.*

Titan didn't answer right away. When he weighed in, he said, *If you must do this, we will do it together.*

Bosse's skin tingled with the relief that rushed through him. *Thank you for being the best part of me. I promise to make it up to you and find us a good place to live in America once we are all free.*

They had just passed a business that smelled of beer and fried food. Titan had captured a rabbit today. Not enough for a wolf who had been going nonstop, but something to eat.

If only Bosse had money. He walked around the back of the restaurant to dig through the dumpster.

Titan shouted in his head. *Shifters!*

Bosse dropped what he had in his hand and swung around. It can't be.

Three men, all dressed in dark blue jumpsuits and smelling of wolves, stepped out from behind the metal garbage container. "Don't fight us, and you won't be hurt."

Titan said, *We might outrun them.*

Bosse allowed his shift to start, giving him claws and

reshaping his head for sharp fangs. He dove at the group to take them to the ground in a surprise attack.

Two went sliding, but the third was bigger and grabbed Bosse by the throat. The two others jumped up and yanked Bosse off the big guy. He fought hard, knocking the two away, and prepared to rip the third one to pieces, but that one held a gun on him. Even with a bullet, Bosse could get away if he took that down and the shooter didn't strike Bosse in the head.

One shifter from the ground jumped up and attacked, forcing Bosse to fight more than one. The minute his attention was divided, a needle stabbed his neck.

That's what the gun had. Not bullets.

Bosse kept blasting his fists, now fighting the two again. They were trying to beat him down. His legs were thick as trees, but they turned to rubber.

Titan moaned in his head. *Drugs.*

Bosse's vision blurred. His arms flopped.

"Not so badass, are you?" one of the shifters said right before he blasted Bosse with an uppercut, sending him to the ground. He could hear a smear of voices as he blinked in and out of consciousness. They carried him for a short distance and threw him into a van, slamming the side door.

How could he get caught again?

He fought to stay conscious, but the drugs were too strong. He passed out, then woke up later, sitting somewhere other than the van. This place vibrated quietly. His mouth was dry as a desert. His wrists had titanium handcuffs, which were chained to the ankle cuffs on his outstretched legs. He looked around. There were four more shifters handcuffed the same way.

He whispered, "Water."

"You gonna act right if I give you water?"

Bosse looked up into the face of his captor and lifted his wrists the few inches the chain allowed as an answer.

"Give him water, Kinter," the big shifter he'd fought said.

Kinter stuck a water bottle to Bosse's lips.

He drank greedily. When he could talk, he asked, "Who are you? Why did you capture me?"

"Our names don't matter. There's a bounty for lone wolf shifters. This is our contracted area. We catch a nice number of you each month. You're not the first shifter that tried to stow away on a ship to America. We're just delivering you to get paid. Nothing personal."

Bosse dropped his head back, disgusted. Was it his lot in life to be captured every time he turned around? Raising his head, he asked, "Where are you taking me?"

"South Carolina."

"Where is that?"

His captors laughed quietly. The big one said, "It's in the United States."

Bosse wanted to roar his anger. He'd failed Alifair and Titan. How could this happen? Determined to escape again, he kept digging for information. He would get away from this bunch somehow. "How many days until we get there?"

Kinter laughed out loud and said to the big guy, "He doesn't have a clue." Even a captured shifter behind him snorted at his question.

Bosse clenched his hands, wishing to get his answer another way, but he was stuck with asking. "Why is that funny?"

"You don't realize you're flying? We're in a Lear jet. We'll be there in a matter of hours, not days."

Now the rumble and soft vibration made sense. He had never flown. Every second, he was getting farther and farther away from Alifair. He had a final question. "Who is buying me?"

"The Black River Pack pays the best money."

Bosse couldn't breathe.

Chapter 13

ALIFAIR COULDN'T FREE her tangled feet. She panicked, twisting and kicking. She couldn't get to Bosse. Couldn't scream at him to run.

"*Nooo!*" She sat up in bed, hair flying everywhere and sweating with a cold chill.

A knock at the door was followed by, "What is wrong?"

That deep voice belonged to one of the guards.

She had to convince him nothing was happening. Think! Best way to make a guard walk away was to babble like an emotional woman about anything. "I saw a rat, and I don't like rats because—"

"Shut up. Do not make so much noise over small things," he ordered and stomped away.

Bosse had to be free.

Just a nightmare from all the stress. A dream and nightmare. He kissed her as if she were the only woman he'd ever wanted.

But that kiss had also felt like a goodbye.

No. She shook her head, unable to accept what her scrambled emotions and terrified brain conjured up. He couldn't be caught again. He said he'd die first. Shifters in dark blue jumpsuits had given him drugs.

They were taking him to the Black River Pack.

Her logical mind stuck its nose into her internal argument. How had they even found him? How would anyone know who he was or wait for him to arrive in a place to be captured?

Okay, she could think more clearly now. Bosse was fine. Some days, she felt like a crazy person ruled by her out-of-control subconscious mind. She just missed him, and her stressed-out brain convinced herself to dream they were together. She should have directed it to dream of Bosse arriving in America and smiling.

Or maybe an image of where Rez had been locked up.

Last night had been nothing more than a nightmare, just like a million other people have when worrying about someone.

With him free, she had to focus. She had one task to accomplish last night and failed.

She dropped her head into her hands and rubbed her eyes, disappointed in herself. She'd meant to grab an hour of sleep and wake in time to hide and watch for someone who might be taking food to Rez.

This was a disaster.

How could she have possibly missed the opportunity to catch her best lead?

It was Bosse's fault.

Really? No, that wasn't fair.

She allowed him to consume too much space in her head, making the screw-up entirely her fault. This second dream of him had not been a fun one. Well, except for the time they had to snuggle and kiss. She'd stayed in a deep sleep, evidently waiting for any sign that he was truly free and on his way to America.

Had that been a prophetic dream of something Bosse would face?

Her dreams usually projected something already in motion.

The short night of sleep would have been fine if she'd had another chance to sleep in his arms. She sat up and chided herself for losing an opportunity to learn Rez's location. Fantasies had no place in her dreams when she was running out of time.

Last night, she'd had a second dream, one she couldn't

brush off as unimportant. She'd once had a prophetic death dream, which had come true.

Now she'd had a second one, and the reality was that she and Bosse had no chance to be together in real life. Even if she could, her clan would shun her for wanting to be with a shifter. Regardless of what happened in the future, she'd never forget the feeling of him holding her against his chest during the dream the night he escaped.

She'd tuck that fantasy into a special place in her heart for later if Krol or his men realized she helped Bosse or caught her trying to free Rez. She wouldn't live long, and her death would be brutal.

Was he the one who would leave her bloody and gasping for breath?

Krol might toss her into the arena just to laugh as some horrible monster like the Beast ripped her to shreds. Blood flying everywhere. Her screaming.

Stop it, Alifair! she ordered.

Thoughts like that would not give her the courage to face another day in this place. Worry about one thing today. Find Rez! She might be losing her mind from all this. If so, she hoped to end up in a nonstop dream world with Bosse.

Jumping up, she dressed, found her water pitcher empty, and scurried down the hall to the group bathroom. Finished with her personal needs, she splashed her face with icy water. That woke her up. On the way back to her room, she passed two more servants yawning as they headed to the community bath area. Not late yet. She wove her unmanageable hair into one thick braid and tied it with a thin leather thong.

Shaking off her dreams to deal with reality, she prepared for a new day of sleuthing for her mother's friend. Alifair had to remind herself of that often. Rez had verbally cut her to the bone at times, but if Alifair's mother still lived, she'd expect her daughter to be the strong woman she'd raised. She knew better than to allow personal differences to get in the way of performing her duty to their clan.

Time to face Hessie. Instead of immersing herself in

kitchen duties today, Alifair offered to prepare and run food to the guards.

Linota hated that task and sent her a smile of thanks.

If Alifair were honest with Linota, she'd admit she had an ulterior motive. Even so, she really didn't mind taking over that task for the easily frightened young woman. First, she had to feed the main floor guards. Even with torches lit along the walls, any activity in this main hall had a dreary feel, but food generally made the guards happy.

On her third trip delivering food to guards stationed along different spots in the hall, she returned to the kitchen and loaded one tray to deliver downstairs for those two guards. She'd been told not to go down there without a guard, but two guards were already present. It made no sense to ask another one.

As she started to depart the kitchen with a loaded tray of steaming stew, she spotted a thin woman with a blue head cloth tied at the nape of her neck and wearing a drab gray dress over her gangly form. Her brown apron seemed to be too large for her as well. She stepped out of the stairwell to the basement food storage, quickly walking across that end of the kitchen. She exited through the side door leading to the hall for Alifair's sleeping area.

The woman had appeared and departed so quickly that Alifair would have missed her if she hadn't been watching intently for anything out of the norm.

Strolling calmly out of the kitchen, Alifair glanced to her right at the guards seated at the far end of the hall, who were all busy eating and talking.

She turned left and hurried toward the hall next to the big stairs where the woman should be. Alifair paused at the corner to peek down the long hall where doors on the right marked servant quarters, including hers.

The woman sporting the brown apron walked away from Alifair, moving nonchalantly with her arms hanging loose and no food tray in sight.

At the end of the hall, she turned right.

What was there?

Alifair had been down that dark passage off to the right once, finding only closets.

One door had been locked, which she assumed held items Krol did not want the servants to touch.

If only she were not carrying a tray of food, she could move around more easily and follow this woman. Gripping the tray, she debated and checked the guards again.

None were looking her way.

Now or never. She hurried down the hall and eased up to the corner, peeking around to the right for the woman. That hall was always unlit, but she could make out the woman holding a flashlight and using a key to open the one locked door Alifair had dismissed.

It squeaked.

Alifair pulled back quickly.

The door squeaked again. Had it closed?

She risked one last look, but the woman was gone. She had carried no food, though.

It didn't matter. Alifair had an idea of where to go hunting next. She pulled back, took a breath, walked quickly without rushing to enter the great room at a normal stride, and crossed it as calmly as her rapid pulse would allow. At the stairs leading down to the guards in the basement cage area, some called the dungeon, she took each step slowly, careful not to fall.

Excitement revved her up in the hope of opening that locked door once everyone was asleep. She'd stay awake for sure tonight. Her mother had been born to gypsies and raised by vagabond musicians in Belgium. She'd been taught useful skills like how to pick a lock. She'd explained to her only child that their magic could not perform every trick.

Alifair knew that better than anyone.

Since her magic was worse than an old-fashioned radio with a weak signal, she'd plenty of time training and adding a few tricks of her own for survival as much as anything.

Taking the last stair step, she had to be careful not to drop the tray that now strained her arms. She wrinkled her nose at the stinky smell of animals, urine, and body odor in the basement. It had to be worse for someone with a sensitive olfactory, like Bosse. His cage had smelled of his wolf and sometimes sweat and blood, but not bad odors.

If he could handle all those days living down here, she could get through this as well.

When the guards playing cards didn't acknowledge her, she announced, "Here's your food." Once they cleared the barrel end serving as a tabletop, grumbling the whole time, she placed the tray so that it balanced on the round surface. Receiving nothing more than grunts as her thanks, she started for the steps again to return upstairs but felt eyes on her.

Hair raised along her neck. Her pulse jumped as if sensing a threat.

Looking over her right shoulder, she met the scary gaze of Beast. He embodied every terrifying physical trait of a boogeyman. Unlike those of legends, he lived.

Why was he staring at her?

Her skin quivered with a strange feeling about that shifter. Had he seen or heard her helping Bosse?

If so, could he communicate with anyone? Based on what she'd gathered from guards who had spent long days and nights here, no one could understand his grunts and grumbles.

They believed he was more animal than man at this point.

She rolled her eyes at herself and stifled a chuckle at her paranoia.

But when she put her foot on the first step, she couldn't help glancing back to see if something else had grabbed his attention.

No. His evil gaze remained pegged on her.

The two guards ate their food and talked, oblivious to what their resident crazy shifter was doing.

Beast turned to look over his shoulder at Bosse's empty cell, then swung back around and locked eyes with her. He sniffed hard in her direction, cocked his head, and pulled his lips back in a scary smile. His eyes gleamed with the look of an animal that had cornered its prey.

He knew.

Her body shook with realizing he could finger her. She had no idea how he'd figured it out, but Beast knew she'd helped Bosse.

Chapter 14

———◆———

BOSSE SLEPT FOR short bursts during the flight. The one time he dropped into a deep sleep, Alifair appeared again. He'd worried he'd never dream of her again, but there she was, sitting down next to him, but he couldn't move his cuffed hands to touch her.

She brushed the hair out of his eyes with her fingers. "I can't believe someone captured you again. What is wrong with shifters?"

"I am not the one to ask. I have met no good ones. You should not be here. These are bad people."

"They can't see me."

He believed her. How could she be here, yet no one sees her?

She leaned in and hugged him.

He sighed at the soothing energy from her touch. If he could just find a way to keep that with him, he could face what was coming.

Sighing softly, she said, "I wish I could help you escape again."

He soaked up the feeling of her next to him and released a sigh of contentment. He had never asked for much in life or been given the opportunity to create a life he wanted to live. He'd spent too many years battling to survive and believed he'd lost the ability to feel anything for another person.

Then sweet Alifair left him cookies.

Not wanting her to stay in case whatever spell shielded

her broke and Kinter found her here, he had to send her home. Bosse would not allow these animals to touch her. He turned his lips to her cheek and kissed her. "You did enough. My wolf and I tried our best. Too many vile shifters in this world."

She hugged him tighter. "You are meant to live free. Don't stop fighting." Then she pulled away, her eyes welling with tears. "Don't quit. You'll find a way out of this. Please keep trying."

He heaved a heavy breath. His mind and body were tired of fighting. "I have no life. Everyone takes it from me."

Heartbreak wracked her face. "Please don't quit. Do it for me."

At that moment, he would have found a way to make this airplane fly to the moon for her. She'd only asked him to continue fighting for his freedom.

Once again, she gave him a renewed sense of hope.

He rubbed his beard carefully over the tender skin of her cheek, longing to keep her next to him, but he couldn't. He had to push her back to safety. These dreams felt too real.

The fact that he knew he was dreaming, but his mind would not accept that as entirely true concerned him.

One look at those sweet lips, and he needed to kiss them again. He moved toward her, and this fearless woman met him halfway, clutching his shoulders and kissing him as if this could be the last.

It very well could be.

His heart thudded hard, longing for this female who felt important. He'd begun to accept his and Titan's fate, but now he did not want to lose her. He'd never felt this deep need for anyone, not like he did for Alifair.

He ran his tongue along the seam of her lips and delved into her mouth, playing with hers. She sucked on his tongue. He bent his knees and strained against the metal constraints so that he could move closer to her.

Too soon, she ended the kiss and sat back.

He glanced past her to see if she'd been discovered. Everything except Alifair was a blurry shape.

Where were the others on this flight to hell?

Was any of this real? No, it was just a dream.

His chest hurt from having to let her go. He wanted… so many things he could never have. Silly to want the impossible. His destiny had been written the moment he'd been born a shifter. His pack had lived as outcasts, and now he was a monster wanted by no one.

"That's not true," Alifair whispered. "You aren't a monster, and… I want you."

Had he said his thoughts out loud, or had she heard the words in his mind?

She urged him, "Stop convincing yourself you can't escape. You got away from Krol. You can break free of these people. Be ready when the opportunity comes and take it."

"I will… try," he mumbled, blinking his eyes. He did not want to sleep. Not yet. A wave of exhaustion rolled over him again. Every time he woke, he could not remain awake long. His eyelids drooped again.

He felt small hands shaking his shoulder. "Wake up, Bosse. What's wrong with you? I watched you battle everything Krol tossed at you and defeat them all, many of them with horns and hooves."

He forced his eyes open. "I have never been so tired, even after battles. These shifters shot me with drugs. I can't fight them off."

She leaned in close and whispered, "Start drinking water. Ask for as much as you can get. That will flush the drugs from your system until your shifter healing can take over."

"Water will work?" He never stopped marveling at the intelligence of this woman.

"Yes. You haven't eaten enough. That's why the drugs hit you even harder."

"I will try to get water, but … you should not come back to me. I don't want you to see me if I fail to break free."

She exhaled on a sob. "Please don't give up. I believe in you." Her body began to fade.

"No, Alifair. Don't leave me." He cursed himself for

asking that of her. "I am sorry. You must go. I want you safe."

"I can't stay. I don't understand how I can be with you in a dream. This never happened in my dreams before, not until I met you. I'm so happy to find you this way. I've been worried about you." She faded again, her last words ghosting to him. "Remember, lots of water and fight for your freedom. You can do this."

Then she vanished, but he kept staring at the empty spot.

Someone yanked him away from her. "Time to go to the Black River Pack!"

Bosse jolted awake, breathing hard from the way that dream shook him. It felt so real. She felt real. He thought over all that she'd said and spoke up. "I need water."

"What's your problem?" Kinter snapped at him.

"I must have water. Has been too long."

Kinter brought him a bottle and held it so he could drink without uncuffing his hands. He'd been allowed to use the urinal once during the flight, but even with two more bottles of water, he'd still been so dehydrated that it had been the only time. He did as Alifair told him and kept drinking water to flush the drugs from his system.

Had she really been in his dream, or was he imagining the whole thing? How would she know to get rid of drugs with water?

He was allowed to use the urinal one more time, but even after three additional bottles of water, he did not go again. The last time he had water, he felt his body relax as it hadn't the entire flight until now. He fell into a peaceful sleep and then woke when he sensed the change in lighting.

Blinking as his eyes adjusted, he sat up to see the first hint of dawn approaching. Were they close to their destination? He silently asked, *Titan, are you okay?*

Better now. Not so sleepy.

Bosse stilled. *I had a dream about Alifair. She told me to drink water to push the drugs out of our body.*

His wolf replied, *She is a good woman.*

Yes.

Muscles in Bosse's chest eased at the clear sound of Titan's voice. Alifair had given him confidence and a new drive to continue. He shared that with Titan. *I know I started sounding like I would give up. That was the drugs. I am better now. We are both stronger now. We will fight to the end.*

Titan sounded relieved. *Good. We are ready. We can win.*

Although Bosse agreed, he admitted they needed food to regenerate to full strength. He still wore the cloth bag strapped over his shoulder and hanging under his arm. It smelled of Kinter's scent from where the shifter had dug through it, probably looking for weapons. At least they had not thrown away the bag. It was a gift from Alifair, the only physical connection he still had to her.

He'd been telling the truth when he said he had not met a decent shifter.

There would always be shifters, like Beast, that were just monsters.

Bosse clenched his fists and muscles, then relaxed his hands. His body would respond when called upon. He had to escape before the ruthless Black River Pack got their claws in him.

He and Titan would take death over being experimented on.

These shifters who kidnapped him and the others had not beaten him while he was handcuffed and given him water might sound decent, but he looked at it from their perspective and came up with why.

They needed their captives to be healthy specimens to sell.

He could use that against them.

Careful to tell the truth when he spoke around shifters, Bosse said, "I haven't eaten in over a day and not much before that. Will I get any food?"

After an exchange with the big guy, Kinter walked to the front of the airplane and pulled several bags from a cabinet. He carried them back, dropping one in Bosse's lap, then continued walking past him and dropping cold paper bags in the laps of the other handcuffed shifters.

Still behind Bosse, Kinter told the other shifters, "If you want to eat, I'll unclip your cuffs from your ankles. Make one wrong move, and I'll hit you with another hypodermic needle."

Grunts of understanding followed.

The big shifter strode up to Bosse, speaking with an accent he couldn't place. "You heard that, yes?"

"Yes."

After unchaining Bosse's handcuffs from his ankles, he handed Bosse a bottle of water with the cap loose, then stood over him as Bosse ate slowly to keep from cramping his stomach. They'd given him a thick roast beef sandwich, potato chips, and an apple. Not a huge meal, but protein.

Bosse eased his head around to see how the other captives were doing.

"*Eyes on me!*" the big guard ordered.

Turning back to the guard, Bosse shrugged as he finished a mouthful. "Just looking to see if I knew anyone."

"You do not. The less you know about the others, the better for you. Just worry about yourself."

The airplane began descending. Bosse's stomach dropped with it. He didn't like flying at all. The craft landed with a bump, but not enough to jolt him. With the sky brightening to a dusky light, he was torn between being ready to get out of this plane to exercise his legs and staying put to avoid the inevitable.

The chain between their handcuffs and ankles was reattached.

Kinter cupped Bosse under the arm and yanked him up to stand. Bosse still had to walk hunched over to move his feet. At the door, with no better way to descend, he hopped down from step to step, then turned around and jumped to the side.

Now he could watch the others figure out how to get to the ground.

The big guard, who appeared to be the kidnapping leader, had exited the airplane first and now held a gun on Bosse. The airport had little traffic. Just a small airplane moving around in the distance. Tall trees were bunched together a hundred yards beyond the end of the runway. He'd spend too much time in the open if he got a chance to run.

Moist heat hit him first. A humid country. He inhaled a deep breath of fresh air filled with a pine scent.

If only he could breathe air once more as a free man.

The next captive hesitated at the top of the stairs with a bewildered look.

Kinter announced from behind him, "You can all get down the same way as the first one."

Three of the captives made it without falling, but jumping on the steps was not as easy as Bosse had made it look. The last shifter missed the second step from the plane and curled into a ball as his body bounced the rest of the way. He hit the pavement and groaned.

"Get up," the leader snarled. He hooked the arm of the captive on the ground and yanked him to his feet. The shifter grumbled and tilted sideways, probably from the drugs. Blood dripped from the cuts on his forehead and shoulder. He wore a pair of faded jeans and looked as if he'd fallen down a rocky embankment in them.

The guard with the gun said, "Kinter. Get the kit. Clean up this one."

"Copy that."

A large van pulled up, driven by another shifter guard. This one wore a dark blue jumpsuit matching that of the others. He had a name on the chest of his suit. Wilson. He jumped out and opened the side door, where Bosse could see chains and hardware mounted to the floor around the inside walls. It smelled of piss and frustration.

This was not the first time they'd captured shifters.

Bosse and the other captives were herded into the van. Climbing in presented another impossible move. Bosse leaned in on his elbows, then his knees, and moved across to the closest spot to sit. Entering first provided him the

He could hear Kinter talking to another man who said, "Sounds good. Bring them out."

By the time the big sliding door on the side opened, Bosse had slumped over. No one seemed to notice, which was fine.

Kinter and the driver began unhooking the closest prisoners and pulling them out. Kinter warned, "We're unhooking the chain for your ankles. I won't shoot you in the head if you get froggy and want to jump any of us, but I can't speak for the man paying for you."

Again, Kinter confirmed his merchandise had to be in prime shape.

When the driver climbed in to get Bosse and the other shifter on his side, he asked, "What's wrong with you?"

Bosse ignored him and heaved hard again.

The driver muttered, "Shit." Then he whispered, "Kinter. Get over here."

Kinter whipped around. "What? Get them out here."

"This big one looks sick."

Cursing, Kinter kept his voice low. "Bring the other one out and watch those four. I'll take a look."

After the sound of struggling to get the other shifter out of the van, Kinter climbed in. Bosse would know that scent to the end of his days when he tracked this bunch down.

Kinter squatted next to him. He whispered, "What's your fucking problem?"

By now, Bosse had a string of saliva running out of his mouth. He gagged and mumbled, "What'd you feed me?"

"Everyone ate the same thing."

"Mine ... maybe bad mayonnaise." That could be possible. He had to avoid lying. "I don't know. I need water to puke." Still true because he could not make himself throw up with his hands tied.

Peeling his eyelashes apart a tiny seam, Bosse took in his captor.

Kinter's shirt showed damp spots where he'd begun to sweat. He clutched his head and finally said, "You have to climb out and stand up."

"Okay. Okay. I…" Bosse rasped. He acted as if his body seized up again and rolled forward but couldn't fall all the way. The chains kept him upright. He begged, "Water."

"Help me get you out of here first, and then I'll give you water. I don't want this van to stink of puke."

Kinter was not as big as Bosse. He unhooked Bosse from the van, then took the chain off between Bosse's wrists and ankles. "Push up when I grab you."

With Kinter tugging and lifting, Bosse made it outside the van to lean against the cool metal surface.

"What is taking so long?" the stranger who must be with the Black River Pack called out.

Kinter yelled, "Getting the hardware off. Give me a minute." Then he shoved a bottle of water at Bosse. "Drink up."

Bosse drank it fast and hard. He needed to throw up to maintain his act. He was almost done when he leaned over and puked. Thankfully, some of the sandwich came up. He sagged.

Kinter grabbed his arm. "No, don't do that. You need to stand and walk."

"I will try."

Kinter told the driver, "Start walking them around the van so we can give that guy a good look." He told Bosse, "Walk."

Bosse stumbled, took a step, stumbled again, and fell into the van.

"Damn it. Hold up." Kinter dropped to his knees and unhooked the ankle cuffs.

This had the potential to work out. Bosse began walking in short steps and swallowing hard.

"Pick your head up," Kinter hissed at him.

Doing as told, Bosse lifted his head and took in the sight of the Black River Pack sent to pick them up. He almost went to his knees for real.

All were in human form, but the large one had to be this group's leader. He stood with his arms crossed and a step in front of four more shifters dressed in tactical gear and carrying rifles.

Bosse had hoped to break free by fighting Kinter and the driver while the buyer loaded the others.

That would never happen with four rifles trained on him.

His life was over.

Chapter 15

BOSSE HAD ALWAYS accepted the day would come when he could not survive. This had to be it.

He and Titan could not escape the infamous Black River Pack of killers who used other shifters as guinea pigs for cruel experiments. He'd talk to Titan first, but the only way out of this might be death.

That sounded easy if you weren't a shifter.

Now he was sick for real. His heart sagged from disappointment.

The leader ordered, "I want to see each captive shift."

Kinter fidgeted uncomfortably. "Nothing was said about having them shift."

"You dare to question me?" The Black River Pack leader swung his attention from the captives to Kinter, staking him in place with a furious gaze. "I am Mort, second to the Black River Pack alpha."

Bosse heard Kinter's heart rate pick up, which meant every shifter here had also caught the sound. If he remembered correctly, mort was another word for death. Had this arrogant jerk taken that moniker to put fear in others?

The only words that concerned Bosse were Black, River, and Pack, synonymous with facing worse than the most excruciating torture anyone could imagine.

Death was preferable.

Mort continued in his superior tone. "I will explain to save time. We pay top dollar for shifters. We recently received one so traumatized he couldn't shift. Shifting is required as a new rule for any deals."

"We have handed you no traumatized shifters in the past," Kinter argued.

Bosse couldn't call him on a lie as Kinter believed he had treated his captives well, but his interpretation of trauma needed updating.

Taking a long moment to stare Kinter into silence, Mort said, "And that is the only reason you remain alive at this point."

Lifting a hand in resignation, Kinter said, "Fine, but are you prepared to handle it if one tries to run or attack one of us?"

"See those four behind me?"

"I'm not blind," an irritated Kinter replied.

"They are trained snipers, and their weapons are loaded with one of our drugs that will drop an elephant shifter in two steps."

Elephant shifter? Huh. Bosse hadn't known those existed.

Mort then directed his words to the captives. "If one of you thinks to use your wolf against us, you'll be restrained, taken to our headquarters, and then tortured for a week as an initiation. As you may have heard, we excel at that with shifters."

More heartbeats jacked up until it sounded like a low rumble of drums to Bosse.

Kinter ordered his captives, "All five of you sit on the ground." He then directed the driver. "Unshackle that one first and let him shuck his clothes. As each one shifts and Mort approves, he has his team contain the shifter and unshackle the next one." He looked at Mort. "That acceptable to you?"

"Yes."

Bosse dropped to his knees instead of sitting, and Kinter said nothing.

Probably did not want Mort to figure out he had a sick shifter on his hands. As each captive shifted, Mort ordered the wolves to leave their nasty clothes behind, lie down to his right, and not even twitch a tail.

When it was Bosse's turn, he told Titan, *Do not shift until I say so.*

Titan confirmed, *I will wait.*

Kinter unfettered Bosse's wrists and ankles, then hooked a hand under his arm to help him stand.

As Bosse shucked off his pants and tunic, he whispered, "It might be easier on my hands and knees."

The look Kinter gave him warned retribution if he failed to shift.

Having never struggled to shift, Bosse had no idea how to fake that. He dropped to his hands and knees, then scrunched his forehead and bulged his muscles. He groaned and moaned, "Come on, wolf. Don't be afraid."

He had Mort in his peripheral vision.

That frowning man glared at Kinter.

Kinter shouted through clamped jaws. *"Change now!"*

Bosse was out of time. If he didn't shift soon, Kinter might kill him for costing his people money. He told Titan, *Let's shift.*

Titan took the body over the next minute, and Bosse's sight sharpened with his wolf's vision.

Shaking off the change, Titan turned to face the Black River Pack.

Mort pointed at the end of the row of shifted wolves lying beside each other. "Take your place." Every wolf had eyes full of sorrow for their future.

Moving tentatively, Titan took a step. Bosse had run out of ideas and felt sick for his wolf to go through this. He thought of suggesting they use their last breath to attack Mort.

Shots rang out from the trees.

All four of the tactical shifters jerked and fell backward from the strikes. The minute they hit the ground, they started ripping gear off.

Kinter had his gun up, backing up to the van. He shouted, "Where are they?"

He was struck in the shoulder. Blood spewed against the white van at his back. He dropped the gun and grabbed his shoulder.

The air filled with the pungent smell of fresh blood. Bosse glanced at the captive shifters. Two stood, shaking and snarling with blood lust. Never starve a shifter.

Wilson tried to run to the van. He took a round to his leg and upper arm. He hit the ground.

Titan calmly asked, *What now?*

Bosse told his wolf, *I don't know. None of the captives have been struck. I think we should wait and watch.*

Mort spun and ran for the woods in the opposite direction the shots had come from.

Now Bosse knew what to do. *Let's get that Mort bastard.*

His wolf launched across the clearing, and shots pinged around him. Whoever was shooting probably thought Titan was out of control. His wolf caught up to the Black River Pack leader as the man shifted into a massive grizzly bear.

Standing on its hind legs, the bear roared.

Fearless after years of battling far worse, Titan leaped for the throat, latching his jaws on the soft area.

Vicious six-inch-long claws slashed across Titan's side, but Titan dug his claws faster than a wheel spinning on a race bike, shredding the bear's chest as he began to slide down.

Huge paws latched onto Titan, yanked him away from the bear's body, and threw him against a tree like a rag doll.

The bear dropped onto all fours, roaring and raging. It came for Titan even though blood flowed from its throat.

Bosse realized, in addition to blood running a stream down Titan's side, that one of his front legs had also been slashed. He told his wolf, *If you can't end this now, you have to run. We're losing blood fast.*

Without saying a word, Titan raced toward the bear and zagged unevenly to the right just out of claw-swiping distance. Titan ran around the bear, cutting hard despite the damaged front leg that threatened to buckle any minute. Adrenaline kept the pain at bay.

The brown bear jumped about, trying to claw Bosse's wolf.

Titan stayed ahead until he had a tiny lead. When he circled the bear again, he wrenched hard to stop and slashed his claws across the bear's back legs.

The back end buckled hard, dragging a long howling moan of pain from the bear.

Bosse praised, *Good job*, but Titan limped away, moving slower. His wolf had given all he had.

Still fighting, the bear came after Titan, dragging its rear legs that flopped loosely behind.

Titan tried stepping farther away, but his front leg collapsed. He pushed up to hop on three legs. Even Bosse started seeing stars—a bad, bad sign.

The wild-eyed bear snarled and clawed deep into the ground, pulling its body forward with two useless hind legs. That demon would not stop.

Titan struggled to move and weaved sideways, dizzy.

Bosse could feel the pain from the gash in his wolf's side. If that bear didn't stop, they couldn't outrun it. Titan would fall soon.

Titan stumbled hard as the bear continued to close the distance to Bosse's wolf, slapping one huge paw down at a time.

Everything blurred in Bosse's vision. He told his wolf, *You fought well. Thank you for being the best friend I've ever had.*

Titan said, *I feel the same, but do not like to fail.* He fell over on the ground, panting hard. He raised his head to watch the bear make one last lunge.

A paw as big as Bosse's head lifted with razor-sharp claws extended for a killing strike.

A boom sounded close by.

Blood spewed from the bear's head. It fell forward. The paw raised to gut Titan dropped an inch short of its goal.

Bosse would like to think this was a hopeful sign, but

it might only be another group preying on them—even humans who would love to brag about bagging a shifter of any kind.

Titan panted hard and stayed down.

Bosse kept giving his wolf encouraging words, hoping to survive this or at least ease him into death.

The sound of someone walking through the woods preceded a big man who smelled of bear. He was built like a freight train, wore his hair short, and had concerned eyes, but power radiated from him.

Not just an average shifter. What was he?

Someone who could easily kill them with one strike right now.

The bear shifter stood over Titan. "Damn, he gouged you good. Can you shift back?"

Titan asked, *Shift or not?*

Bosse replied, *Let's try.*

While he shifted, the man spoke into a radio. "Need the medic now. Shifter down. Slashed badly by a bear. The Black River Pack team leader is dead."

It took time for Bosse to end up in human form. He was in incredible pain and lightheaded. He kept losing blood fast. Slapping a hand over his chest where warm liquid oozed through his fingers, he rasped, "Who are you?"

"Justin." Not a word more about his identity.

Bosse wheezed another breath. "You going to sell us, too?"

Justin raised his eyebrows. "No. I've got a medic on the way. Try to stay with me." He squatted down, and his power withdrew. This shifter was something unusual for sure. Justin proceeded to keep Bosse talking. "Where'd you come from?"

"Escaped Slovakia… imprisoned two years." Bosse fought for air and squeezed his eyes shut every time pain ripped through him. "Lion shifter… captures different shifters to… fight in an arena. He's insane."

Justin didn't comment immediately.

Another shifter in human form showed up smelling of

wolf and wearing a disgruntled frown. He carried a medical case. He asked, "Who killed that Mort guy?"

Sighing, Justin said, "I had to order the strike, or he'd have slaughtered this one."

That sounded like this man chose to save Bosse over keeping Mort alive to interrogate, which made no sense.

Who was Bosse to him or his people that he'd lose a resource?

Scowling, the medic dropped to one knee to start working on Bosse's side first.

Bosse asked, "Are you a doctor?"

"No." He glanced at Bosse's ravaged arm and scowled harder.

For someone tasked with healing a shifter, this one sounded pissed about his line of work.

Stepping a distance away, Justin made a call on his mobile phone and spoke quietly into it.

Bosse only heard muffled words over the wolf shifter medic grumbling about the massive damage Bosse and Titan had suffered. Did he think they hadn't noticed? Maybe these shifters were really going to help him, but help depended upon the point of view once they chose to move him.

Justin returned and asked Bosse, "Are you with a pack?"

"No." That question gave Bosse pause. With no pack affiliation, what would these shifters do with him? Alifair had warned him about being caught as a lone wolf and sent somewhere he'd be expected to stay.

It wasn't as if he and Titan could get up and fight again for any hope of escape. Not yet. His vision got darker. "Please… don't lock me up."

Justin frowned instead of replying, which was not an encouraging sign.

That look sank Bosse's hope of remaining free. His head throbbed, and he couldn't feel his good arm.

"Put pressure on that arm. *Now!*" the medic yelled.

Bosse closed his eyes and fell into a dark hole.

Chapter 16

$\sim\sim$

FOR THE REST of the day, Alifair hung around the kitchen to avoid Eriko's attention. The hours passed too slowly for her anxious nerves.

She'd spent yesterday in quiet panic as Krol had walked out with his Lammogo. She'd expected to be called in front of Eriko at any minute, but that hadn't happened. Krol's right-hand man left the castle at midday for a reason she only learned about now.

While they all were preparing food for the guards or cleaning up, Linota had asked the kitchen help around her if anyone knew when Eriko would return. She was naturally nervous, but the prospect of being interrogated over her possible involvement with Bosse's escape had to rattle her even more every minute.

Servants started speculating about Eriko's whereabouts.

Hessie shut them all down, saying, "He had to take men to close off the tunnel. It's none o' your business what he does. Get back to work."

Thankfully, that had delayed his interrogation schedule, but Alifair still had to come up with a solid alibi for where she was the night of Bosse's escape and practice her answers. Maybe she could use a simple spell to confuse him.

That might backfire on her, like when she had tried to get out of trouble at fifteen.

She threw herself into helping everyone in the kitchen,

glad when another guard killed a deer and delivered it to Hessie dressed and ready to be skinned.

Nothing would put a smile on that woman's face, but fresh game kept her content for a while.

Where could Rez be?

Alifair punched down the bread dough that had risen. The harder the punch, the finer the crumble.

She'd like to punch a certain lion shifter instead of preparing tasty bread for him and his gang of guards. She shook off the unproductive thoughts and folded the dough into itself while mentally running through the list of places she had not searched for Rez.

She still came up with only one possibility, and that was upstairs in Krol's private area. Getting caught there would mean immediate consequences, but no worse than being fingered for her part in Bosse's escape.

She couldn't keep waiting around.

The woman with the blue headscarf had to be going up there through that locked door.

Alifair had seen no other servant moving around on her own and unbothered by guards. Someone had to be feeding Rez. Krol didn't like to lose any of his captives to starvation when he lived to watch their pain and death. Killing Rez would be a wasted value. It made more sense that he might trade her for a shifter or some other benefit. If so, wouldn't he want to keep her healthy?

Yet one question stomped on her hope daily.

Was Rez even here?

She had to be. Alifair saw this castle in a dream after falling asleep during a trance she induced for speed and efficiency, where she asked how to find Rez. She'd waited until she could replicate the dream a second time before informing her clan. The second dream showed her a shape she took to be the country with the castle. She'd looked at locations of countries until her eyes were bloodshot from trying to match that shape, then realized it had to be Slovakia. At that point, she narrowed down this castle by using the internet searches, which showed it as abandoned.

All of that matched what she'd seen in her dream.

The stand-in leaders who managed the clan while Rez was gone declared Alifair should stay in Europe and hunt for Rez. She had the best chance of finding their leader.

That's how she'd ended up hiking and camping near the castle like some lost tourist.

Literally, she made herself a sitting duck for Krol's men to snatch. She'd hoped that part had been correct, worrying she might get captured by someone else.

The first night in the castle, she fell into an exhausted sleep and dreamed of Rez sitting alone in a room walled in stone.

She'd awakened, ready to find Rez and get out of there just like she had awakened after prior informative dreams. Frustrated by week two, she worked harder to narrow the scope of her dream, asking for better details.

That's when she began to see Bosse and Rez.

It didn't take long to realize he would be crucial to saving Rez.

After witnessing multiple battles where Bosse stood like a tower of muscle waiting to destroy every opponent, she realized he showed up thinner and not healed some days. She'd been leaving the wolf shifter extra food when she could drop it off unnoticed and thought that was why he'd entered her dream world, but the dreams showed him battling someone to keep them from Rez.

Only Rez.

Not Alifair, but that was okay.

She couldn't blame him for how a dream worked out. He'd pleaded with her to leave with him or let him help her save her friend. The only person who had shown any concern for her in too long to remember had been a wolf shifter.

Her clan feared shifters after losing three to a pack of vicious wolf shifters and believed they shouldn't even exist. Those three young men had gone looking for trouble, but her people still claimed shifters were unnatural.

Really? Every person in the clan had some form of gift or magic. How were they above other supernatural beings?

She believed there were good and bad beings of all kinds.

This trip opened her eyes to developing her own views.

She'd feared all the captives in cages that had slammed up against the bars when she walked by and snarled at her. Not Bosse or his wolf. Neither one had acted aggressively around her, and everyone here knew Bosse could kill anything.

Then he'd kissed her before escaping.

She'd almost walked out with him in that one moment until her conscience scolded her. How could she explain to anyone in her clan she would never regret that kiss and last moment? She'd never see him again, which was fine if he found freedom and safety.

Keep telling myself that.

Why didn't she deserve to have a life like other women?

Because she'd been born a woman in a long line of female protectors.

Whatever. Her attitude had been crumbling for a while, but watching Bosse go after he'd kissed her like a man who wanted her pretty much kicked her fragile sandcastle life to pieces.

She had yet to see how her dreams would turn out with him helping rescue Rez. He'd had no money or resources when he left her. Time to stop wondering about how he could return and accept that saving Rez was still on her shoulders.

Her mother had told her to trust her dreams.

As a child, Alifair had thought her mother meant for her to believe in the dreams she held in her heart until she began having clairvoyant dreams. That's what her mother had been talking about.

She punched the flour again hard enough for Hessie to frown at her.

Smiling like the simpleton she was supposed to be, Alifair calmed down and stopped mistreating the innocent dough.

If she did escape, she would rethink her place in a clan

that expected her to face all this alone and didn't blink an eye at tasking her with an impossible mission. At this rate, she'd never experience the happiness of having a family when her duty came first.

Why waste time thinking about having a family and life?

She'd seen her bloody demise in the last dream where Bosse stopped a threat to Rez.

Her future would be short and not include a happily ever after. That should convince her Bosse was far better off being in another country. Her rushed plan to get him out of here may have altered the projection of him being present to help Rez, but he would be safe, and she'd do her job as long as she could.

"Are you done with bread?" Hessie shouted.

Alifair looked down, and she folded the bread in the strangest shape. She folded it in half again and said, "One minute." She had to make it look right before handing the dough to the gloomy woman.

Hessie groused about lazy servants.

Folding the dough one last time, Alifair decided that was her best rendition and took it over to show Hessie, who scowled at the shape. "That is not good bread."

"I did as I was told," Alifair defended herself even if she had worked the bread three times too many. She had probably just stepped out of line with that reply, but she'd never had the personality to be ordered around.

Hessie snarled at her. "Go chop vegetables. Try to do that right."

Relieved at not being sent out of the kitchen, Alifair found the vegetable chopping station and turned her body so she could watch for someone to leave with food for one person.

Alifair had worried often that Rez was not being fed until seeing the woman with the blue head covering. She'd carried no food, but her trip from the kitchen to the back hallway gave Alifair hope that someone was nourishing Rez.

Hessie never turned when she said, "Kylie," in the kindest

voice Alifair had heard from that woman. The thin servant wearing the gray dress to her ankles, the same brown apron, and a blue cloth tying back her long black hair walked over to Hessie. She whispered in the frowny woman's ear.

As Alifair covertly watched her now, she realized she had seen this servant work in the kitchen or setting the table, but rarely. What did Kylie do the rest of the time?

Maybe she washed laundry.

Or maybe she warmed Krol's bed and did as she pleased.

Icky thought.

Hessie nodded and spoke softly in reply to Kylie's whisper. She tilted her head toward a cupboard where they stored dried fruit and jerky. Kylie turned in that direction, her gaze sweeping across the room.

Alifair kept her head down, eyeing the scene through her peripheral vision.

Walking calmly through the busy kitchen, the woman opened the cupboard, stayed maybe a minute, and walked away with nothing in her hands.

Argh! That was no help. She needed a good lead.

Then Alifair did a double take at the side view of the woman, which she had not seen before due to high counters and boxes of supplies blocking her view.

Kylie's apron pockets were full.

Could that be the food delivery service for Rez?

Crud. Alifair couldn't just walk out right now, or everyone would point fingers at her suspicious action. How often could they be feeding Rez? Was this a lunch meal? If Kylie was feeding Rez, it seemed she'd also do it at night.

Alifair would stay up tonight and watch the kitchen from a sunken alcove she'd used before.

If she found Rez, could tonight be the time to spirit her out of here?

That would be difficult with the guards on high alert, but she had to try or face the possibility of missing her best chance before Krol returned.

Her heart banged around in her chest like a chipmunk on crack stuck in a cage.

There was no way Bosse would be here to help her this soon. He might not even be in America yet. She'd have to do this alone.

She needed a weapon.

The knife in her hand would be as good as it got, but if Hessie found it missing, she'd flay the skin off the back of whoever took it before Krol got to them.

The day had been chaotic, with guards jumping on anyone going outside without permission and ordering the servants to stay at their work locations until they were released for the evening. Once freed from work, servants were expected to remain in their rooms.

Alifair would wait as long as she could, maybe until one in the morning. If her theory of feeding Rez around two or three in the morning when the castle slept was correct, she had to be in her hidden alcove spot early.

She'd washed off the cinnamon and cardamom scent she'd created as a powder to be boosted with a spell and put it in a small vial before leaving home. The guards had taken all her other possessions except her ragged coat when they captured her. The vial had traveled with cash in a false panel she'd sewn inside the coat and clutched to her body while shivering from the temperature that night.

That plan had worked. What guard would want a threadbare coat with patches and a size too small for a man?

She needed tonight to pay off. If not, she had to return to the kitchen before Hessie arrived for any hope of putting the knife back in place.

If she did get lucky, she intended to keep the knife and try to escape with Rez. Should guards find out and race to catch them, she was expected to stay back and slow them down so Rez could escape.

Once again, she felt no sense of value in this position. Had her mother experienced the same feelings or just accepted her place in the clan?

Alifair should be carrying a bucket of guilt over being

angry at the clan, but she was more disheartened than anything.

So many ifs and maybes to hang a risky plan on was like building a house with a deck of torn cards. It could work if no one came along and touched a weak card.

When her workday finally ended, she paced her room, ready to leave. She wore her coat in case she did not make it back to the room. When the time came, and the castle slept, she snuck around corners, keeping her body plastered to the dark shadows crowding the corridor the thin woman had taken. Once in that hallway, Alifair hurried past the door she prayed would take her to the upstairs and found a place at the end of the hall to kneel out of sight.

Minutes ticked by as sweat pebbled on her forehead, disregarding the chilly air surrounding her.

The woman who had food stuffed in her apron showed up around what Alifair estimated to be two or two-thirty in the morning. Kylie carried a flashlight that beamed on her hand and the key as she unlocked the hallway door. As she entered, Alifair rushed to catch the door before it closed completely and held her breath, but the woman had not paused to lock it.

Was that because it would lock on its own?

She counted to twenty, then pushed the door open a tiny bit and caught sight of the flashlight glow as Kylie moved higher up the stairwell.

This had to be the right place.

Alifair quickly pulled out the tiny strip of material she'd torn from the hem of her work dress and stuffed it deep into the hole where the bolt latch would insert. She filled most of the hole and allowed the door to close. She had initially hoped to follow the woman inside and find a place to hide while waiting on her to leave, but there was nowhere to hide at the bottom landing of the stairs inside this doorway.

Going back to her little hidey-hole, Alifair crouched. It wasn't long before the woman stepped through the doorway and allowed the door to shut behind her. She used a key to lock it but had trouble getting it to engage.

No, no, no. If a guard were called, they'd assign someone to watch the door until it could be fixed. Then, the person fixing it would find the material stuffed into the slot.

Every second of watching ticked up Alifair's pulse to a faster pace.

Her heart couldn't take much more.

Giving the knob a little turn back and forth, the woman finally seemed content that it was working. Too content. Maybe the cloth had failed.

Again, too many maybes to depend upon.

Allowing five minutes to pass first, Alifair tiptoed over and tried the door lock. It was set. Crud. She pulled out a hairpin she'd had fabricated by a metal worker in her clan that was sturdier than most pins. Within thirty seconds, she had the door unlocked and opened. She checked the cloth stuffed in the doorjamb.

It had held up, but the latch was fitted so well that it only needed an eighth of an inch to keep the door locked. She pulled the cloth out, stuffed it in a pocket, and headed up the stairs.

At the top, she opened another door into a wide hallway with what must have been beautiful walls at one time. Candle sconces gave the area a warmth not found in the lower level of this castle. Tall walls were covered in gold-and-gray-striped wallpaper. Carved four-foot-square wooden murals of people riding horses and dogs as if on a hunt hung between four towering doors along the corridor.

Those might shield bedrooms or a library.

Could Krol read?

Maybe he had a library filled with picture books.

Yes, she was feeling mean, and he deserved her disdain.

She checked every door carefully, finding perfectly neat bedrooms behind two and an office area behind one. That jerk had a very old computer and tall cabinets filled with things like batteries, a flashlight, and tools. What powered the computer? She followed a cord from the computer to a door that opened into a large storage room with a generator. This room smelled of gas. With no internet service, based on what she'd heard from the servants, she didn't want to see what a sicko like him had on his dilapidated computer. Closing that door, she did a visual scope of the office. Framed pictures of different sizes covered the walls.

All were of Krol. Of course.

The last door hid a library of sorts. Only half of the lovely dark wood bookcases held any books. Most of them had different types of medieval weapons displayed. Swords and a metal ball with spikes had her shaking her head.

What a lunatic.

She stepped back into the hallway. Was there another level above this one? Rushing from one end to the other, she found no additional door hiding a stairwell. She would have noticed one in his office. Then again, maybe one of the bookcases doubled as a secret entry into a hidden room.

While still in the library, she checked every bookcase. Nope.

Time stood on her shoulders, warning her it would soon abandon her at the worst moment.

Moving faster, she searched the two bedrooms. Nothing.

Crud! Just the office left to look through again.

Inside the office, she ran her hands over every vertical surface and had almost finished when she heard footsteps.

Krol shouldn't be back yet, should he?

Why would she think he'd ever give the true time of his return? He was the kind of suspicious person who liked to show up and catch people not doing their jobs.

She found a closet full of musty books and papers. Squeezing inside, she pulled the door almost shut behind her. With the tiny crack of the door being ajar, she could watch who showed up.

The door to the hallway opened, and Eriko walked in with a second guard. He strode around the room to the desk, pulled a drawer open, and moved his hands around. "Got it." When he closed the desk, a key on a metal chain dangled from one hand. He handed it to the other guard and said, "Give this to Davoot. Tell him to open the stable doors and remain outside to relock them when instructed. This key will be returned to me no later than daylight."

"Yes, sir."

They both headed for the exit. Eriko said, "Don't forget to stop by the room of the servant with the two different eye colors."

Alifair froze still as a deer staring into headlights. Why would they be coming by her room?

The men exited into the hallway, their footsteps clicking on the hardwood floor in the direction of the stairwell to the main room.

No more time to search for Rez.

Alifair wanted to kick something. She had to be close to finding her.

Instead, she had to beat the guard back to her room, which meant racing through a hallway partially exposed to the great hall. No moving slowly to hide her presence.

As soon as she heard the door click shut, she hurried over and tested the knob. Still unlocked.

She stuck her head out and checked.

Both men were headed for the wide stairs to the main hall at a leisurely pace. As soon as they stepped around the corner to the other stairs, she rushed to the door that led her back downstairs and out the unlocked door, which she now had to relock.

Her fingers trembled with the hairpin. Relocking was more challenging for her because she never practiced that.

She felt the latch catch, tried it once, and took off down the hallway and around the corner, almost skidding to a stop.

Eriko spoke to two guards at the bottom of the stairwell.

Whispering, she uttered a don't-look-at-me chant in their direction, repeating it continually as she slowly eased down the wall. They wouldn't hear or see her if the chant worked correctly. The door to her room awaited thirty steps from where Eriko and his two men talked.

Swallowing hard, she decided speed would be more

in her favor than moving around the end of the wall at a snail's pace—no time for second-guessing.

Hurrying and chanting softly, she never took her eyes off Eriko.

She'd made it almost to her door when he held his hand up to the men, silencing them.

She did her best to emulate a statue.

Eriko turned slowly, his gaze taking in everything around him.

This was one of those times she had to be all in to survive. She whispered the mantra faster and faster, her gaze watching his, and pleaded for him not to turn her way.

But he did.

Still murmuring the chant, she kept every muscle in her body still except her heart. Not much she could do about that without terminating her life.

Eriko stared right at her.

She wanted to whimper in fear. The only reason she didn't was due more to her throat closing tight than any wise action on her part.

He had to be able to see her. Why else would he be staring so hard? Then he blinked and seemed to shake off whatever he'd been thinking.

She leaned against the wall to keep her knees from buckling and control her breathing.

Then her internal alarm clock warned her to move or be caught outside her room.

Never stopping her don't-look-at-me chant, she took careful steps to her room, opened the door, and pulled it closed, locking herself in. She'd made it. Relief had her laughing quietly like an insane woman. The chant she'd learned as a child had worked when the one her mother had tried to teach her never did. Her mother had warned that the simple don't-look-at-me spell would not last long enough to help her evade someone hunting her—only the no-one-can-see-me spell, which held more power.

But it also required greater power, which Alifair had

never had. She'd practiced for six months and finally admitted defeat.

Then came the knock at her door.

She was not dressed for bed.

Taking a moment, she asked, "Yes? I'm not dressed to open the door."

"You will open the door any time we order you to."

While he instructed her, she'd taken advantage of that time to shrug off her coat, then yank her shirt, shoes, and pants off she'd intended to wear for an escape. She leaned over to snatch her plain tan-colored shirt off the bed and put it on, buttoning it as fast as she could. Then she stepped into the dark beige skirt with elastic at the waist. Clearly, Krol spared no expense for his slaves.

The guard shouted, "Do you not understand?"

"No, I understand." She tossed her coat and other clothes in a corner. Let them think she was not tidy. She unlocked the door and opened it slowly to find the guard Eriko had spoken to upstairs staring daggers at her door, then at her.

"Follow me."

"May I grab my coat?"

He grumbled under his breath and nodded. "Be quick."

Where was he taking her that she couldn't get dressed first? She didn't have her special scent on either.

She shoved her arms into the coat, intentionally leaving her shoes off. Then she returned to the door, closing it behind her.

He took off at a fast pace. He still carried the key for the stables.

Was she going to the stables? That couldn't be good. "Could you please tell me where I'm going? I don't even have shoes on."

Without turning around, he said, "You don't need shoes. It is time for your meeting with Eriko."

He wanted to see her *now?*

A cold chill washed over her.

Eriko was going to interrogate her about Bosse's escape. She had never been good at lying.

Chapter 17

———— ⌇ ————

BOSSE CAME AWAKE, lying in a bed. A real bed. He'd never had a bed, even as a kid.

That wasn't what frightened him.

The room smelled fresh and clean. He tilted his head up, suffered dizziness, and blinked to clear his swirling vision. Floral wallpaper gave the place a lived-in look. The room had a comfortable smell of having been a family home for a long time.

Using his uninjured arm, he reached for his chest. It was bandaged but didn't feel as painful as he would have expected.

How long had he been out?

Long enough to dream about Alifair again. That had to be why his dick was hard. Not wanting to be found in this condition, he made himself think of the women in his clan for several minutes. That killed the tent pole beneath his sheet.

Looking over at his damaged arm, he found it splinted and bandaged as well. Before being stuck in that cage for two years, his arm would have healed naturally in a day or two. His chest might have in another day, but the medic had been a shifter. He must have been able to tell that Bosse and Titan couldn't heal the damage before they died of blood loss.

He immediately called out telepathically, *Titan, are you okay?*

I am here. The woman takes good care of us.

Woman? He doubted his wolf meant Alifair. That would be beyond amazing.

Where are we? Bosse asked, surprised he'd slept when Titan had been awake.

His wolf admitted, *I do not know. I woke once during the night while she checked bandages.*

Is she a doctor?

Maybe a healer, Titan replied. *She has energy in her hands.*

The medic hadn't been a doctor either. Bosse didn't feel drugged. The guy they called a medic hadn't tried to give Bosse pain medicine while he was conscious, which Bosse would have refused. He didn't trust any shifters or humans with a needle.

Not with the Black River Pack making dangerous drugs.

This was a whole new country to Bosse. He'd heard of rare shifter doctors, but did those exist here?

He hoped Titan had an answer to his next question. *Do you think we are safe here?*

Yes. Feels safe. She is powerful but careful not to harm us with power.

That was interesting. Justin had also possessed a load of power he'd pulled back around Bosse.

The door opened, and a woman came in. He took in her face first and found it peaceful, then sniffed. Wolf shifter.

Bosse could feel the powerful energy she possessed pushing at the edge of his consciousness, but she clearly kept it locked down. Who were these shifters?

Or *what* were these shifters?

"Glad to see you're awake." She had a commanding voice for a woman. She was tall, probably around five-foot-ten, with a crown of short, scattered black hair. The style looked as if it came from running her hands through it in irritation.

Not a woman he'd call pretty. Too light of a word for her. Attractive in a no-nonsense way. She hadn't beamed a polite or nurturing smile at him, which he liked. He didn't trust overly happy strangers.

While she dragged a wooden chair over from where it had been next to the wall, he said, "Thank you for healing us. I don't know who you are, where I am, or what's going on, but you and that Justin guy are the first decent people, especially shifters, I've met in years."

"You're welcome. I'm Jaz. Justin is a friend who brought you to our pack house in North Carolina." She sat and held her hand above his damaged arm.

Then she put her fingers around his wrist as if checking his pulse, but she was not listening to his chest like he'd seen other healers do. He felt energy begin to flow through his arm. The sensation was comforting, and the pain in his arm eased. She must be a healer as Titan thought.

The door opened. She didn't turn or stop her healing when she said, "This is Adrian, my mate."

Adrian moved around to the end of the bed. His thick head of black hair appeared scattered in a different way than Jaz's. Adrian's hair looked to be growing out from a short cut and had locks sticking out in different directions as if he'd been fighting someone. With his build and being a dominant shifter, plus having power similar to Jaz's, Bosse would rather not have to battle either of them.

Even so, he fought against the need not to rise from a vulnerable position. When he started to sit up, pain lashed through his arm.

"Stay down," Jaz said in a firm but calming voice. "Adrian is not a threat as long as you're not a threat to any of us."

"I'm not." Bosse dropped his head back to the soft pillow, glad not to hold it up any longer. He stayed silent while Jaz finished whatever she was doing with her energy. Better to let these two start the conversation.

"You're healing fast now," Jaz announced and sat back. She glanced at Adrian, who cocked his head at her and then nodded.

That was strange.

He addressed Bosse. "Justin said you'd been imprisoned in Slovakia by a crazy shifter."

"That's correct." Bosse kept his answers simple, waiting to see where all of this would go.

"Are other captive shifters there?"

"Yes, but most do not last long." Bosse watched their faces for any reactions but couldn't read these people.

Jaz asked, "Why not?"

"We were captured to be Krol's entertainment. That's the name of the lion shifter who rules a castle in a remote area. I don't know if that's a real name or just what he wanted to be called because I have heard it translates into king."

Jaz snorted at that. "No ego there, huh?"

Bosse's lips twitched. He hadn't felt like smiling in a while. Definitely not since walking away from Alifair. An urgency to reach her pressed on him. "What else do you want to know? I'll answer any questions and only ask you not to lock me away again."

Adrian said, "There's a good chance of that not happening if we find we can trust you and your wolf. Do you have good control of your wolf?"

"Yes, but I wouldn't call it controlling my wolf so much as partnering. We are a team in everything."

At that, Adrian cocked an eyebrow. "That's good to hear. We have a pack of wolves with varying degrees of control, mostly not very good."

He caught Bosse by surprise with that statement. "Why not? As alpha, they must listen to you, right?"

"No, they don't because I'm not alpha. She is."

Bosse swung his attention to Jaz. "I apologize. No insult meant. I made an assumption based on other alphas I've known."

"None taken." Jaz ran a hand through her hair, raking locks in all directions. "I'll give you the short story of what we have. We took this pack over not long ago. I was looking for a missing female shifter and discovered the male alpha here and his son were trafficking female shifters. In confronting the alpha about a woman who I was hunting, I had to battle him in defense. He died. His daughter was the only remaining direct heir to the pack and did not want to be alpha. She pretty much ordered me to take it."

Bosse said, "I find it hard to imagine anyone ordering you around."

"You nailed that," Adrian murmured.

Jaz sent her mate a narrowed-eyed but sweet look and then turned back to Bosse. "We're working to heal this group and help them gain control so they can have productive lives. We want them to be able to work and eventually have mates. We're willing to invite you to join the pack, but we value honesty above all. Do you have plans to run as soon as you're healed?"

Her question stalled Bosse's brain.

"You're hesitating to answer," Jaz pointed out, no longer sounding as positive as she had before.

Bosse took a deep breath and hoped his words would not condemn him and Titan to an unwanted future. "I want to tell you the truth. I would like to find a place to live. You offer what sounds like somewhere my wolf and I would be happy. A woman helped me escape Krol's prison. She had heard Krol was angry over the last arena battle he made me fight. My wolf and I won against a Cape buffalo."

Adrian whistled at that, sounding impressed.

Nodding briefly, Bosse said, "Krol had tired of us winning for so long, which was nothing more than fighting to survive. The female came to tell me he intended to put two shifters against us the next day. We were underfed and not healing our injuries. He wanted to watch my wolf die a painful death." His chest hurt so much when talking about Alifair. "In two years, no captive shifter had ever escaped from the castle, but this woman came to me with a way to escape. She pretended to be a servant. Without her, it would not have happened. I begged her to come with me, but she said she had to stay and find the woman she had gone there to rescue. I offered to stay and help, but she said she could not leave yet and that I would put her in danger if I remained. She told me how to find an old tunnel underneath the castle and the direction to take to reach the ports in Italy."

He paused, still questioning his decision-making in Italy. "As bad as my wolf and I wanted to hold on to our freedom, leaving that night without her was the hardest thing I've ever had to do."

Silence settled over the room, and Adrian asked, "Did they send trackers after you?"

"Yes. We were close to being caught when a thunderstorm and lightning gave us a break. A flash flood wiped out our path. We were fortunate to cross it without getting swept away. We found a cave on the side of a mountain to rest in until daylight, and then we took off again. I'll spare you how we reached Venice, but by the time I made it over a bridge to the shipping docks, I could not go across the ocean and live with myself. I discussed it with my wolf. We agreed to return to the castle for the woman. That's when a shifter gang caught me."

Jaz stretched her legs out and crossed her arms in a comfortable pose. "Who were they?"

"I don't know."

"What can you tell us about them?" Adrian asked.

"They said they contract routes where they know shifters often try to escape and expect them to show up near shipping docks like where they found me. They had four other shifters in chains before capturing me. I had never been on an airplane and used that time to drink as much water as I could to get the drugs out of my system for us to have a chance to escape."

"They took you to that meeting with the Black River Pack," Adrian said, prodding Bosse to continue.

"Yes. The shifter, who called himself Mort, said he was in charge. I knew the minute I met him and his snipers I could not escape. My wolf and I decided we'd rather die fighting than be taken to be experimented on or worse."

"Mort?" Jaz asked, looking up at Adrian.

"Yep, we had intel on that guy," Adrian confirmed.

Intel sounded as if this was more than just a wolf pack. Bosse let that pass to share more.

"That Mort shifted into a grizzly bear." Bosse thought back and added, "I don't know the name of the wolf shifter in charge of the kidnappers, but the driver was called Wilson, and the one who handled the exchange was named Kinter." He looked at each of them. "Did Kinter or his driver survive?"

"No." Adrian sounded disappointed. "Our people only wounded them. Mort's hit squad shifted and ripped out their throats before our people were able to reach the kidnappers. Justin had been chasing the leader, that guy Mort, for a couple of weeks, or our people would not have been on the scene so quickly. By the time he reached Mort, your wolf was a bloody mess, and the bear was coming at your wolf for a strike. I doubt our medic could have done anything about that to save you. Justin approved the headshot."

Having expected to die at that moment, Bosse was still surprised they'd lose someone as important as Mort to save an unknown shifter. "I'm sure you wanted someone to interrogate. Please tell your people Titan and I thank both of them for saving us."

"Your wolf is called Titan?" Now Jaz smiled.

"Yes. Best friend I've ever had."

Titan's words floated in Bosse's head. *We have always been a good team.*

Bosse replied, *We finally found a way to escape. I'm glad. I want to save the woman, too.*

I understand. I am ready when you want to go.

Standing, Jaz announced, "You're well on your way to mending. I'll bring food in. You'll feel stronger soon, probably better than you have in a while. I'd like you to rest more until I say you're good to get out of here. Once you do, Adrian is training our bunch to fight without shifting. He'll want to include you. By that time, we want you able to heal yourself quickly."

"Whatever you say." Bosse smiled and felt appreciation deep in his bones.

Adrian said, "I have one more thing to mention."

"Okay."

"The man who leads our shifter teams has his own questions. I expect him to visit this week. He may have questions because our people always want to stop shifter trafficking."

"I am willing to help your people in any way I can."

Adrian turned to Jaz. They stayed quiet while staring at each other, and then Adrian asked her, "We've heard enough for now, right?"

"Yep." Jaz headed for the door.

Before she and Adrian left, Bosse spoke up. "I have a question."

Adrian swung back to him. "Shoot."

"You two feel extremely powerful, unlike any other shifters I've ever met, and I've fought some very powerful shifters. What are you?"

Jaz looked at the floor for a moment, then lifted her head. "We are different. We can't tell you right now, but you may ask our leader who is coming to visit."

"I will," Bosse confirmed.

Adrian laughed. "I'm looking forward to that conversation."

Bosse relaxed, something he hadn't been able to do in so long it felt foreign. He asked Titan, *Do you think this sounds too good to be true?*

Titan pondered a bit before replying, *Maybe. I believe what those two said. We are safe here, but their leader must be more powerful than them. That is when we learn what will be asked of us.*

Bosse couldn't argue with that.

In fact, he looked forward to finding out what this leader wanted from him and Titan.

The sooner, the better.

Bosse would use whatever information he had in exchange for their helping him get back across the ocean. From there, he would find his way to Alifair.

Chapter 18

IN JUST ONE day, Bosse felt stronger than he thought he ever would again. How could that be? After spending the entire first day sleeping and eating, Jaz declared him physically ready to train on day two.

Adrian did not ask the impossible.

There were four other shifters. Not a large pack compared to where he grew up, but there had been more pack members in this one at one time, based upon what Jaz told him last night.

Before Bosse walked out of the house in clean jeans and a T-shirt supplied by Jaz, she'd made a point of saying that he was not a prisoner here.

He would find out for sure how true her words were when he decided to go after Alifair, but he had thanked her in the meantime.

She'd also given him a word of advice while they talked yesterday. "Since you're not familiar with our country, you need to know there is a shifter law enforcement group called SCIS. Shifter Criminal Investigation Service. When they capture a lone shifter, it's probably the last time anyone will hear from that one. They put shifters in underground cells. They captured three shifters, who took off from here without a word. We can do nothing to help you if you land in SCIS jail. It's not a way any shifter wants to die."

Bosse sucked in a breath at that. Now he understood why the kidnappers feared SCIS. He had to return for Alifair, but he would not make the mistake those three shifters had by leaving without Jaz and Adrian's support.

He'd been straight with them. If they refused to help or asked him to wait more than another day, he would still thank them and then tell them he'd take his chances getting back to Slovakia.

She'd added, "Yep, landing in a SCIS jail is as bad as it sounds. I'm not a fan of that group, but they are the shifter law enforcement run by humans with the aid of some shifters. The jackal shifters they use as enforcers only care about their position and safety within the system."

"Understood. Thank you for telling me this."

Bosse stepped outside, standing on the wide porch of this old house. It had been well-kept and sat in an idyllic wooded location.

He turned to the sound of fighting, but not in a rabid way, and found Adrian working with his pack. Bosse had agreed to do a few rounds with Adrian as he showed his men ways to win a battle without shifting into their animals.

From so many battles in the castle arena, Bosse knew much of what Adrian shared, but he respected this man and listened to what he had to say.

He had no trouble executing any defensive move asked of him.

Adrian explained he took on a different shifter each day while the others paired up. His goal at this point was to teach the shifters to fight in human form, allowing them a better chance of moving around humans without risking drawing attention by giving up their human form.

It hadn't taken long for Bosse to see the problem Jaz and Adrian faced.

These shifters had been in a broken pack run by a sick alpha for too long.

They had almost no control over their animals.

Adrian and Jaz offered motivation for them to hold back from shifting until given the go-ahead at the end of each day. If the entire pack stayed in human form until Adrian called a halt to training, they all ate a great meal cooked by Jaz and drank beer around a fire in the backyard of the house.

If not, the entire group had to hunt for their food on the one hundred and ninety acres, with no beer provided.

When Adrian paired up with Bosse the first time, he held back nothing. Bosse had never enjoyed fighting, but this training was good for him. He needed exercise every day after the life he'd led.

At the end of their round, Adrian said, "You're more than ready to train with the other shifters. Watch out for Badger. He's got issues with control. I'm sure you can handle him, but I'd rather not have Jaz spending all night patching someone up."

When Bosse turned to locate who Adrian had pointed out, he saw Badger on the far side of the clearing doing all sorts of strange things, like jumping around and stabbing his hands at the other shifter called Corbin.

Adrian commented, "You have excellent timing and moves. Do you have any military training?"

"No." Bosse chuckled. "I learned from standing my ground in the pack I was born into, then by quickly figuring out the best way to win a match in the castle arena."

"You've got natural ability. It won't be long before I can find a job for you." Adrian's eyes continued to check on every shifter, then came back to Bosse. "We want you all to earn money and become independent pack members."

"That sounds good." Bosse did not add that he could not see how he'd stay long enough to enjoy that opportunity, but he would stick to his word no matter what.

Adrian turned to the one called Corbin. "Okay, you and Bosse next."

Corbin finished having terse words under his breath with the camp crazy, then backed away, pointing his finger at Badger.

Did that work? Bosse waited as Adrian headed over to Badger.

"Come on," Badger yelled at Adrian. "I'm ready to fight you for alpha status."

Every other shifter groaned and cursed.

When Corbin walked up, Bosse asked, "Will Adrian fight him? I thought Jaz was alpha."

"She is." Corbin swiped wet brown hair off his face with both hands. He wore it longer on top and short on the sides. Glancing back at Adrian, who stood with his hands on his hips, Corbin commented, "Badger isn't wired right. He may get what he wants the day he steps over the line and releases his wolf out here, but it will be a short battle." He returned to Bosse and extended his hand.

Bosse kept his arms folded. "Is this a trick?"

"What? No." Corbin gave him a confused look. "Other than Adrian introducing you to the group, I hadn't met you yet. Where do you come from that people don't shake when they meet?"

"I come from a place where someone would break my arm if I stuck out my hand."

Corbin grinned. "Okay. Sounds like places I've been. I don't give a shit about shaking. Adrian's the one pushing us to be civil."

Bosse gave him a short nod in agreement and opened his arms to prepare for a battle. All of them had pulled off their shirts and hung them on branches, fighting in jeans only.

Corbin's build topped out around six feet, two inches, just shy of Bosse's height, but with plenty of muscle. He moved around to one side. Bosse mirrored what Corbin did, watching for his first move.

He understood that every shifter out here would want to test the new guy.

He'd been tested time and again in the past. The best defense was to wait for their first move.

Corbin came in fast, moving in one direction, then slashed back the other way at the last second. Bosse had to be quick on his feet to stay ahead of him. He had an opening and reached out to grab Corbin.

The guy spun in place, whipping away.

Not bad for practice.

Bosse would not be so careful if it were a fight to the

death. They moved like that, one taking a shot and the other avoiding back and forth until Corbin lifted a hand. "It would be easier to fight you for real than this pussy footing around."

"True."

Jaz called out, "Adrian, the Guardian is here."

Everyone stopped.

Bosse couldn't believe he hadn't realized she'd joined them or that she had another person with her. A man dressed in a fine suit and expensive-looking shoes, even if Bosse had no idea what humans bought to wear. Short gray hair at his temples blended in his groomed cut of black hair. He held his head with confidence befitting a leader. He reeked of power that felt capable of overtaking everyone in sight.

"Who is that?" Bosse asked to confirm this was the leader Jaz had said he could question.

"That's the head honcho over Adrian, Jaz, and other shifters like them."

"His eyes are not human," Bosse pointed out as those eagle-like eyes moved quickly, missing nothing.

"No. He shifts into the biggest sea hawk you've ever seen and is more powerful than Jaz or Adrian. We saw him once when he showed up after Jaz killed our alpha, but it was self-defense, and that alpha was a sicko."

Someone should kill Krol, another sicko.

As Adrian neared Bosse, he said, "I need you to come with me."

He fell into step with Adrian, who grabbed Bosse's T-shirt and his own. By the time they both had shirts on, Adrian addressed the eagle shifter. "You're a little early. Has something happened?"

"Yes. We have a critical situation." This man's words were as stiff as the crisp white shirt beneath his dark gray suit.

Adrian turned around and called out, "Corbin, you're in charge of finishing the training. You've got a half hour left before the pack can shift to run, then have everyone get cleaned up for dinner."

Corbin's eyebrows rose to his hairline as if he had no idea why he had been handed that task. "Uhm, okay, got it."

Jaz led the way to the front porch shaded by ancient oak trees. She had a pitcher of cold water on a wicker table with four glasses and four chairs arranged in a circle.

Once everyone else sat, Bosse took the only seat left. Immense power surrounding the eagle shifter remained under control. It rolled and churned, unlike anything Bosse had ever experienced. He had no doubt this man could unleash more to intimidate him, but he didn't. There sat a man with confidence, someone like Krol would envy and never understand. This eagle shifter had a fit body for the age he displayed, though the hair and face did not fool Bosse.

This man felt old, very old.

Jaz sat back, watching everyone.

Adrian leaned forward with his elbows on his knees and hands clasped.

"I am known as the Guardian," the eagle shifter started. "I've been told you're Bosse and that you escaped a castle in Slovakia where a lion shifter kept you captive."

"This is true." Bosse had been told this man was a guardian, but he now believed Guardian was the eagle shifter's name.

"I'd like to know more about the person behind capturing other shifters."

More than ready to share, Bosse explained, "He is called Krol. He is a lion shifter who believes he is a king and, as such, deserves entertainment like battles fought long ago in the Greek Parthenon. Everyone is expected to live as if we are in medieval times. He's insane. He pits two shifters against each other to fight to the death." Bosse wished that did not sound so civilized. "I was there two years. At first, he cheered when I continued to win my battles against other wolf shifters, but then he grew bored and sent me into the arena with other larger types of animals. The last one I fought was a Cape buffalo."

Jaz showed a tiny reaction—respect—because she'd been raised by a Kodiak bear clan. Adrian smiled as if telling himself Bosse would be a great addition to the pack.

That would only be if he stayed.

"I hated every minute," Bosse admitted. "My opponents were as innocent as me, but I had to protect my wolf, and he protected me."

"I understand," the Guardian said. "I would not judge you on those deaths. We have heard rumors of this lion shifter over the past year and stories of missing shifters, but we've found no one who knew how to find him—only people who heard of someone going to meet the lion shifter and never coming back. Shifter informants were not able to track these people. Trails ended at the same area each time."

Bosse thought on the lack of information and shared, "That is because Krol keeps his people close to the castle and will kill anyone caught talking about him. His guards are human, but he pays a few shifters well to deliver fish, game, and other food. They feel under his protection and do not go into cities where they might speak to outsiders. As for the trail ending, Krol may be crazy, but he's not stupid. He shows his humans how to wipe a scent trail to prevent unwanted intruders."

Taking a moment to digest that, the Guardian said, "I want to know how he could kidnap shifters without a revolt from their packs."

Bosse opened his hands. "It is simple. He shows up with a small army of human guards plus mercenary shifters who are paid well to do whatever Krol wants. When he captures a shifter, he warns the pack he will return to kill all the mates and offspring if anyone dares to come for their shifter or speaks of the kidnapping. In my case, the alpha did not want me to stay because I refused to breed females I would not take as mates. He sold me to Krol. My mother went along with it all. I had no other family."

A dark look passed through Jaz's face. She hadn't liked to hear that, but she remained quiet.

This Guardian frowned, clearly not liking what Krol had done any more than Jaz had. He switched the direction of their conversation. "We believe he may have captured a female mate of one of my shifters."

Jaz lost all relaxed composure and sat up straight. She asked, "Who?" at the same moment as Adrian.

"I will share that in just a bit," the Guardian replied, lifting a hand to stall more questions. "Since my shifters would track anyone touching a mate to the ends of this world, I wish for Bosse to explain if he knows how this Krol could have taken a shifter while leaving no scent trail."

"No scent? The guy is a lion shifter," Adrian mused out loud.

"Exactly, but there was no animal or human scent to track this time," the eagle shifter confirmed. "The only smell noted was of dark magic in the last spot where the mate's scent lingered. Is Krol more than a shifter?"

Bosse stared at the ground, thinking. He lifted his head, meeting the Guardian's disturbing eagle eyes. "Was it a recent kidnapping?"

"Yes. It happened yesterday in Austria."

"Oh, no." Jaz sounded deeply hurt, as if she knew the pack.

Nodding to himself, Bosse said, "I left the castle a couple of days back. The night I escaped, Krol left for five or six hours earlier that afternoon. Krol wields no magic that I know of, but he returned with something unnatural even in the shifter world."

"What do you mean?" Jaz cocked her head.

"It appears to have been… made, not born," Bosse replied. "I have no way to know for sure, but I have never seen or heard of a Lammogo. The upper body is the head and wings of a Lammergeier. Krol bragged they are vultures from South Africa with eagle-like heads and are very large in natural form. This one has a gigantic wingspan. I believe the lower body is that of a lion, and I am guessing that someone bonded those two together with magic."

"Dark magic," Adrian said as if the very word tasted dirty.

Bosse canted his head in agreement. "Yes. I could smell the stench down in the arena when Krol brought the creature to sit with him above where we fought. This thing is large enough to grasp a man my size with its talons and fly it from one place to another. Other than the magic scent, I never picked up a smell of any sort from it. Since it flies, it would be hard to track. Krol sent the Lammogo after me when I ran, and I barely managed to elude it."

Jaz groaned and covered her eyes with her hand. "That's awful. Ivo must be out of his mind."

The eagle shifter sat back and said, "The mate is no small woman. She is six feet tall and pregnant. You're saying you think this Lammogo could fly away with someone that size when she'd be fighting him?"

Bosse kept feeding them more information. "If Krol is the one who has taken the mate, then yes. I saw his pet lift a full-grown sheep. I believe the creature's claws stunned it. When it released the sheep in front of Krol, the poor animal did not move a muscle. I have not seen this thing harm anyone yet, but I can't say that it won't. The Lammogo seemed to be trained to retrieve."

Jaz asked, "Where is the castle? That could be where he's taken her."

Finally, the moment Bosse had been waiting for had just arrived. He had not expected this but would not allow a golden opportunity to pass. He offered, "I can show you the way."

Gifting him with a polite smile, the Guardian said, "I appreciate your offer, but you have just escaped a horrendous imprisonment. My shifters are powerful, trained, and capable of dealing with Krol. I will have my jet on standby for Adrian's team to leave as soon as they are ready. I would not ask you to step back into danger there again."

"You would not be asking." Bosse deepened his tone, ensuring they understood this was important to him. "I appreciate all that has been done for me here, but I told Jaz and Adrian about the woman who helped me escape. She would not leave that night as she had to find someone else imprisoned there. To this minute, I regret allowing her to convince me I would put her in danger if I stayed. I will lead your people there and help rescue the mate first, but I will not leave again without the woman who put her life at risk for me."

All three of them were quiet.

Jaz caught Adrian's attention, and their gazes locked, but not in an intimate way.

Bosse began to think those two might be speaking in each other's minds.

Jaz leaned back, tapping a finger on the arm of her chair. Adrian tilted his body forward slightly, elbows on his knees and hands loosely clasped. With all that, he still looked ready to move.

Jaz and Adrian waited for the Guardian to speak first.

Bosse couldn't wait. "If you are all special shifters with strong powers, why have you allowed someone like Krol to live? He had to be killing long before he ended up in the castle."

That broke the Guardian from his deep thoughts. "We must have firm information on any shifter who is committing crimes. We are not murderers to kill at will or quick to judge someone as SCIS has been known to do."

"That brings up another thing I have wondered. What kind of shifters are you?" Bosse wanted all the truths.

Jaz glanced at the eagle shifter with a curious expression as if she had no idea what he might say.

Adrian pinched the bridge of his nose. "This is what I was talking about regarding our pack the last time I came to headquarters. They're all pushing for more about us."

Sounding resigned about sharing a secret, the Guardian said, "I understand, Adrian. I knew we'd have to inform your pack at some point, but I wish to be judicious about who we tell and when we tell them."

"Absolutely, sir."

Turning to Bosse, the Guardian said, "My shifters come from an ancient Gallizenae bloodline. It would take a while for me to explain how they become Gallize shifters but suffice to say that not everyone born to a Gallize parent or even a pair of parents will be a Gallize with our powers. The males were to be shifters. The women were to be powerful beings. The original idea was that this small number of extraordinary beings would mate at some point as their powers would kill even another shifter who is not a Gallize. Jaz and one other female Gallize in my local group are even more unusual, as they were born shifters with Gallize powers. That's why I have no concern over sending any of mine to deal with Krol and bring our missing mate back."

Bosse thought he'd seen everything strange in this world, but clearly not. He respected the power of these Gallize shifters and acknowledged he could likely not kill one if he faced that possibility.

None of that changed his mind.

"Thank you for telling me this truth, Guardian." Bosse wanted to show them he could be part of their organization. "I will not share your private information with anyone else."

Adrian let out a pent-up breath. "Great. We need as detailed a map as you can draw and anything you can tell us about breaching that castle."

"No." Bosse took in all three faces.

Jaz and Adrian were clearly shocked he'd said no, with the Guardian expecting his help.

Bosse explained, "You must take me. I can get inside the castle to find out if the mate is even there. Would you want to have a blood bath and maybe harm innocent servants also imprisoned only to find out Krol had not brought her there?"

"Shit fire, sir, he's got a point," Adrian said.

"Language, Adrian."

"Sorry, sir."

Addressing Bosse, the eagle shifter said, "I am not accustomed to being refused a request."

Bosse felt the first inkling of potential trouble. He'd angered a man far more powerful than him. He started to explain more but noticed Adrian making a show of clamping his lips, telling Bosse to be quiet.

During that silent stretch, the Guardian said, "I understand your reason for being determined to return. Adrian tells me you show exceptional battle skills in training. He believes you would work well on his team."

Bosse looked at the mated pair of strange shifters.

Had Adrian just told the Guardian that information? Did they also speak in their minds? He didn't care. He wanted to know for sure he was going. "Does this mean you accept my offer to help?"

In no rush to answer, the Guardian studied Bosse for a long stretch of silence before saying, "Yes, but you should know this. If you put saving this other woman ahead of rescuing our captured mate, that will be an unforgivable action. Are we clear?" His words rolled out on a wave of power no one here missed.

"I understand." Bosse did not know how he would rescue the mate, Alifair, and her friend, but he would have to figure that out when they arrived. Based on her timeline, it was too soon to think Alifair had escaped yet.

Jaz and Adrian both wore expressions of concern.

Bosse didn't need them to warn him that crossing this eagle shifter could be more dangerous than anything he had faced in the arena.

Chapter 19

ALIFAIR HAD BEEN assigned clothes washing, which suited her.

She'd been questioned over and over by Eriko early this morning. She could tell he was suspicious of her. He'd change his tactic to ask about her duties. Then, in the middle of her answering his first question, he'd interrupt to ask the last time she'd been in the downstairs cage area.

A question he'd already asked her once before.

With disruptive sleep since Bosse left, she fought exhaustion and yawned a lot to make sure he knew she was tired.

He hadn't cared if she'd been bleeding to death.

The only thing that had helped her was having thought through everything Eriko or Krol might ask her. She'd given him the same answer both times, but she might have faltered if he'd kept up the interrogation for another two hours. There were moments when he'd sit quietly and say nothing.

A good tactic to make someone guilty start talking.

Not a tactic she'd fall for even when tired.

She'd spent her entire life keeping her mouth shut about her clan, her mother's powers, and her own powers, feeble as they were. When he finally allowed her to go to bed, she'd had no time to sleep if she wanted to beat Hessie to the kitchen. She'd rushed to dress again, braided her hair once more that had come apart, hid the knife in her sleeve, and literally ran to the kitchen.

Hessie was still there first. She had her body angled toward the back of the kitchen and head down, cutting meat into sections while muttering to herself.

Alifair's pulse went mad as she tiptoed over to the workstation where she'd taken the knife. She couldn't just put it back in place and risk Hessie catching the movement. She found a place to slide it between two cabinets.

Hessie hadn't looked up yet.

Hoping the woman remained fixated on her task, Alifair moved six steps back toward the doorway where she'd entered.

She cleared her throat and said, "Good morning."

Hessie jerked and turned fast, grousing, "Why are you here now?"

Talk about looking guilty.

"Eriko just finished asking me about the wolf shifter that escaped. I saw no reason to try to sleep for an hour or two. What can I do?"

She'd clearly caught Hessie off guard.

The woman frowned at the floor as if it had insulted her somehow, then lifted her head. "Kylie will be here with wash crew soon. Go outside with them when she shows up. I will give one of those servants a day of easy work in kitchen."

Easy work. Was she serious?

Alifair wanted to make a fist pump. Finally, she got a work assignment that might help her. She'd gladly follow Kylie around and find out as much as she could about that woman.

Slapping a smile on her face, Alifair said, "I will be happy to do whatever you need." She stopped short of thanking the mean woman for the chance to study the outside structure of the castle.

Hessie shoved a hand in her direction, dismissing Alifair and her words.

That woman must have been with Krol before he took on this castle. She cared only about pleasing him and held some position of power, even if it was only over the female servants.

Alifair stifled a yawn on her way outside.

Women began to show up outside, gathering into a small group. Alifair moved over to act as if she was expected to be there.

A sharp female voice asked, "Is everyone here? We do not have all day to finish the laundry."

Looking toward her right to find the owner of that voice, Alifair stared at Kylie with a blue head cloth. She wanted to grab Kylie and shake her until she told Alifair where Rez was being kept or at least make her admit who she was feeding at night.

One of the ladies said, "Hessie kept Nicci to help her today, Kylie."

Kylie lifted her hand, counting the heads. She stopped on Alifair. "What are you doing here?"

"Hessie sent me out to help." Alifair did not smile at Kylie. She arranged her face into quiet acceptance to match the other women.

Grumbling to herself about training someone new, Kylie said, "Follow how the other servants work, and do not be slow."

Alifair nodded in response. She could probably run circles around Kylie, but that would draw attention she didn't want. No, she needed to sink into the background so that she could track Kylie's comings and goings.

The day dragged on while washing clothes and linens in a large tub outside, then hanging them over a rope stretched between two poles sunk in the ground. She'd never been one to hold hate in her heart, but that organ had a special dark corner for Krol.

He made the servants carry out their work based on ancient practices, but he had a computer and copy machine upstairs. What a jerk.

All during the hours of cleaning clothes on a washboard, she had no better view of the castle than the day she'd been taken in through the front doors. She'd never been so thankful to hand off the final wet shirt to the women hanging them.

Kylie announced, "All of the washing is done. We have another task."

Mentally complaining about this entire fiasco, Alifair dried her water-wrinkled hands and headed over with the other servants to find out what slave work they had to do next. But she kept hope alive that this woman would be important to finding Rez.

"Walk around the castle gardens inside here." Kylie pointed at some vegetation growing along the wall. "Look for vegetables and fruit ripe on the vine. Do not make the mistake of picking anything not ripened."

One of the women asked, "What if it's rotten? Do you want us to pick it and throw it away?"

"You will *not* find any fruit that has rotted. There is a sweep of the gardens made every other day."

Unbelievable. Alifair should have weaseled her way onto gardening duty before now. She snatched up a wide wicker basket perfect for picking flowers. The fact that someone had planted gardens alongside this side of the castle wall made lots of sense. Animals could not wander inside here and steal food.

The poor things would end up in a pot before they finished chewing.

She'd made it two-thirds the way around the castle when she cut her eyes up for the umpteenth time to check for another floor above Krol's living quarters.

No additional floor, but there was a round section about fifteen feet in diameter on a corner at the rear of the castle. She had no idea what that part was called without a way to search the history of castle construction online.

Someone moved up behind her. They worked in a line so no one person stopped long to pick. Alifair plucked a handful of raspberries to drop in her basket, moved three steps forward, and then peeked over her shoulder at that tower again. There were narrow windows without any coverings twenty feet up.

Too narrow to get through and too far to jump.

Picking and walking slowly again, she would be out of range to view the tower soon. She stopped and reached at her neck to grab her braid, sliding the leather thong off, and leaned her head back as she tied it again.

Her gaze danced over that round structure.

The shape of a person could be seen inside the top floor.

Clouds had been floating across the sky, blocking the sunlight at times. The sun broke free, casting a ray of light through that window.

Rez sat with her elbow on the ledge and her head propped on her hand, paying no attention to those below. Probably a common view by now of women working below, which Rez easily dismissed. A few strands of golden hair danced in the light breeze.

Alifair fought for a breath.

After all this time, she wanted to shout, "I found you!" Thankfully, she didn't make that stupid mistake.

"You're holding up the line," the servant behind her snarled. "Move, or I will pass you."

"Sorry." Alifair finished fussing with her hair and grabbed her basket. She had to get back on garden duty tomorrow and figure out a way to catch Rez's eye. In the meantime, she needed to draw a layout of what she now knew about the inside and outside of the castle for any hope of finding that tower room.

No sleep tonight. No problem.

One sighting of Rez and she felt she could run five miles. She beat down the urge to laugh and celebrate. Not while Rez remained a prisoner.

But soon, she would be free.

Alifair had little hope of leaving here alive, but she would accept her fate if Rez and Bosse gained their freedom. Maybe somewhere in her cold heart, Rez would thank Alifair for her sacrifice. Maybe.

Hopefully, Bosse had made it to America. Alifair was so relieved to have heard no word of Bosse being captured.

It would be incredible to escape and find Bosse. Silly daydreaming, but she couldn't forget the dreams she'd spent with him.

She wanted a replay of her dream while he'd been on the run, but in real life, she'd get to see all of him this time. She fanned herself at her wanton mind.

Happiness gave her silly thoughts, but Alifair had never thought of a man the way she thought of Bosse all the time. She'd dated a few, but no one special. Since she had no hope of a future life, of marrying or having a child, she intended to enjoy every time she met Bosse in her dreams if it happened again.

Nothing bad could happen to her there.

At the end of the garden, Kylie waited to direct them to walk through a different door into the castle. One that was not near the kitchen. Alifair mentally ticked off every new piece of information.

She would have an escape plan laid out by tonight.

Following the three women ahead of her, she stepped inside the castle, where her eyes had to adjust to the dimmer torch lighting from the bright sunshine.

A gong sounded once, twice, three times.

Alifair paused to the side of the door and asked no one, "What could that mean?"

Behind the fifth servant girl, Kylie stepped in and said, "That's the alarm to warn all the workers and guards that Krol is close to home. It only happens if he's gone for two days or more. He'll be here within the hour."

No. This couldn't be happening.

How would Alifair find Rez's tower room and get her out with Krol back in the castle?

"You three return to the kitchen," Kylie said, pointing at the designated three. She turned to Alifair and the servant behind her walking the gardens. "You two follow me." She walked off without another word.

Alifair's enthusiasm deflated faster than a popped balloon.

She trudged behind the woman who took them around to the hall where she'd opened the door to carry food upstairs yesterday.

What?

A fresh wave of excitement refilled her balloon of hope over where she might be going.

Kylie unlocked the door and walked upstairs fast, wasting no time. At the top of the stairs, she turned left toward the empty bedrooms, explaining, "You're to freshen a bedroom for Krol's new guest."

At the second room Alifair had found last night, Kylie entered and strode over to a tall cabinet made of neglected dark wood no longer polished. She opened the double doors, removed a stack of bed linen, and handed them to the first servant. Next, she walked into a smaller adjoining room. It had been furnished with an oval mirror and wooden table where a cream ceramic pitcher, pottery drinking cup, and matching basin had been set up. Two large towels and two hand towels were folded and sitting next to the basin.

This room also had sort of a commode. Linota had grumbled how servants were stuck with chamber pots to empty and clean while the upstairs bedrooms had garderobes. At Alifair's blank stare, Linota chuckled and explained a garderobe was a toilet with a straight drop to a pit somewhere below.

A guard walked in carrying a large bucket of water and a matching empty bucket.

Kylie pointed at the bathroom. Once he placed the bucket in the room where Alifair stood, he left. Then Kylie opened the door of a narrow closet and withdrew a small plastic tub filled with old rags and cleaning supplies.

Handing that to Alifair, she said, "This room needs to be spotless in less than an hour. Not a bit of dust. Nothing. I don't listen to excuses. Krol is less patient than me." Nodding at the servant tackling the bed, Kylie said, "She will help you when she's done."

"I understand." Alifair accepted the tub of cleaning supplies. She tried very hard to give an acceptable reply while not saying thank you to someone who treated her like a slave. She got busy cleaning as hard as she could.

Who was this new guest?

If she had not seen Rez today, she would have thought Krol had delayed bringing Rez here even if Alifair's dream had pinpointed this as the location.

The other servant joined her after Alifair had cleaned the bathroom spotless. She dumped the dirty water into the empty bucket, rinsed her plastic tub, then refilled it with fresh water and soap. Standing up and groaning with pain in her lower back, she handed the scrub brush to the middle-aged woman.

Good time to get to know another servant. Alifair asked, "How long have you been here?"

"Long enough to know to keep my mouth shut and not ask questions," the woman answered in a flat tone.

Did they capture sullen women, or had the time spent here as a slave to Krol ruined everyone's attitude? Alifair did her best to clean everything she could find in need of attention. Someone like this servant would report any infraction to Hessie.

Time passed without Alifair noticing until she got off her knees and began picking up the cleaning rags. "That should do it."

The other woman dropped her scrub brush in the bucket. "If you say so." With that, she washed her hands in the dirty water, wiped them on her apron, and left.

Alifair ground her jaws, realizing if the room was not suitable, that grouchy woman had just hung the responsibility on her. Fine. She'd keep moving around and checking every inch in case. Wouldn't it be nice if she found some secret passage to Rez's room?

At least the new occupant of this room would have extra water since Alifair had been frugal in using it to clean.

She was down to wiping nonexistent dust from the furniture when a booming voice approached the room from the hallway.

Krol. He sounded jubilant.

Had someone located Bosse? Please no.

The door opened without a knock because no door was closed to Krol. He stood to the side and gave a short bow as if addressing royalty. "I have excellent accommodations for you."

Who had he brought here?

A woman of significant stature. The kind of female who exuded confidence and power just by the way she carried herself. She had striking white hair, which one might associate with being elderly. Not this woman. She might not be thirty yet and carried herself as one who held respect.

More noticeable than all that was her rounded belly. She appeared to be in the late stages of pregnancy. A gradual energy floated into the room ahead of her, sneaking around corners as if checking for threats.

Who could she be? Better yet, *what* could she be with all that power?

Krol turned to Alifair. "Take care of Magdelina's needs. She is my guest."

Magdelina swung a disgusted gaze at Krol that one would give a slimy rat.

Unfazed by her disgust, he made one thing clear. "You will stay here until told to leave." He addressed Alifair. "If my *guest* tries to leave, you will be killed for allowing her to attempt it."

Chapter 20

ALIFAIR'S JAW FELL at the threat of being sanctioned with death if this pregnant woman tried to escape.

Krol retained his pleasant expression, but his voice dropped to a low, menacing sound. "Is there a problem?"

A problem. Try a thousand problems.

Alifair had to find out how long she'd be stuck in here. She recovered to shake her head and say, "I was only wondering if you want me to make plans to sleep up here?"

"No. She is only staying a few hours while I join Eriko to complete the interrogations."

What else did he intend to do? Hadn't Eriko said she was the last person to interrogate?

The door snapped shut, and the lock clicked as loud as a death knell in the suddenly silent room.

Now she'd have to wait until this woman was gone before she could resume her search for Rez. With nothing else to do, Alifair turned to Magdelina, hoping to find out anything she could about Krol's next plans.

Then she realized she'd been locked in a room with an unknown captive she suspected of having some level of power.

Her life just sucked more by the minute.

She needed to find some sort of mutual ground with this woman who was important to Krol. "I'm sorry for you to be in this position while pregnant. Where did Krol capture you?"

"I'm from Austria. Krol didn't actually capture me."

Then she clarified, "He has a strange bird beast that literally picked me up off the ground and flew me away. Its claws did something to neutralize my ability to fight, but it wore off once it set me on the ground at Krol's feet. I'm clearly no small woman and carrying a shifter's cub. I still can't believe what it did."

Alifair had wondered about that thing's claws after hearing how it had stunned the sheep. "You're a shifter?"

"No. My mate is alpha of a bear clan." Magdelina put her hand on her back and stepped over to the bed to ease her burdened body to the mattress. "My mate will be ripping the land apart to find me."

"Will he bring the whole pack?" Alifair could see possibilities in getting Rez out if a large pack attacked the castle.

"We're a clan, not a pack like wolves." Magdelina smiled as she explained. "He would bring an army of shifters if he could follow my scent. Unfortunately, that bird creature destroyed any hope of my clan tracking me by taking me off the ground."

No help there. Alifair still had the same problems she'd had an hour ago.

She walked over to grab one of two chairs placed around a small table in the corner—a lovely antique set of some sort that belonged in a museum. Alifair had never been good at antique styles or the different eras of furniture, but this appeared authentic.

She pulled the chair around to sit facing Magdelina. "That flying beast is called a Lammogo."

Magdelina paused in rubbing her back. "You know what it is?"

"Only what Krol said when he brought it here a few days ago." Alifair couldn't see that woman trying to take any wild action in her condition but still had to ask, "Do you intend to escape?"

"Not yet." She smiled and winked. "I won't get you killed."

"Thank you. I would be happy for you to escape this place, but I must live at least one more day."

At that, the woman tilted her head as if trying to discern if Alifair was joking. "You don't want to live any longer? What are you doing here?"

Heaving a deep breath, Alifair let it out slowly while deciding what to share. She was so tired of hunting Rez on her own and facing the end of her life. She wouldn't have Bosse again but wanted a friend, even one who would not stay long.

This woman had been taken against her will. What harm could come from talking with her? How could Alifair expect Magdelina to share any information if she didn't qualify why she needed it?

"I'd like to live to old age, but I won't," Alifair started. "Krol captured the leader of our small community, a gifted female I fear he intends to use for some awful reason. I came to this area hunting her and allowed myself to be captured almost a month ago for the sole purpose of getting her out of here."

"Where is she?"

"I had no idea until today when I spotted her at a window while I was outside. She's in the rounded corner part of this castle."

Magdelina took this in, quietly thinking for a moment. "What do you think he will do with her if you don't free her?"

"I don't know. The other captives are servants or shifters."

"Shifters?" Magdelina's voice lost civility. Her eyes fired up with a quick flash of fury. "What does he do with those?"

Alifair explained about the arena and the mix of shifters Krol pitted against each other.

The power surrounding Magdelina swirled between her and Alifair, feeling like a hammer ready to strike even while held firmly under control. She fisted one hand, and her facial muscles struggled to appear calm.

How dangerous was this woman? Alifair asked, "I feel your energy. Can you use it to disarm Krol?"

Relaxing her fist, Magdelina answered in a bitter tone. "No. I must be careful, or I'll harm my baby." Then, wiped out from all she'd been through, she held her back and said, "I'm sorry about your friend. I'm going to lie down for a bit. I have no idea where I'll be taken next and need my strength."

"Sure."

Alifair dug around in the room while Magdelina slept but found no paper or anything to use for drawing her layout.

An hour had passed when a knock on the door made Alifair jump, and Magdelina sat up with her white hair needing a brush.

Since she'd been locked inside this room, Alifair waited as the door opened. Linota brought food on a tray with a smaller water pitcher and cup. A guard stood with a rifle in position to shoot if needed.

"This is for Krol's guest," Linota announced, eyes wide and voice shaking.

Alifair took the tray and waited until the servant had left and the door was locked again. She sat it on the small table near the only window. Unlike Rez's open window, this one had a lead and glass insert set permanently in place. Alifair couldn't even shout for help if she had anyone who would listen.

But this room was not in the right place or in a round shape. Maybe by taking care of this woman, Alifair could stay here to clean up the room after Magdelina left with Krol.

Her heart hurt at the thought of what Krol might have planned for Magdelina. "Do you want to eat?"

With an awkward movement, Magdelina stood and stretched. "I'd rather not eat this pig's food, but I have to think of someone other than myself. Krol needs me healthy for whatever he has in mind. It doesn't make sense to poison me." Sitting at the table, she dipped her spoon into the cabbage stew, but not to eat. She mostly pushed the soup around. "I need your help to get word to my mate."

Alifair laughed. "I would be glad to do that, but if you haven't noticed, I'm just as much a captive as you are." She thought about how much she missed Bosse and wished she could see him one more time or send him a message.

Her heart ached with a deep wound from missing him. Did he miss her as well?

Magdelina lifted one eyebrow. "You said you won't live long as if you accept that fate, but don't you want to see the man you care about?"

That stopped Alifair in her tracks. She whispered, "What are you talking about?"

Magdelina swirled her spoon in the air and pointed at the door. "You don't have to whisper. They can't hear our words, not even a shifter. I can use a small bit of power."

"Okay, but what did you mean about seeing a man I care about?" A frightening thought struck her. "Are you reading my mind?"

Magdelina sounded insulted when she replied, "Of course not. That would be rude and invasive. You are thinking so loudly I can't help but hear you. I started out talking in my head to override your voice, but then realized what you were thinking." She extended her hand and said, "I am not going to harm you, but I do need your help. Just take my hand."

Magdelina offered her hand, a harmless gesture if not for that atomic power she carried around.

Gulping down a breath, Alifair considered touching someone with way more power than her but reminded herself she needed an ally. Pushing down her fear, she took the woman's hand, and energy warmed her skin.

Alifair tried to yank her hand back but could not pull free. Panic rattled her. "What are you doing?"

Pulling her lips up to one side, Magdelina challenged, "Don't be a baby. I'm not hurting you, and I can feel *your* power."

"You can?" Alifair stopped pulling. "I have nothing compared to you."

"That's not exactly true. I do have an unusual level of energy, but yours is simply dormant."

Alifair tried to wrap her head around that possibility and couldn't. She'd lived with this body for twenty-five years and knew her limits. "Have you *always* been this strong?"

"Not as much before I met my mate. Bonding with him unlocked all my energy," Magdelina admitted.

Could that happen if Alifair mated with Bosse?

What kind of question was that? A stupid one.

"Now that we understand each other," Magdelina said, "let's stop dancing around. I need you to take a message to my mate." She had yet to release the handhold.

Alifair smiled sadly at her. "I would help anyone in your situation, but what makes you think I'll ever cross paths with your mate?"

Magdelina lifted her shoulder. "Humor me, okay?"

She was serious. Alifair glanced over at the small desk. "I looked for a pen and paper earlier. I didn't find any."

"No paper. Someone can read anything written down. All you need to do is listen to my message. When you find my mate, tell him I said *kompis budbringer*. He will offer his hand as I have."

"What does that mean?"

"It translates to mate messenger, so he knows it comes from me. Once he takes your hand, he'll hear my words flow from your mind to his mind. He won't harm you."

This was a whole new level of strange for Alifair, and she'd come from prime strange stock. She gave up. "Okay, *if* I meet your mate, which I seriously doubt, what do you want me to tell him?"

Magdelina's face softened with appreciation. "Thank you. I believe he will eventually catch up to me or at least to where I've been, and you'll see him then. I just fear it will not be in time."

At least Alifair had no way to get it wrong if she ever did meet this woman's mate.

"By the way, where are we?" Magdelina asked.

"Slovakia. If I had some paper, I could draw a map, but you said no paper," Alifair mumbled. Then she told her new friend in what area Krol's castle was located.

"Excellent. That's plenty. Thank you." Magdelina instructed her, "Close your eyes and relax."

This sounded like a bad idea, but Alifair closed her eyes. Relaxing was out of the question. She could feel energy wiggling its way from Magdelina's hand to hers.

She tried to think of a way out of this, but…

What was happening to her?

She no longer heard the small castle noises or smelled the freshly cleaned room. A vision began to form. In her mind's eye, Magdelina came to her in a wispy blue gown with gold trim. Her stunning white hair was loose, cascading across her shoulders and down her back. Her eyes stared at Alifair… or maybe someone else because Magdelina said, "My dearest Ivo, I have been captured by a lion shifter known as Krol." She continued by sharing what she knew of her location.

Alifair wondered at the energy now flowing smoothly through her arms. She hoped this did not turn out to be a mistake.

Magdelina continued talking to her mate. "Our child will be strong, like his father. I did not tell you it would be a boy, as I wanted to see your face when you held your son for the first time. I will do all in my power to protect him, and I will put his life first before mine if it comes down to a choice. If I fail to survive this…" She stopped and blew out a shaky breath as if the words were becoming harder to say. "I will see you again when our souls meet in the sunshine of our afterlife because nothing can ever take you from my heart. I know you hunt for me. If you receive my message from this woman, please repay her kindness any way you can, for she has been a comfort to me." Taking a moment to breathe quietly, she ended by saying, "I love you more than words can describe. If my life is taken before I give birth, I will keep our child safe as we both wait for you in the afterlife."

Tears rolled down Alifair's face.

This woman had a bond with a man that would pass through the ages. The two of them should be able to be together, not her locked away here in Krol's castle.

Magdelina gently ordered, "Open your eyes, Alifair."

She blinked and looked around. They were still in the room. "Wait, I haven't introduced myself yet. How'd you know my name?"

"Someone you care about spoke your name while we were connected. I did not reach into your mind, but as we held hands, I heard him call to you not to leave him. He was very loud."

Stunned, Alifair didn't attempt to speak. That's what Bosse had said in the dream where he'd been with strangers as she lost contact with him. "What is your gift?"

"We don't discuss such things, but you have agreed to help me, so I will tell you what I can. The simplest explanation is that I can pick up conversations being spoken out loud in this castle and nearby area or very loud thoughts. Conversely, if I am threatened, I can mentally scream into someone's mind until their ears bleed. I still can't risk using that energy, or I might harm my child as he feels everything I do."

Whoa. Alifair felt like bowing. Compared to this woman, she was the level of a carnival magician.

Magdelina sounded ready to move ahead. "Now that you have my message, what do you need to escape? I can't snap my fingers and make it happen, but I will assist you in any way I can. What do you need?"

Having had no way to prepare a plan in this room, Alifair told her the only thing preventing her from leaving. "I told you I saw my friend today. That was the first time in a month of being here. I saw her in a round corner room in the castle. I haven't had time to hunt for that room yet."

Alifair started to say more to this Gallize woman but paused when something she recalled popped into her head.

She stopped mid-thought and blurted out, "What does Gallize mean?"

For a confident woman reeking of power, this one quieted immediately and studied Alifair. "What makes you ask such an odd question?"

Ah ha! Alifair was on to something. "I just realized I heard that word when we held hands. Now I'm curious and would like to know what it is, but if that's something you don't want to talk about, I'll just wait to find out on my own later."

"You could be annoying if I didn't like you so much."

Alifair tried to take that as a compliment.

Releasing a stream of air that whistled with exasperation, this Gallize woman said, "It's a long story, and I'm bound to protect our history, but given the circumstances, I'd rather you have accurate information and not some twisted tale from Krol. There are a limited number of male shifters in this world who have unusual powers bestowed on them by a Gallizenae druidess many centuries ago. They can only bond with a Gallize female of equal power, which I am one."

"You said you're not a shifter, right?"

"Correct. I've heard of a few Gallize women who were born shifters, very few who have different gifts associated with their power. Most of the Gallize females are not shifters."

Considering she and her mate had crazy power, Alifair asked, "Will your baby be one?"

"I doubt it. That has not happened in any Gallize pairing we know of, and our people have been keeping our history for a long time." She put her hand on her bulging middle. "I believe this child will survive. I just do not know if I will. That is why I must get a message to my mate."

Alifair carried the weight of saving Rez already, but she could not deny this woman on the very slim chance she might be able to pass along a message for her. "I may not escape this place, but if I do, I will go to him as soon as possible. Where can I find him?"

"Thank you for taking on another person's burden." Then the Gallize woman told her where the bear clan lived in Austria.

As if this task hadn't sounded impossible before? Another thing hit Alifair as unusual. "You're from Austria, but your English has no accent?"

Magdelina explained, "I was born and raised in different parts of the Midwest area of the United States. We lack a heavy accent like that of the southerners or those from the north in comparison."

"My home is in the US, too." Realizing what this woman had to face soon, Alifair said, "I'd love to keep getting to know you, but your trip here had to be difficult even if you had not been kidnapped. You should lie down and rest some more. You'll probably need your energy for whatever Krol has planned for you next."

"That miserable pig." Magdelina's eyes flashed with fury. "If he had not threatened to have his flying beast hold me down so Krol could claw my child from my body, I would have risked using my power to… stop him."

That sounded deadly.

Alifair would not judge a woman protecting her child because she would do the same given the chance to have a family. She felt a stab of remorse at being reminded she'd never have a mate or become pregnant.

She wondered about this woman's gift. "What a shame you can't use your power when you're pregnant."

"True. I've been told to keep my energy in reserve unless I have no option because my child draws on the power to grow. If I weaken myself, I risk being unable to give birth. With my mate nearby with his power, I had no worries. He would see me through the labor and make delivery easier. I'll suffer whatever Krol has in mind so long as I can protect my son." The Gallize woman walked over and eased her heavy body onto the bed.

Alifair tucked a fluffy pillow under her legs as she'd seen healers in her clan do for pregnant women. "How close are you to delivering?"

"Too close. I speak to my son constantly, asking him to stay where he is comfortable and warm. He moves around like a bear in battle sometimes, but when I talk to him, it calms him."

This woman could be giving birth at any time.

"Give me the name of the person you are hunting, Alifair."

"She's called Rez." What did this woman intend to do with that information?

"Let me have a moment to search the castle conversation to see if someone discusses her. I'd like to help you find her if I can."

Words stalled in Alifair's throat at hearing the woman would tap her gift to help her. Blessings came from the strangest places. She would not question this one. She would be bursting with excitement if not for the information coming from a woman in a worse situation than Rez.

Unwilling to disturb her, Alifair moved to the chair and waited silently.

Magdelina slept for ten minutes, and then her eyes flew open. "Help me up."

Rushing over, Alifair put her arm under Magdelina's and used her strength to help her rise to her feet. "Are you okay, Magdelina?"

"Yes. I have information."

"You're kidding." Alifair grinned, feeling lighter than she had in the past month. Her head spun with the hope of finally getting a badly needed break. "Thank you for anything you can tell me."

"You may not be so happy when—"

The door swung open.

Krol stood in the opening. Behind him were two guards. One on each side of Rez, who lost her catatonic zombie look when she lifted her eyes that lit with recognition. She made a heartbreaking cry. *"Alifair!"*

"Oh, Rez," slipped from Alifair's lips before she snapped them shut. Her mother's friend had lost her normally robust look. Now gaunt, her short gray hair hung limp past her face. She looked beaten.

For the first time on this journey, Alifair's anger at Rez got brushed away by empathy over her suffering.

Too late. Krol's face lost its gleam. He swung his gaze between Rez and Alifair. "You two know each other?"

Silence dropped heavy as a lead blanket over the room.

Alifair clenched her jaws, sickened by the mistake, but Rez had no way of knowing she was here. It wouldn't take a rocket scientist, much less an evil lion shifter, to realize why Alifair had been captured.

This couldn't be fixed. There was no way she could convince a lion shifter that Rez was confused.

All this time spent working like an indentured servant to prove she was a nobody they'd captured. All the suffering she and Rez had gone through now wasted because she'd failed to find Rez before today.

Rez closed her eyes, and her face crumpled. "I had no idea. I'm sorry you're here."

Even one more word from either one of them would make this worse.

Alifair couldn't draw in a breath.

Nodding to no one in particular, Krol said, "Come along, Magdelina."

Shaking herself free from panic, Alifair turned to help Magdelina to the door, intending to continue downstairs with her. Maybe Krol would take her to help both women.

But at the door, Krol put a hand up to stop Alifair. "Back away. I have guards to care for her needs."

Alifair stepped back, silently apologizing to Rez and Magdelina that she couldn't be with them.

Once the Gallize woman waddled out the door, Rez offered her arm to the pregnant woman, which she accepted. Good. Maybe they could be of comfort to each other.

As Krol reached for the door handle, Alifair took a step forward again, thinking she would still be expected to fulfill her servant duties.

He shook his head at her. "Stay here."

"What about helping Hessie?" Maybe the reminder that

Hessie oversaw her duties would be enough for him to send her immediately to the kitchen.

Krol's eyes narrowed to slits. "I spoke with Beast."

Words piled up in Alifair's throat. She had to maintain her pretense even as her protective walls began to crumble. She frowned and hoped she sounded surprised, which she was. "Beast talks?"

"Not exactly, but I have had him here for a long time and know how to question Beast." The smug castle king preened with his superiority.

She ceased trying to be casual and waited for Krol to confirm her greatest fear.

It didn't take him long. "I now know who helped Bosse escape, and I will deal with your punishment myself when I return." He snapped the door shut.

Chapter 21

KROL LED THE entourage of his pair of guards and two female captives out of the castle, tapping his fingers on his thigh as the guards loaded them into the wagon.

Rez, the strange woman who had called the servant Alifair, still wore the titanium cuff on one arm that the kidnappers he'd paid had put in place. The metal impeded magic and interfered with shifting into another form. When he received word of a scout finding a woman in Romania rumored to be gifted, he'd paid well for her. At that time, he'd needed something of value to trade with the mage in case the mage had asked for something Krol did not possess in exchange.

Now he stood to receive complete control over the Lammogo just for handing the mage a Gallize mate. He hoped to trade the second woman for an additional favor.

Once again, Krol wondered why the mage wanted this specific shifter mate. It could be nothing more than that Magdelina carried an offspring from mating with a powerful bear shifter.

Over the two days he'd invested bringing her to his castle, he'd felt power oozing from her. Gallize were rumored to be outside the norm for any shifter groups. He'd thought it was nothing more than idle gossip to build fear in others. Laughing to himself, he'd certainly put fear in her when he warned her against making any foolish attempt to attack him or his men.

He'd threatened to gut her and take the unborn child.

Magdelina leaned forward before the door to their wagon closed. Her eyes did not hold the fear he expected. To be honest, she acted far more confidently than he'd expected.

She told him, "You will not touch this child if you think to bargain with the mage who sent you after me. I am clearly far more valuable with a cub on the way. If you harm my baby in any way, I will unleash everything in my power against you and your men." She sat back, never pulling her gaze from Krol.

He swallowed hard. How could she know he bargained with a mage?

Could she read his thoughts?

Locking his jaws tight, a muscle pulsed in his cheek. "I have treated you well."

She arched an eyebrow, mocking his claim. "My mate will tear every limb from your body while you still breathe, then use his filet knife on the rest of your worthless hide."

"Shut up, bitch!"

Losing his temper had been a mistake. She smiled brightly and leaned back, looking for all the world ready to travel.

His eyes slid to the other woman sitting next to her. They both harbored power of some sort, though the Gallize female had to be the stronger of the two.

Should he separate the women?

The one called Rez had made no attempt to escape and had harmed none of his guards or the servant he assigned to feed her daily. She'd been a meek prisoner.

If those two were going to attempt an escape together, they would have done so the moment he announced the servant called Alifair would face his wrath upon returning.

That bitch had been the one to help Bosse escape.

If not for Beast, Krol might never have known who had been behind the cage break.

Beast made no sense to anyone but Krol. That shifter could barely talk in his half-human form and could not communicate the first time Krol questioned him. It wasn't until after Krol had asked every shifter in the cages if they could recognize the human scents around Bosse's cage because he had found none except from the guards who had been on duty and one servant who had no backbone for releasing a shifter. That redheaded servant cried buckets of tears when asked her name.

The shifters had confirmed what he'd detected. The only human scent belonged to the young servant called Linota.

Eriko had told him he questioned that servant and the one who was now locked in the bedroom upstairs, Alifair. Linota had bawled through the whole interview until he gave up.

The one Krol now knew as Alifair had given Eriko the correct answers, but something had made his man suspicious.

Krol asked the guards how often the servant with two different eyes came down. They said daily to deliver their meals.

But none of his shifters had smelled a human scent from her, only a mix of cinnamon and cardamom. That's when Krol realized he'd never paid attention to her scent, not with so many servants in the castle.

He questioned Beast again, this time asking if he had picked up the scent of the one who had helped Bosse escape.

Beast had shaken his head, no.

Krol would have stopped there, but Beast pulled his lips back, exposing fangs in what might be a grin. Trying to gain information from Beast was akin to figuring out a puzzle. It required asking the right questions.

Krol had been patient and asked, "Was there a lingering scent of any kind besides the two guards and the redheaded servant Linota?"

Beast shook his head no—another grisly smile.

Krol asked one more question. "Would you recognize the natural scent of the female servant with two different colored eyes?"

Beast's grin widened. He shook his head once more.

Then Krol grasped what he'd been missing. "You're saying she has *no* natural scent?"

Lifting his wide chin, Beast dropped it to indicate yes.

Krol ordered extra meat delivered to Beast and informed Eriko he was off the hook for failing to find the person they hunted. Eriko was not a shifter to figure out that someone with supernatural ability had tricked them by hiding her scent.

His men had reported being in a deep sleep during the hours of Bosse's escape. Alifair had been a very busy woman the night Bosse ran from the castle.

Why would she do that for a man who didn't even take her with him? Or had she stayed to find her friend Rez?

There would be plenty of time to get more answers and then deal with Alifair when Krol returned. He wanted to be creative when he meted out her punishment.

What better way to keep others in line than to have the entire castle witness her penance?

Chapter 22

B OSSE HUNCHED DOWN behind thick vegetation in the forest where Krol's guards hunted for game when the contract shifters were unavailable.

Adrian and two other Gallize shifters surrounded him, all of them watching for someone from the castle to show up along a beaten-down trail. Before arriving in America, he'd had no idea there was such a thing as a Gallize shifter.

For the moment, he was thankful to have met them if this plan worked out.

Hunched down on the other side of Adrian was the Gallize bear shifter Justin, also in human form. The burly guy who had saved Titan from a killing blow had shown up at Jaz and Adrian's compound with a quick smile upon seeing Bosse healed.

That smile vanished the moment he heard of the mission.

This Gallize bunch united to protect their own, especially the females.

Bosse was all in to save the women.

Vic, the third Gallize shifter, was some odd kind of wolf. Energy pulsed from him, just as powerful as Adrian's, but where Adrian would discuss anything brought up, Vic had a tight-lipped personality. He reminded Bosse of someone who stepped up to do his duty even while questioning everything around him.

That would bother Bosse if not for the absolute respect they held for their Guardian and Adrian, the mission leader.

Those three dressed in camouflage clothing and painted their faces with black smudges.

Jaz had shaved Bosse's beard and cut his hair, dramatically changing his appearance. He liked not looking like a vagabond. With his face uncovered except for a neatly trimmed beard and hair cropped short on the sides with an inch of thick hair left across the top, the guards should not recognize him.

But would Alifair know his face?

Adrian's mate had also provided a pair of jeans with a charcoal hoodie worn over a black T-shirt. She'd given Vic extra clothes for all of them in case they had to shift. He'd opted to be in plain clothes to resemble the simple way guards at the castle dressed. Some wore brown jackets, but they were all expected to be in muted colors around Krol.

No one could outshine the castle peacock.

That rule worked in Bosse's favor. A true king would have his guards in unique uniforms with a family crest. Krol was a family of one and needed no crest in his little empire.

Adrian whispered, "Sure you don't want an earpiece, Bosse?"

"No. If I am caught without one, they will put me in a cage. If I am found with any technology, I'll be killed immediately." He had no plans to be caught, even if it meant blood running in streams from the castle.

He would round up the women and get them out.

There would be no second chances.

He had a piece of paper the size of his hand and a stubby pencil in his pocket, neither of which should concern a guard. To allay Adrian's concerns, Bosse confirmed again, "I will find a window somewhere on the second floor not facing the entrance to send a note." He'd fill in the information the team needed, fold the paper into the shape of an airplane the way they'd shown him, and then toss it out one of the three sides.

Adrian had enough people to station one on every side

of the castle. He muttered, "I wish you'd take a weapon, maybe a knife in your boot."

Bosse explained, "They would take it when I walked up. I'd rather have a weapon available later when I'm back with you."

Justin asked, "How long will it take you to send the message?"

All of this had been discussed, as well as their other plans.

Patience was not something Bosse possessed in any significant quantity. He'd been on his own for so long that he had trouble with constantly reviewing what he intended to do. In fact, he generally figured things out on the fly when he fought, but their Guardian would not have sent anything less than his best to save the female Gallize mate.

He had to respect these three.

If this were how they normally operated, he'd assure them he knew what to do.

Bosse stressed, "As we *discussed on the flight*, if I do not send a message before daylight of finding the women and how I plan to escape, then I'm captured or dead. At that point, you go to plan B."

Making a loud exhale, Vic said, "It's not that we don't trust your ability, Bosse, but we always go over a plan many times so no one forgets even a tiny part. It's easy for something to go wrong right off the bat, making it more difficult to succeed. In our world, the saying is 'the best battle plan does not survive first contact with the enemy.' There are unknown elements we can't account for."

Part of him wanted to be here alone to make changes, but Bosse needed these men. He wanted to bring the women out alive, and Alifair topped that list. "I understand, but I have survived a long time by not making obvious mistakes. I will not forget the plan."

At that moment, Adrian became very still. "I see someone moving through the woods."

They all quieted and watched as one of the smaller guards Bosse recognized strolled along with his rifle in hand. No wonder Krol hired shifters to hunt for game. This man made too much noise. He would not be good at hunting.

Two other men had come along earlier, talking about how they were unhappy that Krol had put out the word he was hiring additional guards.

Bosse had smiled at Krol's stupid move.

Sitting upwind from the guard, all four of them remained very still as the guard heading their way came within six feet of their hiding spot.

If Krol had hired shifter guards, Bosse's group would have had to make different plans or end up discovered easily, but this was a human.

No one else followed.

The instant the guard passed by, Bosse leaped out behind him, slammed his big hands against each side of the guard's head, and knocked him out cold. The guard's rifle hit the ground before Bosse lowered him quietly. He rolled the guard over and slashed his knife across his chest three times.

Not enough to kill him. Between the small amount of blood loss and having his head pounded, he'd be out for a long time.

All of that took seconds. Heaving a deep breath of relief at finally doing something, he turned to find all three Gallize standing behind him.

Having backup was new for him.

Adrian stepped up and checked the guard's pulse. "He's fine."

"He will survive, but he may wake up before I'm able to either return on my own with more information or take the women out of the castle," Bosse reminded him.

"That's not happening." Adrian pulled a long plastic tube from a pocket on his vest. "This is a safe tranquilizer, which should keep him knocked out for a day. You will have escaped or contacted us by then, so we'll know when to insert." Adrian injected the guard, then put away his syringe.

"I would rather get the women out, but I will do whatever is safest for them." Bosse handed Justin the knife and then hooked the rifle over his shoulder. He leaned over and tossed the guard across his shoulder, wrinkling his nose at the smell.

Some humans never bathed.

Adrian said, "Move out. We're headed to take up positions on the three sides of the castle." He extended his hand. "Be careful."

Bosse had refused Corbin's handshake but felt he had to do this to show he was part of the team, something he'd never been. He shook hands with each of them, pulled his hoodie up to shield most of his head, and started walking toward the castle.

He covered the half-mile in a short time, slowing as he approached.

Two guards lifted their rifles and pointed at him. One shouted, "Stop."

Bosse obeyed. He'd seen these two with Krol but never in the cage area.

Guards in their drab clothing walked over to him. "Who are you and… Shit, that's Turner. What'd you do to him?"

"I saved him," Bosse snapped in an insulted tone as he would have if he had saved the guy. "I was on the way here to work for the king." It was a gamble in case men coming to work for Krol had been told to use a code word upon arrival. When no one demanded anything specific, Bosse mentally breathed a sigh of relief. "I came upon your friend while he fought a very strong man dressed in rags. I think he was a bandit, but stronger than a normal man. When I attacked the bandit with a rock, he did not fall. He slashed a knife at both of us, then ran. I was faster at escaping than your man. Before he passed out, I asked where to take him. He said he was a guard for Krol's castle."

Bosse waited silently for one of the guards to decide how to move forward. They looked at each other. One said, "Eriko should be here. He's the only one who would know the new men Krol wanted to hire."

Was Krol not here? Bosse tested his guess by saying, "I wish to speak with Krol about a job."

"He's gone. Won't be back tonight."

The second guard turned to Bosse. "Who sent you here?"

Now Bosse had more information to work with and said, "No one. I heard a man talking to a couple of other guys in a bar about work in this area. No one was interested once the man said it was for this castle. Everyone believes your castle is cursed."

"And that doesn't worry you?"

Allowing a smile to split his face, Bosse laughed. "I don't believe in old wives' tales." He shifted his shoulders. "Your man is still bleeding all over me."

The first guard said, "Let's get him inside to Hessie and see what she can do." He ordered the second guard, "You stay and keep watch on the entrance."

Bosse handed the rifle off to the guard who stayed, a move intended to back up his story. He followed the other guard in charge into the castle. His gut tightened just thinking about entering the closest to hell he hoped he'd never see again.

Titan spoke in his mind. *We will not be captured again.*

That sounded final, and Bosse agreed. *We fight no matter what this time.*

Inside the castle, the guard directed Bosse to wait at the open door to the kitchen, and then he called out, "Hessie! We have an injured guard."

"I am not healer!"

"You want me to tell Krol that's what you said?"

She slammed a pot down on the counter and shuffled over to them.

Servants and guards began coming up from different areas.

Bosse had yet to catch sight of Alifair. He figured she'd be somewhere around the kitchen. It was not lunch yet when she might be feeding the guards in the cage area. A chill slid over his skin just thinking about the cage again. He shook it off.

Pay attention, he told himself.

Hessie ordered, "Let me see him."

Bosse pulled the limp guard off his shoulder and lowered him to the floor. More of Krol's men and servants gathered around, creating a decent-sized crowd.

Still no Alifair. Had she escaped already? He hoped so.

Now he understood why Vic had said things might change regardless of a plan.

"He is not waking," Hessie groused as she slapped his face.

"I wouldn't be hitting him," the guard from outside warned. "If you're the last one attending him and he dies, Krol will not be pleased."

"Shut up," Hessie muttered, but the guard had gotten her full attention. She stopped striking the unconscious man.

As everyone focused on the injured guard, Bosse backed away slowly and looked around. If Alifair were here, she would not be in the room under the stairs she'd told him about. She said it was small, and she did not like being in there.

His eyes strayed to the stairs that led down to the basement, torturing him with the horrors he'd suffered. He shook those memories off, reminding himself he was here to help the Gallize and save the most amazing woman he'd ever met.

He would do anything for Alifair.

Those dreams and his freedom had him rethinking his future. Alifair did not see him as the other shifters. He wanted the chance to prove he was better than a monster and to spend long days holding her... forever. Those were his dreams, which might never be if she only wanted to go home to her people without him once he had her safe.

Mate, Titan whispered in his mind.

Bosse couldn't believe what Titan had said. *What?*

She is our mate. No other woman has made you so happy.

His wolf had never shown an interest in teaming up with a woman. *She's a human*, Bosse argued, even though his foolish mind and heart believed he could make it work.

She is more than human. Then Titan ended the conversation when he said, *We must hurry.*

Bosse had to keep his head turned in the right direction, or this would all be for naught. Where could Alifair be?

With Krol gone, she might be searching for her friend.

Otherwise, she'd be in the middle of this group if she were nearby.

Bosse had to move quickly. He could come back down later to search the ground floor, but he needed to determine if he could get to any of the upstairs windows first before Krol returned.

Also, it seemed that Krol would keep the captured mate up there.

Taking soft steps, he backed away to the stairwell while keeping the crowd in sight. When he reached the stairs, he quietly took them two at a time while watching over his shoulder.

At the top landing, he began searching rooms for the Gallize mate and any available window.

The first three rooms were empty, one of which had to be Krol's area. It had mechanical desk machines in it.

Why? The cage area guards often complained about not having mobile phones or internet service. That had made no sense to Bosse until he'd heard two caged shifters talking about how Krol had the perfectly hidden location being off the grid.

Krol might not be as much off the grid as he thought.

The fourth door was locked. He jiggled the door handle. No point in forcing his way in when two of the other rooms had windows.

Titan said, *I smell lion shifter and guards.*

Bosse stopped. He'd been told Krol was gone. *Is Krol still here?*

No.

Still trying to get the injured man's stink from his nose, Bosse waited for more details from his wolf.

Titan always had sharper senses than his and said, *Another scent of frightened human. Not here either.*

Bosse asked, *Are the scents fresh or old?*

Fresh.

Bosse couldn't help his disappointment over not having found Alifair, even if he wanted her to be safe. He was so confused. *So, no one is here?*

Titan took a moment, then said, *Not true. I hear someone breathing in the room.*

What about a scent from that person? Bosse asked, already trying to figure out his next move.

No scent. Could be her.

Bosse's heart skipped a beat. There was only one *her* that Titan would reference in this situation.

You mean Alifair, right? he clarified.

Maybe. She had no scent.

That sent his heart doing backflips at first, and then it tanked. If she were here, Bosse could think of only one reason she might be locked in a room. Krol had figured out that she'd helped him escape.

He took a deep breath and hoped Alifair was in there, not someone who might scream or shout an alarm. He tapped lightly. "Alifair."

Soft footsteps ran to the door. "Yes?"

He dropped his head to the door, thankful to hear her voice but sick to know she'd been locked up. He should want her far from here, but if he had to choose between her being here at this moment and somewhere unknown, he'd take here.

"It's me. Bosse."

She started crying. "You are captured again?"

He smiled a real one. "No, I'm safe. Move away from the door. I'm coming in."

He waited for a heartbeat, then wrenched the doorknob so hard it broke the locking mechanism. He yanked the bloody jacket off, not wanting to smell like that man, then opened the door and tossed the jacket into a corner.

Alifair in person was the only sight better than the vision of holding her in his dreams. She stared him up and down in confusion, then her eyes widened in shock, no doubt surprised at his change in appearance.

Before he could explain, she made a little squeal and ran for him, leaping up.

He caught her to him, swinging around, surprised every time this woman wanted to touch him. Blown away for her to be in his arms for real. Until she came along, he'd been resigned to living what worthless life he had left as a monster until something deadlier killed him one day.

Never to have anyone care if he lived or died.

She kissed his neck, then his face, then… he leaned down and met her lips. He could live in this moment for the rest of his life. Nothing had ever felt as welcoming as the way Alifair opened to him.

He explored her mouth, sweeping his tongue in to meet hers.

She made the sweetest sound of happiness.

He pulled his mouth away, and she moaned. "No, don't stop. I never thought I'd get to do this before… "

Grinning, he asked, "Before what, sweetness?"

She seemed lost in the moment and murmured, "Before I died."

Chapter 23

ALIFAIR SNAPPED OUT of her stupor of joy when she realized what she'd said.

How could she have blurted out about her upcoming death? She opened her eyes to find Bosse's worried gaze tracking all over her face.

She tried to fix her words. "I just meant I feared we would never see each other again."

That confused him. She hadn't expected him to return this quickly.

"Lie." He handed her words back to her. "You said before you died."

She gave up trying to deter him. Cocking her head, she teased, "I was being an emotional woman." Truth in that. "We're all going to die at some point."

He studied her for a few seconds and declared in a raw voice, "Not you. Not yet."

He sounded horrified and wounded. He'd been so happy holding her, and now she'd ruined it.

"I'm getting you out of here, and you will live a full life," he announced, no longer showing any emotion on his face. "Don't speak of dying again. I won't allow it."

His hands shook with the intensity behind his words.

This man who had lived in a cage and fought monsters daily might not be able to share his feelings like others, but his words and being here said he cared about her. She doubted anyone had ever seen him in a vulnerable moment.

She grabbed his face, kissing him all over. "I'm happy

to do whatever will put that smile back on your face." No matter how determined she'd been to keep her tears held back, one streaked down her cheek. "I'm so glad to see you, but you're in even more danger coming back here."

He brushed the tear away with his thumb, kissed her forehead, and lowered her feet to the floor. "Give me a minute." He took a chair from the table and propped it to keep the door shut. That would notify them of someone trying to come in but not stop a real threat.

Walking back over, he took her hand and led her to the other chair. He sat and pulled her into his lap. "Krol found out you helped me, didn't he?"

He'd already caught her in one lie. "Yes." Just talking about Krol had her worrying about how to get Bosse out of here fast. "Krol may return at any time. You must leave."

"*We* will leave when it's time. I told the guards I had to see Krol about a job, and they said he wouldn't be back tonight. We're safe until tomorrow." Bosse returned to quizzing her about his escape. "How did Krol figure out what you'd done?"

"He talked to Beast." She started nodding at the confusion on his face. "I know. Hard to imagine anyone conversing with Beast, right? Evidently, Krol is the one person who can communicate with Beast."

"I thought that monster was out cold when you came to my cage."

She'd gone over that night many times since Krol left after threatening her. "I'm pretty sure he was knocked out, and I wasn't wearing my cinnamon and cardamom scent."

Bosse stared off at nothing with a thoughtful expression. "That could be it."

"What?"

"You have a way to hide your natural scent, right?"

"Yes. I'm not the only one in my clan who can do that."

Nodding, Bosse said, "Beast had seen you down there before. He's one hundred percent predator and might have realized at some point that you had no human scent."

She frowned. "Is it possible for him to realize that?"

"Sure. My wolf had to tell me you had no human scent." Bosse breathed deeply. "I enjoyed your spice scent and hadn't thought that hard on it, but even now, I still can't pick up your human scent."

"It's a protective spell I've worn since coming here in case I had a chance to run with Rez." Bosse inhaled a deep breath close to her neck, which felt intimate. He smelled terrific and looked different. No shaggy hair and unkempt beard. Where had he been? What had happened to him? She had so many questions, but he stalled them when he ran his fingers over her hair, then pulled a strand to his lips and kissed it.

The hand on her back rubbed slowly up and down, relaxing the tension from her shoulders, then down to her waist, where his hand cupped her closer to him.

She put her hands on his shoulders, trying to decide if she should get off his lap or take advantage of the best spot to sit in this room. She wiggled her bottom to get even more comfortable.

He sucked in a sharp breath and cursed. "Don't do that. I can't think straight."

Her body loved the sound of him excited. She'd never had that effect on another man. She'd only been with one other man, and he'd made her feel inferior as a woman when she'd complained he'd hurt when he'd made love to her.

After the erotic dreams with Bosse, she realized that her first time had not been making love at all—just inconsiderate sex.

On the other hand, maybe Bosse's reaction was nothing more than a natural male reaction to any woman sitting on a man's lap. That made more sense. She was no siren of the night.

She ran her hand down his chest and wished he didn't have so many clothes on.

He grasped her hand. "Careful, sweetness. I can't be distracted when I have men outside the castle waiting to hear from me."

She sat up. "What men?"

"From the pack I found. I'll tell you all about that later, but they needed me to get inside the castle to find another prisoner. I said I would so long as I could rescue you, too."

She wanted that more than anything, but her wants never mattered more than her clan's. Her heart hurt at what she had to admit. She'd seen her future and had to stay the course of her dreams, no matter how unfair they were. "I can't leave the castle."

Chapter 24

"WHAT?" BOSSE COULD not have heard Alifair correctly. Why couldn't she leave the castle? He would not hear of it. "I'm taking you out of here."

She was the reason he'd tasted freedom and might just have a chance at a real life if Adrian's team could succeed. Growing up in his family's pack had been difficult at best, and he'd lived day by day in misery for the past two years, expecting death around every corner.

This woman had given him hope and a reason to believe in a promising future.

Cupping his face between her hands, she said, "You don't know what has happened since you left. Krol left with Rez. I have no idea where he's going or if he will return with her. I can't leave with no idea of how to find her, and I feel my best chance at dreaming where they are is while I'm in this castle."

This complicated things considerably, but not so much that they couldn't find a way out of this mess. "Okay, we can figure this out. I'll be very quiet so you can sleep and dream. Then we'll know where she went."

"It's not that simple." She nibbled on her lower lip, a nervous movement.

"Have you been sleeping?"

"Not really." She raked a handful of hair back from her face.

"Then you must be tired enough to sleep." He didn't understand what was going on, but he now realized he would not get Alifair out of here unless she knew where Rez had gone.

"I've tried. I only dream of… " Her lips pressed closed. Her eyes shifted away from him in a guilty reaction.

Why? Nothing she could do would equal all the shifters he'd been forced to kill over two years.

Her hesitation piqued his interest. He smiled at her. "Are you having erotic dreams?"

Her hand slapped over his mouth, but the rose-colored cheeks gave her away.

Gently moving her hand, he teased her. "So, you *have* been having sexy dreams." He considered just what she might have done in these dreams and if she'd been with anyone other than him. "*Who* was in these dreams with you?"

Her pretty lips parted. "Why are you angry?"

"I'm not angry." That might be a lie. He'd never been jealous in the past, but neither had he felt this ache in his chest for another woman. The rest of the men in this world could have any other woman.

He wanted Alifair.

She started laughing and couldn't stop, even when tears spilled from her eyes.

That just pissed him off more. "What's so damned funny?"

Gasping for air, she finally stopped laughing like she'd lost her mind. "I'm… sorry." She took a deep breath. "It's just your face. You're angry over what might have happened in a dream world."

Yes, he was. His glower did not change.

"Are you jealous?" She seemed happy at that thought.

"Who. Was. In. Your. Dream?" He'd had some steamy dreams with her. He didn't want her having any with another man, even a make-believe man. And he didn't care how ridiculous that sounded even in his head.

Her smile poked at his anger. She chuckled a little, then leaned close to say, "It was you in my dreams, silly, but

I'm not telling you what we were doing." She wrapped her arms around him, laying her head on his chest.

Just him. He probably looked like an idiot with a big grin on his face and didn't care. Happiness had never been part of his world until he met a cookie fairy with the courage of a fierce warrior. He brushed his hand over her hair, kissed her neck, and then nuzzled her hair.

That drew another sweet sound from her.

With more time and privacy, he'd get more than a little mewling from her.

None of that would happen if he couldn't get her out of here before Krol returned. Laying his head on her shoulder, he sighed hard enough to blow her curls around.

She asked, "What's wrong?"

He loved that her question came out breathless. Lifting his head, he told her, "Nothing is wrong. You're just too great a distraction for me when I'm supposed to be on a mission to save you, Rez, *and* another woman."

Alifair's pretty lips puckered in irritation. "What other woman?"

Was *she* jealous?

He felt better now but quickly explained before she got the wrong impression. "That's why I'm here with the three shifters from the United States. They're unusual shifters connected to a brown bear shifter living in Austria. They believe Krol might have kidnapped his pregnant mate."

Her head bobbed excitedly. "That's true."

Bosse stumbled mentally, trying to figure out how she could know this. "Did you dream about this woman?"

"No. I met her in person. Her name is Magdelina. Krol brought her into the castle today and shoved her into this room. I had been in here cleaning for a few hours. He told me to take care of her needs. During the time he left us alone, we became friends of a sort."

"Yes, that is the woman we were told to find." This would be great news for the Gallize men. Bosse couldn't wait to send the paper airplane message. "Where is she?"

"That's what I was explaining. Krol came by a little

over an hour before you opened my door. I had not found Rez, but Magdelina was using her gift to see if she could locate her. She did, but before she could tell me what was happening, Krol opened the door and said Magdelina had to leave with him. Rez stood behind him. She looked up and recognized me before I could stop her from saying my name."

Bosse digested all that and zeroed in on the one thing that worried him the most. "Krol now knows you helped me, and you know Rez, which would clearly mean you were here trying to free her as well."

She lifted her shoulders. "Yes. He's not happy with me at all."

Major understatement. Krol would torture her as an example to the rest of the servants and guards before killing her. Bosse had never wanted to kill Krol more than this minute. Rage roared to life in his chest. "I'm getting you out no matter what you say. If he shows up before that happens, I'm killing him."

Her shoulders drooped. "I can't go back to my people and say I found Rez but gave up on rescuing her. I have invested too much time in this place to walk away now. You said the guards told you Krol would not be back tonight. Let me have another chance to find her before asking me to leave."

Alifair was confused if she thought he would only ask her to leave. He intended to carry her out of here if that was what it took to keep her safe. She could be angry, but she'd be alive to find Rez, and he'd help her.

She started fussing with her hair, pulling it back and twisting it into a knot on her head. Stray curls fell loose. "I look awful. I wish I had known you were coming. I could have washed my face. Like a ninny, I broke down after he took Rez away. Now my eyes are red and swollen."

"Your eyes are extraordinary." He kissed her, a light touch of his lips. "You have faced far worse than others with grace and determination." He held his palm against her face. "Nothing could lessen your beauty."

She snorted at that. "Freedom has clearly ruined your eyesight."

He smiled at hearing her smart off at him. He'd scowled and snarled at everyone for the last couple of years while living on the constant edge of fury to survive.

Then she came along and quieted a monster with homemade cookies.

When Alifair calmed him the first time, he'd soaked it up, then ordered her not to do it again, or he'd end up killed. Looking back, he realized what an ass he'd been.

The energy that filled him with contentment had been a gift, one he would welcome for the rest of his life.

He now realized how futile his words had been.

Only a fool would believe this woman could be ordered to do anything against her will.

Memories of her had kept him going through the days apart. He used a finger to tip her chin up so he could look deep into that stunning gaze. "I have shifter eyesight. It is perfect."

That awarded him an unladylike snort. "It is good to know your ego is still intact."

She could always make him smile.

But her lips lost their happy curve, and her brow furrowed. She swallowed hard. "I'm selfish to be so glad to see you. That you came for me means so much."

He scowled at the reminder of the night he'd escaped. "Of course, I came back. If you had not convinced me I would put you in harm's way by staying, I would not have left you." His voice carried the guilt he'd suffered. "I have never been more miserable than facing every minute without you once I left the castle. By the time I found the shipping docks in Italy, I had decided against boarding a ship. I was coming back for you then."

Her lips parted in surprise. "Then how did you meet those shifters in the States?"

He told her of being captured again, which had her fisting her small hands. "I dreamed nonstop about you, sweetness. You were with me in the cave where I hid the first night, then on the airplane, and even when I woke up with the pack."

Her lips parted in a small gasp.

"What?" He couldn't figure out what he'd said to shock her.

"I had dreams of being with you. I didn't know the last place, but I recall the cave and the airplane."

His skin chilled at her admission. How could they be in each other's same dreams? He'd think on that later. Continuing his story, he explained how one of the shifters waiting outside the castle saved him, and another offered him a place to live. "I am now part of their pack."

"You have a home." She'd said that so quietly, as if she missed not being at her home.

"Do not worry. I will take you back to your home."

The partial smile she offered this time had no heart. "Let's find the women first."

Trying to read her face and reactions was beyond Bosse. He liked straightforward conversation but wanted to comfort her, not add to her stress.

When had he been the one to comfort someone? He found he liked this role. "Exactly. My shifter friends will be thrilled if you can help them. What will it take for you to dream of their location?"

She put her face in her hands. "My dreams feel off track. During all the weeks here, I never dreamed of Rez's specific location inside this castle. I don't know if I can find them." Lifting her head to face him, she had never looked as defeated as now.

Her people expected her to enter a dangerous place and save their leader. Alifair now took on an even greater burden.

He would not allow her to shoulder everyone's problems. And not alone. "The shifter mate is not your responsibility."

"But she is," Alifair argued. "We became friends in a short time. She asked me to give her mate a message because she fears dying before seeing him again."

How could anyone expect her to find a mate not even the

powerful Gallize people could locate at this moment? It wasn't as if she could depend upon a dream for everything.

Taking one of her small hands in his rough one twice the size of hers, he said, "Look at me."

Worried eyes glistened with fears of failure.

He carefully squeezed her fingers. He would not risk trying to sneak out to deliver information to the Gallize shifters. He might not make it back in to find Alifair again, which was unacceptable. He'd take his chances staying here and wait to see if she might just dream of a location.

Then he'd send the flying paper to Adrian and the team.

He spoke confidently, which he felt she needed right now. "You *will* sleep, and I will watch over you. With me to prevent anyone from harming you, try to relax and allow your power to guide you. Whether you find Rez and the mate or not, I must send a message to my team before daylight."

"What happens at daylight?" Her voice lifted with hope.

She had to be calm to sleep and dream. For that reason, he told her as much of the truth as he could.

"They will break us out of here." He did not share the gamble he'd have to make for his friends to have a fighting chance at surviving an attack on the castle.

Worrying her about him being the first to step into the line of fire would not aid her in falling asleep.

Chapter 25

⚬⚬⚬

ALIFAIR COULD NOT stop looking at Bosse. His short hair was a shade darker than before, and his trimmed beard was so different from the man who escaped the castle, but he was the same man who had touched her heart.

And the same man who returned to the last place he'd want to be, risking his freedom and his life to save her.

She hadn't felt this protected since she'd been a child.

He walked into the bathroom and returned with the pottery cup full of water. "I can hear how dry your throat is. Drink this and allow your body to relax."

She hadn't realized how thirsty she was until he handed her the water. She gulped it down and handed the cup back. "Thank you."

"Stretch out on the bed and think about a peaceful setting." He stepped over to put the cup on the table.

That might have worked once with her mind before meeting Bosse.

Every time she closed her eyes now, she saw him, thought of him, wanted him. Her mind was not a peaceful place, and she had him to thank.

She didn't know what had happened to the woman who arrived in this castle as a female focused on only performing a never-ending duty to her clan and who feared shifters. That woman had little confidence with men. She'd avoided thoughts of a future that didn't involve serving her people.

That woman was gone, and she welcomed the change.

She still had her share of insecurities, but not about being with Bosse.

How many times had she regretted not having more time with Bosse?

Too many to count. "Will you lie here with me, Bosse? I'm tired of being alone." Tired of missing him and denying herself any happiness.

Her most recent dream, a nightmare, had been crystal clear about what her future held.

His cocoa-brown eyes revealed some deep thoughts going on behind that gaze.

Why was he hesitating?

Had she only imagined he wanted her because of their dream dates? "What's wrong?"

"Nothing with you." Bosse took slow steps toward her as he talked. "I want you, Alifair, more than you can imagine. I can't forget any detail from my dreams of being with you, but I'm trying to do the right thing here and not be selfish."

Contentment rolled over her at his declaration. "Oh, please, be selfish," she cooed to him.

He paused. "Not with you. I've thought about us being together, but I won't let you make that choice until you're free to choose without all this burden on your shoulders."

Such an honorable shifter. Her people had been wrong to judge all shifters by one. She accepted that she had to let him go after tonight because he had to leave this place before Krol returned. She needed Bosse to be free.

She hoped to discover Rez and Magdelina's location, but even if she didn't, she wanted Bosse to know what she held in her heart and that tomorrow was not promised. "I want to be with you as well. I see your value today, the man standing before me right now, and I want more than just being with you in a dream. We have no idea what will happen tomorrow. Please don't take tonight from me."

That last part sounded too close to begging, but he would crush her if he said no.

He huffed out a sigh that sounded like he was losing an

internal battle, kicked off his soft-soled shoes, and closed the distance to the bed.

She scooted back to make room for him. Excitement shivered through her in anticipation of what would happen next.

Or what she hoped would happen.

Lowering his big body onto the bed, he pulled her to him and rubbed her arm back and forth.

That was nice, but not enough. She put a hand over his chest and felt the strong thump of his heart begin to ramp up. Moving up and over, she lay on his chest and smiled down at the face she'd love to see every day of her life.

"What are you up to?" he asked, his eyes twinkling with humor. He ran his hands up her arms and massaged tight muscles in her shoulders.

"That feels good," she murmured before kissing him and nipping his lip.

His hands stilled.

She rubbed her body over the front of his jeans, where he left no doubt what he wanted.

Bosse released a pained groan.

Her heart pounded, wanting to hear more from him. She wiggled her hips.

Arms and shoulder massage forgotten, he gripped her hair, careful not to hurt her, and used his other hand to unbutton her shirt in record time.

Pulling the rough cloth across her sensitive nipples made her bite down from the crazy mix of pain and pleasure. He grasped a breast, his fingers in a playful mood, trying to drive her crazy, and then he toyed with her nipple.

He might as well have reached deep into her womb and stroked her.

She clenched her legs and leaned into him like the wanton woman she'd become for one man.

This was what she'd been missing. To feel Bosse in real life. Energy rippled through her from his touch. Her breasts had never been more sensitive. She ran her hand over his hair, enjoying the feel of his thick hair and the smooth sides.

She leaned to the side to kiss his ear and then his neck. His heated skin smelled nice and manly. Not a guy dressed up in colognes and fine clothes.

Bosse epitomized masculinity.

Her sexy dreams had left her strung out from wanting him.

Touching him for real was a hundred times more intense.

He released her hair, moving that hand to hike up her skirt. His big hand rubbed her back and kept at it, going lower to pause and softly squeeze her bottom.

She had no complaints. He could do as he pleased.

He caught the top of her panties and pulled them down slowly, taking his time to shift them back and forth as he worked the material out of the way.

Breaths came faster as her heart raced to keep up.

That same excruciatingly slow-moving hand finally reached between her legs and drew a finger through her heat.

Her mind short-circuited. All she could manage to say was, "Yes, there. Oh, please, yes."

He whispered, "This is beautiful. You are beautiful." Kissing her lips, he touched her tongue with his, then pumped his tongue in and out in sync with his finger sliding over her folds.

She couldn't think. Didn't want to think, just feel every move his mouth and fingers made. Trembling racked her body. His hand changed breasts, and a new strobe of heat shot through her core again. She cried out this time.

He quickly rolled her onto her back, lowering his head to kiss her with a force she'd never felt before.

When his hand left her breast, she moaned in protest.

But not for long.

He hooked his fingers under her leg and lifted it up, giving more access to the finger that dove inside her, pulsing slowly.

All thoughts fled her mind. She gripped the sheet, shaking

with need and straining for something just out of her grasp. So close. He stroked her folds while pumping his finger inside her.

She arched up, unsure if she could hang on longer but not wanting him to stop.

Bosse changed the speed of his fingers, driving her insane, and urged her, "Come for me."

Everything inside her broke free like fireworks shooting in every direction. He kept her at that peak, demanding all she could give until her arched back dropped and her legs went limp.

When she could focus her eyes again, she turned to him, and he wrapped her in his arms, murmuring, "You are unlike any other woman. Unmatched."

She'd longed for a man to make her feel like a woman. Not like the one who had cared more about the family she came from than her. The young man who had wooed her to exploit her gift. Then he discovered she was flawed and walked away.

Feeling cared for. That's what she'd wanted to experience at least once in her life. She now realized it would only happen with Bosse.

"Alifair," Bosse murmured and kissed her neck. "You are like touching heaven."

For a man mistreated for so long, he caressed her heart with his words.

She had never thought of herself as ugly, but she was far from a striking beauty. Bosse made her feel special and feminine. She'd been so alone for most of her adult life. With little time left of this life, being alone stopped tonight.

To be perfectly honest, she'd have still done this tonight even if she could live until old age. Her heart whimpered at the idea of not having Bosse forever.

His lips found hers, brushing a sweet kiss over her lips. He lifted away, staring at her with wonder. "How am I here with someone so sweet?"

His vulnerability peeked out.

She fell a little harder for him. "Because you thought of

saving me when another person would have gone running to get out of here without another thought. Because you kissed me that night and stole my breath. Because you like my cookies."

"*Love* your cookies." He brushed his fingers through her hair, then wrapped one lock around his finger.

"Because you make me feel desired," she whispered, sharing her own vulnerability.

"You are." He kissed the tip of her nose. "No words can describe how much I desire you."

She soaked in his words, reveling at the sincerity in them.

Yawning, she shook her head to stay awake. Falling asleep would be rude, but she'd need a little time before round two, or she'd lose all feeling in her legs. Sounding more tired than she wanted, she said, "We're not done."

He quirked an eyebrow at her. "You aren't satisfied?"

Laughing, she said, "Of course, I am. But what about you?"

Bosse became quiet in a thoughtful way. "I can wait. You should rest."

Was he saying that because she'd yawned, or did he want her to sleep and dream of information?

She shouldn't feel hurt. That was ridiculous after he'd shown her that he did want her. He wasn't rejecting her. Maybe he was worrying about his shifter friends outside. He'd made a commitment to them, and that had to be weighing on him.

That had to be it, right?

Chapter 26

———∽∽———

BOSSE STARED AT Alifair in wonder. He'd brought other women to climax, but nothing that intense. Watching her had taken his breath.

When she could keep her eyes open, she watched him as if waiting for him to change his mind about stopping now.

Not tonight. She didn't understand what it would mean for them to join fully. She spoke of having tonight in case there was no other. He would give her many more days of life. Until then, she wasn't ready to make a life decision.

He ached to drive into her and take her as his, but to do so would change everything. It would be unfair of him to expect her to make that decision in the middle of this castle with her determined to fulfill this duty she carried.

He'd seen the shadows under her eyes when he walked in and knew she'd sleep if she relaxed. Touching her had not been the plan. He'd told himself he could live with the dreams and fantasies until he had her somewhere safe.

She had changed his mind.

He had no regrets and considered every time he touched her a gift.

"Are you having performance anxiety?" she asked, trying to smother another yawn. She lifted up and looked specifically at his bulging crotch. "I don't see how that's possible from here."

"You're a mouthy thing," he told her with warmth. She had not been overly mouthy until the night she'd demanded he escape. That's when he noticed she had an iron will, even when she shook with fear.

Stepping off the bed, he said, "I'll be back." Then he went into the bathroom, wanting to ease his painful condition but fearing she'd start doubting herself if he were gone too long.

She could be a force to deal with while putting guards to sleep and releasing a dangerous shifter to escape. But he'd seen a different look on her face tonight. She'd talked with confidence, but her eyes warned she worried about being rejected.

Her emotions sat on her shoulders for all to see. She'd been trying so hard to sound sure of herself for him to tell her no without hurting her.

He'd wanted her even more.

But he could not step over a line. During the flight here with the Gallize shifters, he'd thought this through and accepted that he might not see her again after they found her friend.

He would not leave her feeling slighted by going too far tonight if she had to return to her people without him. They feared shifters.

When he returned to the bed, he had a damp rag in hand. Her eyes were drifting shut again. He hesitated to touch her, but he had to do this for her. As he gently washed her, Alifair's eyes came open. "Oh my."

She said the most unexpected things.

He smiled to himself and finished. "Stay there and keep the bed warm for me."

"I will." Her words slurred with exhaustion. "Your turn. Right?" She'd barely spoken the last word.

With one last look into the room, he confirmed Alifair had fallen asleep. He shucked his clothes in the poor excuse for a bathroom and poured cold water in the basin for a chilly washing. That gave him some relief. He had to get control of his libido before climbing into that bed with her again.

There were limits to what he could refuse after so long without.

As much as he'd like to have taken all she offered, he found watching her climax exhilarating.

Never in his life had he wanted anything as much as Alifair and certainly no other woman. Passing on the chance to fulfill his fantasies and take her completely hurt more than losing a limb but restored a part of his soul.

He dried off and dressed, glad his short hair required so little maintenance, then returned to the bed. He did his best not to disturb her while he stretched out and pulled her over against him.

She snuggled up, murmuring some gibberish.

He smiled and brushed the hair off her face. "You will sleep now."

She tried to make light of being together tonight as if it were the last night of their lives, but Alifair was not like the last woman he'd known who had an ulterior motive for being with him and wanted only sex.

On the other hand, he was not like her people either. He carried the blood of many deaths on his hands.

But he'd made an angel happy tonight.

Chapter 27

ALIFAIR STUDIED THE wagon decorated to appear like a gypsy trader and moving along a beaten-down trail. When sunlight flashed just right, she saw Rez and Magdelina huddled together on one side.

Then a lion stuck its head out the back, looking all around. Had Krol shifted?

She struggled to stay with the wagon, watching for landmarks. Exhaustion pulled at her until she was deep asleep again. Wind howling through the trees dragged her back to the surface.

The dream had returned with the wagon in a different location but still on a dirt path.

The lion jumped from the wagon and trotted close behind, its big head swinging from side to side, then staring up at the overcast sky. Krol's Lammogo flew overhead, a creature that truly should not exist.

Finally, the wagon entered an open area with the crumbling remains of another castle. Is that where they were now?

Bosse stepped into view with his back to her. He was looking for something.

How could he be there and here with her?

A movement in the wagon pulled her attention back to the opening at the rear.

Magdelina stuck her head out and... looked straight at Alifair, who jerked back.

Frowning, Magdelina's lips did not move, but her words

came into Alifair's mind. "We will not arrive there for another day, maybe two."

Alifair hadn't had prophetic dreams since being a child. How could she be projecting to a day or so later? And how was Magdelina talking to her?

"Do not question your gift," Magdelina snapped. "I have heard Krol's thoughts. He is truly crazy. You are seeing what he sees in his mind. This is because you and I have a bridge between our gifts." Her words were fading at the end. "Find us there, or we will be lost forever."

Then she was gone.

Alifair began muttering, frantic to wake and send Bosse to save them.

His hands rubbed softly along her back, and he murmured for her to sleep. He kept doing that until she went all the way under again.

She struggled to dream again and finally gave up when her mind wouldn't leave her alone.

Draped across Bosse's broad chest, Alifair could sleep for days after he'd drained the stress from her body. Well, she could have if guilt hadn't started pecking at her. First, she hadn't done anything nice for him after the altered-state climax he'd given her. He had to have been in pain last night.

Second, it wasn't as if she didn't deserve this time with him, but Rez needed her. Magdelina, too.

Alifair could not forget why she came here.

Bosse's fingers carefully pulled through her hair and massaged her neck, sidetracking her good intentions to wake up. She wanted so much more time with him, but she'd accept the stolen minutes now to hold onto until the end.

She had to get her thoughts aligned and be careful about what insights she shared with Bosse.

She had to keep her impending death to herself, or he would try to save her. She wanted to doubt that one prophecy, but those specific dreams had taught her long ago about reality.

The last time she saw her mother, she'd begged her not to leave their house after Alifair had dreamed of her mother's death. Her mother had scolded her for even suggesting she turn her back on saving three children. Alifair had tried to explain that hadn't been her intention. She just could not lose the only family she had left.

Her mother had hugged her and said she understood. She then dismissed the dream by saying just because Alifair had dreamed of her father's death, and it had come to fruition, didn't mean the same would happen to her.

Alifair's magic had been sporadic and undependable from time to time, so no one put a lot of stock in her dreams. She knew in her heart that her death dreams were different. Perfectly clear, with no question about the outcome. A childhood friend had died after walking up on a bear and her cubs, just as Alifair had seen in the first death dream. Those were the only ones that had been prophetic and did not happen in real time.

Or maybe after suffering those losses, her mind had refused to look ahead.

In the end, her mother was captured and killed after freeing the children.

She'd failed her mother by not convincing her of the danger. She would not fail her mother's legacy by letting down Rez and the clan.

Did that brief dream with Magdelina mean she knew how to find them?

Or had it been born of wishful thinking?

The pregnant mate had told her to believe and trust her gift. To be honest, she had no other choice, having only received one dream.

So many people depended on her, including Bosse, even if he did not realize it.

She would not fail Bosse either. He would live to enjoy a life of freedom.

Until he could escape and go after Rez and Magdelina, Alifair would hold onto him every second she could, then send him on his way to finish a duty on which she may have reached her limits.

He would argue. She'd have to figure out how to make him leave again.

That seemed impossible, but she had seen her body torn open and blood running freely. It would be better for that to happen without Bosse present.

For him to know of her coming death and witnessing it in person would not lessen his grief.

She had not seen who killed her but, at this point, believed it had to be Krol. Blood ran in a stream down the front of her. The pain had been unbearable. Then everything had gone dark.

"Your mind is too busy for you to be sleeping," Bosse said in the gravelly voice of a tired man.

Had he not slept?

Time to girl up and tell him what she'd seen about Rez and Magdelina. Lifting her head from his chest, she said, "I'm trying to wake up."

"You slept soundly." His hand had moved from her back to her shoulder, gently working the muscles.

"Keep that up, and I'll probably pass out."

That stilled his hand.

She laughed. "You aren't doing anything wrong. I'm just exhausted from so little sleep and working around this place. Then you turned me into a limp noodle. I'd love some tea, but we don't have room service in this dive."

Eyes alight with humor, he put his hand back on her shoulder. "You say funny things. What is this room service?"

That's right. He grew up in an awful pack in the woods, then lived as a caged animal in a pretend-medieval world. He had not been exposed to many modern features. "It's something guests enjoy in a nice hotel, where people stay for a day or more while traveling. You can call to request a meal and drinks be sent to your room."

"Sounds lazy. I'd rather stay at home and eat a cooked meal."

Just that easily, he made staying at home sound ten times better than traveling. She couldn't stall much longer. "I did dream."

His face went from lighthearted to focused in three seconds. "Good news?"

"I think so. It's odd because I used to only dream in advance when I was younger. Generally, I dream in real time these days, but I saw where Magdelina and Rez are traveling to in a day or two, not where they are right now."

Bosse listened intently, looking away for a moment, then back. "You think we can find this place?"

How do I answer him without lying about it not being us? "I think someone here knows where it is. If Krol is traveling to another spot first, then ending up at these ancient ruins, it feels like he can't be traveling out of the country on the first leg of his trip."

"A wagon?" Bosse stepped away from the bed as if needing to pace.

"Yes, he's got the women in one decorated to look like a gypsy merchant wagon. It appears he's keeping the wagon on dirt roads, which means he's avoiding highways."

"That makes sense." Pausing to stare at nothing meant Bosse was thinking again. "How sure are you about what you saw?"

She considered several replies and dismissed all of them.

The best way to convince him was by giving him all she knew. "You were in this location. I saw you for just a moment before it all ended, but you were there. I dreamed in the first two weeks here that you would save Rez, but I had not known it would be somewhere other than this castle. I also saw you step in to stop a threat from getting to her. Maybe that's how she gets away. Even when you left, I couldn't shake the feeling that you might still return to save Rez."

Bosse had angled his body to face her, not breaking eye contact. "When did you first dream of me saving Rez?"

Yay! He believed her. She jumped up and realized she had not dressed. With her back to him, she pulled her shirt and skirt on while explaining, "It was about a week before I finally came up with a way to get into your cage with no one watching." That took a load of pressure off her chest.

Silence pulled her around as she finished buttoning her shirt.

This version of a quiet Bosse began to worry her.

What was going on in his mind?

Feeling suddenly nervous, she kept talking. "I'm surprised I did not dream of Magdelina before now, but she connected to me in this last dream. That's how I figured out what was going on. She told me to trust my gift. That woman has a buttload of power compared to mine. Her energy is even more intense than my mother's. It's hard to put into words. She's something called a Gallize."

That surprised him out of his silence. "How do you know this? I was told that Gallize is a big secret I could not talk about."

He knew about Gallize? Okay, that was unexpected. "It's strange. Magdelina held my hands to give me a message for her mate that could not be written down but instead stayed in my head. She thinks I'll see her mate. I told her I doubted that would happen. I haven't seen any of that in a dream, but I wanted to help her if I could."

"Like you want to help Rez."

Concern churned in her gut at the way he'd said that. "Yes, I told you that's why I let Krol's men bring me to this castle. Rez is our clan's leader. She was also my mother's best friend."

"This is the first time you told me you had a dream that showed me saving Rez."

True, but why did it sound like bad news the way he said it? "Yes."

He strode over to the table, digging out a paper and pencil from his pocket before sitting.

Feeling embarrassed for some reason, she walked over and put a hand on his shoulder. "What is the plan to save Magdelina?"

"I will send a note to my shifter friends waiting outside

the wall. They need to know Magdelina left with Krol." His curt answer didn't fit with the man who held her last night, but Alifair had to admit they hadn't spent enough time together to understand each other's moods.

She asked, "Will they leave without you? You can't be here when Krol comes back for me."

Bosse stopped writing and ran his fingers over his hair. It took him a minute to look up at her and reply. "Do you really think I will leave you again? I could not live with myself the first time. I'm here until I can get you out. We go *together*."

No, she had to make him understand what had to be done. "Your friends are going to hunt for Magdelina, right?"

"Yes."

"You have to be with them," she stated in a no-argument-accepted voice.

"I said I would search for their missing mate first, which I did. She is not here. I also told them I would not leave without you."

She sat up, hating that she had to drive him away. "You have to go without me."

Another stretch of quiet, warning her she had screwed up somewhere.

The confusion on his face hurt to watch. He blinked slowly as if trying to translate her words into something he could understand. "What's this all about? No woman is more important to me than you."

Tears threatened to break free at what sounded like a vow, but she forced them to stay put. She could not do these things and allow her emotions to interfere. How could she make him understand? "Please hear what I'm trying to say. I need your help to save Rez."

His expression didn't change at first. Then a new expression settled on Bosse's face. She couldn't read it but had a bad feeling about the sudden change.

He stated, "I needed to be free to help Rez."

"Yes." She grasped for anything that would clear this up. "But she is not here."

Sucking in a deep breath, Alifair hoped she could get him on the same page with her. "No. Regardless of where she is, I dreamed you would save her or maybe protect her from a threat, and she managed to escape that way. And now I've seen you at the ruins where the women are headed. You must go with your friends to save Rez and Magdelina."

He crossed his arms over his chest. "Then I will take you with me to rescue her."

Shaking her head, she smiled sadly at him. "I wasn't in that dream—only you and Rez. Our clan needs her. She is the leader and healer. I came here only to find her and send her back home. I can't fail at this point. I can't go with you."

"Make me understand because I do not."

She scrubbed her eyes and pushed the hair back from her face. This would be the end of what little they'd had. "Unlike my erratic magic gift, dreams like the one last night are clear and often true. I've had a few go off-target, but that was back when I was younger. Rez needs you. If I go with you, that might change the outcome of the dream. You might not save Rez."

He put a hand over his eyes. "I do not believe this."

"You have to, please," she urged.

As he uncovered his eyes, his gaze lost all understanding, leaving only anger. "Was your dream the only reason you came to me in the cage?"

Her face fell. That wasn't fair. Everything happened quickly leading up to that night, but she had wanted him to be free.

He would hear a lie. "Uhm, yes. I had that dream first. I had to do my duty and knew you were part of the plan, but …" She trailed off with realization. She couldn't believe what he might be thinking. "That doesn't mean being with you isn't special to me."

"I understand. You freed me so I would come back to save Rez," he concluded, not addressing her last words.

She'd hurt him. The one person she would step into harm's way to save. "It isn't the way it sounds."

His thick eyebrow lifted in challenge. "You say you cannot go with me. Is my number one goal to save Rez? Yes or no?"

She sat quietly, hoping he'd see the corner she'd backed herself into.

Glancing away as if he couldn't face her answer, he asked, "If I leave here without you, then you will be happy."

That sounded so wrong, but it was a fact, even if she would be heartsick. "None of this makes me happy." That was the truth. "All I'm saying is that I don't think I should be there for the rescue to be successful."

"Why is this woman's life more important than yours?"

His question threw her a curve. "She's… necessary to the future of our clan."

"But your people sent you into danger to free another woman with no idea if someone like Krol would have killed you by now."

She'd had her own long nights thinking about her place in the universe, but in the end, she'd accepted her duty. With her mother gone, no one else stood in line protect her people.

She had to take her place. She would show she had honor and do her duty.

Trying one last time, she explained, "I know you don't understand, but Rez and I are both important to our people. We have different gifts. Rez's gift is one of seeing the future of our clan and suggesting choices to be made that would keep us safe, plus showing our people how to make the clan stronger. She took our people from scraping out a living and barely able to feed ourselves to a thriving community. I come from a long line of protectors. Now that they're all gone, that's my role. I can't do what Rez can for our people, but I can do all in my power to send her home for them."

He sat there with his massive forearms still crossed, breathing slowly and taking her in for a long time.

Bosse asked, "Who takes your place when you die?"

Had he guessed about her death?

No, he was just trying to confuse her. "Another will have to step in my place." Not anytime soon since she was the last of her bloodline, but she could only hope someone else would become the new protector.

"I've heard enough. I need to send my message."

His flat tone cut her like a newly honed blade.

She didn't want to part this way. She tried not to show the pain ripping through her.

When he turned to write on the paper, she took that minute to freshen up, hoping the world would right itself while she was gone. She stalked into the bathroom and shut the door. Would he leave before she came out?

Using the basin to splash her face and wash her body the best she could, she grabbed the towel Bosse had left folded to wipe away any water. She felt a little better, but nothing could fix the stricken expression staring back at her from the oval mirror.

She sure as heck never saw this kink in her plans coming.

When she walked back into the room, Bosse put down his pencil. He folded his message into the shape of a paper airplane.

What was he doing with that? "Are you telling your shifter friends you'll meet them outside?"

"I will not bother you with my plans since you never told me *all* of yours."

Her heart whined from that blow. She longed to tell him she never wanted him to leave, that all she wished for was to be with him.

Then what? That would be the opposite of what she'd just said to convince him to leave.

Should she have this wonderful man stay here to not only witness her death but to be killed as well?

No, she would be stronger than that to save the man she loved.

Loved?

Yes, her poor heart sang at that thought.

Now she'd have to watch him leave and never be able to tell him she loved him.

This got worse by the minute.

If she admitted that she'd been angry at her people since being brought into Krol's castle, she and Bosse would be right back where they were twenty minutes ago.

She could not wound him all over again. She also might fold and say she'd go with him, which couldn't happen now. She would not put her happiness over Rez's safety.

Chapter 28

BOSSE TOLD ALIFAIR, "Stay here. I'll be back quickly." Not wanting to hear more, he opened the door to check the hallway in both directions before slipping out. He'd put on his soft-bottom shoes and walked quietly across the wide-paneled wood floor to the bedroom with the window.

His insides warred with trying to decide if he had been used yet again. He had little experience with honest people. Adrian and the Gallize shifters treated him fairly, even if he now served a purpose for them. Had he not put his foot down, they would have come without him to find Magdelina.

He understood that with no problem. They'd been honest with him from the start, just as he had been honest with them.

What about Alifair?

Women had deceived him before. He questioned this deep need he felt for Alifair and how he might be blind to her ways. She had magic and had tricked the guards into sleeping the night she came to free him. She was clearly desperate to save her friend and had known he'd return at some point if he were the one to save Rez.

Had she been using him? Was that why she had been so nice to him? Was that why she opened her body to him?

Just thinking that felt as if he betrayed her.

His mind banged around, confused. He wanted Alifair

and was determined to keep her safe, but could he force her to go with him? Should that be necessary?

He put his hand on the doorknob when Titan spoke up. *Has she lied to you?*

Bosse paused to think on all she'd said. *No, but you were the one who said she told the truth while keeping something hidden. That is lying by omission.*

True.

If not for needing to get this message out ahead of daylight, which he believed would come in about two hours, he'd have continued the conversation with Titan.

Hurrying over to the window, he searched for guards below. Krol mainly wanted the front gate secured, having no concern about someone scaling the tall walls on the sides.

He had one chance to get this to Adrian's group.

Calming himself with several long breaths, he flicked the message out the window the way Adrian had made him practice on the way here.

The tiny gliding paper sailed higher than he expected. Would it land in tree branches?

As it crossed over the wall, the triangle-shaped paper arced down, landing on the ground but out of Bosse's sight. He saw no one emerge from the tree line, but neither had he expected that bunch to expose their presence.

His message had been short to fit on the paper:

I have a way to find the mate. Not enough space to explain. I can't get out of here without help. The castle sleeps. You can attack as soon as fifteen minutes after finding this. I will be ready on the inside.

That would give Adrian's men the advantage of surprise and darkness.

Bosse would likely not be as lucky since the guards inside carried titanium ammo and arrows, but he would do his part.

Chapter 29

B Y THE TIME Bosse returned to the room, Alifair had gone through a flurry of emotions, from trying to convince him he was wrong to surprise at his reaction to feeling annoyed that he couldn't hear how much she cared about him.

Now she waited to see if he'd come to his senses.

Bosse closed the door behind him and faced her. He'd always appeared confident about what he was going to do, unlike now when he stared at the floor.

She refused to say another word until he figured out that, yes, she originally came to him because he could help, but she'd been watching him for weeks. She'd gotten to know him long before they talked.

Then he had done the one thing she hadn't expected.

When she'd tried to hurry him out of the castle, he refused to go without her. A man who had been caged for years hesitated to escape. He'd been adamant about not leaving her behind. She hadn't realized until that moment how much she needed to know someone thought her life was important.

That she should come first.

She'd made up her mind that night to help him escape even while doubting he could return to help Rez after reaching America. Then he'd burrowed into her heart with that one action. Any other prisoner who could escape would have left her in their dust without a second thought.

Bosse had lived this hell for twenty-four long months, day in and day out, yet he struggled to convince her to go with him. When she told him he'd put her in danger, he said he'd find her in America.

That was a man of integrity she'd never known.

How could she reach him so he wouldn't leave here angry with her?

Clearing his throat, he said, "I've sent a message for my friends to come inside in fifteen minutes, but it is probably closer to twelve minutes by now. I want you to stay here until I return. Bar the door with a chair, and do not open it to anyone else."

Her heart leaped. He would come back to her.

"Not just me. If someone named Adrian, Justin, or Vic comes here, then open the door."

A lump lodged in her throat. "Why would they be here instead of you?"

"I'm only saying in case I can't get back up here before one of them."

She didn't need a dream to know he was saying in case he died. "Wait up here with me."

"I will not abandon the men who brought me here." He opened the door.

"Bosse, wait."

"Why?"

If she told him she loved him, he would think she was just saying it and not trust her at all. "Be careful."

Nodding, he never looked back as he stepped out and closed the door. His muffled voice came through the door. "Put the chair in place."

She grabbed a chair and dragged it over, shoving it under the lock. "It's in place."

Leaning close to put her ear against the door, she listened. Had he left? Being a shifter, he could walk as quietly as a ghost, especially in the shoes he wore. She counted to one hundred, then pulled the chair aside.

She peeked into the hallway. No one was there. Closing the door softly, she tried to be quiet but had to get down there to find out what Bosse intended to do. The guards used titanium ammo. They could kill him.

Instead of taking the back stairs she'd initially used to reach this level, she headed for the stairs that descended directly into the main room. Taking a corner too quickly, she almost fell when she spun back around to hide.

Bosse crept halfway down the stairs and stopped, leaning into the shadows.

The only lights below were two oil lamps hanging near the large entrance doors.

She held her breath, peeking around the corner. What did he think he could do? Ten guards slept along the walls of the large room with rifles at their sides.

Had it been fifteen minutes yet?

Where were his shifter friends?

She debated what she could do to help him, but she'd have to know what kind of help he needed.

The doors burst open, and three big men rushed in, shooting the first three guards who jumped up, scrambling for their weapons.

But no one was bleeding. Had Bosse's friends missed? No. The guards dropped their rifles, wobbled around, and hit the floor. Those three hadn't waited to see the result. They were coming in like a military team.

Bosse put his hand on the wooden rail and leaped over, shouting as he landed. "I am the wolf shifter. Put down your weapons, or I'll turn my wolf loose!"

By then, more half-awake guards were up and fumbling. They froze at Bosse's yell and turned to him, looking terrified.

Still too many rifles. Someone would shoot.

She searched her mind for what to do and snapped her fingers. Lifting her voice, she called out a spell to make the triggers on rifles held by guards freeze in place. Though her words had rung clearly through the main hall, she feared her magic had failed. Should she keep yelling it, or would she impact weapons Bosse's friends carried by accident?

Guards lifted their rifles quickly to shoot Bosse, then

pulled the weapons back down. They yanked on the triggers and shook the rifles, trying to make them work.

Shocked at the result, she stepped farther down the steps, ready to do more.

Guards poured in through the kitchen from outside.

Two of Bosse's friends worked their way through the room, tackling guards and ripping the useless rifles from their hands. Bosse started toward them.

The third friend, a behemoth of a guy, shouted something at Bosse and ran past him.

Those watching the cage area raced up from the basement, some with crossbows lifted to shoot.

Alifair pointed her hands at the basement guards. She called out a spell to make the arm muscles in those holding crossbows turn rubbery. Nothing happened. Only guards carried the crossbows, so this time, she chanted louder and louder, hoping to be heard over the din of noise.

One of the guards released his crossbow, and then his arms fell limp at his sides. He stared at his weapon as if he didn't understand.

Two more guards ran past him, unharmed by her magic. Damn!

As they clashed with the big guy Bosse knew, she chanted again and put more force into her voice, booming her spell. It was almost as if she could hear Magdelina ordering her to believe in her gift.

Bosse changed directions, running over to help his friend, who had knocked one crossbow out of a guard's hands. His friend snatched away the second guard's crossbow, then dropped it with his arms falling loose.

Knocking the empty-handed guard down with one blow, Bosse turned to find another, lifting to shoot an arrow at his friend. Snarling, Bosse lifted the guard, who dropped his crossbow and threw him on top of the unconscious one.

He shook his friend, whose arms didn't move, then he glanced at the stairs. He must have figured out what she was doing.

"Free this one from magic. We need Justin."

"Sorry." She panicked and changed her chant, spewing it as fast as possible. Please tell her she didn't get it wrong and do something awful to Justin and Bosse.

Justin came alive with a roar and swung around on Bosse with a fist drawn back.

"Not me!" Bosse shouted. "I'm on your side."

Justin shook it off and jumped back into the fray.

Alifair looked up as more guards ran into the room from the front doors, some carrying blades as long as their forearms. How many had Krol hidden around his fortress?

Bosse shouted at Alifair, "Stay out of this. Go hide."

Did he really think she'd do that? He started toward her, looking terrified when she pointed past him. "Look out behind you. Two more coming from the kitchen!"

He had lightning reflexes, but she'd never seen anyone move so fast as when he went after the new guards. Justin and Bosse worked their way through them, fighting entirely in human form when they would be impossible to defeat in animal form.

They turned to help the other two near the entrance to the hall.

That allowed a guard to run from the hallway to her room and race across to take the steps to the basement cage area.

What was he doing?

An earth-shattering sound of roaring and screeching animals erupted, then the scream of a human. Had that stupid guard thought he could release caged shifters, and they'd just let him live?

A giant white tiger shifter burst from the basement steps first with a raging black bear on steroids right behind, then a honey badger the size of a Volkswagen and a buffalo like she'd seen in the western states, but this one was twice as big as the tiger.

With Justin knocking the heads of two guards together, the last of Krol's men went down. She suspected the other two friends had shot many of them with some drug. Add that to what she'd done, and they'd won the battle with the humans.

She screamed, "The shifters are loose!"

In less than a heartbeat, Justin shifted into a gigantic grizzly bear. Bosse gave Titan his body. Those two massive animals crashed into those escaping the cages. With claws flying and teeth ripping chunks out of bodies, the sound was horrific.

Bosse's other two friends remained in human form but stood ready to stop whatever tried to make a run for the front doors.

While all that went on, up came a repulsive nightmare in half-human form.

Beast had shifted more into a man than an animal, but he was still no human anyone would recognize. The four shifters Bosse and Justin battled blocked his exit to the front doors.

Moving with stealth, Beast turned left and headed for the rear exit that Alifair had only discovered the day she'd picked fruit and vegetables for Kylie.

Beast paused at the bottom of the steps and raised his unholy gaze. He opened his mouth in a sickly smile, showing off fangs as long as her fingers.

Her body froze with fear.

One of the animals fighting screamed. Alifair didn't think that was how a grizzly or Titan would sound. She couldn't move her eyes from Beast.

She gripped the railing as a lifeline.

Running upstairs would not save her.

If she yelled for Bosse and distracted him, he'd be vulnerable to attack.

Her heart slammed into her chest. Another animal made a horrific sound she couldn't identify and would never escape her mind. Would Beast jump in to kill Bosse if he caught Bosse focused on another shifter?

No, he stayed at the bottom of the steps, staring at her with putrid orange eyes.

He wanted her.

She had accepted her upcoming death but never wanted to die as Beast's prey.

He lifted his chin at her as if to say, "Next time." Then he was gone.

She folded to her knees and had to sit down.

All the sounds blurred into a fog of droning noise. She couldn't think or speak. She shook so hard her teeth clattered. One thing became crystal clear. She'd thought she was ready to die but had never really faced that reality until just now.

"Alifair," whispered into her fog. "Alifair, are you okay?"

She fought her way back to full consciousness to find Bosse squatting in front of her. He touched her face with his fingertips. "Are you hurt?"

"No, I just… uh… Beast… He escaped." She blinked, trying to bring her brain back online.

"Shit." Lowering his hand, Bosse said, "We got lucky all the shifters weren't turned loose."

Still breathing hard, she said, "A guard snuck down to release them, but I don't think he lasted thirty seconds. Beast probably got him before he could open all the cages." She finally noticed Bosse was naked. "You need clothes."

He let out a loud sigh. "Naked is not a new experience for me," he joked.

Happy to see him no longer angry, she glanced around and said, "Your friend Justin needs clothes, too."

Bosse's head snapped to his left. "Justin, turn around."

"Why?"

"Just do it!"

Justin noticed Alifair and walked away, shaking his head.

"Don't look at him," Bosse ordered.

"Don't tell me what to do," she snapped right back. "I've seen naked men here for a month."

"I don't want to hear that. No more looking at naked men."

She rolled her eyes at him. "When will you learn that I don't like orders?"

Bosse clammed up, but that did not silence his disgruntled breathing.

His two friends, in human form and still dressed, strode

through the massacre of four animals, stopping close enough to talk to Bosse. "Is she okay?"

"Yes, I am," Alifair replied. "I'm Alifair."

Bosse pointed at one of the two men. "That's Adrian, and the other one is Vic."

Vic had a backpack strapped on and his face arranged in a flat look as if he were discontent with something.

"What happens now?" Alifair asked.

Adrian took in the wrecked hall and asked, "Who was in charge of these guards?"

"Eriko." Bosse pointed at a body slumped next to the kitchen doorway. "You got him with a drug shot."

"We need to talk to him." Adrian asked Vic, "You got clothes for Justin and Bosse, right?"

"Hell, I guess so." Vic had a deep voice and slight twang like he was from somewhere south back in the States, maybe Georgia or Tennessee. He lowered his backpack and dug out warm-up pants and T-shirts he tossed to Bosse and Justin. He told Adrian, "That leaves one full set and the small vacuum-packed bags for any more wardrobe changes."

"Got it. Let's talk to Eriko," Adrian said, leading the way with Vic behind him.

"You may want to wash the blood off first," Alifair suggested before Bosse put on pants that appeared to be made for athletes.

"You're right. I don't want to go upstairs in case they need me down here."

"There's a big sink in the kitchen with buckets of clean water next to it on the floor." She stood on wobbly legs but held onto the railing as she followed Bosse to the kitchen.

By the time he'd finished cleaning up and put on the clothes, which included a black T-shirt, Adrian and Vic had roused Eriko.

She stepped from the kitchen in time to hear Eriko say, "I'm telling you nothing." Eriko turned to her. "Krol should have killed you before he left, you bitch."

Bosse stepped out and slapped his head so hard it would

have spun around if not for being against a wall. "Say one more word to her, and I'll take your head off this time."

Lifting a hand to wipe the blood from his mouth, Eriko glared at her but said nothing more.

Vic sounded tired and impatient when he told Krol's right-hand man, "You're gonna talk and soon. We don't have time to waste on you."

Squatted down in front of Eriko, Adrian informed him, "We're in a hurry, and my friend here has never failed to get answers."

"I'm not afraid of you." Sweat rolled off Eriko's chin, making him a liar that Alifair didn't have to be a shifter to realize.

Vic shook his head and said, "I'll give you a demonstration." He walked over and shook a guard back to life. The guy was disoriented and mumbling, "Krol's going to kill you."

Vic looked back at Eriko. "Pay attention to his crotch." Then he focused on the confused guard who suddenly jerked awake and screamed, grabbing himself. He rolled into a ball, crying and rocking.

Eriko's jaw went slack.

Alifair's did, too.

Vic walked back over and announced, "There are no second chances. I don't have that kind of patience. When you're asked a question, you answer immediately. This is your only warning. If you hesitate, I'll give you a nudge to wake you up. Oh, and just in case you missed the show while you were napping, we're all shifters. A lie gets you the same treatment as not answering fast enough."

Chapter 30

BOSSE HAD NEVER been around shifters like these. How had Vic used his mind to strike pain in the still-keening guard?

Eriko, Krol's arrogant lead guard, began to tremble. "I'll talk."

Vic shifted his stance to be even cockier. "Yeah, I thought so."

Adrian started hammering Eriko with questions. "What is Krol doing with those two women?"

"He didn't tell me," Eriko replied, then quickly added, "But he said he was going to Košice for temporary guards called wilkotauks to take on his trip. Said he would not bring the wilkotauks with him when he returned in three to five days."

"What are wilkotauks?"

"Powerful werewolves. Assassins."

Adrian smirked. "Powerful compared to what?"

"I've never seen one. I just heard they are witch-born."

That sounded challenging, but Adrian and his people were Gallize. Bosse asked, "Why does he need assassin werewolves?"

Alifair offered, "Does it have to do with that Lammogo thing?"

Eriko almost hesitated but took one look at Vic and kept talking. "Krol recently made a trip and came back with the Lammogo. I think he owes something to the person who gave him the pet. I'm only guessing, but it might involve using the pregnant woman in trade because he took the Lammogo with him and brought her back. Whoever made that flying creature must have strong magic. Krol probably does not trust him."

"Where is he meeting that person?"

Eriko just lifted his shoulders.

Vic snapped his fingers in front of Eriko's face.

The guard clutched his head and cried out, "*Stop!* My head will explode. *Stop!*"

Once the guard calmed down, Vic said, "That is the only nudge you'll get. The next delay will result in major pain."

Red flooded Eriko's face. He breathed as if his lungs were quitting on him. "Please don't hurt me. I don't know where that meeting will happen, only where he's headed to get the wilkotauks. I'll draw you a map to the estate, which is hidden from the road."

Justin walked up wearing clothes similar to Bosse's. He dug out a pen and paper, handing it to Krol's right-hand man.

Eriko's hand shook as he drew the map. He told them, "Krol can't use the major highway because the women are in a horse-drawn wagon. It looks like a gypsy drifter. These are the trails he'll have to use." He added some lines that paralleled the highways vehicles used most of the time, allowing Krol to avoid being on public roads.

Adrian stood and cast a look around the main hall. "We need somewhere to put them until a team can get here."

Alifair asked, "What about the female servants? They're innocent in all this and are probably hiding in their rooms."

"Are they a danger to anyone?" Justin asked.

"No." Alifair moved her lips as if counting to herself. "The woman in charge of the servants is very loyal to Krol, though. She probably can't get word to him because he doesn't use a mobile phone, but she might undermine anything you left in place. The other nine women are captives. What will happen to them?"

Scratching his head, Adrian said, "First, we'll need a secure place to hold sixteen guards but keep them safe until our people arrive. If the women are willing to stay put, our people will be here before dark and can arrange to send them home."

Those words lifted Alifair's tired spirit. "I'll tell them, but I'm not talking to Hessie, the one I warned you about. That's up to one of you."

Smiling because he had the perfect answer, Bosse said, "There should be five empty shifter cages in the basement for the guards."

Eriko groaned but clamped his lips shut quickly.

Justin gave him a questioning look. "Five? You and I fought four."

That ruined Bosse's good mood. "Unfortunately, the worst one escaped." He told them about Beast and how dangerous that shifter could be. "I'd like to think he'd head toward whatever is home, but that could be a continent away. Still, I don't think he'll come back here."

His gaze sliced over at Alifair. She rubbed her arms as if cold, but it was not cold in here. Beast had scared her. She'd have a hard time closing her eyes again in this country with that thing loose.

Wanting to give her a task to keep her mind off Beast, Bosse suggested, "Why don't you go with Justin to talk to the women and get them set?"

"Good idea."

Justin had given Bosse a glare loaded with a look of are-you-giving-me-orders? When Alifair turned toward the hall by the stairs where she'd had a room, Bosse caught Justin's eye and mouthed, *Please.*

Nodding that he understood, Justin went off with Alifair.

Bosse could get used to working with a team. He, Vic, and Adrian herded the guards who had come around down to the basement, then carried the others and piled them into cages.

He could do without the smell of dead animals in the hall. "We should probably burn these carcasses."

"I was thinking the same thing," Vic concurred. He

crossed the room and opened the big front doors. "Let's toss them out front."

While Bosse and Adrian dragged bodies into a pile outside, Vic found cooking oil in the kitchen, then gathered dead limbs and smaller kindling to start a fire. Flames engulfed the bodies quickly.

Bosse led the way back inside the castle, but the burning odor followed all three of them.

Alifair and Justin walked back into the main hall. She pinched her nose. Burned flesh smelled just as bad as dried blood on dead animals.

While walking back in, Adrian told Bosse and Vic how he planned to find Krol. "Can't be that hard. We can find something belonging to Krol and track his scent."

Bosse did not believe it would be that simple. "Krol is sly and not that easy to corner. He will probably take some of his clothing and drag his lion's scent in different directions. He'll send the wagon on a roundabout path to further confuse anyone daring to follow him."

Running his hand over his hair, Adrian stared at the fire, then asked Bosse. "What's your intel?"

Bosse waved Alifair over. "Tell them what you know."

She cocked her eyebrow at him.

He closed his eyes, waiting for her to tell him she did not respond to orders. He wasn't ordering her, just moving this along.

She surprised him by not mentioning his poor etiquette right now and explained about her dreams. She finished by sharing that she'd seen the wagon entering an area with ruins from an old castle. "I normally see only when someone has arrived at a place, but I don't think the women are at this place yet. Not for another day or two."

Adrian listened politely, but his wrinkled brow said he had trouble using that information. "Thank you for what you've shared. The problem is we have limited time to reach these women before Krol does something with them. We have gifted females in our group as well. One has visions and is *always* correct. Have your dreams *always* come true the way you see them?"

She had never claimed her dreams were always accurate, but Bosse believed in her.

Alifair gave Bosse a look of apology and admitted, "The majority of the time, yes, but not always."

Taking his time, Adrian huffed out a sigh before replying. "I would not insult your intuitive dreaming for anything and truly appreciate all you've done to help us, but I have a map to where Krol is going right now. I can't risk losing any time on a maybe."

That was crap. Bosse growled. "She found her friend here and spoke to the mate we're hunting."

Adrian didn't hide his surprise. "You did?"

Giving him a quick nod, Alifair said, "Yes. Krol put Magdelina in a room I'd been cleaning and told me to attend to whatever she needed. Unlike how he treated other women, he wanted her to be cared for. I think he needed her in good health." When Alifair paused, Bosse could tell he wasn't going to like what she had to say.

Taking a deep breath, Alifair told him, "I can't fault Adrian's strategic thinking. I feel he's right to make his decisions based on what he trusts. He's not insulting me."

Bosse had come to realize through some of her comments that she was used to being looked at as a faulty piece of magical equipment. That irritated him with everyone.

Adrian said, "Thank you for understanding, Alifair. Okay, I'm leaving Vic here to oversee the castle. We need to head toward the first place the guard told us about."

Bosse could not go along with that plan. "You go there. I will take Alifair and follow her information."

"I don't want you two out there with no backup," Adrian argued.

Justin added, "It's safer to stay in one group."

Not someone to easily fall into line when he felt he had better plans, Bosse asked, "Would you not want us to check both places? What if Alifair's dream is correct and we fail to find the mate because we did not split up?" His gaze swept over the faces of his friends. "I am hard to kill after two years of daily battles in this hellhole. I can protect my, uhm, us, but I have no way of letting you know if or when we find the women."

Adrian and Justin exchanged a look. Then grumbling under his breath, Adrian said, "Shit fire, I don't have a satellite phone to give you to reach us."

Bosse sighed at yet another unfamiliar thing to him. "Does not matter. I don't know about satellites."

Vic snapped his fingers. "Hang on." He pulled his backpack off and dug into it, fishing out a small orange device with an unlit bulb. "We were going to put this on a transport vehicle if we had to follow one. It's like an EPIRB that works off satellites."

Alifair watched Bosse, no doubt waiting to see if he understood any of this, which he didn't.

Instead of repeating what he'd just said, Bosse quirked an eyebrow at Vic. It wasn't as if he'd been educated on electronics.

Adrian held his hand out to Vic, who placed the device on his palm. Holding it up to Bosse, Adrian explained, "Basically, if you find the mate, you activate the unit by pulling this small antenna free and pressing this button. It will send a signal to us so that we can locate exactly where you're standing."

Now that was something. Bosse took the trinket from Adrian. There were so many things he needed to learn about. He handed the little orange thing to Alifair. "Put this in a pocket. If I have to shift immediately, I might destroy it." He added, "Please."

That seemed to work. Alifair put the device away and informed him, "I know what this is."

Of course, she did. He admired the way she'd kept herself together and still had sass. He didn't like not knowing if he could trust what he felt for her.

"Thank you both for doing this," Adrian said. "Don't get captured or killed. I do not want to go home and admit I left you on your own."

Bosse snorted. "Your Guardian is a scary shifter."

Adrian scowled. "Shit fire, I can deal with him. I don't want to face Jaz."

Justin burst out laughing.

Adrian glowered at him. "Don't be so quick to laugh. You'll be in the soup with me."

That soured Justin's mood.

Bosse wanted to get moving. "That big shifter called Beast is a rhino-type animal. I don't think he's a natural rhino shifter, but something altered. I've never seen him entirely in human form in the year he was caged next to me. You need to watch your back if you run into him. I have no idea where he'll go, but I don't trust him not to hunt us."

Vic had trouble wrapping his head around Beast. "A *year?*"

Bosse shouldn't care about what happened to the others, but Alifair had brought out a side of him he was starting to recognize. He wanted to be a better person than the one who had faced killing every day for so long.

That had to be the reason his mind jumped to the shifters still here. "What will happen to the rest of the shifters in cages?"

Justin spoke up. "We have to leave them in cages until Vic's backup arrives. That team will figure out how to deal with each shifter. If they have families and a home to go to, one of our people will escort them home to confirm they have a support group. If they're dangerous, we'll transport them to our country where our Guardian will decide if they're safe and then find them a sanctuary."

Alifair asked, "What is a sanctuary for shifters?"

Justin said, "Similar to a reservation for Native Americans."

She wrinkled her nose at that and then exclaimed, "What about Bosse? He has earned his freedom, right? He's here helping you."

Bosse loved how she stood up for him. No one had done that, not even his mother. He leaned over to reply before

Adrian had to say something. "I have a place to live. These people and their Guardian have been very good to me, but thank you for your words."

Her cheeks pinked. She was already pretty as a freshly bloomed rose and got cuter by the moment. Why did she have to make him question where he stood with her or what she really wanted from him?

Adrian ended the meeting. "Time to get rolling. Justin and I have ground to make up to catch Krol, and we don't know at what point he will do something with his captives."

Vic reached into his backpack and flipped two gray packets the size of a man's hand to Adrian. "The last changes of clothes for you and Justin if you shred yours." Then he pulled out a long knife and handed it to Bosse. "In case you need more than claws and teeth."

Bosse accepted the weapon, glad to have it, but he would not admit as much in front of Alifair. She worried so much as it was.

He would keep her safe no matter how many had to die.

Chapter 31

WHY COULDN'T KROL use a car or a truck? The minute Bosse was done with all this, he intended to live a modern life. Maybe not flying so much, but he could learn to drive a vehicle like the truck Adrian had used to take them to the airport.

He didn't have to keep looking around to see if they were being followed, but he had a bad feeling. No smell had reached him. Maybe he was just on edge with all that had happened. He asked Titan, *Do you scent any threat around us?*

No, but I feel eyes on us. Could be a natural animal staying downwind to keep an eye on a predator.

True. Bosse hadn't considered that. They were moving too slowly to suit him.

He'd never cared for riding horses, but this would be easier on Alifair and faster than walking.

Having her in front of him with her soft bottom rubbing against him with the back-and-forth flow of the horse sure as hell wasn't easier on him.

All that wasn't even close to being as bad as the chilly silence between them.

He missed her genuinely warm, open personality, but he could not get past the idea that he'd been a means to an end. He'd smashed his emotions into dust the first week in Krol's castle. Battling and killing one shifter after another he had no ill feelings toward had left him numb. Watching the life fade from their eyes had taken a toll on his soul.

If not for owing Titan his best effort, Bosse might have allowed one of the shifters to kill him and end his misery. He'd never killed before landing in that castle unless he was fighting for his own life or that of a pack member.

What a waste to have spilled blood for a pack that turned their backs on him.

He'd yanked in any foolish emotions, focused only on surviving one day at a time.

A cookie fairy came along and swept up the piles of emotional dust and reshaped his soul, breathing life back into his dead insides.

Since then, she'd led him on a wild ride of emotional turmoil from anger at her taking risks to meet with him, to shock over helping him escape, to the joy of kissing someone so sweet, to terror over leaving her in the castle.

That many ups and downs would wear out anyone, but it was nothing compared to the mental battle he fought to figure out if the woman he cared for had been using him from the start.

His mind yelled at him not to be fooled.

That was how he'd won so many matches, but this wasn't survival. This was life. He had no experience with figuring out something this complicated.

But his heart had stirred awake and now had an opinion as well. His heart asked what she had done that was so wrong.

After thinking on that for a while, he came up with an honest answer. He had forsaken the word trust in a place where it would only have gotten him mutilated and then killed.

She'd gained his trust by risking her life to help him more than once, even while knowing she couldn't leave before finding her friend.

Feeling that his trust had been misplaced and foolish on his part banged up his heart, which he'd paid no attention to for many years. He couldn't ignore that organ any longer.

He wanted her trust.

He wanted to trust her. Everything hinged on believing he could.

Her stomach growled, and he smiled. Stubborn woman would not tell him she was hungry and very likely thirsty.

Titan must have heard her as well. He said, *Water is nearby. I hear it moving.*

I do, too, Bosse replied. *We'll stop and eat.*

He announced, "We have a good place up ahead to take a break."

"Fine."

That's the only reply he'd heard in the last hour. No other four-letter word had ever sounded so awful.

Once he'd pulled off the dirt road and guided his horse through a thin forest, he paused close to an easy-moving stream running over and around rocks. He stepped off the horse and then lifted her down.

She grabbed the saddle when she wobbled for a moment, then got that pert chin up and walked away.

Shaking his head at the cool reaction, he pulled what he needed from the bags and sent the horse to drink from the stream and feed on what grass grew in spots.

"What do we have in these bags?" he asked her in an upbeat tone, not caring about the food so much as breaking through her icy barrier.

"Bread, jerky, fruit. That sort of thing." She tried to pretend a lack of interest, but her stomach growled again, defying her.

If he chuckled now, she would likely not speak to him again until tomorrow and refuse to eat. Instead, he dragged a thick section of trunk from a dead tree over and waved his hand for her to sit first.

She stared at the trunk with debate, causing her facial muscles to twitch, then shook her head and sat. More silence as they ate some of their supply.

He was ready to break and ask her what it would take for them to be at least friends again. That sounded like a stupid idea. While she might be the best friend he'd ever had, she was way more than that to him.

Emotions sucked. How was he supposed to figure this out?

She stood, brushing off the dark gray pants she'd chosen over a skirt. That had come from the guard's clothing supply. She'd refused to wear their shirts, opting for a simple white one she'd found in the room where she'd been locked. The pants had pockets, so she still carried that gadget Adrian had given them.

"Ready to get moving again?" Bosse asked, then groaned inwardly. Could he not find something better to say to her?

"I need a moment of privacy."

He started to argue that she had to stay where he could see her, but she added, "For my personal needs."

Hell. "Okay, but please don't go too far."

Looking around, she pointed out, "There's not a lot of growth here for a barrier. I'm going down the stream far enough that I feel comfortable."

Worry had him ready to object, but he wanted to make peace with her, and this place looked pretty quiet. "I understand."

She'd been looking everywhere but at him until those two words. Her gaze dropped to his face. Her face had another debate in progress, but she dismissed it quickly and snatched up a paper napkin before walking away.

He had to get past her earlier dreams that sent her hunting him for Rez and not feel gutted by her admission of thinking she found him only to help her. If she hadn't fought so hard to stay back and send him for Rez, he might not have blown his top.

What else had happened?

Memories flooded his mind. She'd shown him the way to freedom even though she had to stay behind and ended up being caught by Krol.

She'd come to him in his dreams, and he'd been in hers.

When he broke the lock and opened the door to where she'd been imprisoned, she'd run and leaped into his arms.

He'd never felt the intensity of happiness that he'd felt at her thrill over seeing him again. She'd been unprepared for his return. That reaction had been a hundred percent honest.

Happy to see him. Not someone else.

Insecurity had never been an issue while in that cage and fighting deadly creatures to entertain Krol. His life had sucked, but survival had been simple to understand.

He'd had no good relationships with women in his pack. They'd all been ready to use him for sex, to breed, or both.

This uncomfortable sense of having no idea how to navigate his feelings for Alifair had caused him to fall back on the only thing he'd ever known, which had been never to trust anyone.

He'd compared her to everyone else who had mistreated him when she'd done the entire opposite.

She had been doing her duty for a month.

Risking her life to help him escape had not been her duty. She'd never once said she'd seen his escape in a dream. She'd wanted him far from Krol when she could have just told him to stay in the woods and wait until she needed him.

She had no idea he would even return once he crossed an ocean.

Bosse slapped his forehead. For someone who could think faster than another predator when in the arena, he'd been a mental slug with her.

Titan shouted in his head, *Mate in trouble.*

No! Bosse jumped up and listened. Alifair's muffled shout reached him, but then nothing.

He tossed the food bag aside and raced along the water's edge to find her. What had happened? She had no scent, not even the cinnamon and cardamom from before.

Then he inhaled deeply, smiling to himself. She had a scent from where he'd touched her last night.

She had his scent.

Panic had him pulling off his clothes as he ran, telling Titan, *I need you to track faster than I can.*

His wolf took the body and put his head down, then slowed and lifted his nose to the air.

Bosse wanted to shout to get moving, but he knew better.

Titan took off running at a blinding speed. He focused on the sound of undergrowth being shoved aside and stomped on. They weren't far ahead.

Thankful to hear sounds of her fighting her captor, Bosse hoped she had not been badly injured. *Hurry, Titan.*

We will save her, his wolf assured him. Then he shoved his big body through dense underbrush, crashing loudly as he climbed a hill. Whoever had grabbed her would know by now they were coming.

He did not want Titan to waste time being quiet. This was not the moment to be subtle.

"Get off me!"

That's our mate's voice, Bosse told Titan. His insides churned at the thought of being too late. He would rip apart anyone who had harmed her. He hated how frightened she sounded.

What he hated more than anything was the silence that followed.

When Titan encountered the beaten-down trail of smashed weeds and broken limbs, he picked up speed. He finally leaped into an open area at the crest of the hill where a storm had brought down many trees.

Where was she?

Give me the body, Titan. Bosse could not handle waiting a second longer to find her. They shifted so fast his eyes crossed, then he shook it off and started hunting for her. "Alifair! Where are you?"

She made a noise, but it was as if she had her head under a blanket.

He climbed over tree trunks carefully. One wrong move, and he could end up stepping on her. He kept going uphill until he saw a massive body face down. It was covered in black fur. What was it?

He didn't care. Stepping over the last log, he reached down and yanked on the body. It was heavy dead weight, but he shoved it aside.

A gorilla still breathing but with its eyes rolled up.

Probably a shifter since he doubted gorillas were native to Slovakia.

Staring down, he found Alifair face down between two logs. He carefully moved one aside and bent to lift her up and flip her over. He pulled her into his arms. She was covered in dirt with weeds sticking from her wavy dark brown hair, but she was breathing.

He hugged her to him, jostling her gently. "Alifair, wake up, sweetness."

Her eyelashes fluttered but did not open.

Had that monster broken something inside her? "Are you hurt? I need you to tell me."

She mumbled a few sounds, then lifted a hand to her face, pushing hair out of her eyes that blinked open. "Bosse?"

Why did she sound surprised he'd come for her?

His legs were weak from finding her safe. He sat on a log and shifted her to sit in his lap. Using a finger, he lightly brushed dirt from her eyes and face. "Are you hurt?" he asked again.

Still staring at him, she slowly moved her head from side to side. "You found me."

"Of course, I did." Guilt smacked some sense into him. He might not understand emotions, but he knew when it was time to come clean. "I'm sorry I was angry about you needing me for your dream. I understand. You scared me half to death."

With one sweet smile curving her lips, his world rolled upside down. She said, "Thank you, but I didn't explain about the dreams very well. I'm not good with people, especially not with men."

He caught her chin. "You don't need to be good with *men*. You are perfect with *me*."

He must have said the right thing.

She put her hand on his face, and his body tightened at her touch. She said, "Let me try again. I did not know who you were before I was captured and brought to Krol's castle, but I began caring when I first saw you battle in the arena. You always seemed to hate being there, unlike some shifters who walked in excited to kill their opponent. That happened before I had the dream where you helped Rez. I lived for those moments when I had to bring food for the guards and shifters, even having to feed that awful Beast. It was worth it every time to see you."

What could she have seen but a beaten and bloody human when he was not in wolf form? Servants had to leave a scoop of gruel in his wooden bowl, just like all the imprisoned shifters received. He would always have the memories of her leaving extra food and sweets hidden in a cloth she dropped in his cage.

Drawing in a deep breath, she released it softly, but her heart still pounded from her ordeal. "I did not tell you about the dreams before you left because I did not want you to return, not even for Rez. I wanted you to find America and be safe. She was, and is, my responsibility."

"*Our* responsibility now." He lowered his head to let her see the determination in his eyes. "Like I told you, I had already decided to come back to get you. I couldn't face leaving this country without you. Then those shifters shot me full of drugs and flew me across the ocean."

Her eyes narrowed with fury. "If I had been there, I would have used a spell and made them pay for harming you."

There was his fierce little warrior. She could never tell if her magic would work as intended, but that did not deter her from facing a threat.

A loud growl sent Alifair wrapping her arms around Bosse's neck. "Is it still alive?"

He stood and pushed her behind him. "Not for long if he even thinks to come for you."

Moving sluggishly, the gorilla snarled and sat up.

Bosse warned, "Come near my mate again, and you will die."

The gorilla shook its head, not in answer, but as if to clear away the fog clouding his eyes. He said, "No. I was wrong."

This one spoke in animal form, but that was not important. Bosse said, "You would be wise to get moving and never return. A crazy lion-shifter named Krol captures shifters and has a deadly creature he can use to fly them away."

Anger simmered in the green eyes that stared up at him. "I am stuck in this country because of that miserable Krol. Kidnappers captured me in my country and brought me here because he offered them a lot of money. I got a chance to kill them and escape, but I have had to live on the land here with no way home. I will kill Krol."

"If you get the chance before I find him, have at it." Bosse wanted this shifter on his way, which might go faster if the shifter knew which direction to head for his home. "Where did they capture you?"

"In the mountains near Uganda. Central Africa. Have no idea where that is now."

Bosse held a mental picture of Slovakia in his mind but could not place the countries this gorilla shifter would have to cross. "I think you probably have to head south, which is that way." He pointed past the gorilla's right shoulder.

Alifair stuck her head out from behind Bosse. "Go south and a little east to Istanbul. The land narrows to nothing there, but you don't have to cross water to reach your continent. Keep going south along the Mediterranean Sea until Egypt. Hopefully, you will have located a map by then."

"Thank you. I'm sorry I scared you."

Feeling more charitable since Alifair was unharmed, Bosse pulled her around but kept her under his arm. "Why did you grab her?"

Scratching his head, the gorilla shifter said, "I was tired of being alone and wanted a mate." His bright green eyes slid to Alifair. "I used to have honor before Krol dragged me from my home."

Alifair gave him a sad smile. "Apology accepted. Good luck getting back."

"Thanks." The gorilla shifter stood, stretched, then asked, "What happened to me?"

Bosse grinned, having figured out what Alifair must have done. "Mighty magic from a tiny woman."

"You're lucky. Good mate you got." Shaking his head, the gorilla stepped up on a log and began leaping from point to point until he vanished down the hill.

Too late, Bosse wished he'd thought to ask the gorilla if he'd been tracking them. That had to be what he and Titan had sensed.

Releasing a long breath that eased the muscles in his chest, Bosse was thankful that had turned out better than he had expected. He'd have fought the shifter if that's what it would have taken to keep her safe, but he didn't want to kill another shifter who'd had his life destroyed as well.

Bosse had not wanted to fight and kill up close to Alifair. She'd seen enough of that from a distance. He wanted her to see the man he could be for her, not a monster.

Swinging his head around to her, he said, "We need to get back to our horse. I'll pick up my clothes on the way. Then we can get you cleaned up and back on the road."

"Hold everything." She stepped away and put her hands on her hips. "What's this bit about me being your *mate?*"

Titan observed, *She doesn't look happy we chose her.*

Chapter 32

—⁓—

CLOUDS HID THE sun's progress toward falling out of sight, but it had to be an hour or so before dark.

A long day of tracking, but Adrian's wolf, Red, had loped along steadily.

They had to be faster than Krol and his horse-driven wagon. With a little luck, they'd reach Krol before he got to Košice in the eastern third of Slovakia.

How were Bosse and Alifair faring on their travels?

Again, he questioned leaving them alone for the hundredth time and hoped he did not live to regret that decision.

Red's rough voice broke into Adrian's thoughts. *Bosse fights to survive, but he did not injure the pack members in human form.*

Adrian appreciated having Red share his opinion these days. They'd gone through so much after surviving a brutal imprisonment and too many days when neither would speak to the other.

He would never take hearing Red's voice for granted again.

Replying telepathically, Adrian admitted, *I saw that as well. I don't doubt Bosse's ability, only that he seems not to think he should have us watching his back.*

Pausing to lift his snout and catch scents floating on the wind, Red continued. Evidently, nothing to worry about. Red said, *He has lived a long time while many other shifters died. He will not allow anyone to harm his woman.*

Bosse's woman? That surprised Adrian. *Are you saying*

they are more than friends? They were barely speaking to each other when they left.

Sometimes, you and your mate do not talk when angry.

Adrian hated any time he and Jaz were on opposite sides of an issue. The good news was they knew each other well and quickly resolved any conflict. After taking a moment to consider Red's observation, Adrian asked, *Do you think she and Bosse are mated?*

Not both of them.

What the hell could that mean?

Red leaped over a downed tree and continued deftly through the woods with Justin's grizzly bear keeping pace in a lumbering trot on the opposite side of a highway they shadowed. Both animals had taken turns splitting off the main trail to track Krol's lion scent several times before dismissing it entirely. Bosse had warned them how Krol would try to throw them off his trail with tricks.

Adrian had learned not to push Red to explain more than he wished to share. Red often studied a situation thoroughly before commenting. He'd hold his wolf's comments for when the time came for them to matter.

Justin spoke to him telepathically, which all the Gallize shifters could do in animal form. *We should be getting close to Košice soon. I'm moving away from the road to see if I can find a higher vantage point than we have down here.*

Sounds good. After choosing a more direct route across the country in hopes of catching up to Krol, they'd each covered different sides of a dirt road to their destination after paralleling paved two-lane roads headed east all day. Now, they had to locate Opátka, a small village short of reaching Košice. At this point, they had no idea if Krol was truly going to Opátka or if he'd lied to his men since they were human guards unable to detect a lie.

Adrian's wolf picked up speed, moving through the dense forest with an uncanny ability to dodge or leap over any obstacle without straying from the straightest path. As he moved closer to their destination, houses began to appear sporadically. Both Red and Justin's bear had noticed the sounds and noxious fumes of cars earlier while traveling near the paved roads leading to Košice, but neither had picked up the smell of horses.

Had Krol taken a different route or switched his gypsy wagon and horse for a faster modern vehicle once he was far enough away from the castle? That didn't sound like him based on what Bosse had shared.

Or did he have a way to hide the scent of horses?

The crazy lion shifter had not been pretending to live in medieval times.

He really believed he was a ruling king of that period.

Justin's voice came quickly. *I've spotted a wagon that fits the description the guard gave us.*

All the tiring, hard miles fell away at the sound of hope in Justin's voice.

Adrian asked, *Can we get to him now?*

No. His wagon pulled off the main thoroughfare and passed through a wooden gate. If you stand on the road, the dilapidated wooden gate seems to shield livestock from predators, but I'm two hundred feet up on the rise. Once you close the gate, you pass through an acre of weeds growing all around the dirt trail. There may be thirty yards of forest bordering all that. Then the land clears into a groomed lawn in front of a maintained estate. Guards are armed with rifles. Can't tell what kind from here, but the way they hold their weapons and move around, they appear skilled.

Adrian hated missing the chance to overtake the wagon before Krol got that far. He told Justin, *Tell me how to find you, and we'll come up with a plan for when he leaves. If the rest of what he told his guards was true, Krol can't stay long if he's only hiring more guards here for his main purpose at another stop. He intends to do all that and return to the castle in a matter of days.*

Justin agreed, *That's a lot to accomplish, depending upon multiple ifs.* He gave Adrian directions to his observation spot.

Red changed course and headed that way.

Gallize shifters were apex predators, unlike any other shifters Adrian had ever heard about or met. What could be so special about the assassins Krol came all this distance to hire?

Why would he need those for whatever he had planned for the women?

Nothing sucked more on a mission than trying to function with inferior intel.

Chapter 33

HAVING SPOKEN A code word at the entrance to the Opátka estate, Krol remained inside the wagon until it rolled onto a stone drive that circled in front of a Victorian estate other shifters would not come near.

He was not just a shifter. He was a king who feared no one.

His lion rumbled a snarling sound. Krol silently warned the animal locked inside his body, *Do not make a sound while in this place or even try to shift.*

Tall guards in black vests and matching pants carried rifles he knew had to be loaded with titanium bullets.

He leaped from the rear opening of the wagon, having shifted back to human form to ride inside for the last three kilometers. The Gallize mate, Magdelina, had skewered him with her black eyes. Not really black, but inside here, any orbs not glowing may as well be black holes.

She could stare all she wanted, but she could not break titanium handcuffs.

The other one, he now knew as Rez, had been captured a month ago based on a tip he'd received. He'd offered money for any unusual woman and double if she had been observed using her gifts.

Since being locked away in his tower room, Rez had said not a word until she called his black-haired kitchen maid with two different eye colors Alifair.

That maid had fooled everyone.

He would have to do a better job of interrogating servants

in the future, but it had never occurred to him that some foolish woman would intentionally get caught to serve inside his castle.

Rez lifted her chin. Her brown eyes had deep shadows beneath them. He'd gone by every night he was in the castle and rattled the door to her room, thinking to shake her up enough to speak.

He would do far worse to make Alifair regret having hunted him.

Stepping over to the back of the wagon, he said, "I will return soon. I suggest you both behave as Jothan rules this place and will not be as nice as me if you cross him."

Rez frowned and flicked her gaze away as if he bored her. He should take time on the way back to make her pay for the insolence since no deal had been struck for her yet.

Magdelina never took her steely eyes off his face. Her lips twitched with the start of a smile.

He would like to give that one a lesson in obedience, too, but he had to deliver her unscathed. She'd infuriated him so much that he wasn't sure he could stop once he started in on her.

Rez was a bonus he might be able to trade to the mage for one more request.

She didn't have to show up in perfect condition.

"Enjoy your moment, bitches. It will not last long." Then he climbed out.

Chapter 34

A MATE.
Alifair hadn't been upset, just curious about Bosse claiming her as his. In fact, she'd loved the idea of being a mate, especially his, but felt he should have at least discussed it with her.

Especially after she'd agreed to leave the castle with him. After her dream about where Rez and Magdelina were going, she couldn't argue for staying at the castle.

Bosse had tried to smooth over what he'd said about mating by stating, "I did not mean it to sound like an order."

"I'm not saying you ordered me, but it's the first I've heard of being a mate," she'd explained, trying not to sound irritated. He had to learn to discuss what sounded like a major decision with her.

Bosse had scratched his beard, now growing out again, then paused and cocked his head as if hearing something. He nodded, then told Alifair, "My wolf, Titan, is often better at explaining things. He suggested I explain why we call you mate. I am a shifter."

Lifting an impertinent eyebrow at him, she said, "I'm not confused on *that* point."

His eyes twinkled. "I do love your sassy side."

She hadn't possessed one until meeting a grumpy wolf shifter. She rolled her hand in a motion to stop stalling.

His words turned somber. "When Titan and I choose a mate, we must agree because it is a forever commitment.

One I had never thought we'd face, but we both want you. I did not go any further with you last night because once you give your body fully to me, everything changes. You would be mine… forever."

She'd remained silent, not asking questions or helping him get his point out because hearing what he said in his own words meant the world to her.

He chewed on his thumbnail, then lowered his hand. "You are all I can ever want in a woman and a mate. I should have explained more before we were even that intimate." His last words fell off into a whisper. "We choose you as ours, but you may… not… want me. You still have a choice so long as we don't complete our bond."

He'd lowered his walls and exposed a vulnerability no one saw to give her his truth. His sincerity in picking her forever sent her heart somersaulting.

No one had given her a gift she never expected to receive.

She'd stepped over and hugged him, happy to feel his arms wrap around her. She owed him words, too. "You are everything I could want in a man. I understand what you're saying. I'm honored you and Titan chose me." She just wished she could keep them both. Thinking of this ending too soon hurt her to the core.

Should she tell him so he wouldn't continue to bond with her?

She'd ask him later but wanted to have this moment she'd never have again. Was that too much to ask for a last request?

They'd hurried back after that to pick up his clothes and find the horse standing around, thank goodness. She had no experience with horses and no idea one would be so considerate.

With the light now waning, the dark would soon close in and force them to stop.

She'd been miserable during the first half of the day riding this horse with Bosse at her back.

Alifair couldn't believe the contentment she carried in her heart now. After all the turmoil of the past few days, she wanted to grasp this happiness and hold it tight so it would never end.

Capturing the wind would be easier.

Funny how a person's mind could tear their insides apart for a while and then, with a few words, make everything feel like a fresh rain had blown through. She'd never questioned her drive to save Rez, but in realizing how it had looked in hindsight to Bosse, she understood his hurt.

Words can hurt or heal.

She'd never been a healer but would use her words more carefully in the future. Bosse could do that as well, but he deserved some time to adjust to a new world of freedom and learn to trust those around him.

He hadn't known Adrian's people for long, which meant he'd made a leap of faith to return with strange shifters who might not do what they said. They had, though. Meeting shifters he didn't have to protect his back against would go a long way toward Bosse living a better life.

Anyone could see he wanted more for his life.

Given a chance to prove himself, Bosse would show everyone he was far more than what Krol had made him be.

Bosse and his wolf had developed their own code of honor. She'd never seen either of them toy with an opponent in the arena. Once the shifter they battled showed signs of losing, they allowed their opponent the opportunity and the chance to decide when to quit.

Krol had screamed at Bosse often to finish off a badly bleeding shifter.

Bosse would never lift his eyes to acknowledge the real monster in the room. That had made Krol even crazier.

"I think we are getting close to the place you saw in your dream," Bosse said, breaking her out of her spinning thoughts.

She'd realized they'd been ascending a hill covered in trees. Bosse had worked the horse back and forth, climbing in degrees instead of straight up what could be a mountain.

When did a hill become a mountain?

She sat up straighter and assessed the area as Bosse leaned closer to her, guiding the horse until they reached a narrow path. It appeared to be more of a deer trail than somewhere humans had walked or ridden.

Of course, if the most recent visitors were shifters, the condition of this path made sense.

Bosse lifted branches out of the way as the horse pushed hard to move forward.

Alifair lowered her upper body over the saddle horn to help Bosse until they cleared the trees.

When the horse stopped, she sat up, taking in what remained of gray stone walls bleached by decades of sunlight. There were no trees around the castle. A wooden bridge two floors above the ground connected two sections. Weeds grew across the ground between the structure and the trees, meaning the land had been kept cleared by someone, though maybe only once a year.

"What do you think?" Bosse asked.

"That looks right based on what Kylie told us once I described the images I've seen." She hadn't understood why Kylie, of all people, would help them until Kylie said she wanted to get as far away as she could before Krol came back or Hessie was freed. She begged for help.

Not one shifter standing around called her out for a lie.

Kylie had been Hessie's go-to servant, but she may have acted compliant to protect herself just as Alifair and others had. Kylie had spoken to many guards during her time and learned of the surrounding areas of Krol's castle.

Adrian had assured Kylie that they would take her home.

"I don't want to stay here tonight," Bosse announced.

Honestly, neither did Alifair, but what did that leave them? "Where do you want to go?"

"How do you feel about sleeping under the stars?"

Her first reaction was a gut clench at the thought of sleeping outside where small creepy things and animals would get to her, but then she realized she'd be with Bosse. "Works for me. What about food?"

"I'll shift once I have you in a safe spot and find something to cook quickly before nightfall. We'll keep the fire small even then."

That's how she ended up stuffing small branches into a protective lean-to structure outline that Bosse had created from fallen limbs. He piled up different-sized, smaller branches, explaining he'd seen no sign of vegetation like vines that he could use to tie them together.

She'd woven cloth and yarn back with her clan community. How hard could this be?

Stripping the longer branches, she crisscrossed those in a way that created a decent wall of interwoven sticks. Then she began pushing thinner branches into place, leaving the green pine needles and leaves from other trees to overlap.

By the time she expected Bosse to return, she was quite pleased with herself.

A stick snapped.

That could be something the size of a deer moving around or a person sneaking up on her. She slowly turned to face a wolf standing taller than her. Her knees knocked, and her hands shook.

The wolf canted its head and then dropped what it had been carrying in its mouth.

Two dead rabbits and a pile of clothes. Food for dinner and Bosse's clothes.

She stopped panicking, now feeling like a fool.

This was Titan. He sat like a gigantic, well-behaved dog.

"I'm sorry, Titan, you frightened me. I expected Bosse to come walking up."

The wolf smiled at her.

She started laughing. "I'm going to have to get used to your size. Thanks for dinner. Uhm, I don't really know how to clean a rabbit."

Energy swirled around Titan as his head began to shrink along with his body.

His change mesmerized her. Bones snapped and moved under his skin. That had to be painful, but a minute later, a naked Bosse sat on the ground.

He raised those beautiful brown eyes to her. "Titan said you're funny… and nice."

What a compliment. "Thank him for me. He was tolerant of me acting like a ninny. I should know him by now, but I have never been close enough to be prepared for just how big he is. He's a good-looking wolf."

Bosse sat for a moment staring at nothing, then broke up laughing. He had to catch his breath.

"What?" Alifair demanded.

"Titan said if not for him, I would be alone for the rest of my life. I think he has a point. He called you our mate before me." Standing, Bosse walked away almost out of sight, returning with his clothes on.

"Why didn't you change here?" she asked.

"It's not easy to watch a human turn into an animal the first time. We're trying to give you a chance to get used to us. Besides, I pulled the saddle off the horse, made sure he was set for the night, and grabbed a gourd of water from the saddle bags." Dressed again but still barefoot, Bosse quickly cleaned the rabbit twenty feet away. When he finished, he carried the skin and other unused parts into the woods.

Upon returning, he said, "Take the small, dried twigs I told you not to use on the lean-to and stack them for a fire."

She wasted no time in getting that done. "Want me to rub sticks together to start the fire?" She had no idea how that really worked.

"No. I've got matches. We don't have to live like we did in the castle."

"So glad," she muttered.

Bosse started the fire, keeping it small, and skewered the two rabbits on a stick. Where had he gotten the sticks shaped like a Y for making a rotisserie? Clever man.

Satisfied with that, he studied her handiwork. "That's a fine job of making a cover for our shelter tonight, Alifair."

She hadn't heard him say her name often. Add that to his kind words and she felt genuinely appreciated. She'd never been the outdoor type, but she might get the hang of it with Bosse. "Thank you. I'm not trained in this type of thing, but I figured I understood enough about weaving to make something."

He reached over and hugged her to him. "I'm so proud of you."

Her mind floated around in a cloud of happiness. Is this what life would be like if she had more time to be with him? Working together for a common goal? Her appreciating his abilities and him complimenting hers?

She pushed back against the hurt dousing her happiness. Anger raised its head again, making her question things she'd accepted without question. Far back in time, someone had designated roles, and everyone accepted their jobs to support her community. That made sense.

To expect her to forsake any chance of a life to do a duty that she was hardly qualified to perform did not make sense. Didn't they think she deserved a relationship with a man and maybe even a family of her own?

Maybe the fault lay with her not speaking up.

They were all safe back in the community, content to have her out here alone.

Because Bosse had made her a priority, he'd gotten her to rethink how she'd allowed others to treat her poorly, even good people.

Had her mother been just as angry at leaving her only child alone to go save children belonging to others? What had she been thinking in her last minutes?

Alifair sidestepped that mental path for the moment, which led into a bottomless void.

If she didn't, she'd waste precious time with Bosse.

They ate quickly so he could smother the fire before dark. Then he set the gourd of water near the blanket.

She'd watched the smoke and didn't think a significant amount had lifted above the trees. Now that it was gone, black shadows began closing in on them.

She'd be a frightened ninny out here without Bosse.

He seemed at peace, unworried about any critter showing up.

Then again, no critter would want to face Titan.

Bosse touched her arm. "Take my hand so you don't fall. My eyes can see better than yours out here."

She reached up and grabbed his hand. He must have noticed her trembling because he squeezed her hand carefully.

"I'm fine," she said to the darkness as much as him. "I'm just not used to camping."

"You're really going to like it."

He made it sound like she would. It had to be better than being in the castle. This would be fine. She'd be safe with Bosse.

He tugged her around until he lifted her into his arms.

"What are you doing?" she asked nervously.

"Putting you to bed. Hard to do when you're rigid as a tree."

"I am not," she lied.

He huffed a laugh at her and lowered her to the ground. She clung to his neck, not wanting to lie on the grass where something would crawl on her.

No grass.

He placed her on a blanket he must have spread out when she hadn't been paying attention. Her shoulders relaxed, and she sighed.

"That sounds better," he said before lying next to her where he could pull her back up against his front. He had her facing the inside of their lean-to, protecting her from all sides.

Still, something could weasel its way in here.

"How did you do all that magic at the castle today?"

"What?" She thought about his words. "Oh, that. I honestly didn't think about it. Magdelina said to trust my ability. I was so worried for you and your friends that—"

His fingers worked unbuttoning her shirt, then found her breasts.

She sighed, and it ended on a shaking breath.

He took his time massaging each one. "Go on. You were saying?"

"Uhm…" What was she saying? The magic. "I… uh…"

Another hand reached between her legs and cupped her.

She sucked in air and lifted her hips to him. The zipper hummed when he pulled it down and began to work her pants past her knees. Wanton woman that she was, she lifted her hips to help him. His fingers brushed along the inside of her thighs, moving closer to her heat but too damn slowly.

She moaned at his hands busy in both places. Nerves in her breasts tingled. Energy flowed between them wherever he touched her and stole her breath. Heat bloomed under her skin and spread from her neck to her toes. She'd longed for his touch all day.

He brushed the pad of his finger over a hard nipple, and she arched. Heat pooled in her groin just as he pushed fingers through the frenzied nerves between her legs. She clenched his hand, but two fingers pinched her nipple gently, and she made a pained sound. Bursts of energy pinged her brain. Sensory overload left her unable to choose what to focus on.

He took care of that decision by teasing the folds between her legs, driving her mad with need.

"Please don't stop," she begged.

"No chance." That had come out like a vow. His hands stroked her with insane awareness of how to hit every nerve that sent lightning strikes to her core.

Then he freed her breasts and abandoned what he'd started down below.

What? No! She breathed out, "More."

"It's coming, and so will you." Big hands rolled her onto her back. He had her pants yanked off and her shirt opened all the way.

"I'm the only one naked," she pointed out, unwilling to accept less than everything tonight.

He chuckled over the sounds of moving around. "You sure about that?"

Then his big body covered her, but he kept his weight

off her, kissing her with what felt like too many years of bottled-up need.

He wasn't the only one.

She brushed her tongue over his lips and ran her hands down the carved muscles covering his chest. How could a man who possessed that much power and strength handle her so gently?

He kissed her face and neck, moving across her shoulders and making a deliberate stop at her breasts. They'd missed him like he'd just returned from a month-long trip.

Sucking her nipple coiled the tension deep inside tighter.

She'd thought last night was incredible. It had been but now felt different, like a bigger moment. Maybe getting loved by him with the knowledge that she'd been chosen as his and Titan's mate made every touch feel deeper and more special.

She'd hesitated to discuss being mated, but she wanted Bosse to know she was in this with him for however long it lasted. Maybe, just maybe, her dream would be wrong.

She scraped her nails over the skin of his hard abdomen and reached for his cock.

He sucked in a deep breath of air, releasing a sound she loved being able to draw from him. He shuddered and kissed her breast, then dropped his head to hers. "I want you every minute, with every breath," he said on a shaky exhale.

Grasping his length, which was as much as her hand could hold, she stroked across his velvet skin and whispered, "I choose you as my mate."

"Oh, Alifair." His hands gripped her shoulders, and his lips plundered hers in a kiss that went on and on, filling her heart with love she'd never be able to contain. Shouldn't have to when she held the only person ever to deserve her heart.

When he slowed the kiss, he nipped sweetly at her lips and placed a palm on her face. "I never dreamed of having anyone like you. Then you climbed into my dreams and saved me."

"You saved me back," she replied in a hushed voice.

"Now, I will make you mine." With that vow, he moved his lower body, pulling out of her hand.

She opened her mouth to complain but lost her thoughts when he licked between her legs. His tongue teased her back to that edge, the one place her body wanted to stay, no matter how difficult it was to hang on.

Reaching for his shoulders, she dug her nails in, clinging to him but wanting to let go at the same time.

He pressed a finger inside her and stroked his tongue over her clit with laser precision.

She arched, and her body splintered into shards of pleasure zinging in all directions. He would not relent, his finger and tongue continuing a mix of torture and ecstasy until she was spent.

Her body flopped back on the blanket, boneless and ridiculously happy. She heaved breath after breath. "Before was terrific, but… making love with a mate is… mind-blowing."

With his body again stretched out over her, he rubbed his hard cock against her. His gruff voice whispered close to her ear. "I love how sexy you are."

No one had ever told her she was sexy. With Bosse, she felt hot and desired. His confidence turned her on. His need for her made her weak in the knees.

"I love how hot you are," she countered, then added, "How big and hard you are, too."

Brushing a soft kiss across her lips, he said, "All yours."

"Finally." She could imagine being with him like this every day for eternity.

He chuckled, and then she could feel his mouth lose the smile and take on a more serious shape when he slowly kissed her neck.

Lifting her hips, she rubbed his hard length.

He made a deep groan.

"Are you in pain, mate?" she asked in a coy voice.

In answer, he rubbed his cock through her wet folds, and

she gasped. "Me, too. I'm ready." Her nipples puckered for him, probably worried he might forget to come back.

Licking one nipple then the other, he sucked hard then lightly bit a beaded tip.

"Bosse, I said I'm ready," she whined, pushing her hips up to him.

"Now you are." Sliding away from her breasts, he used his knee to widen her legs and pushed inside her an inch.

She picked her legs up and hooked them over his back, wanting all of him.

He muttered, "I can't hold back any longer," then pushed all the way in, not moving. Was he worried about doing too much?

Impossible.

She had no words for the relief of feeling him deep inside her. Raking her nails over his shoulders, she stopped and clutched his firm muscles. "I'm not fragile. I don't want slow and easy. I want all you have to give me."

That snapped whatever mental dam was holding him back. He withdrew and pushed inside her again and again, giving her muscles time to accept him.

She squeezed her muscles, gripping his hard-on—a message to let go.

His hips pumped faster, pounding into her. She dug her nails in harder, her heart beating in her ears. Energy swirled faster, twisting tighter and tighter until she didn't know up from down.

He reached between their bodies, his fingers stroking her once, twice, and flinging her off that cliff again.

He fell right behind her. He hammered harder, grinding her name out between his tight jaws. With one hard push, his body went rigid. "Alifair. Alifair. *Alifairrrr!*"

As she tumbled through a haze of aftershocks, he slid in and out slowly as he lowered her boneless body gently to the ground.

She could hear his voice but not understand his words, only the sound of his love. Her mind quieted, hearing the forest murmurs carried on a faint wind.

She thought she knew magic.

What they had together could not be conjured by false methods.

Rolling up against him, she snuggled in his warmth. She loved being close to him for as long as possible.

He'd said that crossing this line together would change everything for them.

She agreed. Now she had to find a way to keep him safe and outwit the fates trying to dictate the end of her life before she was ready.

Chapter 35

KROL SMILED TO himself on making a deal with the Kwilkotauk leader Jothan. He'd heard of these witch-born werewolves for a long time but had never had reason to risk a trip to this dangerous place. They were driven by the full moon and their witch blood. He was no fan of dealing with difficult subordinates.

Jothan's assassins were not house pets but were incredibly loyal to Jothan.

He gave two of them instructions to provide Krol with any help he requested. Krol paid heavily in gold for this service.

If he survived the meeting with the mage, it would be worth every penny.

Tension in his chest eased as soon as the wagon pulled out through the gates and onto the dirt road. Jothan had suggested not shifting into his lion around the wilkotauks. They would immediately neutralize any threat.

Krol looked behind the wagon for the two wilkotauks in human form.

One had vanished.

That gave him pause until he reminded himself that he'd hired the best for a reason. The remaining werewolf followed at a steady jog, a blank look on his clean but hardened face. Golden hair stood out two inches in a thick band from his forehead to his neck, which the Americans called a mohawk. Dark purple tattoos of sigils covered the left side of his face, crossing over his eyelids and down his throat. Not a bulked-up guy, but one with toned muscles and not a bit of fat. Bright yellow eyes, each in a smudge of black against pale skin.

Krol had to allow them space to do their jobs. Now that he did not have to waste time diverting his scent trail, he should arrive ahead of schedule.

That would give him a chance to place his two nasty wilkotauk surprises in prime locations to protect him.

No one could stop him now.

Not even if that mage bastard tried to double-cross him.

Chapter 36

ADRIAN'S WOLF, RED, would take the lead the minute Krol's wagon emerged from the estate. Justin's bear crossed to the other side of the road, choosing a spot to observe until Adrian sent word for their next move.

Red searched until he found the optimum place to watch at ground level as Krol's wagon departed the estate early the next morning. Cool air plump with water fell on Red's coat, which bothered Adrian's wolf as much as a duck.

He and Justin had discussed options, but any attack on Krol might end with him killing either or both of the women before they could stop him.

Justin spoke in Adrian's mind. *This would be a great place to ambush Krol now.*

I think so, too, but we'll have to be patient until he shifts into his lion and leaves the wagon. I'm thinking one of us will take him on, and the other will go after the wagon.

Yep, that's a plan. We should probably give Herc the lion to deal with while Red keeps up with the wagon.

Good thinking, Adrian sent back. That would make the most sense. While Red was the fastest of the two, Justin's grizzly Herc had the size to match the lion since they both agreed Krol would not give up. Herc would take any opening to make the kill.

Waiting had never been Adrian's strong suit, not like Justin's ability. Similar to his bear, Justin could sit silently for days if that was required to accomplish his mission.

Justin said, *I'm surprised Ivo didn't demand to be part of this operation.*

Adrian could understand Magdelina's mate being out of his mind with worry and ready to kill everything between him and his mate. Adrian wouldn't stay put if Jaz were in trouble, but Ivo did not have the military training he and Justin possessed. He might get Magdelina killed with a wrong move, the last thing her mate wanted to have happen.

Adrian replied, *He did. Ivo would have come if the Guardian had shared our intel. We'd have spent as much time and energy keeping him alive as anyone he deemed guilty of aiding Krol.*

I'd be the same, Justin admitted.

But you wouldn't lose your head and kill Eriko before we found out where Krol had taken the women.

You're right about that. Justin was quiet, then said, *I just wish we could keep him updated without putting the women at risk.*

I'd like to as well, but the Guardian tasked us with bringing her home and said he'd deal with Ivo because that bear is going to be pissed at being told to stand down.

The sound of wheels turning in dirt preceded Krol's garish wagon decorated to advertise tinctures, knives, and metal pots. If it had been an authentic gypsy wagon, things would have been hanging on the sides and clanging.

As the wagon passed their observation point, Adrian saw a guard from the estate jogging behind. He didn't have a wolf shifter smell but that of a werewolf. Unlike his wolf shifters and Bosse, those wolves turned during a full moon.

Eriko had said they were witch-born werewolves. Would that make a difference?

Red dragged in a breath full of black magic through his nose and shoved his snout into the loose dirt, breathing through his mouth.

Justin said, *That stinks.*

Adrian told him what Red was doing to prevent sneezing.

Herc has his paws over his nose. I think they're far

enough ahead that we're clear if Red and Herc need to sneeze and knock that crap out of their noses.

Once the animals were set, Adrian agreed with Justin to give Herc the lead to take off and follow closer to the wagon. That way, the grizzly bear could engage with Krol as soon as that lion appeared.

Herc followed the wagon on his side of the road, staying twenty feet off to the side in the trees.

Red hung back, watching Herc for any sign of going after Krol's lion, which was the only reason Red caught Herc shaking his head and slowing down.

Bear is in trouble, Red told Adrian.

Justin called a second later. *We're being attacked. Dark magic.*

Red took that news in stride, but his muscles immediately bunched as he lunged into the hunt.

They'd have to put off catching up to the wagon after backing up Herc.

When Red raced across the road and into the woods, Herc came into view. The massive grizzly stood and roared, paws slashing the air at an invisible threat.

Adrian called telepathically to Justin. *We're close, but we haven't seen the wilkotauk yet.*

Justin murmured something indecipherable.

That was not good.

Red paused before rushing forward and lifted his snout to inhale. He swung his head hard to the left, then snuck back toward the road.

Adrian trusted this wolf with his life. Red would do whatever was possible to save Herc and Justin. Before they reached the road, Red turned to parallel it, then slowed to a careful walk as he stalked something.

Off to the right, Justin's bear came down on all four legs, roaring a vicious sound. If Herc could escape the magic, he'd slaughter whatever attacked him.

If not, Adrian didn't want to think about losing his friend.

Red hunched down, easing forward silently until Adrian finally saw what his wolf hunted.

A yellow-mohawk guard dressed in a black leather vest and black pants like the one following the wagon stood with his legs apart. He held up the head of a dead human, softly calling to some unholy spirit.

The head burst into flames.

Adrian said to Red, *Try not to bite too deeply in case his blood is tainted.*

Yes, was his wolf's quick reply.

Justin called, *We're burning from the inside out.*

Oh, mother. Smoke streamed out of Herc's ears. They couldn't wait any longer for help. Red took two steps and leaped at the black magic conjurer.

The wilkotauk turned quickly to face Red, but Adrian's wolf landed on the wilkotauk's head, ripping his face off and then clawing his upper body as he slid down the front. The wilkotauk screamed and grabbed Red, trying to yank him off.

A raging grizzly, free of the black magic, came running in.

Adrian said, *Great job, Red. Let Herc have at him.*

Red pushed off and jumped to the side as Herc slammed the wilkotauk to the ground. Claws longer than Adrian's hand shredded the body in seconds. Herc was still furious, stomping on the body, then standing and bellowing another rage-filled roar.

Adrian asked, *Justin, are you okay?*

Gettin' there. Give Herc a minute. Never seen him so out of control.

Neither had Adrian, but Red would have been no better if he'd been attacked with magic.

Once Herc settled down, snorting and huffing out deep breaths, he walked away from the bloody mash of arms and legs.

Red circled the wilkotauk to join Herc.

Adrian asked for the body, which Red gave him.

Seeing that, Herc gave Justin the body. Poor Justin's face was blistered, and his eyes were bloodshot.

"Are you sure you're gonna be okay?" Adrian asked,

thinking he might have to continue alone and send help for Justin.

"I'm fine, and I'll be better as Herc heals. Those bastards are carrying some ungodly magic shit."

Now Adrian understood. "That's why Eriko sounded in awe of these werewolves. They're not just capable of changing shape. They're dark magic wielders."

Justin had a determined look in his eyes when he said, "Let's shift and go after Krol and the other asshole."

Their animals took off on the same side of the road. Herc led again, and Red stayed a short distance back to watch for any rear attack on Herc.

Adrian estimated where the wagon should be and told Justin, *We're maybe a half hour behind the wagon. Our animals can overtake them.*

I hope so, was all Justin said.

By the time they reached the main road, Adrian had begun to worry about not seeing the wagon yet. At the speed their animals ran, they should have overtaken the wagon before now. No wagon wheel trail turned down the beaten-down path on this side within sight of the paved road leading up to a major highway. They'd found wheel ruts that disappeared five minutes ago.

After their animals searched both sides of the road a mile in each direction, Adrian and Justin admitted the obvious.

The wagon had vanished.

Herc lumbered up to Red.

Adrian telepathically ranted to Justin, *Shit fire, those magic wielders must be wiping away the wagon trail. We've lost them.*

Justin cursed. *We could go back to the castle to see if anyone has received information from Bosse and Alifair, but if we head in the wrong direction, we might screw our chances of getting to Krol's meet site in time if we get a signal from Bosse.*

Adrian couldn't believe this had happened when the women had been so close. The only benefit right now was being close to where they stashed their clothes. Disgusted, he admitted, *Yep, we're dead in the water unless Bosse or Alifair triggers the EPIRB. Let's get dressed and figure out a new game plan.*

he admitted, *Yep, we're dead in the water unless Alifair triggers the EPIRB. Let's get dressed and figure out a new game plan.*

Chapter 37

KROL HAD YET to see the second wilkotauk catch up to them, but Jothan had warned him these werewolves were the best at stealth. One still followed the wagon, though dropping back occasionally to wipe their trail.

He loved that, but this was why he'd wanted to have two wilkotauks with him.

One to deal with any threat and the other to protect his wagon.

Krol itched to shift into his lion. Anything to get him out of this wagon and away from these two bitches.

Magdelina, in particular.

She smiled as if she'd heard his thoughts, which he sure as hell hoped she couldn't. "My mate will leave no stone unturned until he finds you and takes you apart slowly, piece by piece. He may finally smile if you scream long enough. You have one chance to avoid that fate. Return me along with this woman to Ivo and offer to release us for your life."

Her confidence and the threat of facing a Gallize shifter might cause him to reconsider his plan if not for the mage holding a bigger stick over his head.

Besides, when this was all done, he'd have a Lammogo who could fly him away from any danger as well as attack any threat to him. Krol couldn't wait to receive complete control of his flying surprise.

He sat back and grinned. "By the end of today, you will no longer be my problem." Swinging his gaze to Rez, he added, "You might not as well if I'm offered enough in trade."

Rez had said nothing in an entire month and less than a handful of words since yesterday. She leaned forward to prop her handcuffed wrists on her knees. She neither smiled nor snarled. "I don't have a powerful mate to want vindication if I don't survive this. What I do have is an entire community of gifted people, which you will never find. I ensured that before coming to offer aid in Romania to those believed to be related to my people. Anytime we lose a member, we join our power to provide a smooth trip to the next stage of our member's life. But if that person was killed in any way besides an accident, we join our energy to ask that the perpetrator face their worst possible death and that it be drawn out for no less than seven days."

She sat back, just as calm as Magdelina, who had nodded in approval.

His skin felt as if scorpions crawled over him. If only he could change into his lion and roar in their faces until they cowered. Not yet. Jothan had warned him the wilkotauks might kill his lion.

That didn't mean he had to sit back here with the trash.

He'd been hiding his presence during this trip, but with sunrise still two hours away, he had time to stretch his legs before reaching the meet point this morning.

Krol stood, leaning his head down to keep from hitting the wagon ceiling. "Enjoy your smug attitudes for a couple more hours. I promise you both that will be the end of it."

Two pairs of scary eyes watched him leave.

He shook off a cold chill. They were nothing, just talking a big game. He couldn't wait to see Magdelina's face when she realized she was being handed over to a mage.

That had to be worse than ending up with the Black River Pack.

Once he and the mage were done, Krol would kill the driver to leave no witness of this trade. The Gallize alpha Ivo would have no way to tie him to losing his mate. Krol would turn the wilkotauks loose, as he agreed, only because

Jothan's reputation was everything. If he chose not to do business with Krol, word would get out, and Krol would be alone on an island of his own making.

Ultimately, Krol would get the last laugh on everyone when his Lammogo flew him away.

Chapter 38

----~~----

ALIFAIR CAME AWAKE suddenly. Had a noise pulled her from the deep sleep she'd been enjoying, or was the nightmare still sucking the air from her lungs?

The nightmare won.

She wouldn't have believed she had a dream worse than the prophecy of her death.

After she and Bosse had cleaned up with the cold water in the gourd last night, he'd tossed the edge of the cover over her and wrapped his arms around her chilled body, keeping her warm. She didn't stay awake long enough to worry about some animal or bug getting to her. Bosse had been there keeping her safe.

But she couldn't expect him to protect her from nightmares.

This one had been too vivid.

She'd dreamed of the castle ruins not far from where they'd slept. Bosse had been in it, too, but this time, he never acknowledged her presence.

In her heart, she knew this had been a projection of what would happen today if she didn't stop the vision from coming true.

Pushing hair out of her eyes did little to aid her in seeing until her eyes focused. With sunrise still half an hour or more away, the first tiny speck of light brightening the horizon highlighted trees and branches.

Good thing since she had to find her way to a bathroom spot. Then she could come back and think up a plan.

Squeak!

She froze. That was not a natural sound from the woods. Quieting her breathing, she closed her eyes and focused on her sense of hearing. Another less noisy squeal sounded in repetition… just as she'd expect a wagon wheel to make.

Could that be Krol?

Her pulse raced, and her heartbeat did double time.

If that was Krol, she was out of time for planning.

Bosse moved, getting into a better position, and pulled her closer to him.

He would wake the minute she tried to rise. She took slow breaths, trying to calm her heart, or that noise might wake him. While she pulled herself together, she ran multiple scenarios through her mind.

In the end, she had only one choice, and Bosse might never forgive her for what she had to do to keep him safe.

Chapter 39

WAKE UP!

Bosse stirred, then grumbled and fell back into a deep sleep.

Hurry! Wake up! Wake up! Wake up!

Shaking his head, Bosse fought to open his eyes. What was wrong with Titan? Bosse lifted his head, unable to see anything, and plopped back on the blanket.

Mate is gone!

What had his wolf said? Titan had never shouted so loudly in his head, but the word mate finally got through, snapping Bosse awake. His head banged, and he was still groggy.

Get up! Titan roared again, sending ice water through Bosse's veins. *Mate is gone!* His brain got that. Breathing hard, panic brought Bosse fully awake. He reached for Alifair.

His hand landed on an empty blanket. No!

Bosse rubbed his eyes and forced himself to sit up. Trying to wake up was like trudging through quicksand. *Where is she, Titan?* Bosse pushed up to stand and sidestepped to stay upright as he dressed.

I do not know. I smelled a strange scent that woke me.

Bosse leaned on a tree to keep from falling. What kind of scent?

Magic.

That made his heart stutter. Could Krol be here and the

trade happening? Where was Alifair? Why hadn't he heard her get up or felt her pull away from his embrace?

He lifted the water he'd left beside the blanket, poured the ice bath over his face, and then shook his head to sling the water off.

Now he was awake. He snatched his shirt off the ground and pulled it on, ready to hunt Alifair.

Yelling her name could put her in danger if she had been captured.

His hands fisted with white-knuckle fury.

Someone was going to bleed.

He suffered a heart-stopping moment of worry over tracking her, then realized she wore the scent of their bonding. He dropped his head back, staring up at the lightening sky, and said a prayer of thanks that he'd marked his mate.

Where should he start looking?

In the ruins.

As the light began to grow and spread ahead of sunrise, he noticed a large patch of cleared dirt that looked out of place. He'd been all over this area last night and had not seen that. When he stepped close, he squatted down to read something written in the dirt.

Bosse–

I'm sorry for making you sleep hard. I had a nightmare about you being captured, and I can't let that happen again or for you to be killed. I am shielding myself with a spell that should make me invisible. Freeing Rez is my last duty to the clan. I will do my best for the other woman as well. Please forgive me for leaving like this, but your life and safety mean everything to me. I will always love you.

Your mate.

He struggled to draw a breath. Tears burned his eyes.

What had she done? He couldn't live without her. He read it again, looking for a clue to find her, but the only thing that stood out were the words *Freeing Rez is my last duty.*

Alifair didn't expect to survive.

Chapter 40

ALIFAIR QUIETLY CURSED every branch and rock that made her stumble.

She scratched the thought of getting the hang of being in the woods. She was not a shifter or a mountain girl.

Riding the horse up this inclined slope had been far easier than climbing it on foot. Yesterday, she hadn't noticed how thin the air was, but right now, it felt like an elephant had a foot on her chest, cutting off her oxygen supply. Pausing to catch her breath, she wiped the sweat from her forehead.

To do this with any expertise would require exercising.

That alone disqualified hiking as part of her future, even if she were to survive.

A loud squawk far above pulled her gaze up.

Krol's Lammogo flew overhead. If she'd needed any additional confirmation of Krol being here, there it was. The bird thing folded its wings and dove, vanishing from sight behind tall spruce and pine trees.

Ready to strike out again, Alifair ignored her leg muscles screaming at her and pushed on. She slowed when she began to encounter less-inclined ground where trees grew more sporadically. The ruins had to be close. She was almost out of hill to climb.

Not a hill. This had to be a mountain. Anything over fifty feet was in her book.

She moved from tree to tree, feeling like the worst kind of spy, and taking her time to reach a place where she could view the open grounds around the castle ruins. A small herd of five deer grazed on low branches and wild bushes until they reached the far side of the clearing.

All the does moved along until the one in the lead froze. The others stilled as well. The front doe began backing away instead of turning to walk.

What had she seen or smelled?

As she reached the other four, she must have given some secret deer signal. They all jumped around and ran like demons from hell were after them.

With no idea where to go next, Alifair decided to stay put and avoid that far side, which had spooked the deer. She rubbed her damp hands on her pants and felt a lump in her front pocket.

Fishing it out, she realized she had the EPIRB. What had happened to Adrian and Justin if they weren't here with the wagon?

Sliding her fingernail beneath the antenna tip, she started lifting.

A blood-curdling female scream slashed through the silence.

Alifair looked up. Had that been Rez or Magdelina?

Confident her spell would protect her from being seen, she took off running while trying to activate the EPIRB.

Something invisible and big hit her hard on her side, sending her flying and then cartwheeling. She saw stars. Had her spell failed? This was a disaster.

Not as much as empty hands.

She'd lost the EPIRB before she could press the button.

Chapter 41

A SCREAM FORCED BOSSE to stop fast.

That had come from a woman. Had it been Alifair?

He'd stayed in human form in case he had to talk to someone but wondered if he'd get to her more quickly if Titan took the body.

Titan said, *Krol captured two women to trade. If he captures our mate, he may not harm her if he can trade her.*

Leave it to his wolf to keep Bosse from losing his mind. Not yet. Not so long as there was a chance of getting Alifair back. *Thank you, Titan.*

Sadly, he'd been wrong about tracking Alifair. She must have hidden her scent with the spell she claimed would make her invisible.

If it worked.

He felt bad questioning his mate's ability, but she had admitted her magic came and went sometimes. He truly hoped that the lack of scent meant her spell held up and protected her.

She also had that orange thing Adrian said would call him and Justin when they found Krol and the women. Bosse should have thought about triggering the device last night, but at this point, he still had not seen a wagon.

He and Alifair were on their own.

Chapter 42

WHEELING AROUND FAST to face Magdelina, Krol snarled, "Shut up, or I'll have my Lammogo stick its claws into you again."

That silenced the bitch.

No one was here yet. That mage would have made a grand entrance.

Standing in the shadow of what had been a doorway of a building attached to the crumbling castle, he kept watch, anxious for this meeting.

Krol snickered at how stupid everyone else was compared to him.

He'd told the only wilkotauk still present to remain in hiding unless a threat appeared or if he called them in, making it clear he expected the other one to be nearby.

But he did not want anyone killed, just delivered to him.

He'd hidden the two women in the lower level of a two-story stone structure. It stank of rot and animal feces—a perfect spot for putting two snooty women in their place.

Wind whistled across the castle lands this high up on the mountain.

His Lammogo had taken to the air when he ordered it to scout for anything other than natural animals in the area. His creature could not see through the canopy of leaves, but more than one person would be unable to hide from those eagle-like eyes.

Glancing to his right, he smiled at the Lammogo. "Good job. I have great plans for you."

It continued staring straight ahead at nothing, as usual, and standing immobile as if carved from marble.

That was the most disconcerting thing about the Lammogo. It never showed any acknowledgment of his praise. He'd have plenty of time to bond with it once Zuzani handed over complete control.

Krol straightened, alarmed at seeing the wilkotauk who had stayed with the wagon walking toward his hiding place with his arms outstretched. What the devil was going on with him?

When the wilkotauk reached Krol, he said, "Intruder. Still alive." Then he dropped what he pretended to carry on the ground. It hit with a dull thud.

Krol rubbed his eyes, hoping when he dropped his hand, none of that had happened. No, the wilkotauk still stood there. "What the hell are you talking about?"

Something on the ground made a groaning sound.

Angling his head in confusion, Krol squatted down with a hand extended. He bumped into a shape above the ground and got slapped.

"Get away from me," the invisible person snapped.

A woman? She sounded familiar. He stood and used his foot to push at where he thought her body was.

"Ugh." Another groan.

Who could that be?

Had the mage sent this woman to confuse Krol or make him expose his location? Krol stuck his head out into the daylight, searching the grounds. Nothing stirred. He pointed at the invisible woman and told the wilkotauk, "Put her inside the room and find some way to tie her up."

For the first time, the wilkotauk's face showed a reaction. He frowned, which Krol understood. How would either of them tie up an invisible person?

The wilkotauk stepped back with his arms crossed his arms.

Was he refusing Krol?

Jothan's man closed his eyes and began speaking in a language Krol felt certain hadn't been common in the past twenty centuries. It sounded guttural and born of unimaginable horrors.

Blue dust began to float down from ten feet above the ground like tinted ash from a volcano. As it settled over an eight-foot-wide diameter, the body on the ground took shape.

Krol was not surprised to see a female after having heard her voice, but the face she wiped at to clear away ash shocked him. "What are you doing *here?*"

The servant he knew as Alifair stared at him from the flat of her back. "It should be obvious."

He dismissed the wilkotauk, sending him back on guard duty. Then he grabbed the servant's arm and dragged her inside.

She slapped his hand. "Stop. I can walk."

"Think I care?" He kept going, pulling her past the women he'd tied to part of the structure.

"No! Leave her alone!" Rez shouted.

Ignoring her, Krol pulled another length of rope free, giving himself kudos for having planned ahead in case he'd had to hobble the women. Alifair started fighting in earnest, twisting around to shove up to her knees.

She yanked her hands and pulled back, trying to topple him.

He freed one hand to smack her head hard. Her eyes rolled up, and she fell limp. Rez sobbed.

These women drove him nuts. He might never want a mate.

He finished pulling Alifair into a sitting position and tying her wrists to a stone column used to hold up the ceiling.

She had some kind of magic but likely was no threat with her hands tied above her head to the support beam, or she'd have tried to use her magic on him by now.

Zuzani had better make him a great offer for two gifted women.

If not, he'd kill them both before he left.

Chapter 43

"ALIFAIR."

"Hmm?" Alifair's head throbbed. Had a tractor-trailer run her over?

"*Alifair!*" hissed at her.

Opening her eyes had been a mistake. Her head spun even more. She wanted to throw up but realized her hands were tied above her head. Throwing up would be a bad idea as she couldn't lean over and keep the gunk off her.

"Do you hear me?"

"Yes," Alifair snapped. "Stop shouting."

No one said a word.

Crap. That had been unkind of her, but her head and stomach felt as if she were suffering the worst hangover ever. She rarely drank anything and never overindulged.

Opening her eyes really wide, she blinked hard a few times and tried to focus. Dark room that smelled like… yuk. *Don't think about it and breathe through my mouth.*

When her eyes adjusted to the poor lighting aided only by a smidgen of daylight meandering in through a doorway, she made out two shapes.

Rez and Magdelina stared at her as if she were naked.

"What?" That sounded snippy even to Alifair's ears. "Sorry, I'm trying to get my brain working again."

"Good," Rez said. "It must not be functioning well for you to be here."

That stung. She'd promised herself she would not allow Rez to criticize her again once this was over, but she hadn't expected to live long enough to see her again. Still, she had no patience this minute.

Alifair grabbed the ropes that were rubbing her wrists raw and pulled herself up to kneel. Better.

Since she was going to die soon, she might as well get something off her chest. "Are you criticizing me, Rez?" Before the woman could say a word, Alifair continued. "Because I've been through hell for a month working like a slave so I could find you. I managed to get free after you left with Krol and came here because I saw you and Magdelina here in a dream. I walked away from the one person who actually cares if I live or die to fulfill my duty to our clan."

Rez's eyes widened, and her mouth opened into an O.

"So let me be very clear." Alifair had a head of steam pushing her anger. "I will do this last duty, and all I ask is that you do not give me grief about it."

Magdelina had smiled more and more as Alifair got all that out.

Closing her mouth, Rez waited a few seconds, then said, "I'm… sorry. I've had time to think, too much time, but I came to the realization that I should have long ago. This burden should not have been placed on your shoulders any more than the one hung around your mother's neck. I was just upset to see you here when I'd hoped you would escape Romania to live." Tears ran down her face. "As the clan leader, I have allowed my anger at losing your mother to turn me into a bitter woman. I'm sorry I failed you even more than the others."

Alifair dropped her head back, feeling like an ogre. For many years, she'd loved this woman her mother had thought of as a sister.

Hearing an apology soothed Alifair's raw feelings about Rez and the clan. Her mother would be ashamed of how she'd just spoken to Rez.

Dropping her chin back down, she said, "I'm sorry, Rez. I'm just wrung out from all this and can't handle anyone getting on my butt right now. I may have been caught by that weirdo in the black vest, but I'm not down."

"There is a strong woman," Magdelina said, sounding proud of her.

Rez nodded, her crumpled face smoothing out with a smile. "You're every bit the warrior your mother was, Alifair. I don't want you here with us, but I at least have the chance to say I should have told you I've always been proud of you as you grew up. I just lost my way and wanted someone to fill the hole your mother left. My greatest error was not respecting you for that position."

Alifair swallowed the lump in her throat. None of her clan had ever treated her badly, but they had never believed in her skills.

In all fairness to them, she hadn't either, but she'd called on her magic more in the past few days than in her entire life, and it had answered.

Most of the time. "Where is Krol?"

"He left after tying you up," Rez replied.

Blowing out an air of frustration over her situation, she said, "Okay. Apology accepted. Let's all work as a team now. I've got an idea. I hope it works, or we're all doomed to the same fate."

The two women exchanged a heavy glance, and then Magdelina said, "We're behind you all the way, and I will never blame you if anything goes wrong."

"Neither will I." Rez nodded, her eyes red and swollen but sincere.

Alifair refrained from telling them she'd had disastrous results the one time she'd tried this and hoped they were far enough back to be safe.

Chapter 44

B OSSE KEPT SNEAKING toward the ruins in one
direction to determine the best point of attack.

If only he could see Alifair and the other two women.

Until then, he risked putting them in danger if he just boldly rushed in. He'd seen the wagon parked off to the side of the road. The driver lay dead with his throat cut.

Krol must have another exit point. The wagon would be too slow, but why kill the driver?

Because Krol wanted no witnesses.

Bosse hoped Titan was right about Krol keeping Alifair alive to trade. That would not happen while Bosse had breath in his body.

Titan spoke in his mind. *I smell the dark magic here.*

Lifting his nose to the air, Bosse could not pick it up, but Titan had always possessed a keen sense of smell for supernatural scents. Dark magic would not be Alifair's.

What do you think it is? Bosse asked.

Someone or something nearby.

As Bosse communicated with Titan, a piece of orange off to the right caught his eye. He wove his way carefully to get closer until he could determine what it could be.

The orange EPIRB lay in thick grass an arm's length from the closest tree.

Alifair had kept it in her pocket.

He scouted the entire area, searching for someone watching to trap him. Nothing moved across the open ground or along what was left of the wall connecting to the castle. He lay down on his stomach and pushed his arm slowly to avoid disturbing the weeds, fingers searching for a small ball shape.

He bumped it and clamped his hand over the ball, pulling it back to him.

When he could stand again, he flicked his gaze around to see if anyone was headed his way. Not yet.

The short antenna was partially extended. Had Alifair been caught as she tried to trigger the device? He flipped it all the way open and turned the ball to find the button. Please tell him this would work.

He pressed the button. Nothing happened.

How would he know if it worked?

A tiny light inside the button began to blink. Placing it on the ground, he tossed leaves over it to hide the light. While riding, Alifair had told him about satellites high in the air that this would communicate with, so a few leaves shouldn't interfere.

The sound of someone walking reached his ears as Titan said, *He is here.*

Bosse lifted his gaze to the open space in front of the castle.

Krol appeared as he stepped from a building at ground level, stirring dust as he strolled.

Chapter 45

ALIFAIR MENTALLY REVIEWED the awful dream about her death, which could be irrelevant since so many things had altered from her dreams and nightmares.

In the nightmare where blood poured from a gash in her stomach, she had not been tied up like this. There was still time left. How could she get free? Magdelina's gift would not help her even if the woman were not pregnant. Neither would Rez's ability, which required her to go into a trance to foresee a path for the community.

They both stared at her as if waiting to hear how she'd discovered the secret to life.

Rez had never put so much faith in Alifair to see her in the same league as her powerful mother.

Magdelina had told her to trust her gift.

Alifair could do nothing while watching their hope-filled faces. She closed her eyes and focused. With nothing to cut the ropes, she had come up with a wild idea, which was only better than nothing.

Stop with the negative energy, she told herself.

Focusing on the ropes, she dug around for a spell her mother might have used on ropes but could not recall one. Her mother had been born Romanian and taught Alifair magic phrases as she trained. Looking back at her years of practicing, Alifair admitted she hadn't been the best student because she'd thought her mother would live to an old age.

All that time wasted when she could have gained more tools in her magic kit.

"Alifair." Rez's voice came out softly.

She opened her eyes. "Yes?"

"Stop putting pressure on yourself. Your mother used to say you would one day unlock your gift to its true potential, but you tried too hard to be perfect. None of us are. She was amazing, but she had her own misfires. If you have an idea, just try it. We will be no worse off if it does not work."

Alifair had never seen her mother fail, but her mother may have kept those times to herself. She hadn't dwelled on what would not work. Had that been why her mother had often told her to hold onto her wins and leave the losses behind?

She nodded and drew in a deep breath, letting it out slowly as the pressure on her chest eased. Closing her eyes again, this time, she envisioned all the ways she might affect the ropes.

Could she make them stretch or loosen?

If she got the spell wrong, the rope could tighten and cut her hands off.

Nice pep talk, idiot.

As her mind calmed, she heard her mom saying, "Keep up your Latin studies. If you can't pull up the words of my family's language, that is your fallback." What was the word for loosen? Or maybe elongate? If she'd learned them, they would be buried in her mind beneath all the useless information stored there.

Try harder. She curled her fingers, fisting her hands into fighting mode. How could she say stretch the ropes? Two words bubbled to the surface. *Funes extendere.* It translated to *ropes stretch.* In modern day, it would be *stretch the ropes*.

Licking her dry lips, she began whispering, "I command *funes extendere.*" Nothing happened. Too timid for an order, but she was trying not to embarrass herself in front of two powerful peers. On the other hand, why be concerned about embarrassing herself when she wouldn't be living much longer?

Good point.

If she hadn't sounded serious about a chant or spell in the past, her mother would give her a sharp look and ask, "Do you *really* want that to happen?" That had been the Romanian version of stop being a wimp.

Putting grit in her voice, Alifair called out, "I command *funes extendere!*" She kept saying it, feeling a surge of power rising in her middle.

Her arms had been straight up, but now her elbow bent, and her hands hung slack. She opened her eyes and looked up, then pulled her wrists free of the ropes that moved like giant rubber bands.

Rubbing her raw wrists, she looked over to find Magdelina had tears in her eyes. "That was a delight to watch."

Rez grinned. "Your mother would be so proud of you."

Alifair had to fight back tears. She had never been so proud of herself but had more to do. "Thank you both." She hurried over to free both women, who massaged their bruised wrists.

As soon as they stood, Alifair said, "Stay behind me, and we'll escape before Krol figures out what is happening."

"What are you planning to do?" Rez asked.

Still thrilled at her small success, Alifair hoped she could do what she had in mind now.

This was what she had worried about trying. If her gift faltered now, they'd all die, but they were no safer staying in here.

Chapter 46

BOSSE COULD NOT stand in the tree cover and wait another second when he had no idea where Alifair was or what might be happening to her.

After walking out of a lower level, Krol stepped around the end of the wall and did not come back. Within a few minutes, he appeared at the top of the largest building of three stories and leaped to the ground, landing with the agility of a lion shifter. His head swiveled from side to side.

Was he looking for someone… or something? He began walking forward and lifting his hand, palm out in the direction of the trees on the other side from where Bosse hid. It was as if Krol motioned someone to stay put.

Titan said, *Dirt is moving around with no wind.*

What was his wolf talking about? Bosse searched the grounds all the way back to the room Krol had vacated. That's when he noticed dirt near the ground-floor entrance to a two-story building.

The dust puffed up as if disturbed by someone walking there.

He told his wolf, *I see it, but I have no idea what that is. It's moving to the far right. We need to watch our backs in case that is being caused by a wilkotauk.*

If that was a wilkotauk, Bosse needed to move left to add more distance between them.

Titan said, *I hear whispering from whatever is moving the dirt.*

Bosse kept Krol in sight as he tuned out the sounds of critters scurrying around the woods. His heart lurched when he recognized a voice. Alifair.

Titan said, *Mate is talking.*

You're right. Now Bosse had to make his way quietly around thirty yards of tree line to reach her, but the undergrowth between them would slow him down. That didn't matter. Better to circle through the woods and get her to safety first, then come back.

That would give him time to scold her for running into danger.

Then kiss her.

He heard Alifair tell someone, "You two stay hidden here."

Had she found her friend and Magdelina? He'd have to move all three women to a safe place and talk to Alifair later.

Titan warned, *Beast is here!*

Before Bosse could put his plan into action, Beast strode up the dirt road leading to the ruins. The part-rhino's head jerked in Bosse's direction the minute it caught his scent.

Beast immediately shifted into a black rhino. In addition to a large horn shooting up from his snout, two smaller ones jutted from each side of his mouth. Sharp tips as if filed down.

Even in a full shift, that thing did not look right.

Ignoring Bosse, Beast pounded toward the castle, bellowing a threat.

Oh, hell no. That monster had terrified Alifair when he snuck out during the castle battle and fingered her as the one who helped Bosse escape. If it was true rhinos had poor eyesight over a distance, Beast still might be able to smell the women with Alifair.

Bosse would not risk him getting near her.

He told Titan, *Take the body and protect our mate.*

His wolf pushed hard through the change and felt stronger than he had in a long time. Titan leaped from the woods and howled at Beast.

The screwed-up-looking rhino slid to a stop and swung all that weight around to face the attack.

Bosse warned Titan, *Watch out for all three horns.*

Alifair shouted, "*Nooo!*"

Titan glanced that way.

Alifair must have gotten the women to the trees. She was in full view with hands raised and chanting her strange words while heading toward a two-ton supernatural rhino.

Chapter 47

Bosse's heart took a nosedive. What was Alifair doing?

Titan said, *She calls for wind.*

His wolf nailed it. Wind began to gather, sucking in from the trees and around the building, all rushing to stir up a dust storm in front of her.

That wouldn't even slow Beast down.

Bosse couldn't shout to her in animal form. He told Titan, *We have to reach Beast first.*

Where Bosse and Titan had always waited for their opponents to attack in the arena, this was different. All he and his wolf cared for in this world would be smashed to pieces by Beast if they didn't attack now.

When his wolf swung his attention to the rhino, Bosse noticed what was going on far behind Beast.

Krol once again lifted his hand in a not-yet gesture to someone in the trees. Then the prick crossed his arms and struck a superior pose to watch as he had when enjoying matches in the arena.

Beast pawed the ground, jerking from side to side. Its body didn't even move in a normal way.

Titan took off fast as an arrow flying toward Beast.

Beast jumped around toward Alifair and lumbered into a run.

Alifair continued to walk toward that monster with dust swirling ahead of her.

Bosse shouted to Titan, *Beast will get to Alifair first.*

Titan said, *No!* His wolf angled to intercept Beast and dug deeper for more power.

But they were a step too late when Beast hit the wall of Alifair's energy.

Titan drove into a body four times his size. The collision knocked Beast off balance. With all that top-heavy weight, it fell onto its side.

Hitting hard, Titan flipped in the air and landed in a sickening thump, not rolling up to stand.

Bosse's eyes crossed, and his head felt like a cathedral bell struck with a sledgehammer. He could barely say, *Get up, Titan.*

His wolf struggled to stand and wobbled around, preparing for an attack.

Bosse's vision cleared to look for Alifair where she'd hit the ground. She shook her head and sat up, looking dazed.

That rhino moved awkwardly but managed to roll over to its knees. Now was the best time to attack something with hide like a paved road, but Titan's chest moved painfully with heaving air in and out.

Bosse could feel broken ribs. He couldn't ask more from an injured wolf ready to die to protect their mate. He spoke softly to Titan. *You are an incredible wolf. You've always given your best. I know you will now. If this doesn't go our way, we finally have something worth dying for. I'm proud of you, no matter what.*

Titan sent back, *We will protect her. I hope we live.*

Then Bosse felt power rushing to Titan's ribs. It might be too little too late.

Before Beast stood on all four cloven hooves, Titan got his legs under him and attacked first again, cutting hard to the right of Beast's horned snout that tried to gouge him. Titan folded his legs and slid under Beast's belly, rolling to his back. Wolf claws slashed over and over, barely drawing blood.

Beast leaped away, throwing its huge head back toward Titan.

Bosse's wolf rolled quickly, and Beast's hooves missed

Titan's chest by inches. Pain slashed through Titan when he jumped up and ran between Beast and where Alifair now stood with terrified eyes.

Shrieking a wild noise, Beast came for Titan, swinging its head wide from side to side, those horns looking for a soft target.

Titan and Beast clashed.

Bosse felt every gash Titan took, sick for his wolf to fight this crazed rhino.

Krol had walked closer and shouted, "*Kill him, Beast!* I didn't pay the Black River Pack all that money for you to play around. Get it done!"

Gashed and bleeding from multiple injuries, Titan fought on with total abandon and latched onto Beast's throat. He jerked his head back and forth, ripping into the one spot he could finally damage.

Beast caught Titan's shoulder with a hoof and cracked bone, then kicked Bosse's wolf aside.

Titan rolled until his limp body stilled. He moaned, fighting for a breath.

Give me the body, Titan. Bosse endured the miserable change, and so had Titan. His shoulder bled, and his chest had been slashed open, creating a pool of blood.

His wolf had ripped Beast's throat enough that the rhino stood in one spot. A sickening sound oozed out on each exhalation.

Bosse caught movement far behind Beast. Alifair was chanting again and moving toward the rhino.

He lifted his good arm, waving her to go away. "*Run. Save yourself.*"

Her determined gaze met his. She shook her head and mouthed the words, *Not without you.* Her magic created a haze of blue fog around her, giving his mate a ghostly appearance.

He realized in that moment she was willing to sacrifice herself to save him. How could he have ever doubted any action she took? She said she'd seen him save her friend Rez in a dream. That dream had only been partially correct.

Alifair had saved her friend and succeeded in fulfilling her duty.

She had come to him originally for that help but had proven her love again and again.

Yes, her love. Only his cookie fairy could love someone like him. Because of her, he was no longer a broken wolf shifter. He had gained the heart of an angel. The feeling of euphoria flooding him had to be love as well. He'd never experienced anything like it.

Beast must have heard Alifair. It turned sluggishly to face her.

"Please, Alifair," Bosse begged as loud as his hoarse voice could shout. He could not watch her be crushed by that monster. *"Runn!* I. Love. You. Don't die."

She never stopped her chanting. Her eyes filled with tears that streamed down her face. She sent him a kiss and kept walking. Nothing would stop his little warrior.

Krol screamed at Beast, "The wolf is done. *Kill her!"*

Bosse could not do anything with only one good arm.

When Beast took a step, then another, Bosse panicked and told Titan, *If you can shift, try to get to its legs.*

Beast kept going.

His wolf pulled energy and shifted, but it cost him. Bosse fought against nausea and losing consciousness.

Titan came up on all four legs. Only three worked. He moved as swiftly as he could on those legs and caught the rhino when it stopped quickly and jerked its head up.

Alifair screamed, and Bosse felt her anguish all the way through his body.

Had the monster gotten to her?

Titan clamped his jaws on the rhino's rear left leg. As Titan fell on his side, he clawed the area his jaws hadn't touched and yanked muscles free. Blood poured out from the gash.

The rhino jumped to the left and fell on its side, squealing and kicking at Titan with its rear right leg. Titan was ready and twisted to bite hard on that leg, not giving in as the rhino yanked the leg. Muscles ripped free, and blood poured even faster now from two mortal wounds.

Beyond exhausted and bleeding as well, Titan released his hold and crawled away from the pool of blood, trying to reach Alifair. Titan could barely speak. *I am done. Take the body and talk to mate.*

Bosse and Titan suffered through one last shift.

To the left of Bosse, Krol yelled, *"Mage! Where are you?"*

When Bosse's eyes cleared, he lay in blood-soaked dirt. His heart thumped slower. He ignored Krol and inched his head forward to find Alifair.

He could see her faint image through the fog. She held her hands over her stomach and looked bewildered.

Sounding furious, Krol called out, "Lammogo, come to me! Kill the wolf shifter and woman."

Chapter 48

KROL HAD TOLD his wilkotauk to stay hidden until he called to him. He didn't want his best ace to appear before the mage showed.

That stupid rhino the Black River Pack made had failed to kill Bosse or the servant woman. They might bleed out, but not fast enough.

The Lammogo had landed as soon as Krol called it down. He tried again to give it an order as he pointed at Bosse and the woman. "Kill those two."

His flying weapon didn't move an inch.

That bloody mage had said the Lammogo would only retrieve but not kill until their deal was final. Krol had delivered on his end.

Where was Zuzani?

Sure, Krol was early, but the mage said he'd know if Krol arrived with Magdelina. Krol shouted to the sky, "I have the pregnant mate you want. Show yourself."

No squirrelly mage showed his face.

He'd have to kill Bosse and that servant woman himself.

Chapter 49

———— ∞ ————

Bosse GLANCED AT the rhino to make sure it could not get up.

One labored breath after another squeezed out from the rhino's lungs. That monster was done and would be dead soon.

Searching for Alifair, her shape and face were in focus this time. The fog had cleared. She stumbled forward and fell, but not before he saw her blood-soaked clothes. The rhino had slashed her after all.

Her head curved around with red-rimmed eyes frantic until she saw him. "Bosse." The word came out in a squeak. She sobbed and used her fingers to pull one hand forward until she could lift it off the ground, reaching for him. "Bosse."

He ignored Krol, cursing how he'd have to dirty his hands and kill the wolf.

Bosse had no way to stop Krol from harming Alifair.

Failing her hurt more than all his injuries.

Titan wheezed out words in his head. *Shifters coming. Friends.*

Bosse caught the sound of two people running in from the road. He gritted his way through, making his head turn.

Krol stopped sixty feet from him and flipped around, staring at Justin and Adrian. He shouted, *"Wilkotauk! Protect me!"*

Adrian pointed in Bosse's direction. "Justin, I've got this. Check on him."

A primitive sound that Bosse had never heard rang out of the woods as the thing Krol had called came forth with glowing yellow eyes—a dark magic beast.

Having backed over to the castle, Krol pointed at Adrian. "Get that one first, wilkotauk!"

The wilkotauk walked calmly, arms crossed and speaking in tongues, or what Bosse thought that might sound like.

Black smoke curled around his words.

Justin dropped down in front of Bosse, pulling a buttoned-up shirt over his head, leaving a black T-shirt on. "Shit, I need to hurry and help Adrian."

Pulling in a breath, Bosse said, "Leave me. Go to Alifair."

Adrian taunted the wilkotauk, "You're gonna use magic on me? I thought you wilkotauks were badass. Evidently, your animal is afraid to come out."

"Don't listen to him," Krol ordered.

"That's right. Listen to your *master*," Adrian countered, clearly trying to avoid the wilkotauk's magic. "Your master thinks you're a coward."

The wilkotauk shouted, "Not my master."

Justin balled up his shirt and handed it to Bosse. "Keep that shoved over the hole in your chest."

Bosse wouldn't take it. He begged in a hoarse voice, "Please, save my mate."

Justin had pushed the shirt patch against Bosse's chest and stared at him. "Mate?"

"Yes. Save her as you would your own."

Justin cursed and demanded, "Put your hands here so I can get to her."

Bosse complied.

Krol screeched with his hands fisted. "I fucking hate idiots who won't listen."

Vicious sounds of snarling and howling erupted. Bosse checked on Adrian. He'd shifted into his huge wolf called Red that fought a black wolf Bosse couldn't identify. Had to be the wilkotauk. When Bosse looked back at Alifair, Justin had gone down on a knee next to her. His quiet curse reached Bosse.

Alifair sobbed, "Help me up."

"Just lie here and—"

"Shut up and help me up, or Adrian is going to die!" Her face clenched in pain, and she sniffled.

Hope kicked Bosse's heart into beating harder when he saw Alifair on her feet. The Gallize could save her.

Alifair called out, *"Tranquillitas wilkotauk."* Her words had been too weak to hear. She frowned and took a deep breath, whimpering in pain, then shouted in a raspy voice this time, *"Tranquillitas wilkotauk."* She told Justin, "I can only slow it down. I can't kill it. That's your job."

Conflict smacked Justin.

"Please, let me lay down, Justin. I won't bleed out as fast. Go help Adrian, then come back."

He lowered her to the ground, pulled his T-shirt off, and wadded it up to hand her. "Keep this in place. I'll be right back."

"Go!" she ordered with the urgency of a general.

Justin shed clothes and shifted into his grizzly as he raced toward Adrian.

The wilkotauk had leaped ten feet in the air and arched to hit Adrian.

That monstrous grizzly launched itself into the air with claws reaching ahead of a giant head. Justin's bear slammed the wilkotauk wolf, then flew behind it as they both slammed to the ground.

But the grizzly was on top and ripped into the strange wolf faster than anything Bosse had ever seen.

He'd never want to face an angry Justin.

Turning back to Alifair, he tried to smile as he shared one last time with his mate that Justin had gifted him.

Voice gurgling and face racked with pain, Alifair spoke in spurts. "My death… was in the dreams. Not yours… Fight to live."

No, no, no. She knew she would die here. Bosse started dragging himself with his one good arm. "No, sweetness. Life is nothing to me without you."

Chapter 50

ADRIAN HAD TO keep Krol in sight. Red gave him the body back, and it hurt like a bitch, but he had to be better off than Bosse and Alifair. He had no idea what she'd done to the wilkotauk werewolf, but its eyes had rolled up, leaving black holes right before Justin's bear torpedoed it.

Justin still fought the werewolf, but his bear, Herc, looked to have it under control.

Krol was shouting like a lunatic as he spun in place. "*Mage!* Show your face, damn you, or you'll lose the mate."

Pulling on his ripped pants, the only clothes he had left, Adrian's back hurt as if someone had beaten him with a log. The wilkotauk had not gotten close enough to claw him. That meant the dark magic he'd used on Red had battered his wolf's body. Herc made the wilkotauk pay the minute he stumbled, thanks to whatever Alifair did.

Adrian kept walking toward Krol but cautiously. Too much magic had flowed already.

Krol ordered his Lammogo, "Kill everyone out here except me!"

His bird creature slowly turned its head to Krol and stared, not moving a tiny bit.

"Bring him to me, Lammogo!" Krol screamed and pointed at Adrian.

Then, the massive mix of eagle-like head and shoulders attached to a lion's lower body took to the air and flew toward Adrian.

Herc stepped up beside Adrian, snarling a low, hair-raising sound and smelling of fresh blood. Justin spoke to Adrian in his mind. *Bosse warned us the Lammogo has poison or something in its claws that paralyzes a victim.*

Shit fire. Can you stop him?

In answer, Herc's huge head swung to look down at Adrian. The bear gave him a wry expression. Justin laughed. *Herc said he's just getting warmed up.*

Adrian left the bird creature to Justin and called out to Krol, "Hand over both women now. You have made a serious mistake crossing the Gallize."

Behind Adrian came a loud squawk of pain. He glanced back to see the Lammogo on its back and Herc standing on his rear legs, staring at it.

Turning back to Krol, Adrian started to order Krol to kneel with his hands behind him but hesitated at Krol's panicked look. What was he about to do?

For the first time, Krol appeared cornered and searching everywhere. He had no escape. Adrian would be on him by the time he reached any cover.

Krol screamed, "Zuzani, appear now or lose the pregnant Gallize mate!"

Herc made a snuffling sound. Adrian angled his body to ensure Herc was fine while keeping Krol in view.

The flying bird lion stood again. Its lower body dropped down and then pushed up to leap into the air, even with Herc towering over it with a massive paw ready to swat it down.

The bird's two paws and outstretched body stopped in midair.

Energy began to spin above the walkway that extended from one side of the structure to the other, twenty feet off the ground.

A Power Broker appeared. The damn mage. This confirmed Adrian had been right to be cautious. The Guardian would not be happy about this.

Herc leaped around and took two steps, growling in fury.

The Power Broker pointed at Herc and ordered, "Do not come any farther."

Justin's bear could go no farther and raged as if he'd run into a wall.

Adrian remained still. He'd rather not be locked in a Power Broker's magical grip.

"What took you so long to appear?" Krol's face twisted with so much anger he looked as if his head had been squashed. With Herc blocked, he stepped out into the open to face the Power Broker. "I have the Gallize mate in hand, ready to deliver. You owe me full power over the Lammogo."

Zuzani calmly explained, "You broke your part of the agreement. You were never to say my name or speak of our deal."

Krol said nothing at first. He looked around, his forehead lined with confusion, then turned back to the Power Broker. "Are you worried about *them* knowing? They'll all be dead. Simply give me control of the Lammogo, and I'll unleash it to finish them off."

"I think not." Zuzani spoke in a normal tone when he said, "Lammogo."

The creature broke free from being stuck halfway into a leap and turned to face Zuzani. The mage quietly ordered, "Kill Krol."

"What?" Krol stared at Zuzani. "I did all this for nothing?"

Zuzani shrugged.

The Lammogo flapped its wings and lifted into the air as Krol began to shift into his lion. The flying creature landed atop Krol in mid-shift, claws digging into the body, and slammed him to the ground.

Krol's lion and human body became very still, but his eyes bulged in panic. He tried to talk. The only word that slipped free was "mercy."

Evidently, that word was not in the Lammogo's vocabulary. It stood and bludgeoned Krol's body.

Adrian had seen enough. He accused Zuzani, "You are a Power Broker. You have caused deaths here and put one of our Gallize at risk. You must face our Guardian as well as your superiors."

Leaning casually on the faded wood railing and showing no reaction to a deadly threat, Zuzani said, "I do not possess the Gallize mate. Krol did. There is no conflict between the Power Brokers and the Gallize."

Crossing his arms, Adrian would not back down. "You had Krol steal a Gallize mate. That is the definition of conflict."

"True," Zuzani admitted, straightening to his full height. "But she is being returned because of my intervention. I killed Krol. Do you not wish for that outcome?" The mage paused to turn his head, looking toward Bosse and Alifair. "Is it worth it to you for us to continue to battle when two of yours are bleeding out?"

So pissed he could hardly see straight, Adrian reminded himself his priority was saving the mate first, plus Alifair and Bosse, neither of which were moving much. He wanted all of them safe. He made what he saw as his only choice and one he believed the Guardian would expect of him.

The Gallize would always cross paths with Power Brokers. His people needed to live another day to fight.

Adrian ground out his concession. "I'm taking the women. Do not come near one of ours again. You will not receive mercy."

Zuzani chuckled as if he found the warning funny, then he ordered his creature, "Take to the air, Lammogo." As the bird flew up to the sky, Zuzani took a step back, opened his arms, and vanished.

Chapter 51

WHILE ADRIAN AND that mage argued, Alifair begged the universe to keep Bosse alive. "Don't close your eyes, Bosse."

His eyes remained shut. He barely breathed.

The sickening smell of fresh and dried blood clouded the air. She held her middle with one hand, but nothing could stave off the agony of being torn open. Sweat burned her eyes. Ignoring everything except Bosse, she had to touch him. Straining, she dragged herself the last ten inches until her fingers touched his outstretched hand.

"Please… don't… die," Alifair pleaded with what voice she had left.

His eyes fluttered open. He sounded disoriented when he whispered, "Mate."

Just hearing that word gutted her. She hadn't expected him to die, just her. How could she have failed him this way?

His eyes opened again. "I'm sorry. I wanted… more… time with you, love."

She couldn't stop her sobbing. Using what energy she could call up, she dug her nails in, clawing closer to touch his face.

His eyebrows lifted, then dropped back into place.

Rez shouted, "Alifair, free us so we can come to you."

Alifair hadn't realized she'd pinned her two friends in the woods. She didn't want to waste a breath she needed for Bosse, but she'd sacrificed everything, even him, to save Rez and Magdelina. Lifting her head, she called out four words in a rattling breath to break the spell and hoped it worked.

She tasted blood that trickled out of her mouth.

It wouldn't be long now.

Rez and Magdelina showed up fast and knelt on each side of her. Rez took her hand to hold, and Magdelina brushed the hair off her face. Rez asked, "What can we do?"

Adrian rushed up and shouted, "Magdelina, are you both safe?"

"Yes. We're fine, but they need a healer."

"Shit fire, you both look bad." Adrian squatted next to Alifair.

A rush of hope pumped through her. She rasped out, "Can you heal Bosse? Please. Do something."

Adrian sounded heartbroken when he replied, "I don't have supernatural healing ability, and neither does Justin. My mate might be able to save you both."

"Where is she?" Alifair asked.

"Back home in the US."

Bosse stirred to life. His eyes unfocused when he said, "Titan warns. Shifters coming. Many. Protect... my mate."

Adrian jumped up and turned to hunt for the shifters he now smelled. "Shit fire! Justin, watch your back!"

Sick at not being able to do a thing to help Bosse, Alifair hurt thinking about what they might have had. She didn't care what her clan would have thought of her choosing a wolf shifter. This was the man of her heart.

Bosse deserved to live out his life free, not die in this place. She touched his face.

His trembling fingers stroked her hair. "I love you... forever."

She cried even harder at that and gulped a breath. She would do her best to ease his struggle. "You have fought enough, my love. I will see you in the next world. Rest now."

Magdelina, who had been so strong, cried a moment and then demanded, *"Do not die!"*

Alifair wanted to thank her even though Magdelina was no healer. She had a good heart. Rez shouted, "Do something. You have to save them."

Then Magdelina screamed at someone to hurry, but Alifair wanted to tell them fate listened to no one.

The world darkened. Her hand fell limp against her mate's shoulder.

Chapter 52

B OSSE HEARD STRANGE sounds.
Heaven must be a busy place.

On second thought, maybe hell had claimed him. He'd taken many lives and would face his penalty like a man. He only wished Titan did not have to join him. His wolf had never taken a life unless under attack and facing death.

Sounding half awake, Titan murmured, *Neither did you.*

Was it wrong of Bosse to be thankful he had one friend here? Probably.

As he woke up, so did his body, and it hurt like a mother. Why was he in pain? Wouldn't he at least arrive in the afterlife healed? Maybe not.

No point in putting off the inevitable. He blinked his eyes, glad to find himself in low light.

He reached for the aching gash in his chest, finding an angry scar not yet healed.

"Do not touch that."

Oh, mercy, was that Alifair? He whispered, "I can't be in hell if you're here."

Her laughter tinkled, and then she groaned. "Don't make me laugh. I'm better, but not enough to move too much."

Tracking the sound of her sweet voice, he turned his head to the left, and his eyes focused. She sat in a chair with pillows stuffed around her. Her clean hair fell in fluffy dark waves to her shoulders. Her skin had been a grayish color the last time he saw her. Now, she had healthy pink cheeks and those rosy lips he loved to kiss.

He croaked out, "Are we alive?"

Smiling, she nodded and reached her hand to his.

He closed his fingers around her warm hand and squeezed his eyes shut, fighting back tears. When he opened them, she was still smiling at him. "I am so happy we made it, but how did we survive being so far from a healer?"

Leaning forward, she lifted his hand to kiss. Her unusual eyes shined with joy. "I was as surprised as you. They got me stabilized first because my injury was not as deep as yours."

"Who did all that?" This would be the moment Bosse remembered for all days. Of all the awful times in his old pack and surviving Krol's prison, he had never thought to be here in this minute with a woman who loved him and almost sacrificed her life for him.

He'd never considered himself worthy of anyone like Alifair. Never saw himself as more than a monster, a killing machine.

This woman opened a cage door to free him and gave him a new life.

More than all that, she showed him the meaning of love.

"Are you even listening?" she chastised him lightly, laughing as she did.

"No. I was enthralled by the sight of you." He hoped that would make up for being rude.

She laid her second hand over his and gripped him tighter. Her smile didn't vanish, but it relaxed. "I keep thinking about how I found you."

Maybe he hadn't earned forgiveness for being distracted.

Without pausing long, she said, "And who you are now."

Unsure of where she was going with this, he stayed quiet.

"You kept trying to push me away in that cage area, warning me to get out."

He remembered every second. "I spoke the truth."

"No, you didn't speak the truth. You believed what everyone had said about you. You believed you were something they made you do." Studying him a bit, she asked, "Would you battle and kill a shifter today if ordered to do so if you had no conflict with one?"

"No." He shared this body and owed Titan to have a say and asked telepathically, *You heard our mate, Titan. Am I speaking for both of us?*

Titan spoke this time with more energy in his words. *We lived that life the best we could and survived. I trust you to decide our battles again, but I will kill anyone who tries to harm our mate.*

Alifair watched Bosse as he had that internal conversation. He explained what Titan had said.

"I thought you might be talking to Titan." That seemed to tickle her.

Wise mate to learn his ways. His wolf loved to hear her say his name.

Bosse still wanted an answer to his first question. "This looks like the room in Adrian and Jaz's home I woke up in once before on the edge of death. Jaz healed me then. Who saved us in Slovakia?"

"You're right. That's where we are. I got sidetracked. Easy to do when I'm looking at you alive. I've met Jaz and will never be able to thank her enough for both of us." Alifair stared at their hands. "Right before you fell unconscious, you said something about shifters coming in, and there were many. I lost consciousness right after you."

He gulped, remembering that awful moment. "I was at my lowest point because I could not protect you."

She kissed his forehead and grunted in pain at bending over so far, then sat up again. "The shifters coming in were led by Ivo, Magdelina's mate. He was in a rage. I heard that Adrian tried to talk to him, but Ivo ran past him to reach Magdelina. The last words I heard her say were, 'Do not die,' but I missed the rest. She was telling me, 'Do not die. I feel my mate is near.'"

"Before coming back to Slovakia for you, I recall Adrian telling Jaz that no one was to share where Adrian was going to keep Ivo from showing up. They worried Ivo would just kill everything in his path. I would understand that, but that Guardian might not."

Cocking her cute eyebrow, Alifair said, "No one can stop the power of love."

Bosse could not argue with that.

Alifair explained, "When I was with Magdelina in Krol's castle, she told me she could not use her power until she gave birth because the baby needed it." Alifair stopped and said, "Not the baby, their cub."

Bosse loved seeing her happy. "Very good."

She winked at him. "I'm a quick learner." Then she got back to her story. "Anyhow, while discussing her pregnancy, she said she had no worries while she had her mate nearby with his power. He would see her through the labor and make delivery easier. I thought she meant Ivo would make sure she had everything she needed, but Ivo is a powerful Gallize healer. When Jaz heard what he did for both of us, she paid him a compliment and said they should meet someday to exchange thoughts on healing. Ivo drained himself by jumping between us until he felt I would be okay so he could finish working on you."

"I wish to meet this man and thank him myself."

"Magdelina wants to come visit after the cub is born. She said the Guardian would make that happen. She also told me Ivo wants to thank us in person for helping his mate and cub. While he healed me, the message Magdelina had asked me to carry to him passed into his mind. She said he had tears of appreciation. Speaking of the Gallize boss, I haven't met that man."

"I have. He is an eagle shifter and looks to be maybe in his fifties, but I sensed that he is very old. Powerful, too. As I understand it, he is known as Guardian over the Gallize. Also, we must be careful not to talk about him or the Gallize. This is a secret group."

A tap at the door sounded, and Alifair called out, "Come in."

Jaz walked in, black hair scattered like the last time, but she had dark shadows under her eyes.

He tried to sit up.

Alifair went from sweet to in charge, warning him, "Don't you dare screw up her additional healing. Ivo got us home, but she had a lot more work to do on you." Then she whispered, "She scares me."

Behind Alifair's back, Jaz gave her a look for those last three words, then crossed her eyes and stuck her tongue out.

Bosse busted out a belly laugh, then groaned, regretting the move.

Alifair glared at him.

Jaz spoke with a light-hearted voice. "I hope you are not expecting me to heal you every few weeks going forward."

Still aching from the laugh, Bosse said, "That makes two of us."

"You need one or two days more of bed rest, but you should be able to sit at the table this evening to eat with us."

Adrian pushed the door wider open and walked in, putting his arm around Jaz's shoulders. He told Bosse, "You had us all worried once Ivo got Alifair healed. He said he could put more energy into her if he could stabilize you for the flight home. Otherwise, you would have to wait until later that evening for him to recover from being drained."

Alifair mentioned, "I was just telling Bosse what happened after we both went dark on you."

"Good," Adrian replied, then told Alifair, "My boss said you're welcome to take his jet when you're ready."

Bosse's stomach twisted into one big knot. He waited for Adrian and Jaz to leave before he asked, "Are you abandoning me again?"

Chapter 53

ALIFAIR GASPED AT the disappointment in Bosse's voice. He hadn't been joking. He stared at her with hurt bleeding from his gaze.

She whispered, "That's not fair. I was trying to save you last time."

He pointed out, "You admit you *are* abandoning me. What is the reason this time? Are you returning to your people to wait on the next deadly task they assign you?"

She didn't react to his anger. He had every right to question her people. Exposing a vulnerability to others went against everything a shifter like Bosse had likely been taught or had learned on his own.

She'd hoped to have this conversation tomorrow when they could walk and talk. "I don't intend to go anywhere today."

"What about tomorrow?" He clearly wanted answers now and was not allowing her to sidestep this conversation.

Huffing out a breath, she gave explaining a try. "Rez came here with us and stayed with me while I got better the first day. She said she had never wanted me to take on my mother's role, but pressure from the clan got to her, and she didn't expect me to do much anyhow. She regrets underestimating me as well as allowing the clan to push me into an unfair position. She took full responsibility for being the reason we both almost died and is returning to inform the clan that every able-bodied member starts training to defend the clan, or she will not stay."

He released a sigh. "That is good and should free you from invisible obligations."

She couldn't totally agree with him. Her obligations had not been invisible. She'd just blindly followed the path she'd been given and questioned nothing. Her blinders were off now, which is why she finally realized she could not jump onto another path without more forethought, no matter how much she loved Bosse.

In fact, because she loved him, she needed to discuss her reservations about them being together. "Having this chance to spend time with your people has opened my eyes to many things. One is that you deserve a mate."

"I have a mate."

Hearing him say she was his mate released butterflies in her insides. But she'd taken the time to give Bosse's new life consideration while she could think clearly, which rarely happened when Bosse was near her. "You are *all* shifters here. I do not want to be changed into one."

"I would never change you into something you are not," he declared.

She had mixed feelings about his words. She did not want to be a shifter, but she might not be qualified as the mate of one.

Bosse would argue they were bonded, and that was that, but had he considered being together for years? She hadn't, not until coming here. She felt something inside her that claimed him as hers and had no idea if a bond could be changed. Now was the time to have a talk they should have had before making a life commitment.

She would never regret loving him, but could she make him happy when they weren't trying to survive?

Forcing the words past her tight throat, she spit out what had kept her up all night. "You should have a mate equal to you as a shifter. I will never be equal in that way."

After a long silence, he replied, "You are correct."

Well damn. His quick agreement cut her deeper than she'd expected.

Sure, that sounded contrary, but she'd never been in love

before and tried to do the right thing. If she were honest, she'd admit that she wanted him to beg her to stay.

How could she explain what had her mind and heart battling over when she couldn't understand it herself?

She wanted Bosse to be happy like Jaz and Adrian.

That was the truth. Everything else was selfish. Her eyes stung with tears, but she blinked them away.

Bosse crossed his thick arms over his chest. "You have never been equal."

She wished he'd stop talking. Rubbing it in only made her feel worse.

A twinkle sparkled in that devil's brown eyes. "You are *better* than equal in your own unique way. You are far more exceptional than a shifter mate to me. I can't alter what I am, but I do not need a woman who changes into a wolf. I need a woman who wants me the way I am. Who accepts me with all my flaws. I love you, Alifair. My wolf loves you. We want you as our mate."

Her heart jumped around like she was having a panic attack. Deep inside, she'd longed for a man to want her just as she was, flaws and all, with his whole being. Bosse tackled everything with his whole being.

He was the man she wanted. How could she argue with a vow of love so honest? He had no confusion over what he was getting with her as his mate. That's all she needed to know.

Still talking, Bosse explained, "I understand your clan is like family. I will take you to them and stay with you. You do not have to live with shifters."

When had she been so happy? Never really. She'd struggled to reach her mother's expertise instead of reaching for her own potential. She had people she did love in the clan, but she no longer felt compelled to live a role that allowed her no life of her own.

Impatient to hear her thoughts on what he'd expressed, Bosse said, "You will not need an airplane. I find I don't care for them."

Standing, she leaned down with her hands on each side

of his chest, which kept her from hurting her abdomen. She lowered herself until she could gently kiss Bosse.

He kissed her back with smiling lips and then upped the level of the kiss until he had her breathing hard. She muttered, "Jaz will kill both of us if we go any farther."

His arms carefully wrapped her back. "I will protect you."

Her heart had been breaking into tiny pieces at the thought of leaving him because she wanted him to have a better life.

Now that she thought about it, she still had to address one more thing. "On the flight home, Adrian said you can't be out in public as a lone wolf, or you'll be vulnerable to a group called SCIS capturing you. Sounds like you could end up somewhere worse than that cage."

"I will find a way to spend whatever time I can with you," he said solemnly. "I survived years of misery without having memories of you to hold close. I am willing to face anything to be with you."

His last words came out more as a plea.

Even knowing the risk, he would put his life on the line again to be with her.

"I am never going to let anyone lock you away or harm you again," she vowed. "My magic is not always dependable, but my love is. I'll stay here with you… mate."

<hr>

THIS IS BOOK one in my new Wild Wolf Pack series, which is a spinoff of the League of Gallize Shifters. I hope you enjoyed this story, and I *would appreciate a review* wherever you shop for books.

To keep up with new releases and be the first to find out when the next book will be available, please join my **https://authordiannalove.com/connect**. I send very few newsletters, and I *never* share anyone's information. I hate to have mine shared.

Also, if you'd like to know more about the real Mapogo lions, search for the documentary *Brothers in Blood: The Lions of Sabi Sand*. These six lions took over the largest territory by any pride, but it was not pretty. A brutal but fascinating story.

The lammergeier, or bearded vulture, is real and plays an important role in keeping the Alps clean and free of diseases. The main source of nutrition for this huge bird of prey is bones.

If you haven't read all the League of Gallize Shifter books, click on any in the following list to dive into one tonight.

LEAGUE OF GALLIZE SHIFTERS
Book 1: Gray Wolf Mate
Book 2: Mating A Grizzly
Book 3: Stalking His Mate
Book 4: Scent Of A Mate
Book 5: Wild Wolf Mate

RAVES ABOUT DIANNA'S OTHER SERIES:

Belador Urban Fantasy:

"When it comes to urban fantasy, Dianna Love is a master." Always Reviewing.

"There is so much action in this book I feel like I've burned calories just reading it." D Antonio

"There are SO many things in this series that I want to learn more about; there's no way I could list them all." Lily, Romance Junkies Reviews

Slye Team Black Ops Romantic Thrillers:

*"...suspense, thrills, excitement, danger and a super romantic couple...**Dianna Love** writes romance suspense so well, as I consider her one of the best at creating believability and hooking us in from the start all the way to the exciting climax."* ~~ Barb, The Reading Café

"Dianna never disappoints! ... would have give it a 10 if they would let!!! Very enjoyable read, can't wait for the next one :-)." ~~ Amy, Goodreads

***Red Moon* Young Adult Sci-fi/Fantasy Series**
by Micah Caida (pen name of collaborators Dianna Love
& Mary Buckham):

"Time Trap is amazingly original and unexpected...I loved every second of reading it!" ~~ Alexandra F, 15, who has read *The Book Thief, The Hunger Games,* and *Anna Karenina.*

"Reading this book is like riding on a roller coaster, getting to the top and not knowing when the next drop is." ~~ Alex B, 12 years old, has also read all of *Rick Riordan's* books, the *Hunger Games*, the *Chronicles of Nick,* and the *Rangers Apprentice* series.

To contact Dianna – email her
assistant AT authordiannalove.com

Websites: AuthorDiannaLove.com and
DiannaLoveSignedBooks.com

Facebook – "Dianna Love Fan Page"
"Dianna Love Reader Community" Facebook group page
(You're invited.)

AUTHOR BIO

New York Times **Bestseller Dianna Love** once dangled over a hundred feet in the air to create unusual marketing projects for Fortune 500 companies. She now writes high-octane romantic thrillers, young adult and urban fantasy. Fans of the bestselling *Belador* urban fantasy series will be thrilled to know more books follow with the new *Treoir Dragon Chronicles*. Dianna's Slye Team Black Ops romantic thriller series wrapped up with Fatal Promise, but also launched the *HAMR Brotherhood* spinoff series. *League of Gallize Shifters* paranormal romance series continues with spinoff *Wild Wolf Pack* from the world of Gallize Shifters. Look for her books in print, e-book, and audio. On the rare occasions Dianna is out of her writing cave, she tours the country on her BMW motorcycle, searching for new story locations. Dianna lives in the Atlanta, GA area with her husband, who is a motorcycle instructor, and a tank full of unruly saltwater critters.

Visit her website at www.**AuthorDiannaLove.com** or www.**DiannaLoveSignedBooks.com**

A WORD FROM DIANNA...

Thank you for reading *BOSSE,* and thanks also to all the readers who have written wonderful notes about my Gallize Shifters. I appreciate your feedback so much! As you now know, I'm expanding the Gallize world with *Wild Wolf Pack.* More on the next one coming soon.

As always, thank you to my husband, Karl, who makes it possible for me to write my stories.

A special thank you to Judy Carney, who gets better with every book she goes through, and Stacey Krug, who jumps in super early to read pages before they're totally clean. Also, I appreciate Jennifer Cazares and Sherry Arnold for being terrific early beta readers who catch a number of small things missed by all of us even after multiple editing passes.

I want to send a huge thank-you to my Super Read-and-Review Team peeps, who read early versions and then share their opinions—you rock!!

Sending a shout-out to Candi Fox and Leiha Mann, who work hard to support me in so many ways. Thanks to Joyce Ann McLaughlin, Kimber Mirabella, and Sharon Livingston, too.

As always, the amazing Kim Killion creates all my covers, and Jennifer Litteken saves my butt time and again with great formatting just when I need it. Much appreciation to both of you.

Thank you to my peeps on the Dianna Love Reader Group on Facebook. I love coming out to visit with you.

Dianna